W9-BGA-184

ESCAPE CLAUSE

ALSO BY JOHN SANDFORD

Rules of Prey
Shadow Prey
Eyes of Prey
Silent Prey
Winter Prey
Night Prey
Mind Prey
Sudden Prey
Secret Prey
Certain Prey
Easy Prey
Chosen Prey
Mortal Prey
Naked Prey
Hidden Prey
Broken Prey
Invisible Prey
Phantom Prey
Wicked Prey
Storm Prey
Buried Prey
Stolen Prey
Silken Prey
Field of Prey
Gathering Prey
Extreme Prey

KIDD NOVELS

The Fool's Run
The Empress File
The Devil's Code
The Hanged Man's Song

VIRGIL FLOWERS NOVELS

Dark of the Moon
Heat Lightning
Rough Country
Bad Blood
Shock Wave
Mad River
Storm Front
Deadline

STAND-ALONE NOVELS

Saturn Run
The Night Crew
Dead Watch

ESCAPE CLAUSE

JOHN ▾ ▾ ▾ ▾
SANDFORD

G. P. PUTNAM'S SONS | NEW YORK

PUTNAM

G. P. PUTNAM'S SONS
Publishers Since 1838
An imprint of Penguin Random House LLC
375 Hudson Street
New York, New York 10014

Library of Congress Cataloging-in-Publication Data

Names: Sandford, John, 1944 February 23– author.
Title: Escape clause / John Sandford.
Description: New York : G. P. Putnam's Sons, 2016.
Identifiers: LCCN 2016030850 | ISBN 9780399168918 (hardback)
Subjects: LCSH: Flowers, Virgil (Fictitious character)—Fiction. | Government investigators—Minnesota—Fiction. | BISAC: FICTION / Crime. | FICTION / Suspense. | FICTION / Thrillers. | GSAFD: Mystery fiction.
Classification: LCC PS3569.A516 E83 2016 | DDC 813/.54—dc23
LC record available at https://lccn.loc.gov/2016030850
p. cm.

International edition ISBN 9780735212008

Printed in the United States of America
1 3 5 7 9 10 8 6 4 2

Book design by Gretchen Achilles

ESCAPE CLAUSE

1

▼ ▼ ▼

Peck popped a Xanax, screwed the cap back on the pill tube, peered over the top of the bush and through the chain-link fence, and in a hoarse whisper, asked, "You see the other one?"

The big man with the rifle whispered, "Right by that tree, above the first one. She's looking down at him."

"Get her."

The big man rested the muzzle of the rifle in the V of one of the chain links, pulled the trigger: the rifle made a *pop* sound, not much louder than a hand clap. They waited, staring into the darkness, then Peck said, "Ah, you dumb shit, you missed her. You missed her. She should be down, but she's not. She's moving."

"Might have hit that brush, deflected the shot . . ."

"She's moving out in the open. Reload," Peck said.

"I'm doing it. Get off my back, will ya?"

"Can you see her now?" Peck asked. "She's getting curious about why the guy's just lying there."

Pop.

"Got her. Saw it hit," the big man said.

"Sure she's down? We don't want to make a mistake."

"She's going down now . . ." the big man whispered. "I'm pretty sure."

Peck could smell the nicotine and tar on the other man's breath. The big guy was addicted to Akhtamar Black Flames and almost always had one stuck to his lower lip, but not now. Peck reached out and slapped him on the back of the head and said, "I don't want to hear that 'pretty sure.' You know what happens if you're wrong? We're dead men."

"You fuckin' slap me again and I'll stick the gun butt up your ass and twist it sideways."

A small man, crouched on the other side of the rifleman, said, "I saw them get hit. I saw it, man. Both of them. But who knows if it was enough?"

They all went silent for a moment, squinting into the dark. Two bodies lay in the short grass, unmoving. The fence was twenty feet high and stouter than a normal chain link—a prison fence. With no sign of movement on the other side, Peck said, "Hamlet: cut the fence."

"What if they're faking?" The small guy had half circles under his eyes, so dark they looked like broken blue poker chips.

"You're the one who said they got hit," Peck said. The soapy touch of Xanax was slipping into his brain.

The small guy said, "Maybe we oughta split. I'm not feeling so sure about this."

"We're here. It's done. Cut the fuckin' fence," Peck said.

Hamlet's side-cutters made a *grunt* sound as he snipped each piece of wire. *Grunt-grunt-grunt.* They'd come well equipped: they wore rubber kitchen gloves and black clothing and trucker hats and, in addition to the gun, had brought a roll of black duct tape they'd use to put the fence back together when they left.

Hamlet was cutting a wide oval in the fence, leaving it hinged on one side. He'd gotten halfway around the oval when the big man, Hayk, hissed and touched his brother's arm and whispered, "Someone's coming."

They sank into the brush and Hayk moved the muzzle of the rifle around until it pointed out at the perimeter road. Twenty seconds later, a man in a gray uniform ambled along the road, looking at nothing in particular, talking to himself.

When he was directly opposite them, forty feet away, they heard him say, "I told him not to give her the money. She'll blow it on herself. That's what she'll do, and you know it. It won't get to your mom. She doesn't care about your mom. . . ."

Peck realized that the security guard was wearing an earpiece and was talking into a cell phone. He lost the thread of what the man was saying as he disappeared around the curve of the frontage road. When the guard was well out of earshot, Hamlet whispered, "I think he had a gun."

"No, he didn't—I checked that out," Peck said.

"Not in the middle of the night."

"The guards are *not* armed," Peck said.

Hayk said, "Ham, keep cutting. We're almost there."

Hamlet went back to cutting and, two minutes later, pulled open the cut curve of fencing, like a gate.

Peck said, "Go on. Crawl through there."

"Why don't *you* crawl there?" Hamlet asked.

Peck had no immediate answer for that, and the Xanax now had a good grip on him, so he said, "All right, I will. Hold the fence."

Hamlet pulled the fence farther back. When Peck was through, he turned to Hayk and said, "Give me the gun."

"Not loaded."

"That's okay, I'm gonna use it as a poker."

Hayk handed him the gun and Peck crawled fifteen feet to the first body and poked it with the gun's muzzle. No reaction. That was a good thing. The other body was ten feet farther on. He poked that one, too, got no response.

He turned around and whispered, "We're good."

"Told ya," Hamlet said, too loud.

Peck whispered, "Shut up, you fuckin' moron. Get the dollies in here."

Hayk pushed the dollies through the hole in the fence and rolled them over to the bodies. The dollies were the kind used by garden shops, with a flat bed and wide soft wheels.

"Goddamn, heavier than hell," Hayk said, as they lifted the first body onto a dolly. They couldn't see much farther than fifteen or twenty feet away, and the moon didn't help: it sat right on the western horizon and splashed a silvery light off the trees around them. The contrast made it hard to discern shapes and movement.

"Gonna have to push them through the fence one at a time, right out to the perimeter," Peck said. Despite the Xanax, he was sweating heavily, not from the hot summer night, but from fear. He could smell the stink of it on himself.

They loaded the second body on the second dolly and pushed them one at a time through the fence. Then Peck and Hayk dragged the dollies through the brush to the edge of the perimeter road, while Hamlet pulled the fence back into its original configuration and taped some of the cut ends together with strips of the black duct tape. Five quick repairs and the fence looked like new, in the night, anyway.

When Hamlet joined the others out at the perimeter road, Peck said, "I'm going to scout. When you see the laser, bring them."

They nodded and he moved slowly along the edge of the perimeter road, where he could quickly step into the brush if he needed to. Peck had planned the whole operation and he knew there were only a couple of night guards. From that point of view, having a guard pass by only minutes before was a good thing, if a little unnerving. That meant the other guard was a half mile away, and the one they'd seen probably wouldn't be back around for an hour or more.

The perimeter road curved gently to Peck's right. When he'd gotten to the exit point and had seen nobody, he stepped out to the road's edge, took a laser pointer from his chest pocket, aimed it back toward Hayk and Hamlet, and played the red dot across their hiding place.

A minute later, in the ambient light from the parking lot, he saw them move out onto the road, pulling the dollies with their motionless loads. They moved slowly at first, and then more urgently, and finally began to trot.

The tires were almost, but not quite, silent; there was no one but Peck to hear them. When Hayk and Hamlet came up, Peck led them across the road to another chain-link fence, which they'd already cut. They rolled the dollies through the fence, down a mild slope to the edge of a grassy yard, with a darkened house eighty feet away. They waited there while Hamlet repaired the second fence, this time with silver duct tape. A scummy pond lay off to their left, home to any number of green-and-black frogs. Earlier in the summer, when they were making scouting trips, the frogs had been croaking their froggy asses off. Now that Peck could use the covering noise, they were resolutely silent.

Hamlet finished with the fence, and they eased the dollies across the yard to the back door of the garage, pushed the door open, pulled the dollies inside, and closed the door. Hayk took a flashlight out of a cargo pocket and turned it on.

The van was ready, cargo doors open. They rolled the dollies up a wheelchair ramp into the back of the van, closed the doors. Hamlet and Hayk got into the van, Hayk as the wheelman, while Peck went to the door into the house, stepped inside, and looked out a kitchen window at the street.

He was looking out at a suburban neighborhood, a bunch of three-bedroom houses where everybody worked day jobs and the kids went to school: the houses were almost all dark, and the street was empty.

He hurried back to the garage, pulling the house door closed behind himself, and pushed the wall switch for the garage door opener. The garage door went up, but no light came on, because Peck had thought of everything: they'd loosened the garage light. Hayk drove the van out of the garage; Peck pushed the wall switch again and the door started down.

There was an ankle-high infrared safety light that beamed across the door opening to keep the door from closing on children who might be standing beneath it. Peck stepped carefully over it—he really had *groomed* the plan, he thought, with nothing left to chance—went to the van, and climbed into the backseat.

Hayk rolled it down to the street, took a right, and Hamlet said, "Made it."

2

▼ ▼ ▼

The cloudless sky was blue, of course, but the pale blue that tended almost to green, if you were lying naked in a Minnesota swimming hole on a hot summer day, looking up through the branches of the creek-side cottonwoods, thinking about nothing much, except the prospect of lunch.

Virgil Flowers was doing that, bathed in the cool spring water and the scent of fresh-mown hay. Frankie Nobles's oldest son was windrowing the teddered hay, riding a '70s International Harvester tractor, the all-original diesel engine clattering up and down the eighty-acre field on the other side of the crooked line of cottonwoods.

Virgil usually managed to evade the whole haying process, pleading the exigencies of law enforcement, but with this last cut of the summer, Frankie had her eye on him. All her farm equipment was marginal, and though a neighbor would be over with his modern baler and wagon, two-thirds of the bales—the small rectangular ones—would be unloaded in the barnyard.

From Virgil's point of view, there was one good thing about this—the neighbor would keep a third of the hay for his trouble.

The bad thing was, somebody would have to load the other two-thirds of the bales on Frankie's ancient elevator, and somebody would have to stack it in the sweltering, wasp-infested barn loft.

"Why," Virgil asked, "are barn lofts always infested with wasps?"

"Because that's life," Frankie said, back-floating past him on a pair of pink plastic water wings. She was unencumbered by clothing. They'd have the swimming hole to themselves until the tractor stopped running, and then the boys would take it over. For the time being, their privacy was assured by a sign at the beginning of the path through the woods that said "Occupied," with newcomers required to call out before entering. "In the haylofts of life, there are always a few wasps."

"I'm allergic to wasps," Virgil ventured. He was a tall blond man, his long hair now plastered like a yellow bowl over his head.

"You're allergic to haying," Frankie said.

"I can't even believe you bother with it," Virgil said. "You have to give a third of the hay to Carl, to pay for his time and baling equipment. Whatever hay you manage to keep and sell, the feds and state take half the money. What's the point?"

"I feed the hay to my cattle," she said. "We eat the cattle. There are no taxes."

"You don't have any cattle," Virgil said.

"The feds and state don't know that." She was another blonde, short and fairly slender.

"Please don't tell me that," Virgil said. "Your goddamn tax returns must read like a mystery novel."

"Shoulda seen my mortgage application," Frankie said. "One of those ninja deals—no income, no job. Worked out for me, though."

Honus, a big yellow dog, lay soaking wet on the bank, in a spot of sunshine. He liked to swim, but he also liked to lie wet in the sun.

Frankie kicked past and Virgil ducked under water and floated up between her legs. "You have a very attractive pussy," he said.

"I've been told that," Frankie said. "I've been thinking of entering it in the state fair."

"I could be a judge," Virgil offered.

"You certainly have the necessary expertise," she said.

"Speaking of state fairs . . . Lucas should have been killed," Virgil said, floating back a bit. "I can't believe the stories coming out of Iowa. I talked to him about it last night; he's up to his ass in bureaucrats, like nothing he's ever seen. He said he's been interviewed a half-dozen times by the FBI. The goddamn Purdys almost blew up the presidential election. Would have, if he hadn't been there."

"Lucas is a crazy man," Frankie said. "He chases crazy people. That's what he does, and he likes it. Anyway, that's the Iowa State Fair. I'd enter the Minnesota State Fair."

"Probably do better, as far as getting a ribbon," Virgil said. Frankie's knees folded over his shoulders. "Lucas said the Iowa blondes are really spectacular."

Frankie said, "Wait a minute, are you sayin' that I'm not spec—"

She stopped and they turned their faces toward the path. Somebody was scuffling down through the trees, in violation of the "Occupied" sign. Honus stood up and barked, two, three times, and Virgil and Frankie dropped their feet to the rocky bottom of the swimming hole, and Frankie called out: "Hey! Who's there?"

The scuffling continued for a few more seconds, then a tall, slender, wide-shouldered blonde emerged on the path and chirped, "Hi, Frank."

Frankie said, "Sparkle! What are you doing here?"

"I'm about to go swimming," she said. There was more scuffling behind her, and a heavyset man who probably thought he looked like Ernest Hemingway, with a Hemingway beard and Hemingway gold-rimmed glasses, stepped out of the woods. He was wearing a black T-shirt with a schematic drawing of a host and chalice, and beneath that, the words "Get Real. Be Catholic," plus cargo shorts and plastic flip-flops.

He looked down at them and said, "Hello, there."

Sparkle pulled her top off—she was small-breasted and didn't wear a brassiere—then her shorts and underpants and jumped into the swimming hole. When she surfaced, Frankie snarled, "You really, really aren't invited."

"Oh, shut up," Sparkle said. She looked at Virgil. "You must be the famous Virgil fuckin' Flowers."

Virgil said, "Yeah. Who are you?"

Sparkle frowned at Frankie and said, "You've never told him?"

Frankie looked like she was working up a full-blown snit. "No. Why should I?"

Sparkle turned back to Virgil and said, "I'm Frankie's baby sister."

Virgil said to Frankie, "You have a baby sister?"

"Aw, for Christ's sakes," Frankie said.

"Careful," Sparkle said. "You don't want to piss off Father Bill."

They all looked at the heavyset man, who had removed his

T-shirt, glasses, and watch and was now stepping out of his shorts to reveal a dark brown pelt, speckled with gray, which would have done credit to a cinnamon bear. "That's me," he said. He flopped into the swimming hole, came up sputtering, and said, "Gosh. Nobody told me it'd be this cold."

"What's the Father Bill stuff?" Frankie asked.

"I'm a priest," Bill said, shaking his head like a wet dog. "Part-time, anyway."

"He's a priest nine months of the year, and a bartender and libertine the other three," Sparkle said.

"I work over at the Hanrattys' Resort during the summer, tending bar," Bill said. "I'm a fill-in priest for the Archdiocese of St. Paul and Minneapolis the other nine."

"Must be nice for you," Frankie said.

"It's convenient all the way around," Bill said. He had a mild, low-pitched voice that came out as a growl. "The Hanrattys are always hard up for seasonal help, and the bishop gets a fill-in guy and only has to pay him for nine months."

"And you get laid," Frankie said.

"A fringe benefit," Bill said.

"Hey! I'm a fringe benefit?" Now Sparkle was clouding up, or faking it, pushing out her lower lip. Virgil hadn't seen the family resemblance before: Sparkle was tall and slender, Frankie was short and busty. They clouded up exactly the same way.

"Okay, a major fringe benefit," Bill said.

"That's better."

"Aw, for Christ's sakes," Frankie said again. To Sparkle: "What are you doing here?"

"Well, I thought I'd stop by and see my beloved sister—and I'm also doing the last bit of research for my dissertation." She rolled over on her back and paddled past Virgil, a not uninteresting sight. "I'm interviewing migrants at the Castro canning factory. I thought Bill and I could share your spare bedroom."

Frankie scrutinized her for a couple of heartbeats, then asked, "Does old man Castro know about this?"

"I haven't made what you'd call appointments, no," Sparkle said.

"You're going to get your ass kicked," Frankie said. "He's a mean old sonofabitch. When it's about to happen, give me a call. I want to come and watch."

"I was hoping Virgil could have a chat with the line manager over there . . . you know, about prisons and stuff."

"You don't be dragging Virgil into this," Frankie said.

"What's your problem, Frankie? Virgil's a cop, it's a part of his job," Sparkle said.

"He investigates *after* the ass-kicking, not before," Frankie said.

"What's this all about?" Virgil asked. "Why is . . . Sparkle? . . . going to get her ass kicked?"

Sparkle, back-floating between the cop and the priest, explained: she was working on her PhD dissertation about seasonal migrant labor, both the social and economic aspects, at the University of Minnesota. She'd spent two years among the vegetable-growing fields of southern Minnesota and was now moving upstream to the factories. When she had incorporated the factory material, she'd have her doctorate.

"Why would that get your ass kicked?" Virgil asked.

"Because old man Castro has a deal with this village down in Mexico," Sparkle said. She dropped her feet to the bottom of the pool. "They provide him couples to pick the cucumbers and work in his pickle factory. He pays the man a buck or two above the minimum wage, which makes him look like a hero, but the wife also works and doesn't get anything—so his pickers and factory workers are making a little more than half the minimum wage, when it's all said and done. He would rather not have this documented."

"And you're going to write that in your dissertation?" Virgil asked.

"I am."

"Okay. I can see why you might be headed for an ass-kicking," Virgil said.

"See? Crazy shit," Frankie said to Virgil. "You should introduce her to Lucas, since Lucas likes crazy shit so much."

"Who's Lucas?" Sparkle asked. She'd turned to her sister and stood up in waist-deep water, her back to Virgil. He noticed that she had an extremely attractive back, tapering down to a narrow waist. Backs were largely unappreciated in women, Virgil thought, but not by him.

"Another cop," Frankie said. "Actually, ex-cop. He's the one who saved Michaela Bowden's life down at the Iowa State Fair last week."

"Really!" Sparkle said. "I *would* like to meet him."

"Ah, for Christ's sakes," Frankie said a third time.

Father Bill had ducked his head under water and had come up sputtering. "I don't mean to be critical on such short acquaintance, but do you think you might find some way to employ vulgarity or obscenity, rather than profanity, at least when I'm around?" Father Bill asked Frankie. "A nice round 'Oh, shit' or 'Fuck you' is much easier to accept than your taking of the Lord's name in vain."

"Ah, Jesus," Frankie said.

Virgil said quickly, "She means the Puerto Rican, not the Lord."

The two women paddled up the swimming hole, where the creek came in, nagging at each other. Virgil stayed at the bottom end of the pool with Bill, and Bill apologized for their abrupt entrance, saying, "Once Sparkle starts to roll, there's not much you can do about it."

"Is her name really Sparkle?"

"No, but it's what everybody calls her," Bill said. "Somebody at Hanrattys' told me that her birth name was Wanda."

They looked after the women, who'd gotten to the top of the pool, where the water was shallow. They floated there, still arguing, then Frankie stood up and dove forward. Bill's eyebrows went up as she did it, and he said, "Oh, my. When the Good Lord was passing out breasts, it looks like Frankie went through the line more than once."

Virgil said, "Yeah, well . . . I guess."

Bill: "You're embarrassed because I'm a priest and I'm interested in women?"

Virgil said, in his quotation voice, "'Kiss and rekiss your wife. Let her love and be loved. You are fortunate in having overcome, by an honorable marriage, that celibacy in which one is a prey to devouring fires or unclean ideas. The unhappy state of a single person, male or female, reveals to me each hour of the day so many horrors, that nothing sounds in my ear as bad as the name of monk or nun or priest. A married life is a paradise, even where all else is wanting.'"

"Really," said Bill, sounding pleased. "Who said that?"

"Martin Luther. In a letter to a friend."

"Luther. I don't know much of Luther, other than he had horns, a forked tale, and cloven hooves instead of feet. But he said that? You're the religious sort?"

"Not so much—at least, I'm not that big a believer in institutions," Virgil said. "My old man is a Lutheran minister over in Marshall. He used to soak me in that stuff and some of it stuck."

"Good for him, good for him," Bill said. "You'll have to send me a citation for that letter, so I can read it all. Martin Luther, who would have thought?"

"Is this relationship with Sparkle . . . a long-term thing?" Virgil asked.

"No, no, it isn't. I've spent time with her the last two summers, but of course, the other nine months I'm celibate and she doesn't put up with that."

"That seems very strange to me," Virgil said.

"It seems fairly strange to me, too, but I find both sides of the equation to be rewarding," Bill said. "Of course, I may go to hell."

"No offense, but I don't think the Church gets to decide who goes to hell," Virgil said.

"I'm not offended," Bill said cheerfully. "In fact, I agree. Don't tell the Church I said that."

The two women came paddling back and Frankie hooked an arm around Virgil's sun-pinked neck and said, "Sparkle's going to be here for a while. You keep telling me you're going to get a queen-sized or a king-sized bed, and this would be a good time to do it, because I'm going to be sleeping over a couple times a week."

"I can do that," Virgil said. "That old bed is shot anyway."

Frankie said to Bill, "You can go ahead and fuck Sparkle, but I don't want her squealing and screaming and all that—keep it quiet. I got kids."

Bill said to Sparkle, "Maybe we ought to find another place."

"No, no, no . . . this is convenient and I like hanging out with my nephews," Sparkle said. "Another thing is that Castro's goons won't find me out here. Besides, if you tie me up and gag me, nobody'll hear a thing."

They all looked at Bill, who said, "Sometimes I have to struggle to keep my head from exploding."

"That's called the Sparkle effect," Frankie said.

The four of them paddled around for a while, until, from the bank of the swimming hole, a phone began playing the theme from *Jaws*. Honus stood up and woofed at it, then lay back down, and Frankie said, "Uh-oh."

Sparkle: "What's that?"

"The priority number from the BCA," Virgil said. "It usually means the shit has hit the fan, somewhere. I gotta take it."

He'd hoped the other two would leave before he had to get out of the water, but all eyes were on him as he manfully waded out of the swimming hole, sat on the bank, and fumbled the phone out of his jeans.

Jon Duncan calling. "Jon, what's up?"

"We need you up here," Duncan said. "Right away, this afternoon."

"What happened?"

"That whole thing down in Iowa, at the state fair last week, has upset the apple cart," Duncan said. "You know our fair starts this week, there're gonna be more politicians up here, campaigning. We're worried about copycats."

Virgil groaned. "Man, don't make me work the state fair."

"No, no, we got that covered," Duncan said. "But everybody's committed now at the fair, and we've got a new problem. A big one."

"What's the problem?"

"Somebody stole the Amur tigers from the zoo last night," Duncan said. "Apparently shot them with a tranquilizer gun and hauled them out of there. Since it's a state zoo, it's our problem."

"What? Tigers?"

"Yeah. Somebody stole the tigers . . . two Amur tigers. Pride of the zoo. Listen, man, you've got to get up here," Duncan said. "There's gonna be a media shitstorm starting tonight on the evening news. We gotta get the tigers back: and we gotta get them back *right now*. And *alive*."

3

▼ ▼ ▼

They caged the tigers separately in the bottom of the old barn, in what had once been cow stalls. Since a chain-link fence had been enough to keep the tigers separated from any number of chubby, delicious-looking Minnesota Zoo visitors, they'd wrapped the stalls with more chain link. The cage doors, made from chain-link fence gates, were locked with steel snap shackles.

There'd been no electric power in the barn, the ancient wires gnawed through by rodents, so they'd bought two long orange cables, which they plugged in at the house and then laid across the barnyard into the lower level.

Inside, the Simonian brothers had rigged up three work lights from Sears, hung from the rafters, and screwed in hundred-watt bulbs. The work lights were plugged into a power strip at the end of one of the orange cables. The light was bright, harsh, and threw knife-edged shadows over the interior of the barn.

There were no windows.

Against one wall, they'd installed a makeshift table made of a four-by-eight sheet of plywood, sitting on aluminum sawhorses and covered with plastic sheeting. Five waist-high meat dryers were plugged into the second orange cable. Four plastic tubs would hold discarded guts and unneeded tiger organs. A hose, also strung over from the house, would wash everything down.

Though the barn had not housed cattle for decades, there was still an earthy odor about it, not entirely unpleasant, which took Hamlet Simonian back to happier days on his grandmother's farm in Armenia. Happier at a safe distance, anyway.

They'd wheeled the inert tigers into the barn and into the two separate cages on the dollies, then rolled them off the dollies onto the floor. The male tiger was tough to move, even though they only had to move him a foot or so off the dolly. His formidable muscles were slack as bedsheets and simply hard to get hold of, and the cage was small enough that they couldn't work standing up.

When they finally got it done, they locked the cages, locked the outer door, and went and hid. Neither tiger was yet stirring. They'd give it until the next day before they returned to the farm, in case somebody had been watching and got curious about all the activity in the middle of the night.

They met again at the farm the next morning to start work.

"Shoot the fuckin' tiger, Ham," said Winston Peck VI. Peck popped a Xanax. "Do it."

Peck was a tall, round-shouldered man, brown hair now touched with gray. He had a tight brown Teddy Roosevelt mustache and wore gold-rimmed glasses with round lenses. He looked like a college athlete going to seed in middle age: he was thirty pounds too heavy.

"I dunno, man," Hamlet Simonian said. He was bulb-nosed, with dark hair, what was left of it, and sweating hard. He had a Remington .308 in one hand. The night before, they'd used a tranquilizer gun, shooting darts, to take the cats out of the zoo. "Now it seems kinda . . . terrible. A terrible thing to do."

"You knew what was going to happen," Peck said. "You knew the plan."

"I didn't know I was going to be the shooter. I thought Hayk . . ."

The two tigers looked through the bars of their separate cages with a kind of quiet rapaciousness. They were beautiful animals, gold and white with ripples of black, and orange eyes. They were hungry, since it hadn't seemed to Peck that there was any point in feeding them.

If the snap shackles on the doors were suddenly undone, Simonian had no doubt what would happen: they'd get eaten. Forget about the gun, forget about running, those tigers would eat his South Caucasian ass like a hungry trucker choking down a ham sandwich. A Ham Simonian sandwich.

"Ham, shoot the fuckin' tiger."

"Why don't you do it, man? I don't think I got the guts," Simonian said. "Maybe we ought to wait for Hayk. He'd do it." Hayk was Hamlet's older brother by ten months, and he was much larger, stronger, and meaner than Hamlet.

"Because I don't know how to do it," Peck said. He was getting seriously impatient. Killing the tiger wasn't the only thing he had to do this day. He was a busy man. "I've never shot a gun in my life. And we need to get started. Now."

That wasn't strictly true—he'd shot rifles on several occasions, and a shotgun, in the company of his father, but he wasn't sure of his skills, and mostly didn't want to be the one to shoot the tiger.

"Ah, shit." Simonian edged up to the male tiger's cage. He was by far the larger of the two, though that wouldn't matter much if either one of them got out. The smaller female, Katya, weighed nearly four hundred pounds and to the nervous Simonian, it seemed like twenty pounds of that was teeth and claws. Getting taken down by Katya would be like getting attacked by a four-hundred-pound chainsaw.

And forget about it with Artur, the muscular male. He was six hundred and forty pounds of furry hunger. He could take your head off with one swipe of his well-armed paw, and then squish it like a grape between his three-inch canine teeth.

"Shoot—the—fuckin'—tiger," Peck said.

Simonian lifted the gun and looked down the iron sights at Artur, who stared calmly back at him, unafraid, even though something about his eyes suggested that he knew what was coming. Drips of sweat rolled into Hamlet's eyes and he took the gun down and wiped the sweat away with his shirtsleeve, then brought the gun back up and aimed right between the tiger's eyes, five feet away, and yanked the trigger.

The gun went off and to Simonian's surprise, the tiger dropped to the floor, stone-cold dead. Katya, the female, screamed and launched herself at the cage's chain-link fence, which ballooned out toward Simonian, who scrambled away from the maddened cat. The muzzle blast inside the barn basement had been ferocious, and Simonian could hear his ears ringing; it was a moment before he became aware that Peck was running around the barn shouting, "Whoa! Whoa! Whoa!"

"What? What?"

"You shot me, you asshole," Peck said. He was holding his hand flat on his head, and when he took it away, there was a splash of blood in his palm. His baseball cap, which had been given to him by a crew member of the movie *The Revenant*, lay on the floor. Peck told people it was a gift from Leonardo DiCaprio himself, though he was lying about that.

"Let me look, let me look," Simonian said. Behind him, Katya threw herself at the cage again, a rattling impact that bent the chain-link fence.

"Hurts, hurts, hurts," Peck cried, still wandering in circles.

Simonian nervously watched the agitated cat as he and Peck moved to one of the work lights, and Peck tilted his head down. Through his thinning hair, Simonian could see a knife-like cut that was bleeding, but seemed superficial. "It's not bad," he reported. "Must have been a ricochet, a little scrap of metal or something. You could press some toilet paper against it and the bleeding would stop."

"You sure?"

"Yeah. It looks like a paper cut," Simonian said. "It's nothing."

"Hurts like a motherfucker. I'm lucky I'm not dead," Peck said. "I'm going to go find some toilet paper. You drag the cat out of there."

"Drag the cat? Man, he weighs six hundred pounds or something . . ."

"Use the dolly. I didn't expect you to throw it over your shoulder, dumbass," Peck said. "I'm gonna go get some toilet paper. I'm bleeding like a sieve here."

"Okay."

"Speaking of dumbasses, where is your dumbass brother? He was supposed to be here an hour ago."

"He had to get a knife, a special knife for removing the skin," Simonian said. He dropped the rifle, which hit the floor with a noisy *clank*, and Peck flinched away. Simonian picked it up and said, "No bullet in the thing." He tapped the bolt.

"No bullet in the thing," Peck repeated, shaking his head. "You're a real fuckin' gunman, you know that, dumbass?"

"If I'm such a dumbass, how come I shoot the tiger and it drops dead? One shot?" Simonian asked.

"Blind luck," Peck said. He added, "I gotta get some toilet paper." He picked his hat up off the floor, looked at it, said, "You shot a hole in it. This was my best hat and it's ruined. I'm amazed that you didn't shoot me between the eyes." He tramped off toward the door and out onto the slice of green lawn that Simonian could see from where he was standing. A second later, Peck stepped back and said, "I'm sorry about that dumbass thing. I'm a little tense, you know? That was a good shot. I'm proud of you, Hamlet. I mean, except for the part where the shrapnel hit me. You're sure the tiger's dead?"

"He better be," Simonian said, "or Hayk gonna get one big surprise when he tries to skin that bad boy."

"Yeah," said Peck. "I'm going to get toilet paper."

He disappeared into the sunshine, headed for his truck, where he kept a first aid kit. He wasn't really sorry about calling Simonian a dumbass, because Simonian *was* a dumbass. He had to pretend, though, because he still needed the brothers. For a while, anyway. That was simple good management.

Back in the barn, Hamlet Simonian turned back to the cages, where Katya was making desperate purring sounds at her mate, as though trying to rouse him from a deep sleep.

She knew he was dead, Simonian thought. He could see it in her eyes when she turned to look at him.

Another thought occurred to him: he should shoot her now. He shouldn't wait, despite Peck. If he didn't shoot her now, something bad would happen. Like, really bad.

He thought about it, then started rolling a dolly over to the dead tiger's cage. He didn't have the guts to shoot another tiger, at least, not on the same day that he'd shot the first one.

But not shooting the girl, he thought, was a mistake.

They were going to make it anyway.

4

▼ ▼ ▼

Virgil made a hurried trip from Frankie's farm back to Mankato, where he lived. He left Honus at the farm, and as he left, the dog stood in the driveway and barked once. The bark was a familiar one and translated as "asshole!"

Honus stayed with Frankie and her kids when Virgil was out of town, but preferred to hang with Virgil, because Virgil had the best arm and also took him for long lazy walks, and because out in the woods, Virgil would occasionally pee on a tree, like a good dog. Honus was named after Honus Wagner, the shortstop. No grounder ever got past him, although he was occasionally fooled by pop flies.

Since he would be working in the metro area, where BCA officials might see him, Virgil traded his Creaky Boards band T-shirt for a plain black golf shirt, added a sport coat, kept his jeans, and put a quick polish on his cowboy boots. Heeding advice from his departed boss, Lucas Davenport, he got his pistol out of the gun safe in the truck and wore it, though it was uncomfortably heavy.

"Bureaucrats are afraid of guns," Davenport had told him. "If you wear one, it gives you an edge."

The zoo was on the south side of the metro area, seventy-five miles away. He made the trip in a comfortable hour: Jon Duncan, his new boss, said it was an emergency, so he went up with flashers and an occasional siren to move the lagging left-lane drivers, because it was not only faster, but also because it was fun.

Frankie called as he was headed north: "I got Sparkle and Bill settled in. Bill worries me. He's too nice and normal for my household. He's even made friends with Sam."

"What'd he do, show him how to make dynamite?" Sam was Frankie's youngest, a fourth grader, the kind of kid who'd eventually jump off the barn roof with a homemade parachute.

"Almost as bad. He showed him how to drive Sparkle's Mini. Sam was driving it around the yard when Sparkle and I went to see what was going on. Anyway, they're going to stay. I might spend more than a few nights at your place. Sparkle's already gotten on my nerves."

"How's that?"

"Well, for one thing, you spent an unusual amount of time checking her out in the swimming hole," Frankie said.

"Hey. A good-looking naked woman jumps in a swimming hole with you, you're gonna check her out," Virgil said. "That's normal, been going on for a million years, and there's nothing in it."

"That's good, because you mess around with Sparkle, you could get yourself stabbed," Frankie said.

"She carries a knife?"

"No, but I do."

The Minnesota Zoo was in the town of Apple Valley, a bedroom suburb south of Minneapolis and St. Paul. Virgil left his 4Runner in a no-parking spot, flipped his "Bureau of Criminal Apprehension—Official Business" card onto the dashboard, and walked down to the main entrance. A pack of kids was playing on a couple of full-sized bronze buffalos at the end of the parking lot and Virgil nodded at a pretty mother, and down the sidewalk, more kids were playing on some bronze wolves and Virgil gave another young mother a nod.

Duncan was waiting for him by the admission counter. "Man, am I happy to see you," he said. Duncan was on the tall side, with neat brown hair, thickly lashed brown eyes, and big teeth. TV cameras liked him and he liked them back. "You even got dressed up. You even got your gun. *All right*. They're waiting inside."

"Who's *they*?" Virgil asked.

"Virginia Landseer, the zoo director, she's the one with gray hair; Robert McCall, the chairman of the board, he's got the black-rimmed arty glasses; and a couple of other rich people, a maintenance guy, and an Apple Valley investigator," Duncan said. Duncan had been a fair street cop, but he was happier as a manager. "They were talking about wolf fetuses when I came out to look for you."

"Will I get any help on this?" Virgil asked.

"I gotta tell you, man, after what happened in Iowa . . . probably not," Duncan said, as he led Virgil through an unmarked door to the director's office. "We've about moved everybody in the building over to the fairgrounds. Losing the tigers is bad, losing a presidential candidate would really bum everybody out. Especially if it was one of the liberal ones."

"Great," Virgil said. Two hours earlier, he'd been floating in a swimming hole with two good-looking naked blondes and a guy who resembled a bear. Now he was walking through what looked and felt like a bunker. "One administrative question. Why am I doing this, if Apple Valley already has a guy on it? It's their jurisdiction."

"Because we think it's unlikely that this was done by Apple Valley residents or that the tigers are still around here. It's not really an Apple Valley crime, the way we see it," Duncan said. "The other thing is, there's a druggie going around town kicking in back doors. He's hitting two or three houses a day and he seems to know what he's doing, because the cops don't have a clue who it is. People are getting pissed, and the Apple Valley cops are getting a lot of pressure to stop him. They don't have time for the tigers, if somebody else can do it. And it really is our problem."

"Okay," Virgil said. And, "Listen, Jon, I'll do this for you, but after that thing with the dogs—I don't want to become the BCA's designated dogcatcher."

"These are cats."

"You know what I mean," Virgil said.

"I do. And don't worry about it, we're not headed in that direction," Duncan said. "This is a once-in-a-lifetime thing. You get these cats back and I'll see that you never do another animal job in your life."

They were walking down a concrete hallway to the director's office, and Virgil asked, "Anybody got any ideas about how this happened?"

"Lot of ideas, not so much evidence," Duncan said. "They'll tell you the details. Their head maintenance guy is in there; he seems to know the most. They found a cleanup guy, a janitor, I guess, though he works outside shoveling shit or something, who heard what might have been a couple shots from a tranquilizer gun in the middle of the night."

They got to the director's office and Duncan held the door. Virgil stepped inside to find a half-dozen people crowded into an inner office who stopped talking to look at him. Duncan bumped past him and said, "Everybody, this is Virgil Flowers, one of our very best investigators. He'll want to hear what you-all have to say, and then, well, I'll let Virgil take it from there."

A gray-haired woman who otherwise looked like she might be in her middle thirties and who had to be Landseer, the director, said, "Welcome," as she stood to shake hands. She introduced McCall, the board chairman, with the arty black-rimmed glasses, and two other board members, Nancy Farelly and Gina Larimore, and Dan Best, the head of maintenance, and Andy White, the Apple Valley cop.

Larimore said to Virgil, "You're the man who broke that illegal dognapping ring down on the Mississippi."

"Yes, ma'am," Virgil said.

"That's a worthwhile credential," she said. "We are desperate to get our tigers back. How long do you think it'll take?"

"I don't know," Virgil said. "Anything between this afternoon and never, depending on what the thieves have done with them.

If they put them in the back of a truck and are halfway to California . . . it could be tough."

"Don't say *never*, don't say that," McCall said. He was a red-faced man in a suit and dress shirt, with a two-tone blue and white collar. "We've got to find them, and we have to be quick about it. I know that puts pressure on you, but we can only think of three reasons for somebody to steal them."

"Which are?" Duncan had pulled a plastic chair into the office from the outer room, and Virgil took it and sat down.

"One, it's an anti-zoo nut," McCall said. "Those people are mostly talk, as unpleasant as they can be. Two, it could be somebody who deals in live exotic animals—there's a lot of that down in Texas and owning tigers is more common than you'd think. There might be five thousand privately owned tigers in the U.S. And three, and this is the worst possibility, it's somebody who wants to sell the tiger . . . parts . . . to be used in traditional Asian medicine. Almost all the parts are used in one form or another. That would involve killing the tigers, of course."

"Don't say that, Bob," said Farelly. Tears rolled down her face and she wiped them away with a tissue. "I can't stand even to hear that."

"We all know it's true enough," McCall said, scanning the other faces in the room. To Virgil: "Here's the thing: of the three possibilities, I'm afraid the medicine thing is the most likely. If it was exotic animal dealers, well, you can get tigers relatively cheap. You don't need to steal them and take a chance on going to prison. Anti-zoo people probably wouldn't go after tigers; they'd take something easier."

"Not if they wanted to make a spectacular point," Larimore said.

"If that's what it is, they'll have to go public, and we'll get them back—and we haven't heard a word from those people," McCall said. "The tiger's real value—they're Amur tigers, and they're rare in the wild—would be as ingredients in traditional Chinese medicine. They're DNA certified as real Amurs, of course, since they were here in the zoo. If you wanted that kind of medicine, they'd be all you could ask for. As medicine, they'd be worth a lot."

"How much?" Virgil asked.

McCall said, "All I know about that market is what I looked up on the Internet, and I have no idea of the accuracy of the estimate. The Amurs are highly valued in China and they're on the endangered species list. Depends on your connections with the market, but two healthy certified Amurs could bring, as parts, maybe . . . a quarter million. That's what I get from the Internet, anyway."

"There's a motive," Duncan said.

"If that's who's got them, then they're already dead or will be soon," McCall said, turning his eyes to Virgil. "That's why you've got to find them fast."

Has the media been here?" Virgil asked.

"Oh, yes," Landseer said. "We did a press conference at one o'clock, but I have several requests for further interviews at four this afternoon. We'll have to do it. They're really the taxpayers' animals."

Virgil looked over at Duncan and asked, "Jon, do you know Dave the Rotten Bastard up in the attorney general's office?"

"Yeah, sure."

"Why don't you call him and find out the highest possible level of criminal offense he could charge with this case, and the longest possible prison term." Virgil asked. "Then when Miz Landseer has her press conference, maybe you could step up and talk about all that."

"What good will that do?" asked Best, the maintenance man.

"I'm hoping that it'll scare the heck out of the thieves," Virgil said. "Dave is a smart guy and he'll know exactly what we want. He'll come up with a list of crimes you won't believe. Something like thirty years in prison, if they're convicted. With any luck, the perpetrators will give the cats up or tell us where they're at. If they're planning to kill them, maybe they won't do that."

"That's good—that's very good," McCall said. "First good thing I've heard. Can we get that set up in time for the press conference?"

"I can set it up in ten minutes," Duncan said. He would not be unhappy to be on TV.

Best asked Virgil, "Why's the guy called the Rotten Bastard?"

Virgil said, "When he was a prosecutor in St. Paul, he had a ten-year-old crack runner shoot and kill a twelve-year-old. Dave tried to get the ten-year-old certified for trial as an adult."

"Gosh, that *is* a rotten bastard," Farelly said.

Duncan asked Virgil, "What else do you need, right now?"

Virgil looked around at the group and said, "I need to know what you *think*. You're all familiar with this place. How'd they do this? Did they need special equipment to get in? Did they need night vision gear, for instance? Did they have to saw through any steel bars that would require special equipment? Somebody mentioned a tranquilizer gun . . . Where would they get one of those? Do you have any video cameras?"

Best, the maintenance supervisor, said, "I can answer most of that."

"Good," Virgil said. "Let's talk."

A maintenance worker had noticed that the tigers were missing at eight-thirty that morning, shortly before the zoo was due to open. The tigers hadn't been missed before that because they'd spent the night in their outdoor containment—an area roomy enough that not all of it could be seen from any one place—rather than the usual indoor night containment. "I guess everybody who might have seen them thought they were on the other side," said Best.

The maintenance worker had been dragging a broken food pallet around to a Dumpster when he noticed what seemed to be a fault in a chain-link fence. When he looked closer, he found that it had been cut through. He investigated further and found another hole cut in the fence around the tiger compound.

The man told one of the animal handlers, who checked the tiger compound and found that the animals were missing. "He was like, 'Shit! Where are the tigers?' He was totally freaked out, he was worried somebody had *freed* them, and they were running around loose."

They called the Apple Valley cops, who'd called the local schools and had them locked down, and then had run a sweep through the area, looking for the cats. When they didn't find them, they'd called the BCA.

White, the Apple Valley cop, said, "When we decided they'd been stolen, been taken, we figured the thieves had to come in from the parking lot. There's a surveillance camera out there, but nobody monitoring it overnight. The camera spools to a hard drive, with a monthlong cache. We took a look at last night's recording, and whoever did it knew where the camera was—it's mounted on a light pole—and they climbed the pole from behind the camera and sprayed some paint onto the lens."

Virgil: "You're saying at least one of them came in on foot, messed up the camera, and then they brought in a truck or a van?"

White and Best glanced at each other, and Best shrugged, and White said, "No, that's not what we think, not quite. I don't know why they messed with that camera, but they did, at 1:08 in the morning. The thing is, there's another camera that looks out on the entrance—there's only one entrance—and they might not have known about it, because it's not easy to see. Anyway, they didn't mess with that one, and no cars or trucks came or went between eleven o'clock and the morning shift change."

"You're saying the truck was probably already here, maybe came in during a shift change, and then they waited until there was another change?" Virgil asked.

"Don't know," White said, shaking his head. "That seems really . . . not right. I really don't know what they did. Anyway, they were here, and they probably walked up a service road, where they came to a barred gate. They needed a key to get through that. When we looked this morning, we found that it was open, unlocked, but not damaged."

"Then there's an insider, somewhere along the way," Virgil said. "If the insider arrived in his truck, took out the camera . . ."

"They figured that out even before I got here," White said. "There aren't many people on the overnight and we've been checking them all day. They're all accounted for. Most of them walked out to their cars with friends, and you're not going to get two tigers in a Hyundai. We could eliminate most of the cars by looking at them. There were four trucks and we've been all over those, and I gotta say, they don't look connected with this."

White explained that three of the four trucks had open beds, and that the video camera at the front gate was mounted high enough that they could see the truck beds were empty. The fourth truck had a camper.

"I've talked to that guy, and I don't think he had anything to do with it. He's an electrician who was here to work on some lights. He showed me his truck, the back's all built out with tools and parts and supplies. You might be able to get a tiger or two in there, if you stacked them up, but it wouldn't be a sure thing, and it wouldn't be an easy job. Anyway, he doesn't seem right. Besides, he was working all night where people could see him."

Everybody nodded, and Landseer said, "We hate to think that there was an insider involved, but if somebody unlocked that gate, there doesn't seem to be any other possibility."

"Well, there are, but an insider seems like the best bet," Virgil said. "Are the keys controlled? Or are they all over the place?"

"A limited number of people have them . . . but there have been copies along the way, when keys got lost, so we don't know exactly how many there really are," Landseer said. "We know there are eight authorized keys, six people plus two spares. Unfortunately, the spares are kept where any number of people could access them. Both of them are still on their hook—I checked. If somebody took one of the spares and copied it and returned the original . . . we wouldn't know it."

Huh," Virgil said. And back to Best: "Jon told me that one of your guys heard something that might have been a tranquilizer gun last night. Is that right?"

"Yeah. Joel Charvin. He's a cleanup guy working the overnight.

He was on the other side of the zoo and a tranquilizer gun isn't loud. They're gas-operated, so they don't make much noise at all. Kind of a *boo!* sound. Nothing like a shot."

"Like a pellet gun," Virgil suggested.

Best nodded: "Like that. Loud as a hand clap, maybe, but not as sharp as a shot from a regular gun."

"Does this Charvin guy know what a tranquilizer gun sounds like?" Virgil asked.

"Yeah, he does. We use them from time to time," Best said. "He doesn't do it, but he knows what they sound like. He was on the far side of the zoo when he heard the noises, the shots. He didn't identify them at the time as coming from a tranquilizer gun. He didn't see anything, so he went on cleaning up."

Virgil said, "Okay. So a couple guys cut their way through fences, shoot the tigers with a tranquilizer gun. Would they need night vision gear for that? Or is there enough ambient light?"

"Probably enough light," Best said. "I don't know—it can get dark in some of the corners. You sure as hell wouldn't want to get in the cages with the tigers before you knew they were asleep."

"Then what? They carry them out? How much does a tiger weigh?"

"A lot," Landseer said. "Artur, that's the male, was six hundred and forty-eight pounds at his last weigh-in. Katya, the female, was three hundred and eighty pounds."

Virgil held up a finger. "Wait. That's more than a thousand pounds altogether. A half ton. If they're that heavy, they'd need some kind of mechanized equipment to get them out. Even if they had four people, they'd be humping more than a hundred and fifty pounds each, to get the male cat out. That doesn't seem realistic."

"I asked about that and nobody heard anything mechanized," White said. "The holes in the fence aren't that big. There were fourteen people here on duty at the time, nobody heard anything unusual."

"How many were out in the area of the tiger exhibit?" Virgil asked.

"Twelve of the people are basically cleanup and maintenance; two of them are security guards and the guards circulate. They don't have any set routes, but they cover the whole zoo a few times a night."

"Why didn't they see the cut fences?" Duncan asked.

"Not that easy to see, in the dark," McCall said. "I'm not defending the guys, that's the fact of the matter. You can go out and look for yourself."

"I already did," White said, "and Mr. McCall is correct. It's hard to see."

"I'll take a look," Virgil said. "The big question is, how did they move the tranquilized cats? We have to figure out how and where they took the cats out of the zoo. This place is surrounded by houses, maybe somebody has a security camera."

Duncan said to Virgil, "The crime-scene guys have been up at that Minnetonka home invasion, but they were due back this afternoon. I'll check with Bea, see when she can get over here."

Virgil asked, "Does anybody know if tranquilizer guns have to be registered? Or do you need any kind of prescription or whatever for the darts? I assume the things are dangerous . . . you wouldn't want somebody shooting a human being."

"No, you wouldn't. The dose that would put Artur to sleep would kill a human," Best said. "The rest of it, you'd have to ask one of our vets."

"I'd like to get one of the vets to check your stock of darts and see if they're all accounted for," Virgil told Landseer.

She nodded: "I'll do that right now."

"One more question—this might sound stupid. Is it possible that the tigers are still here in the zoo, in some unused cage or den, and the thieves plan to take them out later? I mean, if they don't seem to have gone through the only exit . . . ?"

Everyone sat up, looked at each other and then the director, and Landseer said, "My goodness, nobody ever asked that question. I will have the zoo searched immediately. There are a few places where they could be kept. Wouldn't that be wonderful? To find them here?"

"Might want to tell your searchers to be careful," Duncan said. "Wouldn't want to unexpectedly walk in on a couple of hungry tigers."

Virgil turned to Best: "Could you show me around? I'd like to talk to the guy who heard the shots last night."

"Joel Charvin. I've got him standing by, and Bob Moreno, he's the one who spotted the cut fences."

"Let's go," Virgil said.

"You gotta hurry," McCall said. "Those tigers are in a world of trouble."

5

▼ ▼ ▼

Virgil and Best found Charvin and Moreno in a break room.

Charvin, a short thin man who looked like he might lift weights, didn't have much to contribute, except the time frame: "I think it was right around one-thirty. I was collecting trash, and I heard the sounds, these *pap pap pap* sounds. I was on the other side of the zoo and I looked over toward where the sounds came from, that's off to the west. The moon was going down, the bottom of the moon was touching the horizon. You should be able to check the time from that."

"I was told these guns are fairly quiet . . . but you could hear them on the other side of the zoo?" Virgil asked.

"Sort of. I didn't know what they were, never even thought they might be a tranquilizer gun," Charvin said. "They were just . . . different sounds than what I usually hear at night. Could have been somebody doing a golf clap, like *clap clap clap*."

"Three times, not two?" Virgil asked.

Charvin thought for a moment, his eyes half shut, then said, "Yeah. Three. *Clap clap clap*. There was some time between the sounds . . . maybe a minute."

"Okay, good," Virgil said. "Anything else?"

"Nope. I was working on the other side of the zoo, like I said, and didn't hear anything more. There's houses on the other side of the zoo fence and McAndrews Road is over there to the south, so there's always some noise. I didn't think any more about it until we found out the tigers were gone."

They talked for a couple of more minutes, then Virgil let Charvin go, and he, Best, and Moreno walked around the animal containment areas to the edge of the tiger exhibit. A chain-link fence kept people on the path, and the tiger area itself was enclosed by a heavy black chain-link fence that Virgil estimated to be fifteen to twenty feet high.

Virgil didn't immediately see the cut in the first fence, until Moreno pointed it out. Whoever had cut the fence had cut from the bottom up, a hole three and a half feet wide and two feet high, with the wires on the left edge left uncut so the fence could be swung open like a door.

When they left, the thieves had pushed the fence back in place and had fixed it there by taping some of the cut ends with narrow strips of silver duct tape, which were hard to see even if you knew what you were looking for.

"Anybody would miss that in the dark. Can't blame the security guys," Virgil said.

Best said, "They cut the hole in the tiger cage right over there."

All three of them clambered over the pathway fence and walked to the tiger enclosure. They found the same shape hole cut in the tiger fence, but the cut ends were taped together with black duct tape.

"Somebody thought about this a lot; there was serious planning going on," Virgil said. He got down on his hands and knees and examined the grass next to the cut, then looked up at Moreno and Best. "Take a look at this. Tell me what you see."

The two men got down on their hands and knees and scrutinized the grass near the cut. Moreno spoke first. "There's a line. You can barely see it."

"Oh, yeah," Best said. "I see it. It's straight. Not a shoe print."

"I think it's a wheel," Virgil said.

"They took them out of here on a dolly," Moreno said.

"I think so. Keep people away from here, especially the grass. Our crime-scene people will want to take a look." Virgil looked into the cage and asked, "Anything in there now?"

Best shook his head: "No."

Virgil grabbed the fence and carefully pulled it free of the tape splices, not touching the tape. He told the other two not to touch it and to be careful where they put their hands, knees, and feet, and all three of them crawled into the tiger enclosure. The enclosure was a pleasant piece of rolling ground, well treed, with a small pond, but not a tiger jungle, Virgil thought. He wondered if the tigers knew the difference.

He looked at the pond and asked, "Tigers swim?"

"Yeah, they do. They're not like house cats," Best said.

Virgil led the way to the highest point and motioned back to the cut fence. "The tigers had to be between here and the fence; couldn't see them from anywhere else. Which makes me wonder, how did they know the tigers would be up here?"

"I was talking to one of the keepers, not today, but a while ago, and he said tigers like to hang slightly below the top of a hill, where they're not silhouetted, but they're up high," Best said. "From there, they can see and hear everything, but they're hard to see themselves. An insider would probably know where they hung out."

Moreno: "Only an insider would know that we were letting them stay outside on hot nights."

They looked around a hillside, and Virgil had just said, "Okay, let's go . . ." when Moreno said, "Look at this."

He was pointing at the bottom of a tree at the top of the hill. Virgil went to look and saw a pencil-shaped dart with a furry red tail. "Dart."

"Must have missed once," Best said. "That's why Charvin heard three shots."

"Could be fingerprints," Virgil said. "We'll leave it for the crime-scene guys."

They eased back through the hole in the tiger fence and climbed back over the pathway fence, careful not to touch the grooves that might have been made by a dolly or wagon. From the hole in the pathway fence, Best said, the animals were carried, or rolled, along a service road to a metal gate, where the key was used. Virgil looked at the lock and agreed that it must have been a key. "Doesn't look like it was picked. Not a scratch on it."

"That's what Officer White thinks," Moreno said.

From the gate, Best said, the tigers were probably taken out to the parking lot—they could see the lot from where they were. Virgil studied it for a while, then said, "The parking lot is the obvious spot, but what are the other options? Say they've got the tigers on a dolly and they're moving them through the gate . . . and they want to stay on a hard surface."

"How would they get them out from there?" Best asked. "That second camera is way out by the only entrance and nobody went in or out."

"Once they had the tigers on a dolly, or maybe a couple of dollies, moving them wouldn't be that hard," Virgil said. "Where could they move them where the camera wouldn't see them?"

Best scratched his head, then said, "Well, they could take them behind the service buildings. There's a perimeter road over there that backs up to a regular street . . ."

"There's a fence around all of it, right?"

"Yeah."

"Let's go look," Virgil said.

The three of them hiked over to the far edge of the parking lot, and Moreno pointed out the adjoining street, through a screen of trees and brush. They walked along the perimeter fence, and a hundred yards up, Virgil saw the tape used to put the chain-link fence back together: "There."

"Kiss my ass," Best said. He looked back toward the zoo buildings: "They killed that camera because they were afraid it could see out here. Even if they didn't come in with a truck, they were afraid that it might pick them up."

"What happened was, they wanted the shortest line to get out of the tiger enclosure to a hard surface, which is why they had to get through that locked gate," Virgil said, as they looked back along the line of flight. "Once they were on the road, with a tiger on a dolly, they could roll it without working too hard. Then they needed to get to a place where it was the shortest distance to their vehicle."

They crawled through the hole in the perimeter fence, which led them into the backyard of a house. They trooped through the yard and around to the front, where they found a "For Sale" sign.

Virgil went to the front door, rang the doorbell, got no response, pounded on the door, then tramped through a flower bed and looked through a front window. "It's staged," he told the others. "I don't think there's anybody living here. Let's go around back again."

The house had a double garage, with a door leading into the backyard. The edge of the door was cracked, with a thin line of raw wood showing around the lock where somebody had used a tool to force the door. When Virgil placed his fingers against the top of the door and pushed, the door popped open. The garage was empty, but in the center of it, they saw a small dark splotch on the concrete.

"That could be blood," Virgil said, squatting down to look at it. He'd seen blood on concrete any number of times. "Let's move out of here without messing anything up. . . . Stay away from the line between the door and the fence; we'll see if we can spot any more wheel marks."

It took a while, but they did.

"Now we know how they did it," Moreno said, looking back at the fence line. "They loaded the cats on dollies, rolled them out of the exhibit, across the road, down here to the garage, where they probably had a truck waiting. Could even have a truck with a lift, like a moving truck."

"They had to have scouted out the house ahead of time," Virgil said. "I need to talk to the neighbors, see if anybody noticed any strange trucks or vans . . . or a truck going in the garage when it shouldn't have been."

"I bet your crime-scene people will be able to make something out of this," Best said.

"I bet they won't," Virgil replied.

Best tipped his head: "They won't?"

"Probably not. They're good at collecting evidence, if there is any, but that's usually most useful in a trial, or maybe in a real long investigation where you're looking at hundreds of possibilities and you're trying to eliminate some of them," Virgil said. "But, you know, you find dolly-wheel marks—how many people have dollies in their garages? You find Nike-patterned shoe prints—how many people wear Nikes? That's not really determinative evidence. This was well-enough planned that I don't think we're going to find a whole bunch of fingerprints. We might, but I doubt it."

"How about the blood?" Best asked. "DNA . . ."

"DNA's great, but that could be tiger blood, if it's blood at all. Then if it's human, and you really push on a critical need-to-know-right-now basis and get priority DNA examination, it'll take you three days to get results. That's chemistry, not bureaucracy," Virgil said. "If it's human blood and if the blood happens to be in the criminal database, then that's good. But three days for processing . . . The way the people back in the office were talking, we might not have three days."

"Jesus, I love those tigers," Moreno said. He was wearing a blue LA Dodgers hat, but took it off and curled the bill in his hands. "If somebody turns them into hairballs for some Chinese hairball, I'll shoot them myself."

"Let's get back," Virgil said. "We need to get Crime Scene down here, and I need to start calling people."

Crime Scene was on the way and Virgil, back at the zoo headquarters, sent them straight to the house outside the fence. He told Beatrice Sawyer, the head Crime Scene tech, about the spot of blood and the splintered door and the tape on the fences, the tracks in the dirt and the dart that waited in the tiger enclosure. "Anything you can get will help," he said. "I have nothing that points in any particular direction."

Then he called the real estate agent who'd listed the house for sale, told him that it had been broken into, warned him not to go into it, but asked him to meet in the driveway in an hour. The agent said he would be there: "The owners are in Moorhead—they relocated there. You want them to come back?"

"If they have any idea at all of who might know about their house . . . yeah, I'd like to talk to them," Virgil said.

"I'll call them," the agent said.

Virgil called the Apple Valley police, talked to the chief, told him about the break-in at the house where the tigers had been taken, and asked him to send a couple of cops around. "Tell them to stay out of the house—the crime-scene guys are on their way. The media's going to hear about it and we need to keep them backed off."

"We can do that," the chief said.

He took a call from Lucas Davenport, who'd been Virgil's boss at the BCA before he got pissed off and quit. "Del called and told me they put you on this tiger hunt, and that some people think the thieves are going to kill the tigers to make Chinese medicine. That right?"

"Yeah, I'm out at the zoo now, trying to figure it out," Virgil said.

"Everybody else is protecting the state fair from the Purdys. The fact that the Purdys are dead doesn't seem to make any difference."

"Listen, when that Black Hole case was going on a couple years back, I interviewed a guy named Toby Strait. He lives down I-35. He sells black bear gallbladders to the Chinese. He's right on the line between legal and illegal most of the time, and I know damn well he handles illegally shot bears during the hunting season. I don't know that he'd handle tigers, but he might. If he doesn't, he might know who would."

"Lucas: I gotta talk to that guy. You got a location?"

"No, we're up north right now, I'm working on my cabin," Davenport said. "His phone isn't listed anywhere, either. He keeps changing them, buying burners. I'll be back home tomorrow and I'll fire up my database and get a number to you."

"Nobody has access to the database down here?"

"No. It's on a hard drive at my house and it's encrypted," Davenport said.

"Get back to me as soon as you can," Virgil said. "If people are right about the medicine thing, these guys will kill the tigers. Might already have done it, and if they haven't, they'll do it soon."

"I'd go back tonight and look it up, but by the time I got home, it'd be too late to do anything," Davenport said. "I'll call you in the morning."

At zoo headquarters, the media had shown up in their vans and were setting up for the press conference. Virgil hung back, but watched Landseer, the zoo director, go through the routine—there was no information on the tigers, the Bureau of Criminal Apprehension was all over the case, they hoped to have the tigers back soon, etc.

Duncan took his turn under the lights, said that the attorney general had promised to prosecute the thieves to the fullest extent of the law. Duncan read a list of felonies that the perpetrators had already committed and said that upon conviction, those crimes would lead to thirty-six years in prison.

He added that since there was no market for tiger parts in Minnesota, interstate commerce was probably involved in the theft, and that Amur tigers were on the federal endangered species list. Those were federal offenses, and the FBI was sending agents to help with the case and federal charges were pending.

Landseer finished by saying, "I appeal to the people who have these animals: for the sake of the tigers and for your own sake, tell us where they are. Return them to us. If you do not, I believe you will spend the rest of your lives regretting your crime."

Not bad, Virgil thought.

Landseer and Duncan had barely finished their statements when the TV people started tearing down lights and hurrying back to their vans, not typical behavior, in Virgil's experience; they usually asked questions so each reporter could get his or her face on screen.

He wandered over to a cameraman he knew and asked, "What's the rush?"

"We're going to a crime-scene house around the block," the cameraman said. "You wanna be on TV, I'm sure the talent would be happy to have you."

"Nah."

He walked back to the house where the tigers had been taken: Beatrice Sawyer was there with the BCA crime-scene truck. The neighbors, Virgil thought, had spotted the truck and had called the TV stations. The vans were setting up a block down the street, held back by two Apple Valley cops.

Sawyer was around at the back of the house, looking at the door. "Where did all the TV come from?" she asked.

"Press conference at the zoo—the zoo's on the other side of the fence."

She looked down the street at the truck, then back to Virgil. "Glad I'm not Virgil," she said.

Neighborhood rubberneckers were out in force, standing on their lawns, watching the crime-scene crew moving back and forth between the van and the house. The real estate agent, whose name was Vance and who was too old and balding for his gelled hair, showed up, towed through the police lines by one of the Apple Valley cops.

Three couples had looked at the house over the past two months, he said, and he would find it hard to believe that any of them were involved in the tiger theft. "They're all middle-aged, middle-income, pre-approved people, FICO scores in the seven and eight hundreds," he said. "We did have an open house two weeks ago, and maybe fifteen people came, but we didn't take names on those."

Vance didn't have much more. Virgil took his card and turned him over to an Apple Valley cop to escort outside the blocked-off area. He was inside the garage talking to Sawyer about the spot on the concrete, which she also thought was blood, when the cop came back with a kid.

"Kid needs to talk to you," the cop said.

"What's up?" Virgil asked.

The boy was maybe sixteen or seventeen, thin, had been through a couple of episodes of acne, and was carrying a skateboard. He looked at Bea, then back to Virgil, and said, "Uh, this is kinda private."

Virgil said, "All right, let's go outside."

They walked around to the side of the garage and the kid said, "You can't tell any of the people this . . . the neighbors."

"Well, whattaya got?" Virgil asked.

"Last night I was up at my girlfriend's house . . ." The kid nodded up the street. "We were, you know, up in her bedroom, fooling around. Her parents were down in Missouri taking her sister to college, and they weren't supposed to get home until today. They got home last night instead. Like really late."

"Caught you," Virgil said.

"Nah . . . It sounds stupid, but I went out her window and snuck through some backyards before I went out to the street. When I went out, I saw a van coming out of this garage."

"What kind of a van?" Virgil asked.

"A white one. Like a panel van, like bands have, with those white windows that you can't see inside of. Pretty big van, but it could get in the garage, even with the door down. When I saw the door coming up, I kinda hid, I thought it was the Schmidts coming out and I didn't want them to see me. They don't like me 'cause I'm a skater, and they're kinda narcs, you know? They're friends with my girlfriend's parents and they'd rat me out. They'd *know* where I was coming from."

Virgil had learned from Vance, the real estate agent, that the owners of the house were named Schmidt. "You know what time this was?"

"I called my girlfriend when I got home to tell her that everything was chill and to find out if everything was chill with her. I saw on my phone that it was a little after two o'clock."

They talked about the van some more. The kid wasn't sure about it, but thought the van might be a Chevrolet. "I don't know why I think that, but I do," he said. The kid had one additional interesting fact: when the van came out of the garage, the garage door light didn't go on. Lights always come on when a garage door goes up or down, he said.

They walked around the corner of the garage and Virgil looked up at the door-lift mechanism, which showed a white plastic cover over what should be a lightbulb. He hit the wall switch and the garage door started down, but the light didn't come on. He stopped the door and ran it back up. Still no light. Bea Sawyer had watched him do that and said, "Somebody unscrewed the bulb?"

"I think so," Virgil said.

"We'll check the whole thing," she said. "That's a good find."

Virgil and the teenager went back outside, where Virgil slapped the kid on the back and said, "You did really good. You've got a sharp eye and some balls to come over and tell me this. Maybe you oughta be a cop."

The kid brightened. "You think?"

"Why not? Take a test or something, see if you got the aptitude. Talk to your school counselor, see what he thinks," Virgil said.

"That guy's a dick," the kid said. "He already told me I'll be washing dishes the rest of my life."

"Fuck him," Virgil said. "I hate people who tell kids things like that. You do the best you can and forget about him."

"Okay . . . but listen, don't tell anybody about, you know, sneaking out of my girlfriend's house."

"You're good with me," Virgil said.

When the kid was gone, escorted back through the police lines by the Apple Valley cops, Virgil called Duncan, who was caught in traffic halfway back to St. Paul. "We're looking for a white van, blocked-out white windows, larger than standard, maybe a Chevy, no other information. The thieves could have had their own, but we need to get Sandy calling all the local rental places."

"I'll talk to her when I get back, if I ever get back," Duncan said. "Sounds like you're rolling."

"Got lucky," Virgil said. "From here on out, it's gonna get harder."

He hung up and from behind him, Bea, who was standing on a stepladder squinting at the lightbulb in the garage door lift mechanism, said, "Hey: we got some prints."

"Really," Virgil said. He was interested, but not excited. "I got two bucks says they've got nothing to do with this."

As the afternoon, then evening, wore on, Virgil walked around to all the houses on the block, introducing himself and asking about the white van, and about possible security cameras. The neighbors were cooperative, but he got nothing but the aerobic exercise.

The Apple Valley chief stopped by, found Virgil, and when Virgil told him what he was doing, offered to send a few more cops around to the nearby blocks asking the same question. Virgil took him up on it, and a half hour later, cops were interrogating people across a five-block range.

The neighborhood was intensely residential, though, and except for one insomniac who had seen a late-night white van in the neighborhood—right time, right place, but not as much information as the kid had provided—there were no surveillance cameras of the kind found on convenience stores and gas stations. None of the three churches in the neighborhood or the elementary school had cameras looking out at the street.

The crime-scene crew had finished with the garage. Bea had gotten good prints off the lightbulb and had sent digital copies to BCA headquarters, to be relayed to the FBI, and she confirmed the spot on the floor was blood, species unknown. The crew was now working along the route that the tiger thieves had taken across the zoo property, looking for anything else that might help.

Virgil walked back to Landseer's office to watch the press conference on the evening news. He and Landseer stood together in front of the TV, and Landseer said, "We're not missing any tranquilizer darts. They're all accounted for, and they all have International Orange tails, not red."

"Okay."

The news came up, and a reporter named Daisy Jones, whom Virgil considered a possible sexual refuge if all else failed, and whom he suspected of classifying him in the same way, did a quick rundown of the investigation so far and a follow-up interview with Jon Duncan.

Duncan was smooth on camera and stacked up the threats of long prison sentences and remorseless investigation. "We *will* get the cats back, and we *will* send these jokers to prison."

When she was done with Duncan, Jones turned back to the camera and said, "Duncan tells us that the BCA's top investigator, Virgil Flowers, has been assigned to the tiger recovery. Flowers has been involved in a number of high-profile cases that have resulted in major convictions. Duncan said that he thought the result here would be the same—that Flowers would get the tigers back to the zoo and send the thieves to long terms at Stillwater prison."

Landseer, who was watching the show with Virgil, said, "That's very flattering. I'm glad to have you on the case."

Virgil said, "Daisy never flatters without a motive. I expect she'll be calling me in the next five minutes."

•

He took a call a few minutes later, not from Daisy Jones, but from Frankie.

"I wasn't kidding about sleeping over and I'm not going to wreck my back on your crappy old mattress. And I've had baby mattresses that smelled better. Anyway, I'm down at Slumberland and I'm buying us a new one. The question is, California king or eastern king?"

"What's the difference?"

"California is a little longer but a little narrower," Frankie said. "I'm thinking we go that way, because I don't take up much space and you need the length."

"Let's do that, then. Will it fit in my bedroom?"

"I measured. If you get back tonight, we can give it a test drive," she said.

"You can get it tonight?"

"I can get it in twenty minutes," she said.

"Well . . . see you tonight. Before you buy it, though, talk to the manager," Virgil, said. "Make sure it can take a vicious pounding."

"I'll be sure to ask," she said.

Virgil got off the phone, now distracted: somehow, buying a bed with his girlfriend felt like an important step. There were, he suspected, extensive implications to the purchase, about which most women could have long consultations in coffee shops. He shuddered and called Jon Duncan.

"I'm going home," Virgil said. "I'll be back early tomorrow."

"Why don't you crash in a motel?"

"I don't have my stuff," Virgil said. "I left in a rush and it's less than an hour from here anyway. I can be back before anybody wakes up tomorrow. I've got some household chores to do and I'll pack up a bag in the morning."

"Hate household chores," Duncan said. "Two days later, you gotta do it all over again."

"I hear you, brother," Virgil said.

Later that night, a sweaty Frankie said, "Let's do that all over again."

"Gotta get up early," Virgil said.

"Not before you finish the household chores," she said.

He was about to finish the chores when an image popped up in his mind, a tall, broad-shouldered, naked blonde about to dive into the swimming hole.

Sparkle? That you?

6

▼ ▼ ▼

Winston Peck VI was standing in his driveway, smoking a Marlboro, double garage door in the up position, when Zhang Xiaomin wheeled his Ferrari California around the corner, dropped it into second, and accelerated up the street, generating enough racket to wake the heavily tranquilized.

He pulled into the driveway, revved the engine a few times to annoy anyone who hadn't already been awake, so they could witness his involvement with Peck.

Zhang got out of his car with a selfie grin, as though he expected to be congratulated and possibly photographed. Peck snapped his cigarette out into the street and said, "X, for God's sakes, what are you doing? Put the car in the garage and get in the fucking house."

Zhang, a slender man of middling height, wearing a black silk athletic suit with a small tiger's face on the breast, poked a finger at him: "You do not speak to me like this. You know who I am."

"Yeah. You're the son of a Chinese rich guy who thinks you're a worthless pain in the ass."

Zhang dropped into a combat stance, two fingers extended in a snake hand. "Bring it," he said.

Peck said, "Oh, fuck you. Get the money."

"I want to see the cats before you get money," Zhang said.

Peck looked at him with what he hoped was a hard, intimidating glare, then said, "Put your car in the garage. I want it out of sight."

Zhang took his time doing that, careful not even to brush any of the various brooms, shovels, snowblowers, or racks in Peck's garage. A one-inch scratch on a Ferrari was maybe ten grand, if you wanted a perfect Ferrari, and his father did; the car was in his father's name, not his.

As Zhang eased the car into the garage, Peck thought about what a perfect dumb motherfucker Zhang actually was. Zhang's father, on the other hand, was not. Zhang Min was a Chinese refugee currently ensconced in Pasadena, California, where he was easing back into criminal activity after fleeing his life of industrial crime in China. The elder Zhang had noticed—this wasn't hard—that there were 2.2 million former mainland Chinese living in the United States, effectively cut off from their supply of traditional and illegal Chinese medicine.

A fast man to sniff out an underserved market, he'd begun weaving a drug distribution network centered in Los Angeles; his problem was supply. Peck was part of his answer.

Peck went into his house and found a ski mask he actually used for cross-country skiing, then backed his Tahoe out. He pointed Zhang at the passenger side of the Tahoe, dropped the garage door. Peck took them out to I-94 and east out of St. Paul.

"How's your father? Still doing well?"

"He is angry, as always," Zhang said.

"Angry with me? With us?"

"With me," Zhang said. "He is impossible to please."

"He *is* sort of an asshole, but we need him, you and I. At least for the time being."

Zhang looked out the window, scowling.

When they passed Radio Drive, Peck handed Zhang the ski mask and said, "Put it on backward. You can roll up the bottom enough to breathe."

"I'm not gonna . . ."

"You do it or we go back and forget the whole thing," Peck said. "That would make the old man happy, huh? Dropping everything? I'm not gonna let you see where we're going, X." Peck couldn't actually pronounce Xiaomin's first name, and they agreed he could shorten it to X, which X seemed to like. "You run your mouth too much; you do stupid shit all the time. It's my ass on the line, too."

"Fuck you," Zhang said, but he pulled the mask on backward, leaving the end of his nose and mouth exposed.

Peck drove on for a few more miles to Manning Avenue, got off the highway, turned north, did a couple of laps around the parking lot of a Holiday station, to confuse things, then went back out to Manning Avenue and turned south.

"Are we there?" Zhang asked. "I'm getting carsick."

"Hang on for another couple of minutes," Peck said. "Don't go puking in my truck."

The farm was eight or nine miles out, a run-down place waiting for the suburbs to arrive. The house had last been lived in by two community college students, two years earlier. It had functioning electricity; a functioning well; a semifunctioning septic system that the day before had leaked water onto the yard, which Peck had stepped in; and a barn out back. The farm was owned by a New York investor, the guy waiting for the suburbs to arrive. They pulled into the barnyard, and Peck said, "You can take the mask off."

Hayk Simonian came out and stood in the headlights, a burly man in a blood-spattered apron, carrying a long skinning knife in one hand. He was smoking one of his Black Flames, a yellowish cloud of nicotine and tars swirling around his head. Peck turned the headlights off, and then he and Zhang walked to the barn where Simonian said, "We still got a long way to go. What are you doing here? Why's this asshole here?"

"I need to show X that we got them," Peck said. "It's a money thing."

Simonian said, "We got more than tigers. We got a whole shitload of trouble. You been watching the TV?"

"No—but we knew they'd freak out."

"More than that. They put the state cops on the case. The state DA says they're gonna catch us and they've got enough crimes already to lock us up for thirty years. Life, if we kill the tigers."

"Nonsense. Besides, they're not gonna catch us," Peck said. "There won't be the hair of a tiger around here in a week."

"Where're the cats?" Zhang asked.

"Inside," Simonian said. He tipped his head toward the barn door. Simonian was wearing cargo shorts, flip-flops, and an LA Dodgers T-shirt under the plastic apron. All the clothing showed splashes and speckles of blood.

He led the way into the barn, where three work lights provided high-contrast lighting over the central part of the barn floor. The dead male tiger was hanging from a ceiling hook, above a big, blue plastic tarp. The tarp was smeared with blood.

The tiger's hide had been removed and was lying on another tarp at one side of the barn floor, like a cheap rug. The naked torso of the tiger might have been a huge, oversized man . . . except for the head, where the bared teeth shone like antique ivory daggers.

The whole place smelled of blood, intestinal sludge, tiger poop, and sweat.

Simonian nodded at a row of Tupperware containers on the floor near the pelt. "Eyes, whiskers, claws, balls, cock, all separate, like you said. I'm looking at the pictures and I can get the kidneys and liver, but I sort of fucked up the spleen."

"You've got to be more careful. That spleen was probably worth a couple grand all by itself," Peck said, peering at the heavy naked muscles of the tiger's body.

Simonian said, "All I got is a comic-book picture of his guts to go by. Anyway, I still got it, only it's sort of mushed up."

"Keep it, then, but get it in the dryer before it goes bad," Peck said. And to Zhang: "You satisfied?"

"Yeah." Zhang had walked a long circle around the hanging torso, continuing to the back where the female tiger stared at them from her cage. A few feet from her cage, he made a sudden aggressive move forward. The tiger reacted, moving forward herself, but faster, harder than anything Zhang was capable of. Zhang jumped back, startled, laughed nervously, and then turned to Peck and said, "Can I shoot her?"

"Not now," Peck said, the irritation riding in his voice. "We don't have a lot of refrigeration here, as you can see, so we need to keep her alive until we're done with the big boy."

Zhang went over and stroked Artur's pelt, then picked it up;

the hide was heavy, and he strained to lift it. "Help me put it on my shoulders—I want to take a picture of it."

"No," Peck said. "Put it down. You hear what Hayk said about thirty years? All you need is a picture of you with a tiger skin on your head on Facebook. Put it down."

Zhang dropped the pelt like a rag. "You guys are pussies."

Simonian said, "What?"

Zhang poked a finger at him, as he had with Peck. "I said . . ."

Simonian stepped toward him and Zhang slipped back in his snake pose. Simonian turned to Peck and asked, "What the fuck is that?"

"A martial art thing," Peck said. "It's the beaver stance or something."

Simonian said, "Yeah?" and casually reached out and slapped Zhang on the side of the head, nearly flattening him. Then he slapped him four or five more times, making a rapid *pop-pop-pop* sound, using alternate hands, as though Zhang's head was a speed bag.

Peck said, "Okay, knock it off, knock it off."

Simonian stopped and said, "Martial bullshit," and Peck said to Zhang, who'd staggered to the side wall and was leaning back against it, "You've seen the cats. Let's go."

Outside, Zhang held one hand to an ear and, with the other, poked a finger at Peck. "I'll come back and kill him. I'll come back and tear his heart out and eat it raw." There was a bit of blood under one of his nostrils and at the right corner of his mouth.

"X, Hayk could beat you to death by accident. You're a silly, useless asshole, and you've got to learn to live with that," Peck said. "Get in the fuckin' truck."

"You will tell Hayk to treat me with respect . . ."

"Hayk's basically your father's man," Peck said. "I don't tell him much."

Winston Peck VI was the son, grandson, great-grandson, great-great-grandson, and great-great-great-grandson of physicians, going back to Winston I, who served with distinction in the Union Army during the Civil War. Peck VI had actually gotten an MD degree, by the skin of his teeth, only to be subsequently banned from the profession for unusually intrusive examinations of young female clients during his residency at a medical clinic in Indianapolis. He had been lucky to escape sexual assault charges. For what? Copping a feel? Nothing that didn't happen every Saturday night behind the local high school. And the women had been unconscious, so they didn't even really *experience* it. All very discouraging.

After that episode, he'd moved to St. Paul to be close to the money of his mother, first wife of Peck V, but when she died young, in her early sixties, he was appalled to find that most of her estate went to her second husband. Peck was dismissed with a hundred thousand dollars, which had lasted a bit more than a year.

Still, he had the MD degree—they might not let him practice, but they couldn't take the degree away—and reinvented himself as an authority on traditional Chinese, Indian, Vietnamese, and Native American medicine: whatever the buckskin-and-bead set seemed to be indulging itself with.

Life was hard, though, and he was considering immigration to Sedona, Arizona, where the pickings might be better, when he'd encountered Zhang Min at a traditional medicine convention. After several friendly conversations, each recognized the innate criminality in the other, and an arrangement was reached: Peck would supply, Zhang Min would distribute.

The early medicines were derived from African and Asian sources, routed through Canada.

Eventually, some of the more demanding clients asked about getting the tip-top quality of product, as derived from endangered tigers and rhinos.

The money was big—and led to the raid on the Minnesota Zoo, though the whole idea had left Peck scared shitless: two certified, endangered Amur tigers. Fewer than six hundred of them remained in the wild, and no privately held tigers were known to be Amurs. A good Amur could provide medicines to increase libido, improve sagging male potency, repair liver and lung damage, and cure incontinence and irritable bowels.

Zhang Min was no fool, and he wanted proof that he would be getting what he was paying for. He supplied assistants in the form of the Simonian brothers, whom he met through Armenian gang contacts in Glendale, and he also sent his ne'er-do-well son to keep an eye on things.

So I have now seen these things," Zhang said through the wool of the ski mask that was again covering his eyes. "I will inform my father tonight. When will we get the medicines?"

"Some of it, like the powdered whiskers, we can FedEx out right away," Peck said. "Other parts will take a while. They have to be dried, purified, and ground up. That takes time. He should start getting the more powerful stuff, like the ground femur, in a couple of weeks. But I've got a lot on the line here. I want to see the money. If I don't, I've got other customers. Your father jumped the line."

"Because of his money."

"That was an important part of it," Peck said, unembarrassed. "So, how old is your stepmother?"

"She is not my stepmother yet," Zhang said, the resentment boiling in his voice. He'd turned away to look out the window.

"Okay. I forget—how old is your father's fiancée?"

"Fifteen," Zhang said, after a moment.

"My, my. Do the police know?"

"This is an internal Chinese matter," Zhang said. "It is arranged between our family and her family."

"Yeah. Arranged in San Francisco, where Chinese arrangements are not always in line with accepted American core values. Or laws, for that matter. Putting the pork to a fifteen-year-old may be pleasurable, right up to the doors of San Quentin, or wherever California puts the pederasts now."

Zhang jabbed a finger at him: "You will keep your mouth shut about this."

"She a looker?"

"She has attractions," Zhang admitted after a moment.

"Oooh. Big tits? Is that what we're talking here? Big tits on a fifteen-year-old? How's her ass? Nice and tight?"

"She . . ."

"I would think this arrangement would make you unhappy," Peck said. "How old are you, X? Forty? Your stepmother will be, what, twenty-five years younger than you? A hot Chinese chick could keep your old man turned on forever. She could be pooping out babies for twenty years. What part of the fortune will you get?"

"Shut up," Zhang said. And, "I am thirty-eight."

"We provide your father the medicine, all right. Maybe you and I could work out another arrangement, on our own."

Long silence. Zhang said, "I'm devoted to Father."

"Of course you are," Peck said. "We will take maximum care that all of these medicines are completely safe and nonlethal."

"Yes."

"When's the wedding?" Peck asked.

"Two months," Zhang said.

"Huh. *Forbes* said your father has more than a hundred million dollars. I'm sure he will leave you with at least a million."

"Shut up."

"How much does a Ferrari cost?"

"Shut up."

They rode in silence until Peck rolled around the gas station again, then back to I-94, where he told Zhang that he could remove the ski mask. Zhang peeled if off and said, "You are a very bad man to make me think these things about my father."

"Yes, I am," Peck said. "I'm bad. Small-time bad. Your father is big-time bad. Evil, in every sense of the word. As I understand it, the women working in his factories were no better than slaves, that he had them beaten if they didn't meet production quotas, that he kept them locked in concrete cells, that some might have died there. Chinese articles on the 'net say he routinely forced the younger women to have sex with him, and that in the end, he took money that should have been theirs and ran to the U.S. The Chinese government says he left behind an environmental disaster at his battery factories."

"All so Americans can have their cheap cell phones," Zhang sneered.

"I don't care why he did all that, to tell you the truth," Peck said. "He's lived like a sultan for years, too much rich food, too much booze, too many cigarettes. The fact is, he'll never see seventy, the way he's going. He'll probably die in the next few years and then this little Chinese flower will get all the money. From your point of view, it's too bad that he didn't die a little sooner, huh? It's the difference between a lifetime of used Toyota Corollas and a lifetime of private jets and new red Ferraris."

"Shut up," Zhang said.

"*Used* Corollas," Peck said. "Of course, they do get a lot of miles per gallon, which is helpful if you're poor."

"Shut up."

They were back at Peck's place fifteen minutes later.

He'd made some inroads, Peck thought.

Old man Zhang would give him a quarter-million dollars, cash, no taxes, for all the various medicines they could squeeze out of two adult Amur tigers. Young man Zhang might do much better than that, if properly blackmailed.

"Get the money," he said, as he rolled the garage door up.

Zhang got an Amazon mailing box from the floor of his car and they went into the kitchen where he opened it to reveal stacks of fifty-dollar bills. He counted out twenty-five thousand dollars, beautiful engravings of Ulysses S. Grant piling up on the dining table.

The pile made Peck's heart flutter. Maybe he wasn't a total sociopath, he thought: he *did* love money.

7

▼ ▼ ▼

Virgil got up at seven o'clock, feeling that all was right with the world, though he knew it wasn't, never had been, and never would be. Honus was sleeping between Virgil and Frankie, yawned, and made Virgil yawn, then Virgil slapped Frankie on her lightly garbed butt and went to get cleaned up.

The new bed was a complete success. His toes no longer hung over the end, and when he needed to dig them in, he could.

Frankie squeezed into the bathroom as he was getting out of the shower, stared at herself in the fogged-up mirror for a moment, then asked, "Why do I look better when the mirror is fogged up?"

Far too experienced to attempt an answer, Virgil said instead, "I hope those tigers are okay."

Frankie yawned, stretched, and then rubbed the fog off the mirror with a *squeak-squeak* sound and asked, "You coming back tonight?"

"If I can. I'm gonna take my bag, though. You've got to walk the dog and feed him; I don't have time this morning."

"All right. Sparkle and Bill are over at the Castro factory," Frankie said. "Probably right now. They want to talk to workers going through the gate."

"You worried?"

"Yep. Me and Sparkle don't see eye to eye, but I don't want her to get hurt. Bill should give her some protection. I don't think they'd beat up anybody with a witness around . . . would they?"

"I don't know that they'd beat up anybody at all," Virgil said. "Most companies will beat you up with lawyers and PR ladies, not with goons. Not anymore."

"Well, this is old man Castro we're talking about. He's a throwback to the bad old days," Frankie said.

"You're sure Bill will be there?"

"Yeah, he speaks good Spanish, if Sparkle needs an interpreter."

"Tell you what—I'll swing by there, talk with them," Virgil said. "If the company people see me around, maybe they'll think twice."

Virgil was on the highway at eight o'clock, listening to radio news programs out of the Twin Cities. The tigers were the first item.

". . . the longer the tigers are missing, the more likely the outcome is to be tragic, according to experts on zoo thefts. We're speaking to Dr. Randolph Bern of the American Association of Zoological Gardens. Good morning, Dr. Bern . . ."

Virgil didn't think too much about the media, except to exploit them when he needed to. The media was like rain: when it was falling on your head, there wasn't much you could do about it. Unless, of course, you were a bureaucrat, in which case you ran around in circles and threw your hands in the air and prepared statements, none of which accomplished anything.

Dr. Bern told him nothing he needed to know, so he switched to a country station and listened to Terry Allen sing "Bottom of the World," a song he didn't hear often enough. On the way north, he detoured off Highway 169 through Le Sueur, threaded his way across town and out into the countryside, where the Castro factory poked up like a brick thumb.

Virgil turned into the dusty parking lot and saw Father Bill leaning against the hood of Sparkle's Mini Cooper Clubman, smoking a cigar. Virgil pulled up next to him and got out.

"Virgil," Bill said, with his square-toothed Hemingway grin. "You look different with your clothes on."

"Bill: Where's Sparkle?"

"She's inside. Some factory . . . functionary . . . came out and asked her what she was doing, talking to people," Bill said. "She told him, and they invited her inside to talk to the manager. I wasn't invited."

"She okay?"

"I hope so. She does tend to bite off more than she can chew," Bill said.

Virgil looked at the factory, which resembled something he imagined a medieval madhouse might look like, dirty-white window frames scattered around a four-story dark brick wall, with massive chimneys belching steam into the summer air.

Down at the far end of the building, trucks were unloading produce across receiving docks, and the odor of hot pickle and rotten vegetables mixed with truck diesel fumes and the smell of the corn maturing in the surrounding fields: altogether, the familiar and not entirely pleasant perfume of industrial agriculture. The smoke from Bill's cigar didn't help.

"Hostile place," he said.

"The people going in looked pretty tough—beat-up, tired. Lots of illegals, I think," Bill said. "Mostly women, here at the factory. Most of them weren't interested in talking to us. The ones that did said that everything was just fine. Sparkle thought maybe I should wear my collar out here, but I wasn't comfortable doing that. Not without thinking about it for a while."

"People look scared at all?" Virgil asked.

"No, no. They looked tired, more than anything."

"Huh." They stood and looked at the factory for another minute, then Virgil gave Bill a business card with his private cell number on it, and said, "If there's any kind of trouble, call me."

"I will. I've got to be to work by four o'clock, so I've got to be out of here before the first shift ends. I think Sparkle will be coming back alone this afternoon," Bill said. He blew smoke, then added, "I don't think there'll be any trouble here, at the plant. If they give her any trouble, it'll be away from here."

"Well, let me know," Virgil said. He handed Bill a second card. "Give one to Sparkle."

Virgil stopped at the zoo, talked to Landseer for a few minutes to see if anything interesting had come in—e-mails with tips, ransom notes, abject confessions. Nothing had.

"I'm frightened and quite depressed," she said. "I think the tigers may be gone forever."

"If it goes a week, I'd agree. If we can get a hint, a crack, anything, soon, then we might be able to save them. If this is an insider job or if an insider provided keys to the tiger areas, then we need to find and locate that guy," Virgil told her. "I know that managers don't like to do anything that would suggest to employees that you suspect them of wrongdoing . . ."

"I won't do that, not without specific evidence," she said.

". . . but what I'd like you to do is to come up with a list of people you *think* would be most likely to be involved," Virgil said. "You don't have to write anything down, do it in your head. Maybe talk it over with somebody else you trust. Then we'll call them together, and mix in a bunch of people you're sure are *not* involved . . . in other words, make it a big meeting. I'll give a talk about the investigation and see if we can generate some tips."

"In other words, you want me to put the finger on a specific group of people, but disguise it so it looks like we're talking to everybody," Landseer said.

"Exactly right," Virgil said. "That way, nobody feels oppressed or anything, but at the same time, we whisper in the ear of the guilty party . . . or somebody who knows who the guilty party is."

"Ethically, I'm not sure how that differs from me giving you a list of people to harass," Landseer said.

"Ethically, there might not be any theoretical difference, but nobody gets their feelings hurt and nobody sues you. There are some practicalities involved."

Landseer thought it over for a few seconds, then said, "I want the tigers back."

Virgil nearly bit his tongue off as he was about to blurt, "Atta girl," but managed to abort the reaction and said instead, piously, "I think we all do. Our ethical positions have to take into consideration the impact our decisions will have on the tigers, with whose care we are entrusted."

"You're a very capable bullshitter," Landseer said.

"Thank you."

"When do you want to do it?" she asked.

"Soon as possible," Virgil said.

"Lunchtime. Twelve noon."

Virgil continued on to BCA headquarters in St. Paul, where he spent some time with the crime-scene crew, looking at what they'd gotten. The blood spot on the floor turned out to be human blood, and fresh.

"There wasn't much. It was a superficial layer on the concrete, not soaked in," Bea Sawyer told him. "It looked like somebody might have cut himself and a drop of blood hit the concrete. I'm thinking it could have happened when they were handling the tigers, all those teeth and claws."

"Think they'd need treatment?"

She shrugged. "We're only seeing one drop. He might've bled all over a tiger or wrapped the cut with a hanky or something, so there might be a lot of blood that we're not seeing. Or it could be one drop. Not enough information to tell. We've got it in line for DNA processing, but you know what the line's like."

"Yeah." The DNA-processing line was short enough that they'd have evidence for a trial, but long enough that it wouldn't do much for solving the case, even if they eventually got a hit from the DNA database. "Why would you think anyone would wrap a cut with a hanky?"

"Well . . . to stop the bleeding."

"But why with a hanky? Who do you know carries a hanky?" Virgil asked.

"It's just an expression, Virgil," Sawyer said.

"You know who wraps wounds with a hanky?" Virgil asked. "People on TV. Somebody gets cut on TV, they've got a hanky. In real life, no hanky. You need a different expression: wrapping the wound with toilet paper. Or Dunkin' Donuts napkins. Something more intelligent than a hanky."

"Right, I'll put it on top of my lists of things to do," Sawyer said. *"Get new expression."*

"It's like people getting hit with lead pipes," Virgil continued. "Who gets hit with lead pipes? They haven't made them for a hundred years. There aren't any lead pipes around, except maybe in water mains, and water mains are way too big to hit anyone with. Copper pipes, steel pipes, iron pipes, plastic pipes—no lead pipes. Nobody gets hit with lead pipes."

"I'll write that in my book of Virgil Flowers tips," Sawyer said, exasperated. "Now get out of my hair."

Sandy, the researcher, saw him in the hallway, said she'd called several van-rental places, and there'd been a lot of vans out during the period that covered the thefts. Not all had been returned, but of those that had, nobody noticed any blood, tiger hair, or anything else unusual, and some of the vans had already been re-rented. She was compiling a list of names of the renters.

"The problem is, if they drove here from California or Washington, they might have rented the vans out there," she told Virgil.

"Why would they be from California or Washington?"

"Because of where you find the traditional medicine shippers dealing with China. Those tigers could be in Salt Lake by now, if they're on the back of a tractor-trailer."

"Could you get me the names of these shippers?" Virgil asked.

Davenport called. He had a phone number for Toby Strait, his contact in the animal parts underworld. "His girlfriend said he's hiding out from an animal rights activist who shot him last year."

"I heard something about that . . . didn't remember his name, though. The girlfriend didn't have a phone number for him?"

"She says not, though she's probably lying," Davenport said. "She also told me that he's moving away from black bear gallbladders and is focusing more on reticulated python skins. She says he can generate more volume with snakeskins with less personnel trouble."

"Pythons? Where does he get them?"

"Mostly from former dairy farmers who've got heated barns," Davenport said. "They feed them, grow them, kill them, and skin them. He deals the hides to Italy."

"Minnesota dairy farmers are raising snakes? Sounds nasty," Virgil said.

"It is nasty. Strait's not a nice guy. And he's a little fucked up right now. That animal rights woman shot him through both legs and he's hobbling around. They let her out on bond and he thinks she's looking to solve both her problems. If she shoots him through the heart next time, she gets rid of an animal abuser and the primary witness for the first shooting."

"You think she's really doing that? Hunting him down?"

"Wouldn't be surprised," Davenport said. "Her name's Maxine Knowles and she lives somewhere up by Monticello. You better find him quick. You know, before she does."

Sandy came back: "Got a name for you. Biggest shipper out of the U.S. Name is Ho, and he works out of Seattle."

Virgil found an empty conference room that was quiet and private and called Ho. The call was answered by a woman with a soft, high-pitched voice that sounded like a child's. She had a musical Asian accent. "Can I tell Mr. Ho who's calling?"

Virgil identified himself, and she said, "One moment, please. I will see if Mr. Ho is in his office."

Ho was in his office, all right, Virgil thought, as he sat listening to an orchestra version of the Beatles' "Eleanor Rigby," but was trying to concoct a reasonable lie about being somewhere else, out of touch.

To Virgil's mild surprise, Ho came up. His voice carried no trace of any accent except maybe UCLA computer science. "This is Ho. We know nothing about it. I wouldn't touch a tiger with a ten-foot pole. Or even a ten-foot Ukrainian."

"Who would?"

"I don't know. What kind of numb-nuts would kidnap a couple of endangered-list tigers? You gotta know that the cops'll be hunting you down like you were a rabid skunk. I'd suggest you go look for lunatics and don't call Ho."

"Mr. Ho, uh . . . what's your first name?"

"Dick."

"Dick . . . really? Okay, I understand that tiger parts are used in traditional Chinese medicine."

"That's correct—but they don't get the tiger parts from me. Or from anywhere in the States. Most of what's sold in the States as tiger product comes from something else—God only knows what.

Maybe alley cats. Anyway, it's all fake. If the feds catch you shipping tiger parts *into* the States, you're looking at three to five in Victorville. If you were shipping them *out*, and they were stolen from a zoo, you'd probably get the needle."

"Which would maybe be one reason to kidnap a tiger *in* the States and keep it here?"

"Might be a reason, but it's not a sane one. It's crazy," Ho said.

"But that's what happened here. Since you deal in traditional medicine . . . are there people in Minnesota that would be knowledgeable in the area of traditional medicine? That you know and work with? That I could talk to?"

"Yes." Long pause. "You didn't hear this from me."

"Okay."

"Let me get my list up." Virgil heard the rattle of a keyboard, then Ho came back: "Talk to four people. Dr. Winston Peck, MD, in St. Paul; India Healer Sandra S. A. Gupti-Mack in Minneapolis; Carolyn C. Monty-McCall, PhD, in Apple Valley; and Toby Strait of Owatonna. I can get you those addresses and phone numbers . . ."

"A couple people have mentioned Toby Strait," Virgil said. "You think . . . ?"

"No. Not Toby himself. Don't tell anyone I told you this, but Toby looks at animals the way most people would look at a turnip or a cabbage. Killing doesn't bother him. But he's not a reckless businessman. If somebody offered him a couple of tigers, he'd do the calculation, and then he'd step back. He wouldn't have any moral problem with killing a couple of rare tigers, but he'd see the practical problems. He'd know that if he got caught, he'd get no mercy from anyone."

"All right. Give me those addresses and phone numbers, if you could."

Ho produced them, and Virgil said, "Thank you," as he wrote them down, then Ho asked, "Say, where'd you get my name?"

"Internet," Virgil said.

"Of course. Why'd I even ask?"

The noon meeting at the zoo was crowded with employees, many of them in blue employee uniform shirts, with a necktie here and there. A rumbling conversation continued even after Landseer rapped on a microphone with a steel ballpoint, and finally a guy stood up and shouted, "Everybody shut up."

Landseer said, "Thank you, Ed," to the man, who sat down again as the talk died, and Landseer said simply, "I called this meeting so that the state agent can talk to you about the theft of the tigers. His name is Virgil Flowers and he has an exceptional record of solving major crimes, so we have high hopes he'll get our tigers back. Agent Flowers . . ."

Virgil got up and gave his talk, and said in part, "I'm sure you've all heard some of the details of the way the tigers were taken out of here, probably on a dolly of some sort, maybe like the flat ones that furniture movers use. You've probably heard that the catnappers cut holes in the fence to get into the holding areas, or whatever you call them. You may *not* have heard that they didn't cut through the lock on the gate. The lock is a good one, and we don't believe it was picked. The thieves had a key, and the key had to come from inside the zoo. They either stole it, or somebody gave the key to the thieves. We're hoping somebody here in the room will know of a way the key could have been stolen, might have seen some unauthorized person in the gear closet where the keys are kept, or might have heard of some unauthorized use of the keys by somebody here in the zoo. We're not asking you to rat out a friend—we're asking you to help us trace the key to whoever has the tigers. We need to do this quickly. Some people think the tigers may have been stolen for use in traditional Chinese medicine, which would mean killing them."

A man asked, "Why do you think it's Chinese medicine? Seems to me more likely that it might be anti-zoo activists."

Virgil said, "We're looking at those people, but there're not many of them, and whatever they say in their literature, they don't have a record of doing things like this. They're more likely to chain themselves to the entry gate. We think somebody did this purely for the payday. The only way there'll be a big payday is if the animals are processed for medicine."

There were a few more questions and some grumbling and Virgil finished by asking for tips at the BCA website: "There's a click-on link at the top of the page that says, 'Select a popular function.' If you click on that, you'll find a link called 'Provide a tip.' You can do it anonymously. Mention my name or the tigers. At this point, we'd appreciate any help we can get."

Landseer took the microphone back and said, "We need to get this done in a hurry, people. If you know anything at all, or even suspect something, please, please call Agent Flowers or leave a tip."

When everybody had shuffled out of the meeting room, Landseer asked, "What do you think?"

"Hard to tell. Not a lot of enthusiasm, but all I need is one guy who saw something," Virgil said.

8

▼ ▼ ▼

Virgil didn't expect any immediate response to the tip line, so he got out the list of contacts that he'd gotten from Ho in Seattle.

One of them, Carolyn C. Monty-McCall, PhD, lived nearby, and he decided to go with her first.

He wasn't very familiar with Apple Valley, other than having slid off a highway into a ditch the winter before, on his way to St. Paul after a snowstorm. The town turned out to be a pleasant and fairly standard middle-class suburb, quiet streets lined with trees, basketball nets beside the driveways, three-car garages everywhere.

Monty-McCall lived on Fossil Lane in an area where all the street names began with *F*, which Virgil found annoying, for reasons he couldn't quite nail down. His nav system took him off 145th Street—perfectly good name for a street, in his opinion—onto Flora Way, then onto Freeport Trail, past Fridley Way, onto Flagstone Trail, down Footbridge Way, and then onto Fossil Lane. It all seemed unnecessary and maybe stupidly precious.

Monty-McCall had a two-story cocoa-colored house with yellow trim and a stand of paper birch trees in the small front yard. A discreet sign under a front window said, "Monty-McCall, PhD," hinting that she might take clients—patients?—at the house.

She was home.

Virgil rang the doorbell, heard a thump, and a moment later, Monty-McCall, wearing a quilted and belted hip-length housecoat and turquoise-colored capri pants, came to the door and peered out at him. He held up his ID and she opened the interior door and through the screen said, "Yes?"

Virgil identified himself, told her that he was looking for the stolen tigers. "I'm told you have some expertise in traditional Chinese medicine, and we're looking for contacts in that . . . er, community," Virgil said.

"Well, I didn't take them," she said. She was a woman of average height, perhaps forty, with heavy dark hair and a single thick eyebrow that extended across both eyes.

"I didn't think you did," Virgil said. "I have a list of prominent experts on traditional Chinese medicine and your name was on that list. We have some questions about that, uh, community, and we're looking for help."

"I don't know what I can tell you," she said, "but I'll answer questions. Come in."

Inside, she pointed Virgil at a couch and asked, "You want a glass of white wine?"

"Can't, thank you," Virgil said. "I'm on duty."

"Well, I haven't had lunch, so I'm going to have one, if you don't mind," Monty-McCall said.

"That's fine," Virgil said. She went away to the kitchen, and Virgil took a furtive look around. Not much to see: a couple of commercial semi-abstract landscape paintings, one above the couch and the other on the wall near the entry, plus the couch he was sitting on, an easy chair, a coffee table, and wall-to-wall carpeting in pale green. The room was opaque, without real personality, and maybe, Virgil thought, by design, if she dealt with clients in her home.

Monty-McCall came back with a frosted beer mug and a bottle of white wine. "What can I do for you?" she asked, as she unscrewed the top on the bottle.

"All I got was your name. . . . What kind of work do you actually do?" Virgil asked.

"I'm a psychotherapist with a subspecialty in traditional medicines," she said. "These are not prescription medicines, but rather nutritive distillations, supportive potions that help clear the body of unnatural poisons. Not drugs."

"Are any of them derived from animals?"

"Some, but nothing that would ever come from tigers, or rhinoceros horns, or anything like that." She poured the beer mug full of wine. "Most of the animal-based tonics come from standard meat-processing plants, as I understand it. Some kinds come from suppliers of game meats and fur processors. The few that I use I buy premade, standard, brand-name things. I don't actually get involved in any animal processing myself." She took a long swallow of wine, as though she were drinking a Pepsi.

"All right. What I really need to know is whether you suspect any suppliers or manufacturers of the animal products of selling illicit products—like tiger or rhinoceros parts."

"No, although I've never given it much thought. They're all

pretty commercial—there's not a big demand for the products, so you have a few small retail suppliers nationally, most of them selling through the Internet. I know anecdotally that there's a demand for some tiger products, and I wouldn't be surprised if there was an underground Internet thingy that sold some of it. I do know there is a man here in Minnesota who collects bear gallbladders and ships them to China," she said.

Toby Strait, Virgil thought. "I've heard about him and I've got him on my list to talk to," Virgil said. "Do you know either a Dr. Winston Peck, MD, in St. Paul, or India Healer Sandra S. A. Gupti-Mack in Minneapolis?"

The corners of Monty-McCall's mouth turned down and she said, "Where did you come up with those names? They can't be on your expert lists—they must be suspects."

Virgil leaned back. "I'd prefer not to say . . . but if you have any information?"

She'd already drunk half the mug of wine and now took another gulp and did a fake shiver as she swallowed. "Winston Peck is a creep. Believe me, I know. He did a seminar on traditional medicines, oh, five years ago, where we met. I was talking to him afterward, and one thing led to another, you know, and he asked me out. We went out a couple times. . . . To cut it short, he's a sex freak. I would have nothing to do with him."

"Violent?" Virgil asked.

"Not . . . dangerously. He didn't try to drug me or anything. He didn't try to rape me. He's simply creepy."

"Do you want to define 'creepy,' or do you want to pass?" Virgil asked.

"Mmm, I'll give you the outline. Winston is a narcissist; he wants women to . . . *service* him. Not, you know, interactive sex; he wants what he wants. When he gets what he wants, his interest in sex goes away. If you understand what I'm saying."

Virgil rubbed the side of his nose, then said, "Okay. What about the tigers? Could he do that?"

She thought for a moment, then said, "Possibly. He lives high and there's a rumor that he can't practice medicine anymore. He might need the money. I looked up his degree and it's legit, but the rumor is, he did something really bad and can't practice."

Virgil nodded: that was interesting. "No details?"

"No. I looked him up a lot on the Internet, but couldn't find anything," she said.

"What about Sandra Gupti-Mack?"

"Yeah. Sandy Mack graduated from high school down in Farmington and sold real estate for years, and then she went off to India for about fifteen minutes one year and came back as a guru with a dot on her forehead and a hyphenated name that she hopes sounds Indian," Monty-McCall said. "Not that there's anything wrong with hyphenated names, obviously, if they're legitimate. She does what she calls psychotherapy and peddles her homemade pills all over the country. She even wrote a book about it: *The Buddha's Apothecary*. Now, I'll tell you what: it would not surprise me at all if she used animal-based medications. She brags about being a traditionalist 'compounding pharmacy,' so she'd need the raw product."

"But you don't think she's totally legitimate?" Virgil asked.

She finished the wine with a gulp, pulled a hand across her lips, and said, "Huh. That bitch wouldn't know an ethic if one bit her on her butt. *The Buddha's Apothecary*. Are you kiddin' me? It's like the Buddha was a drugstore clerk in his spare time. A soda jerk or something. She's gotten rich with her pills. I'll tell you something else that didn't occur to me until right now. If she had some real honest-to-God tiger, she could roll her tiger pills out there for a million dollars. Maybe more. How many pills could you get out of a tiger? A hundred thousand or more?"

"I have no idea."

"Bet she does."

Monty-McCall was refilling her beer mug with wine when Virgil left. Her information had been fairly tepid, with a few interesting raisins: that whole thing about Peck having a questionable history. And Virgil got in his truck thinking about female alcoholics, and how they were less visible than men—except when they got behind a steering wheel. Usually though, they'd sit home and hammer the white wine, instead of going out to a bar and drinking and falling down in public. He liked an after-work beer himself, had no problem with people who liked to take a drink. Sometimes, though, you could see what was coming: Monty-McCall was killing herself.

Sandra Gupti-Mack was next up. She lived in the Uptown area of Minneapolis, in a gray two-story house that probably dated to the prewar years. Two bicycles were chained to the white-painted railings on a tiny front porch, and a bronze statue of the seated Buddha gazed at passersby from a wall niche that once had been a window. The Buddha was positioned on a rug, the rug providing a platform for the bolts that held the statue in its niche. *Evidence*, Virgil thought, *of the existence of Buddha-statue thieves.*

Above the Buddha was a sign much like Monty-McCall's:

"Dr. Sandra Gupti-Mack, Psychotherapy and Traditional Medicine"; beside him was a yellowing copy of *The Buddha's Apothecary*.

Gupti-Mack was home, too.

A tall, heavy, dark-haired, dark-eyed woman who trembled like an aspen when she opened the door, Gupti-Mack was dressed all in white, a blouse that looked like a doctor's hospital jacket with matching white slacks with bell bottoms. She was barefoot; she had a black dot in the middle of her forehead, not quite centered between her eyebrows.

When Virgil introduced himself, she said, "I have a client at the moment. I'll be with her for another twenty minutes, and I have another client a half hour after that . . ."

"I'll walk up to the corner store and get a Coke and come sit on your porch and wait," Virgil said. "Come get me when your client leaves. I won't need a half hour."

She nodded, reluctantly, and closed the door. He walked up the street, got a Coke, came back and sat on the porch, and watched the people go by. Mostly women, getting into their lives. Uptown was where you went after you graduated from the university and got a job in marketing at Pillsbury or General Mills, but still had that butterfly tattoo on your shoulder blade, hip, or ankle.

As he was sitting there, an ancient man hobbled by, assisted by a cane. He looked like he'd been dressed by somebody else, in a floppy-brimmed boonie hat, a T-shirt that said "Chairman of the Board" over a black-and-white photo of Frank Sinatra, and faded madras shorts. He was wearing black over-the-calf socks and sandals. His legs looked like they came off a café table.

He stopped on the sidewalk and eyed Virgil. "What are you looking at?"

Virgil said, "Mostly, the girls going by."

"Oh. Yeah. I used to do that," the old man said. After a moment's thought: "I just can't remember why."

He went on his way.

A half hour after Gupti-Mack said she'd be twenty minutes, a red-eyed woman walked out, dabbing at her eye sockets with a Kleenex. As Virgil stood up, she said, "I hope you're not here to harass Dr. Gupti."

"No, I'm not," Virgil said.

"You'd better not be. My husband's a lawyer and he'd be on you like a permanent wave."

"I'm . . ." Virgil realized he had no place to go with the conversation—he didn't even know what a permanent wave was—so he fished a business card out of his pocket and handed it to her. "If your husband thinks he needs to talk to me, my number is on the card."

"I'm sure he'll do that," she said. She scuttled off down the sidewalk to a blue Prius and stared at him through the windshield with the electric ferocity only a Prius owner could summon, as he knocked on Gupti-Mack's door.

Gupti-Mack let him in and said, "My last session ran long. I'm afraid I couldn't help it. I only have fifteen minutes or so until my next one . . ."

The house smelled like incense, which was no surprise; the only surprise was that it smelled so good. "I'm the BCA agent assigned to recover the tigers stolen from the zoo," Virgil began. "I'm sure you've heard about it, so I've been contacting people with knowledge of the traditional medicine community, seeing if they could point me in any particular direction . . ."

Gupti-Mack asked the usual questions about where he'd gotten her name and why he'd come to her in particular, and Virgil replied with the usual evasions, and finally she said, "I have no idea who might have taken the tigers. I was shocked when I heard. Shocked! When I saw in the paper this morning that you police believe somebody in the traditional medicine community was involved . . . well, I dissolved in disbelief. Absolutely dissolved."

"Do you use any tiger products in your compounding?" Virgil asked.

"Absolutely not! Never! Is that why you're here? Because you think I took these tigers to make medications out of them? That's . . . that's . . . absurd. Should I have a lawyer here?"

"If you're not involved in the theft, of course not," Virgil said. "We're trying to get the tigers back alive and if somebody snatched them to make them into pills, we might already be too late."

"Then if you don't suspect me, what exactly do you want?"

"You know lots of people in this community. If people took the tigers to make them into medicines, they'd have to have a way to market them," Virgil said.

"Two tigers . . . I'll tell you, Officer Flowers, I have no idea who'd be able to handle that much weight in traditional medication. My total sales, if you were to weigh them, would probably come out to ten pounds of medications a year. The newspaper this morning said that the tigers weigh over a thousand pounds, together. I would think that the only way they could be sold is if somebody had a way to get them to China."

"Alive?"

"Oh . . . probably not. They would probably process them in some out-of-the-way laboratory and ship the medications," she said. "The U.S. doesn't care so much about what goes out of here, and the Chinese are quite . . . flexible . . . about what they allow in."

"Any other possibilities that you can think of?"

"There is one man here in Minnesota . . ." She was talking about the guy who bought and sold bear gallbladders, as had Monty-McCall, but she couldn't come up with anyone else except an herbal wholesaler in Chicago and a ginseng dealer in Wausau, Wisconsin.

Virgil had a hard time looking into her eyes: the black dot on her forehead was the tiniest bit off-center, and he found himself watching it, wishing it an eighth inch to the left. He asked about Monty-McCall.

"That fraud," Gupti-Mack sneered. "She calls herself a specialist in traditional Chinese and South Asian medicine, but I don't think she's ever set foot outside the United States, much less India or China. And she has that phony doctorate from some Jesus-Jumpin'-Up-and-Down diploma mill in Mississippi or Alabama. Yet she dares to compete with me, after I have put myself through a rigorous training program in both Mumbai and Beijing, with the highest authorities—"

Virgil interrupted: "Is there any real use for tigers in medicines?"

That brought her up short, and after a moment, she said, "Yes. Just as there is a real use for heroin in Western medicines. Those nostrums are *not* used only because of the ethical issues involved."

"But if somebody knew they were getting real tiger pills . . . there'd be a market?"

She didn't want to say it, but did: "I suppose so."

"What about a Dr. Winston Peck?" Virgil asked. "Do you know anything about him?"

"Winston? Well, he has an MD in Western medicine, but no longer practices. He's an authority in traditional medicines of all kinds—Asian, Indian, Native American, and Inuit, among others. He has written two books comparing traditional and contemporary Western medications, tracing the way traditional societies have often used analogues of modern medicines well before Westerners ever discovered the modern equivalents. The Sioux, for example, used red willow bark as an analgesic, and it turns out that willow bark contains salicylic acid, which we know as aspirin."

She went on for a while, until Virgil asked, "Have you, uh, I don't know quite how to put this . . . have you heard that Dr. Peck has been involved in . . . unusual behavior . . . with women?"

She blushed, but shook her head, and Virgil thought, *So it's true*. The only question was, how unusual. "I have never heard anything like that," she said. "He's a scholar and a medical doctor, with a good reputation in the traditionalist community."

Out in his truck, Virgil dug out his iPad and Googled Peck. He found the usual mishmash of LinkedIn, Facebook, and medical conference listings, often confusing Peck VI with Peck V and Peck IV, the latter two alive only by reputation. The accumulation of Internet stuff was as boring as anything Virgil had ever read.

With no luck on the Internet, Virgil called Peck, but got an answering machine. He left a message and drove back to BCA headquarters, where he found Sandy, the BCA researcher, in her shoebox office.

"How do I find out about a guy who doesn't have a criminal record, as far as I know, and has the most boring Internet personality ever?"

"Boring Internet personality—huh. Gotta be a crook, laying low. Give me what you've got, and I'll go out on the 'net and look around."

While Sandy did her search, Virgil checked with Jon Duncan, who asked hopefully, "Anything good?"

"I'm not stirring up anything I can get hold of," Virgil said. He told Duncan about his talk at the zoo, and his conversations with Monty-McCall and Gupti-Mack.

When he finished, Duncan, who was twiddling a yellow pencil, said, "Jeez. Not much there."

"Not yet. These are unusual people, though. I think we're in the right area," Virgil said.

"All right. Well, pray for rain. Anything I can do, let me know."

Duncan, having been a field cop, knew well enough that even on important cases, sometimes nothing happened when you needed it to.

Virgil checked the tip line, found nothing intended for him, and called Frankie to ask about Sparkle. "Have you seen her this afternoon?"

"Yeah, she's home. She said everybody at Castro was nice enough, but she says they hated her being there."

"That's okay, as long as they don't do anything about it."

"Sparkle says she thought a guy in a red pickup truck followed her for a while, but she lost him in Mankato. She says. Kinda freaked me out, but when I really pushed her on it, she wasn't sure she was being followed at all. I think she expected to be, and when she saw two trucks that looked more or less alike, she got paranoid. She checked her rearview mirror all the way out here, and never saw the truck after she left Mankato."

"Huh. Well, as long as she's okay," Virgil said.

"You coming home tonight?"

"Might as well. Nothing happening here," Virgil said.

"That's not good."

"I've still got a guy to talk to. . . ."

Sandy was tracking Peck through the wilds of the Internet. When Virgil went back to talk to her, he found her pounding on her keyboard. She glanced up at him, held up a hand that meant "stop" or "go away," and he said, "I'll get a Ding Dong. You finding anything?"

"Yes. Give me five minutes."

Virgil got a Ding Dong from the vending machine and gave her ten minutes; he and Sandy had once had a sharply abbreviated romance and she continued to be testy with him. When the ten minutes were up, he went back to her office, where she was peering at a pale green document on-screen. She said, "Interesting."

"What's interesting?"

"Dr. Peck lost his license to practice medicine in Indiana when a medical board found that he'd engaged in unethical behavior with some female patients. I had to go around some circles to find it, but it turned out he'd give women with sprains or muscle pulls or other minor injuries a shot of nitrous oxide to help relax them while he was putting on a splint or a wrap, or manipulating a limb. They'd wake up feeling all funny."

"Uh-oh."

"Yeah. He was lucky he wasn't charged with rape, but nobody was exactly sure they'd been penetrated. One woman thought she might have been photographed . . . for later use. Anyway, the fact that he was disciplined would show up on any background check, and once the details were known, there's no way he'd ever get licensed. Not here in the States."

"But he still calls himself a doctor."

"Well, not exactly. He calls himself Winston Peck VI, MD. And he does have an MD," Sandy said.

"Huh. Thank you."

"Not done," she said.

"More?"

"He filed for bankruptcy two years ago, two hundred thirty thousand dollars in debt, twelve thousand in assets, not counting his house and two vehicles. He had to sell a car; he kept a truck, a Tahoe."

"What business?"

"He had an idea like emojis," Sandy said. "He called them 'the nip family.' They were digital nipple images that you could customize to look like your own nipples, and they could carry messages back and forth. You'd send somebody a nipple on your iPhone, and it'd talk to their nipples, and so on."

"Nipples."

"Yeah. You'd get the nipples for free, but then you go to 'the nip' website and customize them for a dollar, so they'd look like your own, you know, with nipple rings or whatever," she said. "He copyrighted the idea, but he doesn't know how to code, apparently, and he hired a couple of coders who drove him right into the ground with their salaries. And when nobody bought a nipple . . . he was screwed."

"You're pulling my wiener," Virgil said, without thinking.

"No, I tried that, and it didn't really pay off for me," she said.

"Hey!"

"Okay, but what I'm telling you is the truth. He tried to create a nip family thing, hoping it'd go viral and it went more like bacterial—like flesh-eating bacteria. They ate all his money."

"Which would give him a reason to grab the cats." Virgil and Sandy looked at each other for a few seconds, Sandy waiting, until Virgil finally said, "He's the most interesting guy I've run into so far. The only one who'd seem to have the . . . energy . . . to pull this off."

"Which doesn't necessarily mean he did it—there are probably another half-million people in the Cities with his energy level," Sandy said.

"Yeah, but he's been outside the law with these women; he's in financial trouble; he deals in traditional medicine; he's got the energy."

"Certainly worth a closer look," she said.

9

▼ ▼ ▼

Peck still wasn't answering his phone, so Virgil went to his address, which turned out to be a sixty-year-old white-shingled house with a tuck-under garage in a quiet neighborhood not far from the Cathedral of Saint Paul.

Virgil banged on the door for a while and got no response, looked through the garage windows and found enough light to see that the garage was empty.

Back in his truck, he tried calling Peck again, and again got no answer. Stuck for the moment, he looked up the number Dick Ho had given him for Toby Strait, called it, and got . . . nothing. No phone with that number, at least, not on any network, anywhere.

Virgil next tried the number Lucas had given him and connected with Strait's girlfriend, whose name was Inez.

"I already talked to that other cop about this, that Lucas what's-his-name: Toby's hiding," Inez said. "That Knowles bitch is hunting him down, and the law knows it, and they don't do a friggin' thing about it. Toby's afraid to turn on his phone because there are ways of tracking it. If somebody spoofs a number and he answers it, Knowles can figure out exactly where he's at."

"You really think she's still hunting for him? She's lucky to be walking around free," Virgil said.

"I *know* she's still hunting him. She's told people that. You want to know something? If *anybody* has *any* idea of where Toby is, it's probably Knowles."

W*ell, that's an idea*, Virgil thought, and it was good from two angles: Knowles might know where Strait was hiding, and she was among the most radical of animal rights activists in the state. A lot of radical animal rights people didn't care for zoos, so there was at least a slender possibility that Knowles might know about somebody who had taken the animals as a publicity stunt, if that's what had happened.

Lucas had said she lived near Monticello, on the northwest edge of the Twin Cities metro area. He could probably jump the rush-hour traffic and make it up there in an hour or so. He called the BCA duty officer, asked him to find out where Maxine Knowles had been arrested, and to get the address she'd left with whatever police agency had arrested her; and to check her driver's license and see if that matched with her bail papers.

He made it out of town ahead of the rush and was on I-94 driving north when he took the callback from the duty officer, who told him that Knowles lived eight miles out of Monticello. He'd looked at a Google Earth picture of the address, and told Virgil, "It looks like a house with a half-dozen trailers scattered around. It's out in the sticks. I'll tell you, Virgie, I'd call up Sherburne County and get a couple deputies to go out there with you."

Virgil did that. He explained to the sheriff what the problem was, and the sheriff agreed to send a couple of deputies along.

They'd meet in a Walgreens parking lot in Monticello, and then cross the Mississippi to Knowles's place.

Virgil found the two Sherburne County deputies, who were named Buck and James, chatting with a couple of Wright County deputies at the Walgreens. Virgil shook hands with everybody, then ran into the Walgreens and bought a couple packs of cheese crackers and a Coke. The Wright County deputies said, "Keep your asses down," and Virgil, Buck, and James rolled in a three-car caravan north across the Mississippi.

North of the river, they threaded their way through a skein of backroads that ended at a shabby farmstead, with that semicircle of trailers the duty officer had told him about. Behind the trailers, they could see a maze of eight-foot chain-link fences, which appeared to be much newer and in much better shape than the trailers. Two gray Subaru station wagons, one with a flat front tire, were parked in front of the cages.

They crossed a culvert into the farmyard, and within a minute or so, people began wandering out of the trailers. Virgil, out of his truck, was joined by Buck and James, and Buck whispered uneasily, "Jesus, it's a zombie outbreak."

A dozen people came out of the trailers, most of them dressed in ragged farm-style clothing, denim overalls and long-sleeved shirts and gum boots, both men and women; and they were old, with long badly cut hair, gone gray, and all but one or two were noticeably thin. The combination of age, hair, and spindly bodies did give them the look of zombies, Virgil thought, along with the shuffling gait that one or two of them had.

A tall, sunken-cheeked man asked, "What can we do for y'all?"

"I need to talk to Maxine Knowles," Virgil said.

"Can I ask what for? She's legally bailed out," the man said.

"I'm not here about her legal problems," Virgil said. "I actually need to talk to her about her area of expertise. I'm the cop looking for the stolen zoo tigers."

That set off a rash of commentary among the crowd and the tall man shook his head and said, "Well, that's a disaster. I can tell you, we don't have them, and I don't know who would."

"I believe you, but I still need to talk to Maxine," Virgil said.

The tall man looked at them for a few seconds, then pulled a cell phone from his pocket and poked in a number. After a few more seconds, he said, "Maxine, there are some police officers out in the yard looking for you. It's about the tigers."

He listened briefly, then hung up and said to Virgil, "She'll be right out."

Maxine Knowles came through the back door of the house, nodded to the group facing Virgil and the deputies, and said to Virgil, "I don't know about the tigers. I hope you find them before they're killed." She was a tall, stocky red-haired woman wearing an olive knit blouse, black jeans, and hiking boots, who added, "I have no idea who'd take them."

Virgil said, "Is there somewhere you and I can go to talk?"

She pushed out a lip, considering, and said, "I guess so. We could talk in the kitchen." To the group, she said, "I think we're okay here, everybody. Let's get ready to feed."

The group began to break up, some people going to their trailers, others walking out toward a couple of sheds set off to one side of the chain-link fences.

"What's the chain link for?" Virgil asked, as he followed Knowles through the house's mudroom and into a funky-smelling kitchen, redolent of old potatoes and overripe tomatoes.

"Our animals," Knowles said. "We have fourteen horses, four cows, six pigs, one broken-wing crow. All rescued. We've got a bunch of cats and dogs, also rescued, that mostly run around loose, unless they've been too abused and we have to sequester them. No tigers."

Virgil explained his mission and his thinking: "You're pretty well hooked into the animal rights people. Do you have any ideas for me, who might have been radical enough to grab the tigers?"

She started shaking her head before he got through explaining. "I really don't, and I think you're barking up the wrong tree. You want some nutcakes who are processing them for Asian medicines."

"That's what we're all afraid of," Virgil said.

"There's a man named Toby Strait—"

"That's the other reason I'm here. He's apparently in hiding, ever since you made bail."

"That sonofabitch." Her eyes grew wider and her face turned red. "You know what he does for a living?"

"I think so . . ."

"If he's allowed to keep doing that, he'll kill off every bear in the state and in Wisconsin and the Dakotas, too. For their gallbladders! So some Chinese assholes can make a medicine that doesn't even work! People get all weepy about rhinoceroses, and they should, but who's crying for the black bear, that's what I want to know! Who's crying for the black bear?"

"Well . . ."

"If you asked me for one likely man to steal the tigers . . ." She paused, settled a bit, and then said, "I'm not going to talk to a police officer about my case."

"I don't need that," Virgil said. "What I need is any idea you might have about where Strait might be hiding."

"I don't know," she said.

"Have you looked?"

She shook her head. "I'm not talking to you."

"Do you have any ideas? Anything? We're pretty desperate here."

She got up and got a glass of water, and leaned against the kitchen sink, considering, then said, "He won't be processing bear gallbladders, not at this time of year. I'd have to guess that he's out at one of his snake barns. Even if he isn't, I know they're processing the skins now, so his snake barn people must be able to get in touch with him."

"You haven't been sneaking around to his snake barns, checking up on him?"

"I'm not . . . No, I haven't, and you know why? If I did, I believe I'd get shot. He'd be willing to do that, to get me off his back. And I have to believe that the law would take his side, if I was found creeping around him. He'd shoot me and get away with it."

"Do you know where one of his snake barns is at?" Virgil asked.

She nodded. "Yes. Yes, I do."

"But you haven't been sneaking around?"

"Of course not."

She got a map up on her laptop and pointed out the snake barn. From a satellite view, it looked like a nicely kept place, nothing at all remarkable—another pretty Minnesota dairy farm. Best of all, it was straight south from Monticello, and a little west, two-thirds of the way back to Virgil's home in Mankato.

Virgil thanked her, got up to go, and asked, "What's the story on all the old folks?"

"Volunteers," she said. "Help me with the animals. You know, they sort of moved in on me; mostly old people, living on Social Security, who care about things. They figured if we got some old trailers—didn't even have to pay for them, they're rescue trailers, like the rescue animals—and came out here as a group, they could pool their money, live better, have friends around as they get old and start dying off. It works for us."

"Huh. I hope that none of you really has anything to do with the tigers," Virgil said.

"We don't. I'm not too happy about the whole concept of zoos, as a philosophical matter, but for some animals, like Amur tigers, zoos are about the only thing standing between them and extinction. For that, we need the zoos."

Outside, Virgil found Buck and James watching through the chain-link fence as the old people fed the horses. Most of the horses looked solid enough, but two were radically thin. "We got those a week ago. Don't yet know if they're going to make it—you can't just stuff them full of hay all at once," Knowles said. "What I want to know is, how in the hell can you starve a horse to death, in Minnesota, in the summer? All you have to do is let them out in a ditch and they'll feed themselves."

"I don't know," Virgil said. "I don't understand it, either."

From Monticello to the snake barn, located south of the town of Gaylord, was ninety minutes or so, the blacktop roads shimmering with heat mirages. Virgil ate the cheese crackers before he made it back to Monticello and on his way south stopped at a

McDonald's in Norwood Young America for a Quarter Pounder with Cheese, small fries, and a strawberry shake.

He thought about Knowles as he ate, and why God might create somebody like her. She'd seemed sane enough, not somebody who was hunting down another human being so she could shoot him to death. But she'd been caught more or less red-handed doing exactly that. People, he thought, were never one thing. Knowles was an intelligent, thoughtful lover of animals, and a potential killer.

Virgil could feel his heart clogging up with grease as he finished the sandwich, but continued on to Gaylord, and out the far side of town to the farm of Jan Aarle, "Jan" being pronounced like *Yawn*.

Aarle's wife came to the side door of the suburban ranch-style farmhouse and said Jan was working in the barn. She called him on her cell phone, and a moment later, he walked out of the barn and across the yard to the house.

"I don't really know where Toby is, but I could probably get a message to him," Aarle said. He was a fat, pink-faced man with an accent that sounded German, but not quite German—maybe like an American-born kid who grew up speaking German around the house. "What I'd have to do is call around the other barns, and somebody probably has a working number."

"I need to talk to him today," Virgil said.

"I can start calling right now," Aarle said.

"I'd appreciate it."

Aarle went inside the house to start calling—he said he needed to sit down—and Mrs. Aarle stood in the yard with Virgil and said, "Real nice day, isn't it? A little too hot, though."

Virgil looked up at the blue sky and puffy white fair-weather clouds and said, "Yep, sure is. Looks to go on like this. For a while, anyway."

"Not that we couldn't use some rain," she said.

"Most always could use some rain," Virgil said. "As long as it's not too much."

"Sure got it last year, in July," she said. "Way too much. I think it was heaviest on the sixth."

"I remember that," Virgil said. "We got something like three inches in Mankato."

"Five inches out here, on our rain gauge," she said.

Virgil said, "Whoa. That must have been something."

"Sounded like we had a drummer up on the roof," she said. They both turned to look at the roof.

And so on. Aarle came out after ten minutes and said, "Well, I spread the word. I expect you'll be hearing from him. You're welcome to stay for dinner if you like."

"Had a McDonald's up in Young America; thanks anyway," Virgil said. "I'd kind of like to get home before dark."

"Mr. Flowers lives in Mankato," Mrs. Aarle said, as they walked over to Virgil's truck.

"That must be real nice," Aarle said. "Nice town. We've talked about retiring there."

"Probably not for a while yet, though," Mrs. Aarle said.

Virgil waved and got the fuck out of there before his ears fell off.

He was three miles out of the Aarles' gate when Strait called.

"This is Toby. Who are you, again?"

"Virgil Flowers. I got your name from Lucas Davenport."

"He quit," Strait said.

"Yeah, but he's still got his database," Virgil said.

"All right. I'm going to call Davenport and I'll call you back if he says it's okay."

"Do that," Virgil said.

Strait called back five minutes later: "He says you're okay. Where are you?"

"I left the Aarle snake barn maybe ten minutes ago, heading south," Virgil said.

"Then we could meet up in New Ulm. You go straight on south until you hit the river, take a right, come across the bridge," Strait said. "There's a Taco Bell off on the right side of the road, couple blocks in."

"When?"

"I'll be waiting for you," Strait said.

Beans and corn, beans and corn, beans and corn, all the way down.

Strait was leaning against the back of his Chevy pickup, a soft drink cup in his hand, when Virgil pulled into the Taco Bell parking lot. Strait was a short, husky man in a canvas outdoors shirt, worn loose, and jeans and boots. He was wearing a camouflage PSE hat and mirrored sunglasses.

Virgil climbed out of his 4Runner and noticed the lump under Strait's elbow and said, "You're carrying."

Strait lifted his shirt to show Virgil the butt of a full-sized Beretta, and said, "Wouldn't you, if you were me? I still can't walk right and maybe never will. I do got a carry permit."

"Where'd she hit you?"

"Back of both legs. Didn't lead me enough."

"Looks like she got the elevation wrong, too," Virgil observed.

"Well, it was a snap shot, and I was running. I got to give her that much," Strait said. "She ain't a bad shot. I saw her get out of her truck and I knew what was coming—this was back at my place in Owatonna—and I started running to get behind my truck. I was carrying, then, too, and when I went down, I got behind the tire and emptied a whole goddamn magazine at her. I measured it off later at three hundred and twelve yards. I gave her about six feet of elevation shooting my Beretta, which turned out to be right. That was the clincher when they arrested her—bullet holes and bullet dings on her truck. They got a slug with rifling marks that matched my gun."

"Lucky that she didn't have time to get set up," Virgil said.

"You're telling me," Strait said. He hitched up his pants. "What can I do for you?"

"I'm looking for those stolen tigers."

"I don't have them. I got enough to do with my bears and my snakes," Strait said. "To tell the absolute truth, you'd have to be crazy to snatch those tigers. I mean, Jesus Christ, didn't those people know what was gonna happen? That they were gonna have a world of shit rainin' down on their heads? All of our heads. I knew goddamn well that when somebody stole those tigers, somebody would be coming around to give me a hard time. It's just ain't fair to legitimate businessmen to get painted with this broad brush."

"I don't know what they were thinking," Virgil said. "That's something I'd like to know."

"They wouldn't have done it, if they knew about *my* situation—that goofy twat Maxine hunting me down like I was a rabid dog."

"You're an expert in this stuff," Virgil said. "If they're processing these tigers for medicine, how long would it take?"

Strait took his hat off, brushed his hair back with one hand, and looked up at the sky. After a while, he said, "They were full-grown, right? I'd say a couple, three days apiece, if they got access to a good commercial dryer. That's if they're processing the whole animal. With tigers, over in Asia, sometimes the poachers will only take the eyes, heart, whiskers, teeth, penis and balls, and femur bones. You could do that in an hour, maybe, put everything in a sack. When you do that, you leave a lot of money on the ground."

"What are the femurs for?"

"Well, all ground up, they're supposed to cure about anything," Strait said. "Everything from ulcers to burns. Then there's the baculum—that's a bone in the penis. You could get anything up to five thousand dollars for an Amur tiger baculum alone."

"Really?"

"That's the fact, Jack."

"Who would you look at for this?"

Strait stuck a pinky finger in his ear, wiggled it around, then said, "Well . . . Amur tiger's gonna be worth some serious money, but you'd have to be able to prove it was real. That's probably why they don't care about the publicity—maybe even want some of it, to prove it's real Amur they're talking. There's a premium for endangered species. What I'm saying is, I don't know anybody local who could handle two tigers, but there's enough money involved that it could be an outsider. Crew goes around, looks at a bunch of zoos, picks out the most likely one, hits it."

He hesitated, then said, "Of course, grabbing the tigers seems totally batshit anyway. Too much risk, no matter what the payoff is."

"Nobody local."

"There are some local people who handle animal products, I just don't see them hitting the zoo."

"Give me some names," Virgil said.

"Three that I can think of. There's a company in St. Paul called Carvin Exports, which mostly deals in wildlife hides—not furs, but deer hides, wolf skins, bear skins, that kind of thing. I sell them bear hides and some snake, though they're at the lower end of the market. I can't see them involved in this because they're too corporate. Too many people would know, although I suppose the company business could have given the employees some ideas, and they went off on their own. . . ."

"But doesn't seem likely to you?"

"No, it doesn't. Then there's a guy in St. Paul named Winston Peck . . . a doctor . . ."

"I've been looking for him already," Virgil said. "Haven't been able to find him."

"All right. I don't think he could handle a tiger on his own. He buys in small amounts for his retail clientele. You know, for patients, and for people who go to his traditional medicine website. There's a woman over in western Wisconsin who does deal in animal musks and so on. Her name is Bobbie Patterson, don't know exactly where she lives."

Virgil said, "Toby, I really hope you're not involved in this. If I find out you were, I'm going to call up Maxine and tell her how to find you."

"C'mon, man, don't even joke about that," Strait said. He looked nervously up and down the street. "In fact, I've been standing around too long. I'm getting the fuck out of here . . . but, uh, why don't you get out first?"

"Don't trust me?"

"I'm not saying that . . . but why don't you pull out first."

"All right, but give me a phone number. I might need to call you," Virgil said.

"Don't be giving this out. Maxine's mad as a goddamn hatter."

"You're good with me," Virgil said, as he entered Strait's phone number into his cell phone's contact list. "As long as you don't have those tigers."

10

▼ ▼ ▼

Virgil pulled out first, going a block down Seventh Street to Broadway, got caught at the light. A left turn on Broadway would get him home in a half hour or so. As with any kidnapping, time was crucial in finding the victims alive . . . if they weren't already dead. At that very moment, though, he didn't know what he could do in the Twin Cities that he couldn't do in Mankato.

Still, he thought, he was probably on the wrong side of the Minnesota River, which didn't have a heck of a lot of bridges. If he stayed on the south side, where he was, he'd wind up back in Mankato—but if he left New Ulm on the north side of the river, back across the bridge, he could tend down toward Mankato, but also leave open his option of returning to the Twin Cities by a much shorter route.

He could try to call Peck again, and check with the BCA tip line, the zoo director, and whoever else might help, before he had to make a decision whether to go south to home or north to the Cities. How had he survived in the job before cell phones?

In his rearview mirror, he saw Strait driving down Seventh in the opposite direction, then turn a corner, on Minnesota Street. Minnesota didn't lead out of town, and Virgil wondered if Strait might be hiding in New Ulm itself.

The woman in the car in front of him was texting and didn't pull out when the light went green, and Virgil waited patiently for one-half second before tapping the horn, and the woman looked up, saw the green light, gave him the finger, and drove on through. New Ulm was getting more like LA every single day, Virgil thought.

He took the turn, drove a block, then took another left, around the Walgreens block, and then another left, back to Seventh, and a right turn toward the bridge. He passed Minnesota, looked down the street and saw that Strait was four blocks down, still heading west. A small gray car nearly cut him off as it turned down Minnesota, and Virgil went on, considering himself lucky not to have gotten another finger from its elderly driver.

He punched up Peck's cell phone, and somewhat to his surprise, Peck answered on the first ring, sounding sleepy. Virgil identified himself, mentioned the tiger investigation, and said, "You were recommended to me by a number of people as an expert on traditional medical practices in Minnesota. I need to come talk with you. I'll be in St. Paul in an hour, if you're at the same address as on your driver's license."

"Well, yes, I am," Peck said. "I could accommodate you, I suppose, but maybe . . . Could we make it two hours? I'm a writer and I work early and late: I just got up from a nap and I need to run out for dinner. So . . . seven o'clock?"

"That'd be fine," Virgil said.

Took him a minute before he thought, *Wait. A small gray car? Kind of a small station-wagon-looking car? A Subaru? With an elderly driver?*

Virgil was in traffic, with a concrete center divider between himself and the opposite lane, but he did a screeching U-turn anyway, bumped over the divider and headed back toward Minnesota Street—and a black New Ulm cop car was on him like holy on the Pope, both lights and siren. Virgil said, "Shit," out loud, and hit his own flashers and pulled over, hopped out, jogged back to the New Ulm car.

The cop didn't get out, but looked worried, and Virgil held up his hands to show that they were empty, then made a rolling "window-down" motion with his finger and the cop dropped the window and Virgil said, "I don't have time to explain, but there could be a shooting about to happen. My name's Virgil Flowers, I'm with the BCA . . ."

"I've heard of you—"

"Call in and tell them you're following me and we might need more help. Could be a woman with a rifle and she's supposedly a good shot. Follow me now."

Virgil ran back to his truck and took off, hit the siren as he did it, made the turn on Minnesota, didn't see either the gray car or Strait's truck, said "Shit" again, thumbed through his phone's contact list, got Strait's number, and called it.

Strait came up and Virgil shouted, "Man, this is Virgil. You got a gray car behind you?"

A second later, Strait said, "There's a car, but it's quite a way back. I think it's gray."

"That might be Maxine."

"What?!"

"She might have followed me. I'm coming after you with a New Ulm cop," Virgil said. "Where are you?"

"I'm on North Broadway, going out west on 14."

"All right, we're coming after you. If that's Maxine and she has a gun in the car, she's going straight back to jail, and this time, she won't get out."

"She *did* follow you, you silly shit," Strait said.

"Yeah, yeah, we're not sure that's Maxine," Virgil said. "Stay on 14, don't let that car get too close. We're coming . . ."

Up ahead, Strait dropped the hammer, unholstered his Beretta and stuck the barrel between the seat and back on the passenger side, so it wouldn't slide off the seat if he had to hit the brakes hard. He cranked the speedometer up to a hundred, but backed off to ninety-five and then ninety because the highway couldn't handle the truck's weight and speed. He swooped around the wide turn where Broadway turned into Twentieth Street, past a couple of body shops, going out of town, the truck's passenger-side tires running off the road at two spots, leaving his heart up in his throat.

Around the turn, past the cemetery and the liquor store, then a shallower turn took him into a straightaway and he ran it back up to a hundred and . . .

That piece-of-shit Subaru was gaining on him.

Up ahead of him, the highway narrowed from two lanes to one, and he picked up his phone and looked at the screen and punched up his most recent call and Virgil answered and Strait shouted, "It's her: they're chasing me. I'm doing a hundred and they're still coming up on me and this truck don't got no more."

Virgil shouted back, "Keep going, we're right behind you, got lights and sirens going, I'm hoping we can scare her off when she sees us in her rearview."

He looked down at his speedometer: they were still in town and he was going seventy-five and scaring himself. If somebody poked out of a side street, he could kill them. He chickened out and slowed to sixty. That meant that Strait and Knowles were actually getting farther away by the second.

Virgil shouted into his phone, "Do you know the country out there?"

"A little bit," Strait shouted back.

Even through the phone, Virgil could hear the wind noise ripping off Strait's truck. "Is there any place where you could lead her around in a square, you know, take a right, take another right, take another right, and bring her back to us?"

"I already went by Highway 12, I got a left turn coming up pretty quick that I could take down to 27 and back to 12 and circle around past the airport and bring it back, but she's gaining on me, man, she's way faster through the corners. . . ."

"Take the turn," Virgil said. "Don't let her pass you, it's hard to shoot out of a moving car, take it back to 12. We'll come down 12 the other way, so we'll meet you."

"Aw, shit, here I go . . ."

Strait must have dropped the phone or tossed it on the passenger seat, Virgil thought, because he could hear the bumping of the truck and what might have been a round of cursing from Strait, then the roaring sound of the truck engine being overstressed.

Virgil and the New Ulm cop car were coming up on Highway 12, and Virgil slowed and took the turn and headed on south, the cop car right on his tail. A minute later Strait was back on the phone. "We're both on whatever this road is and they're still closing up on me. I lost some yardage going around the corner."

Maxine Knowles was in the Subaru, but she wasn't driving it. What she was doing was crouching on the passenger seat, trying to get her rifle out the open sunroof without dropping it. She was using a cheap but accurate .223, with a twenty-round magazine. The first time she shot Strait, she'd done it with a Remington .243, and she much preferred that rifle and that caliber, but the cops had the gun.

Now she screamed down at the driver, "Get in the middle of the road where it's smoother. Where it's smoother. Smoother. This ride is rattling me around too much, I can't get a decent sight picture."

"I'm trying, I'm trying. I don't see the cop," the driver shouted back.

"Don't worry about the cop. I'm going to try to stand up now. Stay in the middle . . ."

She was too thick to fit easily through the sunroof, but once up, the tight fit helped brace her upright. She lifted the rifle, clicked off the safety, and aimed at Strait's truck, which was a hundred yards or so ahead of her and bouncing even more violently than her car.

The front gun sight wobbled wildly over the back of the truck, but she took a breath, softened her stance as much as she could to absorb the bumps, and opened fire. She worked through the first twenty rounds in ten seconds, pulled the mag, dropped it into the car, and the driver handed her a second magazine.

Up ahead, the back panel on Strait's camper-top seemed to be showing some holes, but it was hard to tell: she was aiming at the window on the back, and what could be bullet holes could also be reflections and dust. Strait, in the meantime, had put his right tires onto the shoulder and was kicking up dust and gravel, which started hitting Knowles in the face. She squinted into the dust, slammed the second magazine into place, and emptied it at the fleeing truck.

Strait shouted into the phone, "She's shooting at me, man, she's shooting at me, I can hear the slugs hitting the back of the truck . . ."

"We're on 12, we're coming fast, stay ahead of her, get down in your seat as far as you can . . ."

Strait did that, which cramped up his right leg, and so he missed the brake when he tried to make the turn onto Highway 27, and he lost the road and crashed through a ditch and out the other side and tried to switch his foot over and sideswiped a tree, and then another one, and the steering wheel seemed to rise up and hit him in the lower lip, slicing his lip on his upper teeth, and then he was in a dense windbreak, rolling over brush, and then his car stopped, involuntarily: he was jammed up between trees and thought maybe he'd lost a tire.

He didn't take the time to worry about that, but grabbed the Beretta and crawled out the passenger-side door, which was away from the road, and a burst of gunfire rattled through the sides and top of the truck. Strait peeked around past the grille, saw Knowles standing on the side of the road near the back of the Subaru. A couple more shots rattled off the top of the truck and through the side windows, shattering them, and he took a chance, poked the Beretta around the front of the truck, and unloaded all fifteen rounds in the general direction of the Subaru and Knowles.

Virgil couldn't get Strait on the phone, but he heard the gunfire and with no other way to call the cop behind him, thumbed through his directory for the New Ulm police department, called it, and yelled at the cop on the other end. "Me and one of your guys are in pursuit of a woman we think is trying to shoot a guy."

"Yeah, we heard. We're talking to Ross; he says he's right behind you."

"He is, but I can't talk to him. Tell him we've got gunfire up ahead; he's got to be careful. I don't know what happened, but I'm hooked up to the victim and he says the attacker is shooting up his truck and now I'm hearing what sounds like him shooting back . . . Tell your guy to be careful."

"We're telling him; we got a couple sheriff's cars headed your way, and two more from us, but we're all way back."

"Gotta go . . ." Virgil said, and he made the turn onto Highway 27, and far ahead, saw the gray car stopped on the side of the road, and a person—he couldn't tell whether it was a man or a woman—standing behind the car.

With a gun, he saw, as he got closer, firing into the ditch. Strait had run off the road. If that was Knowles, she had a rifle, and all he had was a weak-ass nine, and not only that, the nine was locked in the safe behind the seat.

Given all that, Virgil got as close as he dared, which was perhaps fifty yards, close enough to recognize Knowles. She paid no attention to him, his siren or his flashing lights, or to the cop car behind him, but slapped another long magazine into her rifle and kept shooting into the ditch.

Strait realized that Knowles was focused on the truck and was punching a hundred holes in it, and he slipped backward and got behind a tree, and then another one, always keeping a tree trunk between himself and the other gun. When he was behind the second tree, he stretched out on the ground, reloaded his gun—his second and last magazine—and waited to see if she'd try to sneak around his truck.

He'd been so focused on staying down, out of the line of fire, that he hadn't heard the police sirens. He heard them now, and they were close.

Virgil got the 4Runner sideways on the highway, kicked open his door, opened the back door, and got his gun and two magazines out of the safe.

As he did that, the New Ulm cop ran up beside him, carrying a shotgun.

"Want me to nail her?"

"Let me yell at her first," Virgil said. He shouted, loud as he could, "Maxine! Stop!"

She heard him, because she turned her face toward him and then she stepped behind the Subaru, apparently kneeling out of sight, and kept firing. Then an older man slipped out of the Subaru, lifted his hands over his head, and wobbled into the ditch on the other side of the road and sat down in the weeds.

The cop said, "I could take out her window glass."

"Yeah, maybe you better do that," Virgil said. The cop popped up and fired the twelve gauge four times. As far as they could tell, nothing happened—the buckshot either bounced off the car, or the deputy had missed it.

"I can guarantee I didn't miss," he said.

"See if you could bounce a shot under her back tire," Virgil suggested.

The cop stood up and fired a couple of quick shots at the back of the Subaru, low, and forward of the back tire. No response.

"I've got to reload," the cop said.

Then, suddenly, there was no more noise. No more shooting. A few seconds later, Maxine was waving her gun over her head and shouting, "I give up. I give up."

Must have run out of ammo, Virgil thought. He shouted, "Throw your gun into the road and come out in the open with your hands up." The rifle landed on the blacktop and then she came out with her hands up. Strait wasn't shooting and Virgil shouted, "Toby—she quit. Don't shoot, but stay where you are until we check her."

There was no reply and Virgil said to the New Ulm cop, "Let's go. Keep the shotgun on her and if she pulls another gun when we get close, blow her up. Can you do that?"

"Yup."

"Good man. I gotta check the other guy, make sure she didn't kill him."

They moved out from behind Virgil's truck, Virgil around the front, the New Ulm cop around the back with the shotgun mounted to his shoulder, and they stayed that way as they jogged down the road toward Knowles.

Virgil hadn't felt much during the chase except stress and intense concentration, but now the anger was coming on. He'd been chumped and because of that, he'd led a bona fide crazy woman to her victim—forget about the fact that the victim was a notorious asshole, Virgil had still been chumped and that had resulted in two people trying to shoot each other to death.

When they were close, Virgil shouted at the man in the ditch, "Up! Up! Hands in the air. Up on the road!"

"I don't have a gun!" The old man stood up, hands overhead, and stumbled up to the road. Virgil recognized him as one of the men from Knowles's farm, dressed in faded overalls and a tattered Vikings hat.

Virgil said to Knowles, "Get down on the ground."

"Uh-uh," she said, "I don't bow down for anybody."

Virgil was still moving fairly quickly and he came up beside her, grabbed her by the back of the neck, and used his shin to kick her legs out from under her. She went down, yipping in surprise. Virgil broke the fall with his thigh, then let her slip onto the road, when he pinned her with a knee between her shoulder blades, caught her flailing wrists, and cuffed her, as she sputtered into the blacktop, then patted her down for a pistol.

She didn't have one. He pointed his gun at the old man and said to the New Ulm cop, "Cuff him and put him on the ground."

That took three seconds and then Virgil walked to the Subaru and shouted over it, "Toby, we got them on the ground. Where are you?"

"Down behind the truck. I'm coming," Strait shouted back.

Strait came up from behind his truck with his gun in his hand and Virgil went down to meet him and asked, "You okay?"

"No thanks to *that* bitch."

Virgil: "I gotta take the gun."

"Man . . ."

"I know, but I gotta take it," Virgil said.

Strait reluctantly handed it over, then looked at his truck: "Shit. It's ruined. It looks like the Nazis machine-gunned it or something. Then I hit a couple of trees."

There were, Virgil estimated, dozens and maybe a hundred bullet holes in the side and back of the truck. "You were lucky."

Strait bobbed his head and then said, "I got a whole load of snake hides in the back, all curled up in bundles. They soaked up the incoming when I was on the road. Then, when I ran off the road, she must've thought I'd stayed in the truck. She really hosed it down."

They walked together to the road and around the Subaru and Strait took three fast steps toward Knowles, who was still facedown on the road, and cocked a leg to kick her in the face.

Before he could do that, Virgil caught him by the collar of his shirt and yanked him back. "Don't do that," he told Strait. "At this point, she's going back to jail and won't see daylight for fifteen years. You'll complicate things if you kick her."

"I was only going to do it because I was overcome with emotion," Strait said. He sounded like he was asking for permission.

Virgil said, "Uh-uh. Stay back."

More cop cars were closing in on them, lights and sirens. The New Ulm cop said, "I can't believe that nobody got hurt. There're six empty magazines in that Subaru and on the ground.

That's, what, a hundred and twenty shots?" He looked at Strait and asked, "How many did you fire?"

"Thirty," Strait said.

"I did six, with a shotgun," the cop said. "A hundred and fifty-six shots and nobody got a scratch."

"I cut my lip on the steering wheel," Strait said.

"You'll take that," Virgil said.

"I guess," Strait said. He plucked at his lip. "Hurts, though."

Knowles looked up from the ground and snarled at Strait, "Sooner or later, your luck—"

Virgil cut her off. "Shut the fuck up." He was easily pissed off by gunfire.

The first of the backup cops arrived in a cloud of dust and the New Ulm cop who'd followed Virgil out said, "There's one really good thing about this whole situation."

"What's that?"

"I got a total lock on 'Officer of the Month.'"

11

▼ ▼ ▼

The New Ulm cops said they'd handle the processing of the crime and the crime scene, which would be pretty straightforward. Given that, Virgil would be treated mainly as a principal witness, with the arrest going to New Ulm.

Knowles and her companion would be taken to the Brown County jail, eventually to be charged with attempted murder, then Knowles would be transferred to Steele County district court, which had freed her on bail. Bail would no longer be a possibility.

The elderly man began to sob as one of the New Ulm cops put a hand on his head and guided him into the back of a cop car. The cop said to him, "Look at the bright side. You're going to get lifelong free health care."

They were at the scene for more than an hour before Virgil could leave. He'd have to file reports with the BCA and the New Ulm cops, but not for a day or two.

The chase and the shooting had left him feeling disoriented, and as he drove back toward New Ulm, the anger began to burn out and he started to get scared: all those bullets flying around like bees. He tried to put the thought aside and called Peck. Peck answered—Virgil could hear the sounds of dishes and silverware clinking in the background, so Peck was at dinner—and Virgil said, "A major problem came up. I'm going to be a little late . . . probably half an hour."

"I'll still be around," Peck said. He sounded impatient, though, put-upon.

Virgil called Duncan and told him about the chase and the arrests, and Duncan said, "Does this have anything to do with the tigers?"

"Only peripherally—I was checking out a possibility, and one thing led to another."

"You gotta think *tigers*, man."

"Thanks for the tip, Jon."

"Hey, I'm not trying to be tiresome, but a lot of people are looking at us, and if something doesn't happen soon, we could be headed for a pretty unhappy conclusion."

"I know, I'm out here pushing the boulder up the hill. We'll get there."

Virgil called Davenport and told him what happened; Strait was Davenport's guy and he needed to know.

"Did you have a gun with you?" Davenport asked.

"Yeah."

"You didn't shoot it, did you?"

"No."

"There's the fuckin' Flowers we all know and love," Davenport said.

"I was chumped," Virgil said.

"Happens to everybody, all the time," Davenport said. "At least you got Maxine off the street. She was goofier than a fuckin' Packers fan who's lost his cheese."

Virgil pulled into Peck's driveway shortly after seven-thirty and climbed the steps to the front door, where Peck was waiting, smoking the butt end of a cigarette. He was wearing a knitted cardigan over a T-shirt, black jeans, and slippers.

He pushed the screen door open, said, "Come in," and led Virgil to the living room, where two beige couches, a faux-wood coffee table, and a blue reading chair made a conversation group. He stubbed out the cigarette, took the blue chair, pointed at a couch, and asked, "What can I do for you?"

"We're trying to track down the tigers taken from the zoo," Virgil said, resisting the temptation to wave away the secondhand smoke. "We're trying to figure out who in Minnesota, or close to here anyway, would have the knowledge and ability to process a dead tiger into traditional medications. We understand that you're an expert in the area and might have some ideas about that."

Peck rubbed his forehead, thinking, halfway scowled, and said, "The compounders of traditional medications here in the Twin Cities area work with herbs and other vegetation. Roots and so on. Not with fauna. Well, there's one exception that I'm aware of. . . ."

"Toby Strait?"

Peck frowned. "Is he still working? I heard he'd been shot by some animal rights nut."

"He was," Virgil said. "He wasn't killed and he's up and around again. You weren't thinking of him?"

"No, I was thinking of Bobbie Patterson—Roberta Patterson. She processes roadkill, the carcasses of animals trapped for their fur, and bats."

"That's . . . unusual."

"Not a profession I'd choose for myself. She was a biologist, failed to get tenure a couple of times, and decided to make some money," Peck said. "She has an operation over in Wisconsin, east of Hudson somewhere. Always been legal, as far as I know."

"You have an address or number for her?"

"No, but I think she's called Patterson Biologic Resources or something close to that. She has a website."

"I'll talk to her," Virgil said. "Exactly what kind of equipment would you need to process biologics?"

Peck shrugged. "Not my area. I'm more interested in traditional medicine as an academic discipline. I publish books and papers in the field; I don't engage in the production of herbal or animal compounds. And to tell you the truth, those that do, around here, are usually a bunch of shitkickers stumbling around in the woods, trying to get something for free. They're not exactly high-end biologists. Bobbie Patterson is the exception there."

"But you do use some traditional medicines from time to time, right? Or at least buy some?"

Peck nodded. "Sure. I have a small, select patient list. Some of these things have a long history of efficacy against certain kinds of illnesses. Rheumatism, for example, or gout. Karl Marx suffered from gout and so did Henry the Eighth."

"Didn't know that," Virgil said. "Do your medicines work?"

"Like Western medicine, they work some of the time. Some of the time, they don't," Peck said. "But they do no harm."

"Hmm," Virgil said. Then, "I don't mean to offend you, but I have to ask a few questions. We're asking these of everyone we speak to. Could you tell me where you were two nights ago?"

"Well . . . here," Peck said, waving toward a wall-mounted television. "Two nights ago, let me see, I was working here until midnight or so and watching some television—*The Freshman* was on, an old movie, but it always makes me laugh. Marlon Brando reprising *The Godfather* as a comedy. Anyway, I was making a few notes from a book, a catalog really, called *Life in the Bengal*, about primitive medicine in India, as it was preserved into the 1890s."

Virgil would check the movie time later. "Nobody here with you? No visitors?"

"No . . . I did see my neighbor when I was pushing the garbage out to the curb. That's Maxwell Broom, next house down the street. That was late, probably ten o'clock."

"I've been told that a fully processed tiger would be worth quite a lot in terms of medicine, and again, not to be offensive, I understand that you ran into some financial difficulty recently."

"Been doing some research on me, huh? Well, it wasn't a difficulty, it was a goddamned disaster," Peck said. "Started out simple, made a little money with an iPhone app aimed at people who are hard of hearing. Most ringtones are high-pitched, see, and people suffering hearing loss can't hear them, even when they're loud. I had an idea: ringtones based on lower-frequency sounds. I hired a coder, put together the ringtones based on lower-frequency tones, bought advertisements in *AARP Magazine*, which were quite expensive, and made some money. Then this coder started pressing me with this idea for an emoji-type figure. He said it would go viral and make us millionaires. . . ."

"Nipples," Virgil said.

"Don't even say the word to me," Peck said. "I must have been out of my mind. But: the *Star Tribune* article was wrong. I assume that's where you got your information? I didn't declare bankruptcy, the company did. I was the nominal head of the company."

"Said they took your car."

"They got it wrong. That was the company van," Peck said. "Don't ask me why we had one; my accountant suggested it. A tax thing. Anyway, I did have to sell it to pay off creditors, along with a couple computers and some office equipment. The company's remaining assets, is what it was. I don't deny that I was hurt, but . . . I still have considerable personal assets."

Peck was up-front and calm, yet his left leg bounced against his toes for the whole time of the interview. Nervousness, Virgil thought, brought rigidly under control in his voice and face, but tipped off by the leg. Not necessarily an indictment: most people were nervous when being interviewed by a cop.

Virgil asked him, "If you had to throw out three names—you know, if somebody put a gun to your head—who'd you say, in the traditional medicine market, might do this?"

Peck frowned, and after a moment's thought and a couple of facial scratches, said, "Well . . . nobody. Nobody here in this area. Most of these people involved in traditional medicine, to be honest, are somewhat timid. Backwoods people, the ones who actually produce the basic flora and fauna. They're not the kind to be sneaking around stealing tigers. They tend to be reclusive, rather than aggressive. And I'd say . . . poor. They usually don't have a lot of resources. I couldn't see them organizing anything like this raid on the zoo."

"So . . ."

"I think you're looking in the wrong direction. You want somebody who's more confrontational, somebody who's not afraid to go to jail. Somebody with money and lawyers. I'm thinking the anti-zoo people or animal rights people. People who lie down in front of bulldozers. Not some lady who goes mushroom hunting."

Virgil's phone buzzed, and he looked at the screen. Bea Sawyer, the crime-scene specialist.

He said, "I've got to take this."

Peck said, "Sure, walk into the kitchen, if you want some privacy."

Virgil walked into the compact kitchen and, on the way, punched up the call.

"Virgil, this is Bea. Hey, we got a hit on those prints we took off the lightbulb, believe it or not. The feds say they're from a small-time crook named Hamlet Simonian: three convictions for burglary and one for hijacking a Best Buy truck."

Virgil was astonished. "Convictions here? Do we have an address?"

"No, not here," Sawyer said. "He was busted in Brooklyn, New York; Camden, New Jersey; and Glendale, California, on the burglaries, and Phoenix, Arizona, on the Best Buy truck. He's never done any serious time and has apparently either been clean or clever for a few years now, but we've got lots of mug shots."

"Bea, let me call you back in a minute. One minute."

"I'll be here."

Virgil checked through his list of contacts, found the name of the people who owned the house where the tigers had been taken: the Schmidts. He poked in the number he had, and Don Schmidt answered.

Virgil: "You know anybody named Hamlet Simonian?"

Schmidt: "Never heard of him."

"He wouldn't have installed a lightbulb in your garage door opener?"

"I don't think so. Let me ask Marge." A minute later, a woman came on the line: "No. I do that. I haven't done it for a couple years, at least. It was still working the last time we were there."

Virgil: "Thank you."

He called Sawyer back and said, "We got one of them. Good job. You gotta get down to the office and start cranking out mug shots for the newspapers and TV stations. I want to get this on the ten o'clock news."

"I'm there now, I'll get it started."

Virgil walked back to the living room and said, "Something's come up, I've got to go. I'd like to talk to you some more, though."

"Well, I'm working," Peck said. "I'm usually most available after my morning writing session, after lunch."

"I'll stay in touch," Virgil said.

Out in his truck, Virgil called Duncan: "Jon, we got a name on the tiger theft. A Hamlet Simonian. I'm going back to the BCA to look at his file. We've got mug shots. If you could . . . I'd like you to get in touch with the TV stations and get this guy's face on the air."

"Yes! Virgie, goddamn it, you're rolling," Duncan said.

"Bea Sawyer's putting the mug shots together; she'll tell you about finding them. You need to get the TV people to put up the pictures and our phone number, in case somebody knows where this guy is living."

"Yeah, yeah, I got that. See you at the office."

Winston Peck VI had handled the interview with Virgil with the aid of a double dose of Xanax, which was now leaving him feeling tired. He was stressed, scared, freaked out, but chemically calm.

He sat staring at the television for two hours, some baseball game, he was never sure which one, when Hayk Simonian called and said, "You better turn on the TV."

"It's on."

"Did you see it?"

"What? I'm watching a ball game." Maybe too much Xanax: he was having a hard time focusing.

"A teaser ad for Channel Three news. They have Hamlet's picture; they say he stole the tigers."

"What?"

"I don't know how they got it, but he's gonna have to run for it. If he can make it out to Dad's place in Glendale, they can fix him up with a fake ID. He's gonna need some cash. You got cash?"

"I could give him a couple of thousand, maybe," Peck said. "How did this happen? How did they find him?"

"I don't know. Shit happens. Anyway, I'll tell him to come over to your place," Simonian said. "He's at the Olive Garden in Coon Rapids; he could be there in a half hour."

"What about his license plates? If a cop spots his car . . ."

"Like I said, man, shit happens. Not real likely, though."

Peck hung up and looked at his watch: two minutes to ten o'clock. He sat through a bunch of ads, then the news came up, *Three at Ten*, and the first thing on the news was a mug shot of Hamlet Simonian, taken by the Phoenix police, followed by another one, taken by the Brooklyn cops. The Brooklyn shot wasn't so good, having been taken when Simonian was younger and fatter with short hair, and shiny with what appeared to be sweat.

The Phoenix photo nailed him, might have been taken by *National Geographic*: "Our Survey of Cheap Hoods."

"Shit. Shit, shit, shit."

The problem with the Simonians was that they got caught. He'd known that, from his talks with old man Zhang. Zhang had said that they could lift heavy weights, they could butcher a tiger, but they had the IQs of small rocks. They were that kind of guy, but their job in the tiger theft was so simple that Peck hadn't worried too much. He should have.

Hamlet had always seemed to be the bigger liability, because he didn't think. About anything. Peck didn't know exactly how the police had identified him, but it would turn out to be something thoughtless and stupid.

Hayk, on the other hand, was a sixty-watt bulb, compared to Hamlet's backup light, but Hayk had an honor problem. Almost any little thing could turn out to be a stain on his honor and would require revenge. He'd get his revenge and then the cops would come, and they'd take him away and fingerprint him, and everything he was wanted for would then come up on their computer screens.

Peck still needed Hayk for processing the tigers, at least for a while, but he didn't need Hamlet anymore. He thought about it and started to sweat himself, but eventually went out to the garage, pulled a junk box out of the way, and dug the nylon bag out from behind it.

Inside the bag was the dart gun they'd used on the tigers. Still had two darts . . . didn't make much noise.

He thought about it some more, exactly how this would work. He put the gun back in the nylon bag twice, and twice took it back out. Eventually, he left it sitting on the hood of the Tahoe, ready to go.

Hamlet Simonian didn't make it in a half hour, leaving Peck in a constant and prolonged state of agitation that even another Xanax couldn't help. Finally, an hour after his brother called, Hamlet Simonian pulled into Peck's driveway. Peck had been waiting impatiently behind the access door to the garage and popped it open when Simonian got out of the car.

"Where in hell have you been?" Peck hissed. He checked the street: almost all the houses were dark. "You were supposed to be here half an hour ago."

Peck backed into the garage as Simonian walked up to the door. "Shut the goddamn door," Peck said.

Simonian stepped inside the dimly lit garage, pushed the door shut, and said, "Dark in here. Where are you?"

Thut!

The dart *hurt*. Simonian looked down at his chest, could make out the syringe sticking out of his shirt, right through the left nipple. "You motherfucker!" he screamed.

The garage was dark, but there was enough ambient light coming in through the back access door that he could see Peck, in his white shirt, crouched behind the hood of the Tahoe. Simonian yanked the syringe out of his chest and threw it on the floor, then lurched down the side of the truck and around the nose. Peck had run down the opposite side, and now stood at the back of the truck, waiting for Simonian to fall down: there was enough sedative in the syringe to knock out an eight-hundred-pound tiger.

Simonian pursued him. They did two laps around the truck before Simonian failed to make a turn and crashed into the outside wall, where Peck had hung some garden tools. He bounced off the wall, fell on the floor. A shovel fell on his head. Peck, afraid that he might be faking, waited for a minute or two, peering over the hood of the car, then reached out, grabbed a rake off the wall, and used the handle to prod Simonian. Simonian didn't even moan.

Peck moved closer: he could hear the other man breathing. The thought flashed through his mind that maybe he ought to strangle him or hit him with the shovel, but his more rational mind told him that the sedative should be enough.

So he waited: and it was. Six or seven minutes after he shot Simonian, the breathing slowed, slowed, and finally stopped.

While he was waiting for Simonian to show up, Peck had worked out a plan to dispose of the body. Not a great plan, but it would have to do. At the back of his garage, he had a half-sized refrigerator that he'd bought for his office, when he had an office. Stripped of the shelves, he thought he could squeeze Simonian into it.

He pulled the refrigerator to the empty garage space. He had an ice chipper leaning against the wall, a six-foot steel rod with a point on one end and a one-inch blade on the other. He used it to punch a dozen holes in the refrigerator: he didn't want decomposition gas to float it.

When he was sure Simonian was dead, he turned on the garage light, dragged the refrigerator around to the back of the Tahoe, and opened the hatch. The refrigerator wouldn't fit upright, so he laid it on its side, with the door opening down. Then he dragged Simonian around to the back of the truck, removed his iPhone and wallet, and tried to stuff the body into the refrigerator. Didn't fit. There was space, but like a wrong piece in a jigsaw puzzle, one lump or another always stuck out—either an arm stuck out, or a knee did.

As an actual medical doctor, Peck had never been queasy about other people's blood. He got a meat cleaver from the kitchen and cut off Simonian's left arm at the shoulder joint. That took a while, but there really wasn't much blood because Simonian's heart wasn't beating anymore, and what blood there was, he managed to contain on a garbage bag. When the arm came off, still wrapped in a shirt sleeve, he tucked it behind the body, and tried to slam the refrigerator door. Still didn't fit, though there was empty space inside.

"Goddamnit, these guys . . ." Hamlet remained an uncooperative pain in the ass.

He cut off Simonian's other arm, and by rearranging all the

parts, managed to get the body to fit. The door kept popping open, though, and he wound up using a half roll of duct tape, wrapped around the length of the refrigerator, to keep it shut.

Now for the scary part, he thought. The garage had been private: now he'd be transporting a murdered body on the public roads. If somebody rear-ended him, he'd be spending his life in Stillwater prison.

He ran the garage door up, backed the Tahoe out of the driveway past Simonian's Buick, and began sweating heavily: fear sweat, the worst kind. He drove out to I-94, then east, turned north on I-35, drove precisely at the speed limit to Highway 97, took it east to Highway 95 along the St. Croix River, and turned north again to the Osceola bridge to Wisconsin. He was familiar with the bridge from winter ski trips. There was never much traffic across it, even in daylight hours. At two o'clock in the morning, there was nothing.

Unlike his brother, Hamlet Simonian hadn't been a large man—probably a hundred and sixty pounds. The refrigerator added fifty or sixty. Normally, it might have killed Peck to lift more than two hundred pounds out of the truck, but all he had to do was swivel it over the railing of the bridge, and let go . . . and he was so pumped with fear and adrenaline that he hardly noticed the weight. He pulled, lifted, turned, and dropped.

He heard it splash and, one minute later, did a U-turn on the bridge and headed back to the Minnesota side. Waited for the blue lights to come up. None did. He allowed himself to begin breathing again.

What he would do, he thought, was drive Simonian's car to the basement level of a downtown parking garage, where people often left their cars for extended periods. From there, he could take a cab home. By the time Simonian's car was found, and Hayk Simonian realized his brother was dead, Hayk Simonian would also be dead. No other choice, at this point.

He left the car in the parking garage, threw Simonian's wallet into a sewer, after taking out $106 and all the IDs. The IDs would go through a shredder and into the garbage.

But the iPhone . . .

Early the next morning, he drove over to a FedEx store and sent the phone to a Jack in the Box in Glendale, California, by FedEx Ground.

And he was done, he thought, with Hamlet Simonian.

12

▼ ▼ ▼

With the break on Hamlet Simonian, Virgil called Frankie and said he wouldn't be making it home that night. "Something could happen up here—we've got this guy's face on every TV set in the state."

"I know, I saw him. Anyway, go ahead and stay," she said. "Me 'n' Sparkle and Father Bill and Rolf are playing canasta. You be careful." Rolf was her oldest son.

"I will. See you tomorrow, probably." He didn't mention the afternoon chase with Maxine Knowles and Toby Strait.

Virgil bagged out at the Radisson Hotel at the Mall of America, and a few minutes after midnight, he'd been asleep long enough to be deeply annoyed when his phone rang.

The BCA duty officer: "Landlord over on West Seventh says he's got a renter who he's pretty sure is Simonian. He says it's ninety-nine percent."

"Jenkins and Shrake still out?" Virgil asked.

"Probably. It's early for those guys."

"Roll them over there, if you can find them," Virgil said. "Call

St. Paul, tell them to wake up the judge and get a warrant. I'll be there in half an hour: give me the address."

Shrake called him twenty minutes later, as Virgil was passing the airport. "Me and Jenkins are over on West Seventh. I hope your suspect is a dirtbag."

"He shows all the signs," Virgil said. "Why?"

"His apartment's above one of those twenty-four-hour car washes. I don't know how in the hell anybody could sleep up there. No lights on, that I can see. Anyway, it's the kind of place only a dirtbag would wind up."

"Where are you guys?"

"Parked on Snelling right at the bottom of the hill. We're talking to St. Paul, they woke up Van Dyke and got him to sign the warrant, and they got a key from the landlord. They're sending a car over."

"Good. I'll be there in a few minutes."

Jenkins and Shrake were sitting in Jenkins's aging Crown Vic. Virgil drove up the hill, did a U-turn, and pulled in behind them. He crawled into the Crown Vic's backseat and Shrake said, "Good thing that St. Paul cop isn't here, he would have ticketed your rural butt for the U-turn."

"Already been through that today," Virgil said. He looked through the front window at the car wash. "What do you see over there?"

Jenkins pointed at a line of barred windows above the wash and said, "Nothing. No movement. The plan is, I pull the car into the car wash, which starts the noise up, to cover the approach. Then you and Shrake and Bowers go up the side stairs, kick the door, and bust Simoleon."

"Simonian," Virgil said. "A 'simoleon' is money, in obsolete British slang."

"Whatever," Jenkins said. "If you guys don't fuck this up, I get a clean car on the company's nickel and we're heroes because we bust the tiger thief. If you *do* fuck it up, I should be available for backup, right after the no-spot rinse."

"The side stairs are what? Metal? Concrete? Wood?"

"Concrete. We did a quick turnaround in the parking lot to check it out. Everything over there is concrete—it's one solid concrete-block building. There are two apartments, front and back. He's in Apartment One, which is at the front."

The St. Paul cop called a minute later and said he was on his way, the warrant in hand. The landlord, he said, rented the place furnished, by the week, and Simonian had been there for three weeks. He'd told the landlord that his name was Gus Smith. "I mean, hey, somebody's gotta be named Smith."

Jenkins and Shrake were both large men, in overly sharp suits and nylon neckties. Both had thin webs of scars beneath their eyes, from being punched; both had fluorescent teeth, having had their real teeth knocked out while still young.

"We heard you had some excitement over in New Ulm this afternoon," Shrake said, as they waited for the cop. "What happened?"

Virgil told them about the chase and the arrest of Maxine Knowles. "There's gonna be an ocean of paperwork."

Jenkins said, "Yeah, but at least you had some fun. Nothing good like that ever happens to us anymore. Shrake hasn't hit anybody since, what, June?"

Shrake was probing his large ceramic teeth with a toothpick, took it out to say, "Don Carmel. Wayzata."

"Okay, since two weeks ago," Jenkins said.

"A pretty long dry spell for you guys," Virgil said.

"Yeah, not much you can really do about it," Jenkins said. "Gotta be patient, wait them out."

The St. Paul cop showed up in an unmarked car and parked behind Virgil. They all shook hands and the cop, Bowers, asked, "You don't think they got the tigers in the apartment, do you?"

"There's a question that hasn't been asked," Shrake said.

"No, I don't. The two tigers together weigh more than a thousand pounds. Even if they were dead, getting them up to a second floor, without an elevator, is gonna be a load and a half," Virgil said.

"That's good, because I really don't have my tiger-shooting vest with me," Bowers said.

"Enough bullshit, let's get it on," Jenkins said.

Jenkins and Shrake took the Crown Vic across to the car wash. Shrake got out and put his back to the wall under the stairs and Jenkins took the car into the car wash, which started up with a roar.

Virgil and the St. Paul cop crossed the street and parked on the side of the wash unit, where they couldn't be seen from the apartment. They joined Shrake next to the staircase, and Shrake asked Virgil, "You got your gun?"

Virgil patted his hip. "Right here."

"Try not to shoot anybody with it; I mean, one of us."

"Yeah, yeah. Let's go."

They went up the stairs walking quietly, in a single file, and found Apartment One at the front of the building. The apartment had a steel door and the two visible windows were barred with fake ornamental wrought-iron window guards. There were no lights on.

"Okay, so nobody's gonna get through the iron bars," Shrake muttered under his breath. "My question is, how do you get out if there's a fire?"

"What's gonna burn?" Virgil asked. "The whole goddamn place is made of concrete."

They listened at the windows and at the door and heard nothing at all, though it was hard to hear anything over the noise from the car wash. Shrake whispered, "What do you want to do?"

Virgil shrugged. "The key. He won't hear it with the car wash running."

Bowers dug it out of his pocket and passed it over and Shrake slid it into the lock, turned it, and pushed the door open one-handed, while keeping his back to the wall. No sound, no reaction.

Virgil, on the other side of the door opening, reached around the wall, groping for a light switch, found it, and turned on the porch light, which fully illuminated all of them. "Damn it." He turned it off, and found another switch, and turned it on.

Virgil backed up to the window. He could see the interior of the apartment now that the light was on, and it appeared to be empty. He could see a dark hallway leading to another room.

"Don't think anybody's home," he said. The car wash suddenly went silent, and Virgil said into the sudden silence, "Let's clear it."

They did. The apartment door opened directly on the living room, and Shrake led the way in, both he and Bowers pointing their weapons at the hallway to the back. Shrake found a light switch that turned on the hall light; the hallway led to a small bedroom and a motel-style bathroom, tight and cheap, and both empty.

Jenkins had come up the stairs to join them, and now said, "Look at that fuckin' TV set."

They all looked at it.

"Lucky guy," Shrake said. "Having an appliance like that. Football season coming up."

The TV occupied most of the middle of the living room and must have been seventy inches across, perched on two metal folding chairs with a cable leading to a cable box that sat on the terrazzo floor under the chairs.

Bowers, who'd been wandering around the apartment, said, "Here you go." Without touching it, he pointed at a paper map of the Minnesota Zoo, sitting on the breakfast counter.

"Okay, he's the right guy," Virgil said. "Wonder if he took off?"

"If he's got any brains, he did," Jenkins said. "Shrake and I were sittin' in a bar . . ."

"No . . ."

"We must've seen his face twenty times between nine o'clock and the news. If he was here, watching that thing"—Jenkins waved at the giant TV—"he couldn't have missed seeing himself."

Virgil looked around at the bleak little apartment, the dirt-stiff ten-year-old chintz curtains, the dusty, rugless terrazzo floors, the few pieces of furniture, the near total absence of dinnerware: two cups that he could see, a glass, a couple of spoons, one knife, and a fork in the sink. "Let's take the place apart. We need any kind of hint we can find about where he hid the tigers. Anything."

What they found was an apartment that was little lived in. Almost everything looked like it came with the apartment, except the television, a few pieces of clothing hung in the single bedroom closet, and some underwear and socks packed into the single chest of drawers. A pair of new, unworn pointed-toe black dress shoes, with white sidewalls, lounged next to the chest.

"Guy must like to boogie," Shrake said.

A green plywood box sat at the end of the bed, with a Master padlock fastened through a simple latch.

"It's an old army footlocker," Virgil said, touching it with his toe.

"I got a bolt cutter in the car," Bowers said. "I'll run and get it."

He did, and they cut the padlock off.

Inside, they found a lot of junk—earphones; an old Apple iPod filled with music of a style Virgil was unable to identify; a short-barreled Smith & Wesson .38 that looked to be a hundred years old, though loaded with fresh cartridges; a short stack of printed porn, plus some car magazines; and at the bottom, a thin address book that contained no addresses, but did contain a list of what appeared to be passwords.

"This could be useful," Virgil said. "If we can find his computer. If he had a computer."

"I don't see anything like a router," Bowers said.

"I don't think he lived here and I don't think he expected to stay long," Shrake said. "Looks like he came here for the job and planned to go back home when it was done."

"Should have left sooner," Bowers said.

13

▼ ▼ ▼

Two-thirty in the morning on the St. Croix, the river air cool and redolent with the odors of beached fish and automobile exhaust. The sheetrocking Yoder brothers, Curt and Hank, known to their friends as the Yos, were expecting some serious channel-catfish action; they'd be fishing right up to daybreak, barring thunderstorms and zombie outbreaks.

The Yos had stopped at an all-night convenience store for a six-pack of Miller Lite, a tin of Copenhagen Wintergreen for Curt, and a couple of Fudgsicles before heading down to the water.

Once off the road, they sat licking the Fudgsicles and drinking the first of their beers, while Dwight Yoakam finished singing "Long White Cadillac" on Outlaw Country. When the song, Fudgsicles, and beers were finished, Curt stuck a plug of Copenhagen under his tongue and said, "Let's get 'er done."

Curt got his gear from the truck bed and headed upstream from the bridge, while Hank believed that there were major catfish holes below the bridge piers, so he went that way.

Both men were wearing LED headlights, the better to bait their hooks and unhook any catfish. Hank turned his light on to more easily mold some stink bait on a treble hook—he had his own homemade formula, concocted of chopped chicken liver, diced night crawlers, nacho cheese, canned corn, and cornmeal, thoroughly mixed in his girlfriend's Waring blender when she wasn't around, and suitably aged in the hot sunlight on his back porch—and threw his first cast out next to a pier.

A big slab of gray stone shelved out of the river below the bridge, and while the bait sank into the hole, he walked back and forth, looking for a place to sit and smoke, where his line wouldn't drag over the rock. He was doing that when he saw, in his headlight, a corner of the safe about a foot down in the water.

For a moment, he couldn't believe what he was seeing, then he called, "Hey, Curt! Curt! C'mere. Quick."

Curt caught the tone in his brother's voice, so he reeled in, turned on his headlight, walked down under the bridge, and asked, "What?"

Hank pointed to the water under the bridge. "Am I nuckin' futs or is that a safe?"

Curt peered into the water, asked, "Where?" and then, before Hank could reply, "Holy shit. I see it. That's a safe all right."

Hank: "What do you think?"

"I think somebody couldn't open the sonofabitch and threw it off the bridge," Curt said. He was so excited he inadvertently hawked his whole plug of tobacco into the river.

Hank: "Like it's stolen?"

"Of course it's stolen, bonehead. If you owned a safe and wanted to get rid of it, you could sell it on Craigslist or even take it to a junkyard," Curt said. "You wouldn't throw it off a fuckin' bridge. I bet there's a million bucks in there."

"What do you think we ought to do?"

Curt scratched his forehead for a moment, mulling it over, then said, "I think we fish that bitch out of there and get it back to your place. You know what? Maybe the people who stole it couldn't open it, but Jerry Pratt could."

Jerry Pratt was an unemployed machinist, with metal-cutting skills.

"You think we could lift it?"

"Somebody had to lift it over the bridge railing, so yeah—I think we could lift it," Curt said.

"I wonder why he threw it in the shallows?"

"Probably didn't know any better, or maybe he did it at night," Curt said. He walked back to the shadow of the bridge, sat down, and started untying his boots. "Get your pants off."

Hank looked around: nothing to see but brush, and not even that, if they turned off their LED headlights. An occasional car drove over the bridge, out of sight. "What if somebody sees us?"

"You ain't got that much to see," Curt said.

"That's not what I'm talking about. What if somebody sees us with the safe?"

"We'll tell them . . . that we thought it was an old refrigerator and we were taking it out for, you know, cleaning-up-the-river reasons. We're, like, tree huggers or some fuckin' thing."

That sounded good. Hank nodded and said, "Better leave our shoes on. Lots of hooks been broke off in there."

Five minutes later the naked brothers were chest deep in the river, trying to get a hold on the safe. "Fuckin' heavy," Hank said.

"Yeah . . . but . . . it's movin'," Curt said.

With more grunting and a few groans they got it out of the water and up on the rock, where Hank said, "Fuck. You know, it looks more like a refrigerator than a safe."

"Too heavy," Curt said.

"It's a fuckin' refrigerator, man. Probably full of water." The refrigerator was loosely wrapped with water-soaked duct tape to keep the door closed. Hank yanked the tape off, pulled open the door, and in the pooled light of their headlamps, Hamlet Simonian's left arm flopped out on the rock.

"Jesus Christ!" Hank shouted, dancing away from the arm.

There was a brief discussion of possible choices—throw the refrigerator back in the river and then run and hide; call the cops anonymously then run and hide; or just run and hide. But their truck had probably been seen up on the road, and somebody might have seen them in the water, and there was a house not far away. In the end, for a lack of reasonable alternatives, they called the Polk County sheriff's office and waited.

A deputy showed up ten minutes later, took a look, and said, "Now you boys wait right here," and Curt asked, "We got any choice?" and the deputy said, "No."

After that, the Yos found themselves deeper in bureaucracy than they'd ever been in the river, but nobody seemed to think they had anything to do with what was obviously a murder, and they were eventually told they were free to go. The Polk County medical examiner took one look at the body, still stuffed in the refrigerator, and moved it along to a better-equipped facility in St. Paul.

Not much got done in St. Paul, except that an assistant medical examiner took fingerprints from the hands on the severed arms and sent them off to the FBI.

Virgil had gone back to bed at the hotel and was sleeping soundly when the BCA's duty officer called him at five a.m. Virgil crawled across the bed to the nightstand, where his phone was playing the first few bars of George Thorogood's "Bad to the Bone."

"This is Virgil."

"Hey, man, this is Clark, up at the office."

"If I can find my pistol, I'm gonna kill you," Virgil said.

"Pretty unlikely scenario, right there, you finding the gun. Anyway, I thought I better call. This Hamlet Simonian guy's been found. We got a call from the FBI."

Virgil sat up. "Terrific. Where is he?"

Clark said, "In the ME's office, here in St. Paul."

"What?"

"Somebody killed him—they don't know how yet—and tried to stuff his body in a compact refrigerator. He didn't fit, so they cut off his arms and squeezed them in around the body."

"Cut off his arms?"

"Yeah. Of course, I'm assuming it wasn't a suicide . . ."

"Hey, Clark . . . ?"

"Yeah, yeah. Anyway, the killer threw the refrigerator into the St. Croix, up by Osceola," Clark said. "It landed in shallow water and a couple of fishermen spotted it. They thought it was a safe."

Clark told the rest of the story, which he found amusing, and finished by saying, "Now you got a murder."

"Aw, shit. Give me the ME's number."

As long as he had to be awake, Virgil thought the ME ought to be, as well. He got hold of an assistant, who said nothing would be done with the body until eight o'clock. "I had a look at it, while they were bringing it in. I don't see any obvious trauma . . . other than the dismembered arms, of course."

"No gunshot wounds? Nothing like that?"

"Nope."

"Tell the doc that the murder is related to the tiger theft," Virgil said. "I'll be up there to talk to him, but soon as he gets in, ask if there's some chemistry that would pick up the kind of sedative overdose you'd get if somebody shot you with a tranquilizer gun, the kind used on large animals."

"Huh. I can tell you that kind of chemistry is routine, but I'll be sure to mention it. Could get some results back pretty quick."

"Great. I'll be up."

"Sounds like you've got an interesting case here," the assistant said.

"Provocative, even," Virgil said. He reset the alarm clock, rolled over, and before he went back to sleep, he asked himself, who'd cut off a dead man's arms? Who would even think of it? A medical doctor, maybe?

He had to talk to Peck again.

Two hours later, while he was pulling on his socks, Virgil called the Polk County sheriff's office in Wisconsin and spoke to the sheriff, who'd been to the scene. "It's another one of your damn Twin Cities murders that you keep unloading on us," the sheriff said. "If he'd dropped the refrigerator fifteen feet west, it'd technically be a Minnesota case, which it should be."

"You're breaking my heart," Virgil said.

"Yeah, sounds like it," the sheriff said.

The sheriff told Virgil the story of the Yoder brothers and a description of the murder scene. "From eyeballing it, I'd say the guy hadn't been in the river long at all," the sheriff said. "I've seen any number of drownings, been down for anything from an hour to a couple of weeks, or even a couple of months. This guy was probably dumped earlier in the night. If the ME tells you different, he's wrong and I'm right."

Virgil and the sheriff talked for a few more minutes, Virgil extracting as many details as the sheriff had, then he hung up and drove across the Cities to the BCA building.

Clark, the duty officer, had gone home at seven o'clock, and since he'd notified Virgil, the lead investigator, he hadn't bothered to leave a message for Jon Duncan, who freaked when Virgil showed up and told him about it.

"Cut off his arms? Cut off his arms? What have you done, Virgil?" Duncan cried, rocking back in his office chair.

"I haven't done anything," Virgil said.

"Why do your cases always wind up like this?" Duncan asked, running a hand through his hair. "Why can't you have a straightforward missing-tigers case?"

Duncan was only half-joking. "You know, most of my cases don't involve any violence at all," Virgil said. "Most of them are really straightforward."

"I can't remember even *one* that was straightforward," Duncan said. "What about the one with the spies? What about the one with, with . . . the dognapping one that turned into a triple murder or something and you arrested the school board? Are you kiddin' me? You arrested the school board?"

"Not all of them," Virgil said. "One of them is still on the run."

"Ah, man, does the media know yet?"

"I wouldn't be surprised," Virgil said. "A Wisconsin county sheriff's office handled the case when the body was found. I expect they got the Simonian ID as soon as I did, and they know Simonian was wanted on the tiger theft."

"So they'll be calling. TV, radio, the whole shooting match," Duncan said. He looked at his office telephone as though it were a cockroach. "I gotta talk to the director."

"That's not a good idea. He's gonna be a little testy right now."

The director was about to be fired, if office rumors were true. Since the building contained a couple of dozen professional investigators and the usual garden-variety snoops, the rumors were generally accurate.

"No help for it," Duncan said, about calling the director.

"I thought you liked being on TV," Virgil said.

"I do, most of the time," Duncan said. "But I like it to be on the credit side of things, where I'm the hero. You know, I smile at the camera, show off my dimples. This is gonna be debit. Big-time debit."

"Good luck with it," Virgil said. "You do have the cute dimples. Here's a tip: I'd stay away from the phrase 'The suspect was disarmed.'"

Virgil left Duncan to his media problem and drove to the medical examiner's office, a single-story gray building with all of the charm of a shoe box, built next to a Regions Hospital parking structure. The medical examiner, a chain-smoking doc named Nguyen Ran, asked, "You want to see the body?"

"No. What I want is some clue that'll get me to the killer. And the tigers."

"Don't have any of those," Ran said. "I also don't have any chemistry back yet and won't have until tomorrow, but I can tell you that you're probably right on the means of death. No sign of the normal types of violence, not even defensive wounds, but I did find a small bruise next to his left nipple. When I looked closer, I could see a point of penetration that would be consistent with a wound made by a big needle. I dissected that area and found a lacuna in the underlying muscle, and bruising that would be consistent with the violent injection of a substantial quantity of fluid: almost like an inch-long blister in the muscle."

"It's what I thought," Virgil said. "He was shot with a tranquilizer gun."

"Yeah. I looked at his lungs . . . you don't need the details, but it all points toward a massive dose of a fast-acting sedative. Big enough that the dose killed him. They didn't have to finish him off with any of the conventional methods. The cheeseheads sent the whole refrigerator over. No tranquilizer dart inside, no dart was found at the scene."

"*Anything* else? Anything that would help me?"

"Nope. Wearing a T-shirt and jeans. Underwear, socks, and Nike brand shoes. No ID—no wallet or anything, no jewelry. Fingers were all intact, got a fine set of prints, about as good as you could hope for."

"What about the arms?" Virgil asked. "Were they cut off with a scalpel? Hacked off with an ax? Anything I could look for?"

"More like sawn off with a sharp knife. I'm thinking a butcher knife. Postmortem, of course. No effort to carefully disarticulate the shoulders. They were cut right through. Nothing particularly neat about it. From what I get from my investigators, it was probably done because the killer couldn't fit the body in the refrigerator any other way."

"You wouldn't say off the top of your head that it was done by a doctor . . . somebody with a knowledge of human anatomy?"

"No. The way it was done, a deer hunter could have done it. Anybody who'd ever taken apart a carcass. I mean, it wasn't sloppy, but it wasn't so skillfully done that I'd suspect a surgeon. You looking at a surgeon?"

"No," Virgil said. "Maybe at a regular doc."

Ran shrugged. "Couldn't prove it with me."

Virgil sat in his truck and thought: if you had to hide a tiger-skinning operation, you wouldn't do it in a tightly packed suburb. You'd probably want to do it where you had a piece of land around yourself, free of snoops. Like out in the countryside.

The closest big patches of rural countryside were on both sides of the St. Croix River, and Simonian had been found under a bridge over the St. Croix. And Peck had given him the name of a woman who processed animals . . . in Wisconsin.

Need to take a look at her, he thought.

14

▼ ▼ ▼

Peck was lying in bed, listening to WCCO radio, when he heard the news. Hamlet Simonian had been pulled out of the St. Croix River.

"Oh, mother of God," he groaned to the thumbtack in the ceiling. He'd used the thumbtack for meditation exercises, before he'd discovered the full efficacy of Xanax. With his luck, he thought, the thumbtack would come unglued some night and land point-down on his eyeball.

After a while, aloud, he said, "They found Hamlet. How could they find Hamlet?"

He'd managed to keep his shit together during the interview with Flowers with the help of an extra tab of the Xanax. Drugs wouldn't help him with Hayk Simonian, not after the bullshit he'd laid on the older brother.

He'd told Hayk that Hamlet Simonian was driving back to Glendale, California, where their family came from, where he planned to hide out until the heat dissipated. When Hayk had later complained that he couldn't reach his brother on his cell phone,

Peck had told him that Hamlet had turned it off, so the cops couldn't check his call history. He'd suggested that Hayk go to the Apple lost-phone locater service and look for the phone's location. Hayk had done that and the phone was shown as being in Des Moines, and later, moving west from Kansas City.

Hayk had been satisfied with that and had gone back to work, drying out tiger meat. He'd planned to work most of the night, finishing the soft-tissue part of processing Artur, and then he'd move on to grinding the bones. He was probably still asleep in the farmhouse: but Hayk spent a lot of time listening to Minnesota Public Radio and when the noon news came up . . .

Only one thing Peck could do about that.

Peck went down to the garage and got the rifle out—not the tranquilizer gun, but the .308 that Hamlet had used to shoot the male tiger. Peck didn't know a lot about guns, but he'd fired a few, knew how to load the rifle, knew how the safety worked: guns were simple machines and a child could operate them. Children often did, as illustrated by the accidental death statistics.

He left the gun unloaded and worked the bolt a few times and pulled the trigger, getting the click of the firing pin, then slipped a .308 round into the chamber, put it in the Tahoe, and headed out to the farm.

The Xanax was still at work. He was worried, even frightened, but functioning.

In the run-up to his company's bankruptcy, he'd been handling the daily stress with Ambien at night to help him sleep, and Xanax during the day to smooth himself out. That had worked for a while. Then one night, while on Ambien and Xanax simultaneously, he'd had a couple of evening margaritas at a St. Paul bar, had gone outside, and had physically frozen on a street corner. For nearly half an hour, he'd been unable to pick up a foot to move.

Since it was St. Paul, nobody had noticed. He might have stood there for a week if something in his brain hadn't finally broken loose, and he found himself able to walk again.

He had thrown the Ambien away, but kept the Xanax and now was rolling through the warm morning with a smooth chemical calm. He didn't think about the consequences of what he'd done with Hamlet Simonian, or what he was planning to do with Hayk Simonian, because the consequences were simply unthinkable. The Pecks were physicians: they did not go to prison.

Were the Pecks psychopaths? He didn't think so. Sociopaths, probably, since he had to admit that he really didn't feel much for his fellow human beings. He even had a hard time figuring out what it would be like, feeling something for his fellow humans.

His father, he thought, was probably the same way, since he hadn't apparently felt much for his wives or his only child. He didn't know about Pecks IV, III, or II, but his father had owned a photograph of Peck I standing next to a wagonload of severed legs, supposedly taken during the fighting at Cold Harbor in the Civil War. Peck I was leaning on the wagon, a cigar in his hands. He was smiling.

Basically, Peck VI thought, he was carrying out an old family tradition.

At the farm, Hayk was up and sitting on a stump outside the barn, smoking a cigarette, wearing a wifebeater shirt and jeans. He yawned, apparently just up. Peck parked and got the gun out of the back. The safety was off, so he kept his finger away from the trigger as he carried it toward the barn.

"Gonna shoot the girl?"

"No, but you are, when the time comes," Peck said. "I thought I better leave the rifle here. It makes me nervous having it around the house."

"A lot of shit makes you nervous," Simonian said. He yawned again.

"Because I think ahead," Peck said. "You should try it sometime. How's the drying going?"

"Should be done by tomorrow, then we can start on the girl. The testicle slices came out good. You can start grinding and bottling if you want."

"Probably tonight," Peck said. He could hear classical music coming from inside. Public radio. "You hear from Hamlet?"

Simonian shook his head. "Nobody has. I called Mom, she hasn't heard a thing. You'd think he'd call from a pay phone or something."

"You tried to find a pay phone lately?" Peck asked.

"There's that," Simonian said. He stubbed the cigarette on the stump, then snapped the butt into the driveway. "Back to the salt mine."

Peck led the way inside, which stank from the electric dryers; the temperature in the place must have been over a hundred. Peck pulled the door shut behind them. A collection of bones lay on a blue plastic tarp on the floor and a pile of tiger meat on another tarp. Simonian had pulled all the teeth and they lay on an improvised table, along with pans of dried flesh. Still carrying the rifle, Peck bent over the table, looking at what amounted to tiger jerky.

"Good," he said. "You're doing good here. Anybody been snooping around?"

"The mailman stopped this morning—I was out by the road and he asked if we were moving in. I told him no, we were getting the place ready to sell off. Probably take the buildings down. I told him we wouldn't be using the mailbox or getting mail, and he went away."

"All right," Peck said. He looked at the tiger meat, including the defleshed, toothless skull, and said, "We'll grind up all the bones separately, by type—keep the femurs away from everything else. Anything we're not gonna use, we can bury out back. You ought to use a hammer and break up the skull, but keep that separate. I'm not sure, but I suspect we'll get more for skull bones, or brain-pan bones. I'll ask old man Zhang about that."

"How would anybody know if it was brain-pan bones or leg bones, after it's ground up?"

"Well, *I* would," Peck said. "There are some ethical standards involved here."

Simonian yawned and turned away from Peck to look at the bones, which was what Peck had been waiting for. He was five feet from the other man, and when Simonian turned, Peck lifted the rifle and shot him in the back.

Boom!

Again, the muzzle blast was deafening; and at the last second, Peck flinched, remembering the ricocheting bullet the first time the gun had been shot in the barn. He wasn't hit this time, though, and he looked on with interest as Simonian lurched away, one step, two, and reached out toward the remaining strip of tiger bone and meat hanging from the overhead hook, turned, and gave Peck a puzzled look, then fell facedown on one of the blood-spattered tarps. Nothing dramatic happened—no last words, no struggle for life, scrabbling across the bloodstained floor.

Peck looked at the suddenly deceased for a moment, then went to the barn door, pushed it open a crack, and looked out. The barn was set well back from the road, and nobody was on the road.

So it was done.

Peck had known from the start that he'd have to get rid of the Simonians, though he'd hoped it would be later than this—now he'd have to finishing processing the tiger meat on his own. As that thought occurred to him, he felt the prickling of hair on the back of his neck, and turned to see Katya peering at him with her golden eyes. She seemed to be waiting.

"What do you want?" Peck asked the cat.

Katya stared back at him, unmoving, making no noise.

A pan sat inside the cage, empty. They'd known they'd want to keep the female tiger alive for a few days, until they were finished processing the male, so they'd provided a water pan. Hayk apparently hadn't been filling it.

A hose came in from outside—Hayk had been using it to wash down the tiger carcass—and now Peck set the rifle aside and dragged the hose over to the cage, turned the nozzle on, and filled the pan through the fence. Katya didn't move.

"It's there if you want it," Peck told her.

He turned to the problem of getting rid of Hayk's body. He could back the Tahoe up to the barn door and get the body out without being seen, but getting a 240-pound body into the truck would be a problem. Three of them had struggled to get the male tiger onto a six-inch-high dolly, when they'd only had to lift a bit more than two hundred pounds each, and Hayk had lifted a lot more than his share.

Katya made a rumbling sound from her cage, and Peck glanced back at her. She hadn't eaten in three days, probably hungry.

He turned back to the problem of moving Hayk, and then thought, *Wait, a hungry tiger?* He had 240 pounds of fresh meat. Hayk was heavily built, especially from the waist down and one of his legs probably weighed between forty-five and fifty pounds, if he remembered his medical texts correctly.

Removing the legs would seriously reduce the load, he thought, and all the tools for doing that were right here in the barn. Two birds with one stone. He looked at the cat.

"Got the munchies?"

Katya didn't say anything, but lay back and watched him.

15

▼ ▼ ▼

Roberta Patterson lived out in the countryside, in a ranch-style house with yellow siding and an oversized mailbox surrounded by dusty-looking cone flowers, out on the county road. She was getting her mail when Virgil pulled into her hosta-lined driveway. Virgil knew a man who bred hostas, but he was not confident of that man's intelligence.

"Do I know you?" Patterson asked, as he got out of his truck, stepping carefully to avoid the hostas.

"Nope. I'm a Minnesota cop looking for the tigers," Virgil said.

"Ah. I wondered if you'd come around here," she said, as she thumbed through the mail. "You got some ID?"

Virgil showed her his ID and they walked up the driveway to the house, talking about what a nice day it was, and how last week's rain had kept down the dust after a dry summer. A metal garage or work building sat behind the main house and was nearly as large as the house. Patterson said, "That's where I work; I guess you know what I do."

"Yeah, but I don't know exactly how you do it," Virgil said.

"Come on inside. You want a root beer? I just bought some."

"That'd be good," he said.

"Scoop of vanilla ice cream?"

"Yeah, that'd be great."

They sat in her compact kitchen to talk; the kitchen smelled of country vegetables like carrots and onions, with just the barest undertone of soil and skunk. As Patterson put the root beer floats together, she said, "To keep it simple, I collect a variety of fauna and flora, animals and plants, and dry them and prepare them and bottle them and ship them to people who distribute them through traditional medical channels."

She was a tall, thin, dark-haired, blue-eyed woman in her middle forties. She was wearing a white blouse with a wolf's head embroidered into it, jeans, and hiking boots. "I get the animal parts through a local fur dealer and some from roadkill. The plants I collect myself, usually from river bottoms, and I have a patch of ground I lease from a local farmer for growing marigolds and mint and a bunch of other herbs."

"You haven't heard anything about the tigers?"

"No, of course not, or I would have called the police," she said. She handed him the float in a ceramic mug. "I'd never be involved with anything like that, or anything that involved endangered animals. The animals that I use are members of the weasel family—mink, otters, martens—brought in by trappers, and I'll get striped skunks from the same place. Or from roadkill. They're all used for their musk. In the fall, I'll get bear gallbladders, which are collected for the bile. Animals are a relatively small part of the business. I do a ton of herbs. That's most of it."

"Do you know anybody who would have heard about the tigers . . . if there's anything out there to hear?"

"Honestly? If there was anything to hear, it'd probably be me," Patterson said. "There hasn't been a hint, so if the tigers were going to be used for medicine, I believe it has to be somebody working on his own. Or it's not people who are going to use them for medicine. There are animal rights people . . ."

Virgil spooned up a chunk of ice cream, ate it, and said, "We haven't ruled that out, but there's a problem: one of the people who we strongly believe was involved was found murdered. Dumped in the St. Croix, not far from here. The thing is, he was a professional criminal. A professional thief. Not the kind of person you find hanging around with, um, you know, radical do-gooders."

"Do you even *know* any radical do-gooders?" she asked, with a tinge of skepticism.

"As a matter of fact, I do. I talked to a couple of them and they say they haven't heard a thing. I believe them," Virgil said. "Besides, they pointed out that the zoo is part of a project to save the Amur tiger from extinction. Even the most radical animal rights people would support that."

"All right—but here's the problem," Patterson said. "Tiger parts are illegal in the U.S. and most of the rest of the world. They're even illegal in China, though the law is mostly ignored there. So, you've got, say, a thousand pounds of tiger that you need to distribute. How do you do that? To put it another way, since you're a police officer, how would somebody get rid of a thousand pounds of cocaine or heroin?"

Virgil considered that for a moment, then said, "You'd need a distribution network."

"Not just a distribution network," she said. "An *illegal* distribution network. As illegal as a Mexican drug cartel. Everybody involved would be committing a felony."

"Hadn't thought about that part," Virgil said. "Where would I find a network like that?"

"Ask your drug people," she said. "I suppose it'd be out on the West Coast, where you've got a lot of older Asian residents, who'd be the main customers. Unless, of course, it's being shipped directly to China."

"Huh."

"I'd point out that somebody with access to a large illegal distribution network is not going to be a debutante. You said this man who was murdered was a professional criminal. That fits."

Virgil asked, "You have any idea of where I'd look?"

"None at all, except what I see in the movies. Los Angeles, San Francisco, Seattle, maybe . . . Vancouver, I guess."

"Jeez." He drank the last of the root beer. "I wonder if they might have already moved the tigers out?"

She shrugged. "Could have, I guess, although that'd be a problem. I have horses, and moving them around is a pain, even with a good horse trailer, when you're going any long distance. With tigers? Be a heck of a lot easier killing and processing them here. Once they're processed and the products get fake labels, who would know that they're looking at illegal tiger parts and not legal cattle parts? Ground-up bone looks like ground-up bone. You'd need a DNA test to tell the difference."

"Okay," Virgil said. He was at least semiconvinced. He took a business card from his pocket and slid it across the table to her. "Thanks for your help. And the root beer float. Call me if you hear anything or think of anything else."

She picked up the card. "I will. I do hope you find these guys. They're the kind of people who give traditional medicine a bad name."

Virgil headed back to the Twin Cities. He was crossing the St. Croix bridge at Hudson when a call came in from an unknown number.

When he answered, Patterson said, "This is Bobbie Patterson again. Listen, I did think of something else. It's possible that they killed the tigers and then froze them to take them somewhere else to process them. That involves refrigerated trucks. Keeping a thousand pounds of meat at freezing temperatures isn't all that easy, if you're moving. It'd be easier to buy some meat dryers and do it right here. They're not expensive; people use them to make deer jerky. They'd probably need four or five of the smaller dryers. I doubt that they'd buy a big commercial deal . . . so maybe you should call up the dealers of meat dryers, see if anybody delivered a whole bunch of them to the Cities."

"You are a very smart woman," Virgil said. "Thank you."

Virgil called Sandy, the BCA researcher, and got her started on that, then called St. Paul's gang guy, who said he had no idea about Chinese gangs, though there were a couple of Hmong gangs. "I can guarantee they're not up to smuggling tiger parts, dried or not. These guys are hustling a little Mexican Mud and hillbilly heroin; they wouldn't be involved in anything more sophisticated."

He said he'd call a guy in San Francisco and ask who'd know about Chinese gangs. "If you've got this dead guy from Glendale, it seems like you're looking at California. I don't know if my guy would know anything about LA gangs, but he might know another guy who'd know."

Virgil had just crossed into St. Paul when he took a call from another unknown number. "Virgil? Bob Roberts from Mankato PD."

"Hey, Bob-Bob. You got my tigers?"

"Uh, no, man. Listen, I hate to be the guy to tell you this . . . but somebody beat up your girlfriend."

Virgil nearly drove off the highway. "What! What!"

"Frankie. She's hurt, man, she's on her way to the hospital. A couple guys jumped her outside a Kwik Trip. Nobody knows why, there wasn't any argument or anything. They didn't even talk to her. They jumped her and beat her up and took off. Looks like it was a setup—one of the cops out there says they were wearing masks."

"How bad? How bad is she?"

"Don't know yet, but she got smacked around pretty good. That's about all I know. I mean, she isn't gonna die or anything, but she's beat up."

"I'm coming," Virgil said.

16

▼ ▼ ▼

Virgil got south in a hurry, cutting through traffic with his lights and siren. On his way, he called Jon Duncan to tell him what happened. Duncan asked if he had any idea who'd attacked Frankie, or why, and Virgil said that he didn't.

"I've made a lot of people unhappy the last few years, but not many who'd know that I've been hanging out with Frankie," Virgil said. "Or even if they knew, nobody who would go after her. Besides, nobody goes after a cop's girlfriend; if they're going to do anything, they go after the cop, and they don't do that very often."

"Okay. I'll tell you what, Virgil—you go down there and do what you have to do, and take care of Frankie, and keep me informed," Duncan said. "I don't want you investigating this. I want you to stay away from it."

"What? Jon, I've got to, this is . . ."

"You don't investigate attacks that might be aimed at you," Duncan said. "I'll get Sands to pull somebody off another job to do it."

Sands was the BCA director. "He doesn't like me much," Virgil said.

"Who cares? He's about to get fired, and his boss, and his boss's boss, both *do* like you. Even Sands can't say that we don't take care of our people, so . . . I'll get somebody good," Duncan said.

Frankie had been taken to the emergency room at the Mayo Clinic, an orange-brick building on Marsh Street. Virgil dumped his truck in the parking lot and hustled inside, where a nurse told him that Frankie was in the ICU. "That's temporary until we get test results back," she said.

"How bad?" Virgil asked. "How bad?"

"Don't really know yet, but not so bad, I think. She apparently lost consciousness for a while, back where the attack took place. That's what we were told, anyway. She was conscious when the ambulance got there, so she wasn't out for long," the nurse said. "She was having trouble breathing when the paramedics got to her. We put her through a CAT scan; she had cracked ribs and a partially collapsed lung. The docs put in a chest tube, and the lung's reinflated. Didn't see any brain damage, but she's got a mild concussion."

"Man, that sounds bad, that sounds bad, man," Virgil said. He felt an urgent need to do something, anything, but there was nothing he could do.

"It's never good," the nurse said. He added, "There's a lot worse comes through here every day, and they walk out a few days later."

A cop was sitting in a plastic chair at the end of the emergency room and he got up and walked over when he saw Virgil. "Hey, Virg. I talked to Donnie Carlson a minute ago, and he said they don't have any names yet, but Frankie took a piece out of the arm of one of the guys who jumped her. Bit out a piece the size of a quarter, so when we get a name, we'll have DNA and he's probably got a pretty good hole on his arm."

Virgil nodded. "Hang here for a minute, Al, will you? I want to talk, but I want to go look at Frankie . . ."

"Sure."

With the nurse on his heels, Virgil went into the ICU, where the nurse opened a crack in the curtains around Frankie's bed. Frankie's eyes were closed, but when he stepped in, she must have heard the heels on his cowboy boots, and she asked, "Is that you?"

"Got here as fast as I could. What the hell happened?" Virgil asked.

Now her eyes opened. "How shitty do I look?"

Virgil shook his head. "You look like somebody who got held down and sandpapered. No permanent damage, no big cuts or anything; you won't have scars, if that's what you're worried about."

Her face was a massive bruise, and though her nose was straight and unsplinted, and so probably not broken, there was dried blood around her nostrils and at the corners of her mouth. He could see her bare arms and they were scraped as badly as her face. Both eyes would be blackened for a while.

"That's what I was worried about," she said. Then she asked, "You okay?"

"What? Of course . . ."

"I don't want you killing anybody," she said.

Virgil looked at her for a few seconds, then said, "I can't make any promises."

"Virgil!"

"Fuck you. I'm not making any promises." Virgil started to tear up, looking at her, wiped the tears away with the heels of his hands. "Ah, Jesus, Frankie . . . We'll find the guys who did this. Have you pissed anybody off lately? Bad enough to do this? Unless you know somebody, it's gotta be aimed at me."

"No, no. It wasn't." Her voice was quiet, almost rusty. "It's Sparkle. She wanted to visit a migrant trailer park on a farm out west of here; it's off a rutted dirt road. She borrowed my truck to get up there. I was driving her speck."

Specks were cars that Frankie thought were too small to be useful. "They thought I was her," she said.

"Ah, shit . . ."

"They kept saying, 'You get your nose outa our business. Go home, bitch.'"

"There's a cop out in the emergency room, Al Foreman. You know him?"

"I know Al . . ."

"He says you bit a chunk out of one of them and the cops picked it up," Virgil said. The guy's gonna have a hole in his arm and we can nail him with the DNA. We'll get him, I swear to God."

Frankie said, "That's nice . . . I feel really sleepy . . ."

The nurse, who had trailed in behind Virgil, said, "You're filled up with painkillers, honey. You'll be sleeping a lot."

They talked for a few more minutes, but Frankie was slipping into sleep, and when she was gone, Virgil kissed her on the forehead, backed out of the room, and found Foreman, the Mankato cop. "What do you know?"

"Nothing but what I heard from the guys. She went over to the Kwik Trip around three o'clock. She went inside and bought some groceries and when she came back out, she was jumped by two guys who caught her between her car and a truck that was parked beside her," Foreman said. "Donnie can tell you how big they were and all that, but I can tell you that they parked in the street, so the cameras didn't get the license plate number. A witness says the vehicle was a red Ford SuperCrew pickup. Probably a couple years old."

"Get their faces on the video?"

"No. They wore ball caps without any brand markings, which means they must have bought them for this job, and rubber Halloween masks. Somebody says they were Mitt Romney masks. They wore canvas work gloves. The guys have the video down at the shop, if you want to see it. Can't really see too much after the first few seconds, because Frankie goes down between the cars. They were wearing work shirts and jeans."

"Do you . . ." Virgil trailed away as a pretty but tough-looking blonde walked into the emergency room. She was tall, square-jawed, and wide-shouldered, with small, barely discernible boxer's scars under both eyes. She wore dark slacks, a tan blouse under a dark blue jacket, and black marginally fashionable boots that could be used to kick somebody to death.

She said, "Virgil. How's your friend? Is it Frankie?"

"Yeah, Frankie. She's pretty roughed up, but she'll be okay," Virgil said. He knew Catrin Mattsson, but not well. "Catrin—good to see you. This is Al Foreman, Mankato PD. Al, this is Catrin Mattsson, she's with us at the BCA."

"Oh, yeah," Foreman said, as they shook hands.

Foreman said "Oh, yeah" because he recognized the name: Mattsson had been a sheriff's deputy famously kidnapped, raped, and beaten by an insane serial killer. She'd been rescued at the last minute by Lucas Davenport, and she had killed her captor with a steel bar, as Davenport had been reeling with a smashed nose. That was their story, anyway.

Her ordeal and her resilience had brought her to the attention of the governor, who'd pressured the BCA into hiring her. Davenport had supported the appointment, having worked with Mattsson on the serial killer case, before she was kidnapped. She was building her own reputation at the BCA as someone not to be messed with and who carried more than her own load.

Foreman filled her in on the details of the attack and Virgil told her what he'd gotten from Frankie: that the attack was probably aimed at Frankie's sister, Sparkle, and why that might be. Mattsson listened closely, one fist on her hip; a full-sized black Beretta was clipped to her waistband just ahead of her fist.

When they were finished, Mattsson said, "Virgil, Jon wants you back on the tigers. Soon as you can reasonably do it. He knows you've been making progress—Sandy said to tell you that she's found a shipment of meat dryers and has e-mailed the details to you. I'll find the guys who attacked Ms. Nobles."

"Frankie," Virgil said.

"Yeah, Frankie."

"She's asleep; she's full of pain medication," Virgil said.

"Okay, I'll be here overnight. I'll check every once in a while, see if she's awake," Mattsson said. "In the meantime, I need to talk to this Sparkle."

"She's staying at Frankie's farm."

"Why don't you wait here for a minute," Mattsson said. "I want to talk to the doc. Then we'll go look at the video, see what the locals have, and then I'll follow you out to the farm. You better get back to the Cities tonight. The tigers are still number one on the media hit parade."

She went off with the nurse to find the doc and when she was out of earshot, Foreman said, "Whoa."

Virgil looked after her and said, "Yeah."

Foreman: "Hot and scary. I mean, totally jumpable, but then she'd probably eat your head, like a black widow."

"I'm not sure I'd say that out loud," Virgil said.

"I hear you, brother. You okay with her on the case?"

"More than okay," Virgil said. And he was: nobody at the BCA would go after Frankie's attacker harder than Mattsson. He owed Duncan for that one.

Mattsson came back a few minutes later and Virgil led the way across town to the Mankato public safety department. Mattsson had called ahead, and the Mankato detective, Donnie Carlson, had the video ready to run.

"The store has a digital recorder tied to the cameras, and the whole thing is hooked up to the Internet," he said. "We had the video a half hour after Ms. Nobles was attacked. Two cameras cover the gas pumps, a third one is mounted above the pumps and looks at the front door to catch a stickup man coming out. We can see the attack on the edge of that one."

They bent over the desk watching the full-color video, which had no sound. It began as two men, one rangy and athletic looking, the other too fat and built like a door, walked up to the side of the store and passed out of sight. The video then skipped forward three or four minutes to show Frankie walking out the door carrying a sack of groceries. As she turned down the slot between Sparkle's Mini and a truck, the two men jogged back into the video frame, then into the slot between the vehicles.

Frankie saw them coming and turned at the last second, as one of the men swung an open-handed slap at the side of her head. The slap connected and she dropped the bag and flattened against the car, her hands going up to protect her face, then the man hit her with a gloved fist, once, twice, and she tried to squeeze past him but the second man, the heavy one, blocked her retreat and shoved her back to the first one.

The athletic man swatted her across the forehead and this time she began to sink down, and he grabbed her blouse with one hand and wound up to hit her again, but she turned her head and bit into a length of exposed arm above the work glove, and they could see him shout or scream as she wrenched her head away from the arm and she fell out of sight, but the man kicked her twice, and then ran out of the picture, followed by the fat man.

Without sound, the video was flat and looked something like a puppet show: the punches and slaps didn't have the sound effects of movies.

A few seconds after the attackers ran out of the picture, a third man hurried around the nose of the truck and looked at her, then turned and shouted to somebody out of sight, and went to his knees over her, although the camera still couldn't see her, and they saw a heavy brown-haired woman in what appeared to be a hairstylist's nylon uniform run into the store and then, a moment later, two more men run out to where the third man was now standing over Frankie, shouting. One of the newcomers turned and ran back into the store.

The video then skipped ahead to an ambulance arriving. The paramedics hurried up to the small crowd between the cars, and a moment later brought a backboard, and then loaded Frankie onto a gurney and wheeled her to the ambulance and loaded her inside. A moment later, the ambulance was gone.

Virgil hadn't really been aware that the two attackers had been wearing masks, and said so.

"It's hard to see," the Mankato cop said. "Watch this."

He typed in a number and the video recording skipped back to the point where Frankie turned between the two vehicles and the two men appeared. Mattsson muttered, "Watch out!"

At that point in the attack, the men's heads were up and looking straight at the cameras. That lasted for only a second or two, but Carlson froze the photo as the two looked toward Frankie. With the image frozen, Virgil could see that they wore pale rubber masks. "Don't think they look like Mitt Romney, but I've been told that's what they are," Virgil said.

"Yeah, they are," Carlson said. "We matched them with some masks you can buy from a Halloween place on the Internet."

Mattsson spent five minutes quizzing Carlson, with Virgil chipping in from time to time, then Mattsson closed her notebook and said to Virgil, "Let's go talk to this Sparkle person."

Frankie's farm was northwest of Mankato, across the Minnesota River and out in the countryside, a fifteen-minute ride from the public safety department. Frankie's truck was parked on the side of the driveway past the house. Virgil parked and Mattsson pulled in beside him, and as they got out, Sparkle came out of the house. She was smiling, but when she saw Virgil's face, the smile fell away like a dead leaf off a tree.

"What? Virgil! What happened?"

Virgil told her, and she pressed her hands to the sides of her head, and kept saying, "Oh my God! Oh my God!"

When she'd recovered a bit, Sparkle said that she hadn't seen anyone following her that day; that her interviews had been congenial, but she had names of all the canning factory people she'd spoken to. Mattsson took notes and asked more questions, and Virgil realized that he wouldn't be able to help much, wouldn't do anything that Mattsson wasn't already doing.

As Sparkle was answering questions, Frankie's youngest son, Sam, came walking up the driveway wearing his Cub Scout uniform, carrying a BB gun, and trailed by Honus the dog. Virgil went to meet him and before he could say anything, Sam said, "I finished second."

"In what?"

"Marksmanship," Sam said.

"How many people in the competition?" Virgil asked.

"Seven other ones. I shoulda won . . ." He squinted, just a bit, and then asked, "What's wrong?"

"Ah, man, your mom got hurt," Virgil said. "Not real bad, but she's going to be in the hospital for a couple of days."

"What happened?"

Virgil told him, and Sam said, "If I catch that motherfucker, I'll kill him," and he was deadly serious.

"No, no, the cops are taking care of that," Virgil said. "And don't say 'motherfucker.'"

"You say it."

"Yeah." Virgil slapped Sam on the shoulder and looked around and then said, "Basically, you're right. The guy's a motherfucker."

Sparkle and Mattsson were still talking when Virgil left, driving back to Mankato and the clinic. Sparkle said she'd come as soon as Mattsson was finished with her. At the hospital, Frankie was soundly asleep and a nurse said she'd be down for a few hours.

He called Sparkle to tell her that, but Sparkle said, "I'm coming anyway. I called Bill and he'll take the night off and stay here with the kids. I'll sit with Frankie until she wakes up, whenever that is."

Virgil sat with Frankie for a while; signed onto the hospital Wi-Fi and checked his e-mail. Sandy the researcher had left a note that said five meat dryers had been shipped to an address in St. Paul's Frogtown, from Bug-Out Supplies, a St. Louis survivalist supplier. She left a link to a website, and when Virgil went to it, he found a red headline that said, "When the SHTF, BOS's Got Your Back." Virgil figured out that "SHTF" meant "shit hits the fan," a refrain he found throughout the online catalog. The dryers Sandy highlighted cost $231 each.

She included the address to which they were sent, and the buyer's name: Bob Smith.

"Bob Smith," Virgil said to himself. "Right."

Sandy added a note: "BOS said the order came in with a postal money order for the full amount. They said that's not uncommon with survivalist types—apparently they don't want you to know that they're making survival jerky in the basement."

Virgil headed back north toward the Cities as night was falling.

As he did that, Winston Peck VI was driving the remnants of Hayk Simonian out of the farm and onto a Washington County back road, heading south. He no longer much cared if the second Simonian's body was found—he'd been afraid of Hayk, but now Hayk was dead. Killing Hayk wouldn't mean much, in terms of penalties, if the police ever figured out who'd killed Hamlet Simonian.

His main objective was to get Hayk's body well away from the farm. He drove south, slowly, not to attract the attention of any roaming cops, past small farms and orchards and truck gardens, crossed the bridge at Prescott, and drove into Wisconsin toward River Falls.

After a couple of random turns, he found himself in the middle of a long, shallow valley with a wet, overgrown ditch on one side. With no headlights in view, he stopped the truck, dragged the Simonian load out of the back, wrapped in plastic, then staggered over to the ditch, waded into the weeds, and finally gave the body a heave.

That would do it, he thought. If somebody wanted to fish it out of there, good luck to them.

Virgil called Jenkins and Shrake.

"If you guys got the time, I got a target," he told Jenkins. "We'll probably need Shrake to add a little IQ to the expedition."

"Well, shoot—we were planning to go out drinking tonight and pick up some loose women," Jenkins said.

"You can still do that, as long as you don't shoot anybody while you're with me and get stuck with the paperwork," Virgil said.

"Fine," Jenkins said. "Where do you want to meet?"

"At the office—we won't be going far."

When Virgil got to the office, the duty officer said, "Jenkins and Shrake are upstairs, but there're some guys looking for you. They're out in the parking lot in an RV."

"I saw the RV," Virgil said. "Who are they?"

"Don't know," the duty officer said. "They came looking for you, said they needed to talk to the guy in charge of the tiger investigation. We told them you were on the way in."

"Huh. Call Jenkins and Shrake. I'll take them with me," Virgil said.

Jenkins and Shrake came down the stairs a minute later, dressed in their usual overly sharp suits, pastel dress shirts, Frenchy pointed shoes, and nylon neckties. "Where're we going?" Jenkins asked.

"First stop's out in the parking lot," Virgil said.

Jenkins and Shrake flanked him as they walked out and down the slight hill to the RV. As they approached, Virgil could hear the engine running. At a lit back window, they could see four dark-haired men, apparently sitting at a table, playing cards.

Virgil knocked on the door. A minute later, the door popped open, and a swarthy, black-haired man in black slacks, a black T-shirt, and Frenchy pointed shoes, wearing a heavy gold chain around his neck, looked down at him.

"You're this fuckin' Flowers?"

"That's not . . ."

"That's what they said you were called," the man said, nodding toward the BCA building.

"Yeah, this is him," Shrake said.

Jenkins added, "Say, those are some nice-looking shoes."

"Thank you. Yours are also attractive." The man turned to the back of the RV and said, "This is the Flowers."

A moment later, six heavyset men, all wearing gold chains, in T-shirts and slacks or black jeans, with muscles and ample guts but no visible tattoos, dropped down out of the RV and lined up facing Virgil, Shrake, and Jenkins. Like the OK Corral, Virgil thought, except that he didn't have a gun.

"You have information about the tigers?" Virgil asked.

"No. We know nothing about tigers," the first man said.

"Then what . . . ?"

"We are the Simonians," he said. "We are here for Hamlet. To get justice for Hamlet."

17

▼ ▼ ▼

Virgil looked at the six Simonians for a moment, then said, "I hope 'justice' doesn't mean 'revenge.'"

Their spokesman said, "They can be the same."

"Revenge can be a crime—usually is," Jenkins said. "Whatever your shoes look like."

One of the other Simonians said, "We want to know what is being done to capture this killer of Hamlet."

"Everything we can," Virgil said. He did a little tap dancing; he didn't mention he was the only investigator on the case full-time. "The three of us are on the way to do another interview in the case. In the middle of the night. We don't take murder lightly in Minnesota."

A third Simonian nodded and said, "This is good. We need to look in the face of this Hamlet Simonian you say is dead. We have Hamlet's cell phone number, and the Apple company says it is presently traveling through Kansas City, Kansas."

Virgil's eyebrows went up: "Really? We could use the number for his phone. It's possible the killer took it from him."

The spokesman said, "We will give you that number. When can we see the supposed dead Hamlet?"

"Right now, if you want."

The six exchanged a long series of glances and nods, and the spokesman said, "Take us to him."

They were five minutes from the medical examiner's office, more or less, and when they got there, Virgil didn't bother to go in with the Simonians. Instead, he stood in the parking lot and briefed Jenkins and Shrake on the Frogtown address where the meat dryers had been delivered.

When he was done, Jenkins asked, "We don't know who lives there, or even if they're involved?"

"That's right. Don't start shooting until we're sure," Virgil said.

"Okay. But . . ."

"What?"

"What if we kick in the door and find out we're in a roomful of tigers?" Shrake asked.

"I'll tell you what—you shoot a tiger, you'll have to move to Texas," Virgil said. "Don't wait for a moving truck or anything. Get out of the state."

They all thought about a house full of loose tigers for a minute, then Shrake asked, "How's Frankie?"

He told them and about Catrin Mattsson taking the case.

Shrake nodded and said, "Catrin. That's good. The main thing is, you won't be around to kill whoever did it."

"If either of those guys gets killed by a BCA agent and anybody finds out that Frankie's the girlfriend of a BCA agent . . . there'll still be a shitstorm," Jenkins said.

"Maybe a little less with Catrin," Shrake suggested. Because of her history.

One of the Simonians who'd gone inside came reeling back through the door of the ME's office into the parking lot, making gasping, crying sounds, his hands pressed to the sides of his head.

"Guess it was Hamlet," Jenkins said.

All six of them were out in a minute and one said to Virgil, "They cut off his arms. They cut off his arms."

Virgil said, "I should have warned you."

The man said, "They cut off his arms."

Another one agreed. "His arms, they cut them off."

The first one asked, "What do I tell his mother? They cut off his arms?"

Shrake said, "There can be some . . . adjustments . . . in a good funeral home."

"They cut off his arms . . ."

Virgil tried to empathize, talking quietly to the Simonians about how he'd run down the killers, devote his life to it, if necessary, but in his heart, he worried a lot more about his injured girlfriend than a dead Simonian.

The Simonian, in his view, was another asshole who'd volunteered for a Bad Thing and paid for it. Given a choice, he wouldn't have chosen for that to happen, but neither did he really agonize over it. The other Simonians may have sensed that, turning away from him and back to each other. Their head guy gathered the others around him and said, "This cannot stand. We will avenge our brother, I promise you."

Jenkins said, "Hey, chill out, there," but they ignored him.

The Simonians never did calm down. Virgil took out his ID case, pulled out several business cards, shuffled through them, found the one he wanted, handed one to the lead Simonian, and told him to call with questions. They said they would check into a motel and the original spokesman said, "We will call you and you can call us if you find anything." He gave Virgil what had been a blank business card, with the name Levon Simonian and a phone number written in pencil.

As they drove away from the medical examiner's office, Jenkins said to Virgil, "Better you than me."

"What?"

"Giving those guys your business card. They got nothing to contribute, but they're gonna call you every fifteen minutes."

"Don't think so," Virgil said.

"You saw them, how freaked out they are," Jenkins said. "I got a hundred dollars that says they call you fifteen times a day. *At least* fifteen times a day."

"You're on," Virgil said.

Jenkins examined him for a moment, then said, "You're too confident."

"Because I gave them one of Shrake's business cards," Virgil said.

Shrake, in the backseat, said, "What? What?"

Jenkins snorted and said to Virgil, "You're my new role model."

"You really couldn't do much better," Virgil said.

Shrake's phone rang and Jenkins started laughing.

Frogtown was a low-income neighborhood in St. Paul, mostly built in the later nineteenth century for working-class families. Although a few old Victorians still spotted the neighborhood, the streets were dark and close and many of the houses were failing.

Virgil turned down one of the narrower streets, and Jenkins said, "What the fuck?"

Up ahead, not far from what Virgil supposed was the address of the target house, two white trucks were parked on the side of the street. Television trucks.

"How did they know?" Shrake asked.

"You know goddamn well how it happened," Virgil said. "Somebody at the office tipped them off. Sandy must have mentioned it to somebody, and the word got around. I don't think she'd have done it on purpose. Never has in the past."

"That ain't right," Jenkins said. "If they were there, they're gone—unless they're inside waiting for us."

"Doubt that they'd hang around," Virgil said.

The address where the meat dryers had been delivered was worse than most of the houses around, a crumbling two-story with a narrow porch. Virgil stopped the truck a few houses away, and they all looked at the unlit windows of the target house until Shrake said, "Well, shit. Let's go knock."

"You guys got your guns?" Virgil asked.

"Does a fat dog fart?" Jenkins asked. "Which doesn't mean you shouldn't get yours."

"You're right," Virgil said. "Shrake—pull up the other seat and hand me the safe."

Shrake pulled up the backseat that he wasn't sitting on, dug out the gun safe, and handed it to Virgil. Virgil punched in the safe's combination and took out the pistol and the belt-clip holster.

Jenkins, watching, said, "You know, chicks don't go for guys who carry Glocks."

Virgil said, "Yeah, but they go for guys who carry what I'm carrying."

"Hope you got a safety on it, whatever it is; unlike a Glock."

"Let's shut up now, and stop being all nervous, smile for the cameras, and go knock on the fuckin' door," Virgil said. "Shrake, there's a flashlight in the door pocket. Bring it."

They got out of the truck and Shrake muttered, "I hope a Glock can stop a tiger."

As they walked down the street toward the target house, ignoring the TV trucks, a girl came out on the porch of a house they were passing and said, "Hi, policemen."

Shrake said, "Hi, honey. Listen, who lives in the house two doors up? Not the next one, but the one after that? Who lives there?"

"That's a rent."

"So you don't know who lives there?"

"Nobody, now," she said.

An older woman came to the door, carrying a dish towel, and asked, "Janey, who're you talking to?"

"Some policemen."

The woman looked past the girl and said, "Oh. Oh, are you the policemen? We've been waiting for you. The television reporters said you were on the way, but that was a long time ago."

Shrake: "Ah, boy."

Virgil said, "We're going to the house on the other side of your neighbor, here. Your daughter says it's a rental?"

"Always has been," the woman said. "Nobody there now. They moved out a couple of weeks ago."

"How long were they there?"

"Not long, hardly ever saw them."

They chatted for another couple of minutes: the renters had been two men, one large and one much smaller, but who looked alike—brothers, the woman thought. "You know who'd know better? Mrs. Broda. She lives right across the street from them, the house with the porch light. She's an old lady, she watches everything."

They continued up to the target house, moving slowly, looking for any movement at all. There was none, and while Shrake and Jenkins waited on the sidewalk, Virgil climbed two steps up to the narrow board porch, looked in the mailbox—it was empty—and knocked on the door. There was no movement inside. He knocked louder, still got no movement, and the house lacked the organic feel of an inhabited place. Virgil couldn't have explained that feeling, but a lot of cops experienced it, and it was rarely wrong.

Shrake came up on the steps and said, "Window shade's up over here." They walked down the porch to the front window and Shrake turned on the flashlight and they looked inside.

The place was empty: no furniture, no rugs, no nothing. They could see the corner of a small kitchen: no glasses, no soap.

"Goddamnit," Virgil said.

Jenkins, from the sidewalk, said, "Let's go talk to Ms. Broda."

"I want to look in the side door," Virgil said. He took the flashlight from Shrake and walked around to the side of the house and looked through the window on the side door. He could see a mop in a corner, dried out, no bucket.

He turned the flashlight off and walked back to the front of the house and said, "Old lady."

As they walked across the street, the doors popped open on the TV trucks, and cameramen hopped out, and the lights came up.

"Ignore them," Virgil said.

Across the street, the door opened as soon as they started climbing the porch. An old iron-haired woman in a dark brown sweater was talking on a cell phone. Her hair was neatly combed, and she wore dark red lipstick, though she hadn't entirely managed to keep the lipstick inside the lines. "Yes, they're here now. The blond one might be a cop, but the other two look like Mafia. Yes, yes, I know. Talk to you as soon as they're gone."

Shrake said, "We do *not* look like Mafia."

"Yes, you do," Broda said. "Can I see some ID?"

"You do, kinda," Virgil said to Shrake, as he showed Broda his ID. "But it's a good look for you guys. They'd like it in Hollywood."

"That's true," Broda said. "Anyway, that house is owned by Chuck Dvorsky, who lives over in Highland Park. He rents it, when he can. He rented it to two thugs a month ago and he says they skipped on the next month's rent. Don't think they ever lived there—I only saw them a couple of times. Once when a UPS truck delivered a bunch of big cardboard boxes. Wouldn't be surprised if they were full of drugs. Anyway, they were pretty heavy. They were driving one of those orange trucks you rent from Home

Depot for nineteen dollars. They loaded up the boxes and took off—haven't seen hide nor hair of them since."

"You know when this was? The date?" Virgil asked.

"Nope. About a month, I suppose, give or take." She scratched her chin, then said, "I take that back. Probably three weeks. Less than a month."

"Definitely a Home Depot truck?"

"Oh, yeah. People around here rent them all the time when they're moving. People here move a lot."

The cameramen were on the street, lighting up the front of the house, making movies of the interview.

Jenkins asked Broda, "How come you're all dolled up, hon? You going on TV?"

"I thought they might ask," she said. "When I saw the trucks arrive, you know, I walked down and asked what they were all about, and they said you'd be coming. About the tigers. I haven't seen anything like a tiger, though."

Virgil asked for descriptions of the men she'd seen, and Broda described Hamlet Simonian in some detail, and another, larger man who she said resembled Simonian. Like the first woman, she thought they might be brothers. Virgil took out his cell phone, called up the Channel Three website, and showed the woman the Simonian mug shot. "This him?"

She looked and said, "That's him."

When Virgil, Jenkins, and Shrake finished with Broda, they thanked her and started back to the truck. The cameramen had been joined by reporters who pointed their microphones at the cops and one of them asked, "No tigers in there?"

"Nothing in there," Virgil said. "House is empty, as far as we can tell. I don't know about tigers; we had reports of a defenestration and had to check it out."

"Defenestration? That's a pretty big word for a cop," one of the reporters said.

Behind Virgil, Jenkins muttered, "Fuck you and the horse you rode in on."

The reporter said, "Hey, what?"

Virgil said, "Broda. He said you should interview Mrs. Broda. She's waiting." They all looked at Broda's house and saw her smiling through the screen door.

Back in the truck, Virgil took out the cell phone number for Levon Simonian and called it. Simonian picked up on the second ring, and Virgil asked, "Listen, did Hamlet have a brother?"

After a moment of silence, Simonian said, "Hold on."

He then muffled the microphone on his phone; Virgil could hear speech-like sounds, but couldn't tell what was being said. A full minute later, Simonian came back on and said, "Yes. He possibly had a brother."

"Big guy, powerful? Looked like Hamlet?"

Another few minutes of silence, then somebody in the background blurted, "Oh my God. Did something happen to Hayk?"

Virgil asked, "How do you spell 'Hayk'? And do you have his birth date?"

He got the name and birth date, called them in to the BCA duty officer, told him to run the name, and also asked him to find a phone number for Chuck Dvorsky, the landlord of the vacant house.

The duty officer put them on hold for a moment, then came back with Dvorsky's home phone number. Virgil called it. A woman answered and said she was April Dvorsky, Chuck's wife. She said, "Chuck's in El Paso, Texas, buying a Porsche 928."

She said she did the accounting on the rental units their company owned and that the man who'd rented the Frogtown house had moved out before he moved in. "He never did put any furniture in it and then he skipped out on the lease."

"Big guy, small guy?"

"Kinda small. Not light. Short and a little stout."

"Has anybody else been in it since?"

"No, nobody—I mean, except to clean and get ready to offer again," she said. "I was over there this afternoon with the cleaning crew."

"So it's been cleaned."

"Yes, it has."

Virgil asked her to stay out of the house; he was going to check to see if it would be worthwhile to have a crime-scene crew go over the place. "We can get a warrant, if you want," he said.

"That's okay. I'll stay out and if you decide to send CSI, I'll meet them there and let them in."

"Thank you. I'll call you tomorrow."

Shrake said, "Cleaned up, so probably no prints, especially since it sounds like they didn't even live there. They rented the house to have an address where UPS would drop the dryers."

"Yeah," Virgil said. Virgil got on his cell phone, switched it to speaker, and called the duty officer at the BCA, who said he had a response from the FBI on the Hayk Simonian inquiry.

"He's had a dozen arrests, mostly from working security at nightclubs around Los Angeles," the duty officer said. "He beat up people. Sometimes, a little too much. He also did some jail time—not prison time—for receiving stolen goods. That was in Los Angeles, too. The feds picked him up on suspicion of distributing counterfeit bills in Glendale, California, but the witnesses failed to identify him."

"Not a good guy," Jenkins said.

"Not a good guy," the duty officer said, "but a small-timer."

"Let's get the best and most recent mug shots we can find and give them to Jon Duncan," Virgil said. "We need to get them out to the TV stations and the papers."

"Too late for tonight," the duty officer said. "The news is on now."

"Yeah, but let's try to get them out for the early morning news, run them all day tomorrow."

With nothing more to do, Virgil dropped Jenkins and Shrake back at the BCA building, thanked them for their time, and drove home. On the way, Daisy Jones, the TV reporter from Channel Three, called and asked, "Why'd you go to that house? I know it wasn't because somebody got thrown out a window. I got about two minutes before I've got to go on the air. Tell me."

Virgil considered. His attitude toward information differed from the attitude of most cops. He figured if he knew something about a crime, and other cops knew it, and the crook knew it, who were they hiding the information from and why? Sometimes, there was a good answer to that question; most of the time, there wasn't. One reason for parceling it out carefully was to get reporters obligated to you, because sometimes they knew things that you didn't, and if they owed you, they might cough it up. And sometimes, putting information on the air, or in the papers, stirred up new information . . .

Daisy Jones was one of those willing to trade.

"You didn't hear it from me," he said.

"Of course not. Talk faster. I've now got one minute and forty-five seconds."

"If the tiger thieves are processing the animals for traditional Chinese medicine, then they need to process quite a bit of meat—internal organs, gallbladders, eyes, all that. They need to dry it. That house got an order for five jerky dryers. The two men who took the delivery never really lived there—they rented it for one month, took the delivery, and disappeared."

"That would mean that they were planning to kill the tigers. Might already have done it," she said.

Virgil considered for another moment, then said, "Daisy, you are going to owe me big. I don't know how you're going to pay me back, but I'll think of something."

"No time, no time. Just tell me," she said.

"Okay, you heard from local police sources and I'd appreciate it if you'd say it came from Minneapolis. One of the men seen at the house was Hamlet Simonian."

"Oh my God, Virgil, you've nailed it down," Jones said. "They're killing the tigers or already have. I owe you big, thank you."

Click. She was gone.

Virgil got to Mankato at eleven-thirty, washed his face, brushed his teeth, put a can of beer in his jacket pocket, and drove down to the Mayo.

Frankie was awake; Catrin Mattsson, Sparkle, and Father Bill were sitting next to her bed in side chairs, and the four of them seemed deeply involved in conversation. When they saw Virgil coming, Frankie said something to the others and they all stirred around and then Frankie asked, "Where you been, cowboy?"

"Trying to find those fuckin' tigers," Virgil said. He leaned over the bed and kissed her. "Got nothin'."

"Now you've got a murder," Mattsson said.

"Yeah, at least one." He popped the top on the beer and told them about the missing Hayk Simonian and the Simonian justice crew.

"Interesting," Mattsson said. "Could have two murders, with more on the way. I ought to be done down here in the next day or two at the most. If you haven't found the tigers, ask Jon to let me help out. I've been working a cold case up in Isanti County and it's not going anywhere. I don't even think the dead woman's from Minnesota."

"Okay. I could use the help. It's getting complicated," Virgil said. He looked at Frankie: she was badly scuffed up, but the scuffing was superficial and would heal soon enough. "How's your head?" he asked her. "I mean . . . headaches? Anything more about the concussion?"

"They say that looks okay," Frankie said. "The boys were here. You've got to talk to Rolf. He's been going around to bars, asking about who might have jumped me. You know he's got a temper."

"I'll talk to him," Virgil said.

"I already did," Mattsson said. "I don't know if it did any good."

"Rolf has been known to engage in criminal behavior of a minor sort," Virgil said to Mattsson. "Sometimes, with his mother. If I have to, I'll bust his ass on suspicion of something and stick him in the county jail until we get this figured out."

"Oh, don't do that," Frankie said. "With his priors . . ."

"We'd let him go for lack of evidence," Virgil said. "It's better than having him find the guys who did this and then spending thirty years in Stillwater for killing them."

She stared at him for a moment, then said, "You know, there's a little too much testosterone floating in the fishbowl. First you and then Rolf, and if Tall Bear was in town, he'd probably scalp them." Tall Bear was her half-Sioux second son, who was on a towboat somewhere down the Mississippi.

"I'll talk to him, too, if he comes back," Virgil said.

Sparkle and Father Bill hadn't said much, and Sparkle stood and said, "Come on, Bill, we ought to get some sleep while we can. Gotta be up early tomorrow."

"What's tomorrow?" Virgil asked.

"More interviews," Sparkle said. "I'm almost done. I'd like to get inside the factory, but that's not going to happen. Not unless I find a way to sneak in."

"I wouldn't allow that," Bill said. "I'd tie you up and lock you in the trunk of the car if you tried."

"Too much testosterone," Frankie said again, and the other two women nodded.

When Father Bill and Sparkle had gone, Mattsson told Virgil that she hadn't gotten anything solid on the men who'd attacked Frankie, but she had the names of a few possibilities.

"I leaned on Lucas for his asshole database and he gave me two names down here. I talked to them and they pointed me at a half-dozen guys who might do that sort of thing. I'll be rounding them up tomorrow. If I find somebody who won't show me his lower left arm, I'll be going for a warrant."

"Good," Virgil said.

Mattsson left to get some sleep and Virgil asked Frankie what they'd all been talking about when he arrived. "Everybody looked pretty involved."

"Well, you know Sparkle," Frankie said. "She recognized Cat's name and that whole case. Sparkle and Father Bill—they're, I don't know, effective bullshitters when it comes to psychology. They got her talking about it and it all kinda came out. Bizarre doesn't even cover it; it was like a war crime, what that man did to her. Then Father Bill started doing therapy . . ."

"Oh, boy. I hope she doesn't regret that. Or worse, start flashing back," Virgil said.

"She already has flashbacks. She said so."

"How about you?" Virgil asked. "How's your head, aside from the concussion?"

They talked for a while, about the attack and what it meant. "The cops told the paper, and a couple of reporters tried to call, but the hospital pushed them off," she said.

"Yeah, that's gonna happen," Virgil said. "Do what you want—talk or not."

"I'll think about it," she said.

Virgil's phone rang and he glanced at the screen: BCA.

"Yeah?"

"Virgil, a guy called here and he wants to talk to you about that house up in Frogtown. He says it's urgent."

Virgil took the number and called it; finished his beer while the phone was ringing. The man who answered said his name was Joe

Werner. "I work at the zoo. I wasn't at your meeting, but I heard about it. I might have something you should know, but I don't want it to get out that I told you."

"If I can keep it to myself, I will," Virgil said.

"Okay. It might not be anything . . ."

"I'd like to hear it."

"I saw that TV thing about the house, where you went looking for the tigers, where they delivered the dryers, where that Simoniz guy lived," Werner said. "There's a guy here at the zoo, works here, named Barry King. He lives on the next block down from that house."

"Huh. Interesting. What are you thinking?" Virgil asked.

"Well, uh, I really don't want it to get out that I told you this, but Barry's basically a jerk and he's always got money problems. If you told me that you'd arrested Barry for stealing the tigers, I'd have said, 'Yeah, I can see that.' Anyway, I was thinking, if somebody asked Barry where you could get those dryers delivered . . . and if he knew a cheap place for rent . . ."

"Got it," Virgil said. "You keep quiet about this, okay? I'll be on it first thing in the morning. Thank you."

Got the tigers?" Frankie asked.

"Not yet, but I might have a tail," Virgil said.

His tip to Daisy Jones could have a nice payoff, he thought, and as far as Jones knew, she'd still owe him. A twofer.

18

▼ ▼ ▼

Virgil left a phone message for Jenkins and Shrake and suggested that they meet at the BCA building at eight o'clock the next morning for another trip over to Frogtown. Jenkins was still up and sent a text back, saying that Virgil wouldn't make it to the BCA at eight o'clock unless he got up at five o'clock in the morning—"No fast way to get across the south end of the Cities at that time in the morning."

Virgil thought it over, agreed, and changed the meeting time. "Nine o'clock or as soon after that as I can get there."

Virgil made it to the BCA at ten after nine. He'd stopped at the Mayo before heading north again, but Frankie was asleep and he left her that way. Shrake, looking fresh and smelling of French cologne, said he and Jenkins hadn't gone out the night before because the trip to the possible tiger den "broke our focus. You want to nail yourself a cougar, you can't be thinking about tigers."

They drove in Virgil's 4Runner to the same neighborhood

they'd been in the night before, the two thugs giving Virgil a hard time about his vintage black "Hole" T-shirt.

"I reject your ignorant criticism," Virgil said. "Courtney Love had a terrific voice and a good band behind her."

"Wasn't that hard to look at, either," Jenkins conceded. "That doesn't mean your shirt isn't ridiculous. For one thing, it's a size too small."

The conversation continued, but they got to the target house about two hours too late. When they arrived, a St. Paul cop car was parked in the street in front of the house. "I'm suffering from a sudden lack of confidence in our mission," Jenkins said.

"Ah, man. Let's go see what's going on," Virgil said.

A St. Paul police sergeant named Random Powers came out the door as they walked up to the house. Powers knew Jenkins and Shrake and said he'd just taken a missing persons report from the girlfriend of a man who'd disappeared that morning, two hours earlier.

"Is his name Barry King?" Virgil asked.

"Yeah. You know where he is?"

"No, I don't," Virgil said. "Goddamnit."

Virgil told Powers about the BCA investigation and the cop said, "Go talk to Gloria. Be my guest. And . . . try to look in her eyes."

Virgil, Shrake, and Jenkins found Gloria Ortiz sitting on the living room sofa, drinking a glass of green stuff. Ortiz was a pretty, brown-eyed woman with blond streaks in her dark hair and a gold crucifix dangling down her intriguing cleavage. She identified herself as Barry King's live-in fiancée.

"I don't know what happened. He got up, he said he was going out to run. He was wearing his running shorts and shoes and a T-shirt, and he went off. Then he didn't come back. He's supposed to be at work—when he didn't come back, I got worried and called the police and asked if a runner had been hit by a car or anything."

Powers, who'd followed them inside, said, "We got nothing like that."

Shrake asked Ortiz, "You guys been getting along? Any chance he, you know . . . might be looking for a better opportunity?"

"No," she said. "I can tell you that for sure. He left his wallet, watch, and iPhone on the bathroom counter. I promise you, Barry would *never* leave his wallet and cell phone behind, if he was planning to take off. There was a hundred and forty dollars in his wallet, and all his IDs and credit cards."

Virgil: "Barry come into any money lately?"

Her eyes drifted sideways and Jenkins said to Virgil, "That looks like a big yes."

"I don't know where he got it, but he bought some neat new shoes last month—he likes shoes. I looked in his wallet and there was more than a thousand dollars in cash in there," Ortiz said. "We had an argument about it. Oh . . . his shoes are still here. He didn't take any of them, except his running shoes."

"He ever mention the tigers to you? The missing tigers from the zoo?" Virgil asked.

Her hand went to her mouth. "Oh my God. Is that what this is about? You think Barry helped steal them?"

"We would like to talk with him," Virgil said. "See if he had any ideas about what might have happened to them."

"I don't think Barry . . . he's not the kind of person who could organize a thing like that. You know, stealing the tigers. Barry can be nice, when he tries, but he's not the sharpest knife in the dishwasher."

"Did he spend any time watching the news about the tigers?" Virgil asked.

She bobbed her head. "Oh, yeah, I guess. Everybody has been, right? Especially if you worked at the zoo."

"Do you know . . . has he had any new friends? Anybody you thought might be a little unusual?"

"No, but he has his own friends. I don't hang out with them much. The boys, you know, go drinking with the boys. I go out with my girlfriends."

Shrake: "You didn't talk about the zoo, about the tigers?"

"Only about how terrible it was, the tigers being stolen. Anything more, he hasn't said a thing to me. Not a thing."

King wasn't saying much to the Simonians, either. He lay facedown in the RV and bled into the carpet, and occasionally groaned.

One of the Simonians had talked to Hamlet and Hayk Simonian's mother, who'd given them two names: Larry King, who she said worked at the zoo, and Simpson Becker, who'd hired them.

Her mistakes with the names occurred because Mother Simonian had been born and raised in Iran and had fled when the revolution made things difficult for Christian Armenians. Surrounded by family in California, speaking Farsi and Armenian, she'd learned only basic English—but she had watched a lot of television, Larry King and *The Simpsons* included; she in fact may have unconsciously modeled her blue-tinted hair on Marge Simpson's. When her elder son called and said she should take down a couple of names, "just in case," he said Barry King and Winston Peck, and she heard Larry King and Simpson Becker.

The Simonians in the truck had managed to identify Larry King as Barry King by searching references to zoo employees, but hadn't yet located any doctor named Simpson Becker.

Still, Barry King was a start. When he went for his morning run, they'd pulled him into the Simonian RV and proceeded to question him. When he failed to cooperate, they beat the shit out of him. When that didn't work, the youngest and most violent of the Simonians suggested breaking his fingers, one by one, but one of the older men rejected the idea.

"I can't stand that sound, you know? That popping, cracking sound."

King let them beat him and never admitted a thing, except to moan and proclaim his innocence. He knew, from television news, that Hamlet Simonian had been murdered, and he suspected that Peck had done it. If he admitted any knowledge of it, he believed the Simonians would throw him off a bridge or some even more colorful Armenian equivalent, like off a bridge in front of a train.

He took the pounding and eventually the Simonians got tired of doing it, gave him a paper towel to wash off his face, and dropped him off on St. Paul's East Seventh Street with a wad of toilet paper to block up his bloody nose.

As they let him go, the young, violent Simonian asked, "Why you got a fly tattoo on your neck?"

King said, around the toilet paper, "I thought it looked cool."

The Simonian said, "You ever go to Amsterdam?"

"What? No, I never go any farther than Wisconsin. Amsterdam?"

"The Amsterdam airport, all the urinals in the men's rooms got flies like that, right down in the bottom. You're supposed to aim at them. You got a piss-pot fly on your neck, man."

"Goes with the daisy tattoo I got around my asshole," King said.

The Simonians all laughed and slapped him on the back and said he wasn't a bad guy, but if they found out he'd had anything to do with Hamlet, of course, they'd find him again and kill him.

"Got that," King said. "If I hear anything, I'll call you first."

Once free, King walked to a convenience store, told the clerk that he'd been mugged, and the clerk reluctantly allowed him to use the house phone. He called home, and Ortiz told him that the state cops had been looking for him. He told her to collect his clothes, shoes, phone, wallet, and car keys, and bring them to him at the convenience store.

"You're gonna get me in trouble, aren't you?" she asked. "Did you steal those tigers?"

"Of course not. I was home with you when they were stolen," he said.

Ortiz agreed to come get him. She did, in his car.

"Tell me what happened," she said.

He told her: "A total mistake. I had nothing to do with those tigers. They must be going around picking up zoo employees and beating them up."

Ortiz figured he was lying. He was in the backseat, as they drove across town, and she watched him in the rearview mirror as he got dressed and stuffed little twists of toilet paper in each nostril.

He had her pull over six blocks from the house, took the driver's seat, and told her to walk the rest of the way. "I'll call you when I've got this straightened out," he said.

In the six-block walk back to the house, Ortiz gave the situation serious consideration. Somehow, she thought, King was involved with the tiger theft, and at least one man involved with the tiger theft had been murdered.

Ortiz was a hairdresser with a wide breadth of knowledge involving men, lying, and criminal justice that beauty shops generated through their daily panel discussions. If the cops busted King for any aspect of the crime, they might get him for the murder as well. They would take a long look at her, too, to see if she was an accomplice. She was sitting out there like a clay pigeon, she thought, totally ignorant of the crime, but also totally exposed.

She got Virgil's business card out of her bureau drawer and called him.

"I found out what happened to Barry," she said. "Some guys in a big RV picked him up off the street and beat him up."

"Big RV? He's there now, with you?"

"No, he took off."

"What kind of car is he driving . . . ?"

Virgil got off the phone with Ortiz, called the duty officer, and told him to call the local emergency rooms in case King went to one of them. Then he got the registration for King's car from the DMV and put the make, color, and license plate out to Twin Cities police agencies and the highway patrol. He cursed himself for not getting the make and license plate of the Simonians' RV.

But the Simonians had landed on King, which meant they

knew something. They'd had at least one name, so they might have more.

He called his Simonian contact. When Levon Simonian answered the phone, Virgil could hear traffic sounds in the background: they were in the RV.

"We need to get together and chat," Virgil said.

"We're going fishing in Wisconsin," Simonian said. "We will call when we get back."

"We need to talk now," Virgil said. He lied a little: "I've got a description and make on your RV, and your license plate number. If we can't get together and talk, I'll have the highway patrol track you down."

Simonian said, "Good luck with that. And don't call us any more today; we're busy."

"Wait! What are you fishing for?" Virgil asked, trying to keep the conversation going.

"Marlin," Simonian said. He hung up.

When Virgil tried to call back, he didn't even get a ring. Something bad, he thought, may have happened to the Simonians' cell phone.

King, in the meantime, had called Peck.

Peck was working at the barn, drying tiger meat. The smell was awful, nothing at all like barbeque, and now mixing with the funky stink of tiger poop. Katya was sitting in her cage, staring at him. Hayk Simonian's femurs, tibias, fibulas, patellas, and a number of foot bones were scattered around the cage. The femurs had been cracked open, and Katya had scratched out all the marrow.

When King called, Peck listened to his complaints, then said, "I'll meet you. Uh, I'm not at home right now, but I can meet you at the Cub supermarket parking lot off Radio Drive. You know where that is?"

King could find it, he said.

They met an hour later. When King got out of his car, Peck looked at him and said, "I don't believe you didn't tell them my name. Did you tell them my name?" He looked wildly around the parking lot, saw nobody approaching. "Is this a trap?"

King said, "If I'd told them the truth, they would have killed me. They're here to kill whoever killed Hamlet, and there's only one way they could have gotten my name—Hamlet must have given it to them. If he gave them my name, he must have given them yours. Anyway, I'm going to Chicago. Right now."

"What's in Chicago?"

"Not the Simonians," King said.

Peck had been considering the situation since the moment that King called him. The conclusion was straightforward: King had to go.

The cops would believe, correctly, that the tiger thieves had to be the killer of Hamlet Simonian. King could tell the cops that there were only four people involved in the theft: the two Simonians, Peck, and himself. Hayk's body would be found sooner or later, which meant the killer had to be either Peck or King. If King talked to the cops, he might convince them that he neither participated in the murders nor knew that they were coming. He might, in other words, roll over on Peck, make a deal for his testimony in return for a lighter prison sentence.

He might not even wait to be caught—he might talk himself into approaching the cops preemptively.

He had to go.

But at the moment, Peck asked, "You didn't tell your girlfriend about this, did you? Gloria what's-her-name?"

King had been thinking about that himself. "No, of course not. We need to hold this tight."

"Okay. Thank God for little favors."

"I gotta tell you, I'm a little nervous about this. I figured you'd killed him. Hamlet."

"No! No! I didn't kill him! I didn't kill Hamlet! I'm not a fruitcake," Peck shouted. He turned away, ran both hands through his hair. He was sweating like a steam pipe. He turned back to King. "I paid him off, I gave him ten thousand dollars and when the cops found his body, I asked Hayk what the fuck had happened. Hayk and I were processing the tiger that whole time; he knew I didn't have anything to do with Hamlet's death. Hayk said Hamlet had made a deal to buy a couple pounds of meth and run it back to Glendale. He could make five hundred percent on his money. He could turn ten thousand into fifty thousand. That's how he got killed: he tried to hook up with some meth dealers and he wasn't smart enough to pull it off. I didn't kill him, Barry. I'm actually a goddamn doctor, you know. Do no harm and all that shit."

King said, "I'm sorry, then. I didn't really think you did it. I had to consider the possibility."

Peck said, "Listen, Barry, if you run to Chicago, you'll be skipping out on your job and the cops will know exactly who gave us the key to the tiger den. Then they'll hang you for Hamlet's murder, even though you didn't do it and I didn't do it. You've got to go back to work, pretend nothing happened."

"How am I going to do that?" King asked. "The cops are gonna find out that the guys in the RV kidnapped me and beat me up. I should be talking to them right now, asking them why I got picked up. If I don't go to them, they'll know I was involved."

"Ahhh . . . shit. Then maybe you ought to go to them . . . you could say . . . I dunno." Peck looked around the parking lot; an elderly couple, pushing a shopping cart and pulling along two tow-headed boys, paid no attention to them. He said, "Look. We're processing the tigers out at a farm, not far from here. Five miles. Let's go talk to Hayk, see what he thinks. He knows how to deal with cops. You can follow me out."

King agreed, and as they left Cub supermarket and turned east on the interstate, Peck watched in the rearview mirror to make sure he didn't change his mind.

As they drove to the farm, in addition to monitoring King, Peck considered his own psychological condition. Was he now a serial killer, or about to become one? You probably had to kill three, didn't you, to be considered serial?

On the whole, he thought he was not a serial killer. Serial killers got off on the killing. In Peck's case, he didn't feel much at all. Killing didn't get him sexually excited or emotionally wrought. Killing was simply a work-related task.

Would he be classified as a spree killer? Again, he thought not. Spree killers didn't kill as work-related tasks. They went nuts and killed everybody they could see.

Peck had no political motives, wasn't interested in politics, held no grudges, so he wasn't that kind of psycho. No, he decided, he was clearly a sociopath whose life had been shoved into a difficult corner. Lots of people were sociopaths, some of them very successful in life.

Furthermore, killing people was actually a pain in the ass. Kill somebody, and there were all kinds of logistics to work out: how to keep your DNA off the victim, how to get rid of the body, what to do with the dead man's car. The last matter was particularly perplexing. You could drive the car someplace and drop it off, though you'd have to be careful about DNA and fingerprints. But you wouldn't want to drop it off near the murder scene, and if you didn't, how did you get back to your own car? Walk? That seemed inefficient. Take a taxi? Then you had a witness. He was sure there were ways to do it, but he'd have to research it on the Internet.

When they turned into the farmyard, Peck pulled up to the barn, hopped out, and waved at King, who'd pulled up behind him. Peck walked straight to the barn door, and as he pushed it open, called, "Hayk? Hey, I've got Barry King here. We need to talk."

Hayk didn't answer, being dead, and now lying in a ditch fifteen miles away. The rifle was leaning against the wall next to the meat-cutting table, along with a box of cartridges. Peck picked it up, pulled the bolt, slipped a cartridge into the chamber, and walked back toward the door.

When King pulled it open and stood there in a halo of sunlight, Peck shot him in the chest. King fell heavily against the door and slid down it, closing the door in the process. When Peck tried to get out, he found the body was blocking the door, and because there was a small cavity in the earth outside the door, and King's body was in it, he couldn't immediately get the door open. He had to kick it, and then push it, and then kick it some more, growing increasingly panicky—the body was in plain sight if somebody drove past the farmhouse—until finally he could squeeze through the crack between the door and the doorjamb.

When he did get outside, he found that King was unconscious but not yet dead. Peck dragged King's body out of the cavity, got the door fully open, and pulled him inside.

Still breathing.

Peck walked around the barn, looking at the body. Still breathing. He didn't want to risk another shot, so finally, impatient, he went over and kicked the wounded man in the head. King sputtered out some blood, and Peck lost it, and kicked him in the head another half-dozen times. That did it and the breathing stopped.

Being a doctor, he also checked for a pulse in King's neck. Nothing.

"I feel much better after the workout," Peck told Katya. He needed the conversation; a way, he thought, to resolve the situation in his own mind. The big cat stared at him from behind the chain-link fence and didn't contribute a thing. "You know, you figure out what you have to do and then you execute. That's so important. Execution is. You have to carry through. A lot of people can't do that."

The cat said nothing.

19

▼ ▼ ▼

Virgil was working the phones, spreading the word among police agencies about the search for Barry King and the Simonians. He wasn't getting anywhere, and he had to be content to sit and wait and think about something he might do.

One thing he didn't do was watch the local television news, where the BCA—meaning him—was getting ripped for not finding the tigers. The talking heads had no suggestions about how that might be done; they simply wanted it done, never mind that the BCA was looking for one or two people in an area with a population of three and a quarter million.

Virgil still believed the tigers were nearby, but he had resigned himself to the idea that they were probably dead. He also had the sense that they weren't down in somebody's basement in suburban Woodbury, or any other suburb, because there were too many people around. But where would they be?

In the meantime, following up on a tip from the Simonians themselves, he gave Hamlet Simonian's phone number to Sandy, who talked to Apple about lost phones, found out how you tracked them, and determined that the phone was moving west out of Denver, down I-70.

"We need to find the guy who's got it," Virgil said. "Any ideas would be appreciated."

"Lots of cars on I-70," Sandy said. "I don't think the Colorado highway patrol is going to shut down an interstate and start searching cars for a cell phone."

"We gotta do something—we need that phone," Virgil said.

"I can call around," she said. "I wouldn't count on getting it."

"I gotta think," Virgil said. "I mean, I *am* thinking, but I'm not coming up with anything."

While they were doing that and Peck was murdering King, Sparkle was sneaking into the Castro canning factory with a woman named Ramona Alvarez. Alvarez's husband unloaded trucks, while Alvarez worked on the topping line, where open jars coming down a roller track were topped up with pickle slices.

"Not as many people here as I thought," Sparkle muttered to Alvarez, as Alvarez walked past the time-card rack. She wouldn't be checking in; the ghost workers didn't have time cards.

"There are a lot of people here; you don't see them so much, except down at the loading docks," Alvarez said in good but heavily accented English. "Here, it's mostly machines. We got to watch for Stout. If he sees you here, there'll be lots of trouble. They put you in jail for trespassing."

The factory, Sparkle thought, looked like what she imagined the inside of a coffeemaker might look like—hot, lots of moving parts, saturated with a wide variety of odors, ranging from fresh cucumber to the smell of the spices and vinegars that made pickles. While the exterior of the place was foreboding, that big dark brick wall, the interior was painted a uniform beige, with a slick easy-wash finish.

A few minutes after Sparkle and Alvarez entered the factory, the pickle-packing machinery shut down momentarily for a shift change. Alvarez changed into a blue apron, hairnet, and plastic gloves, and took her spot next to a bin of wet pickle slices, waiting for the jars to come down the roller track.

Four other women worked the line, two facing Alvarez and a third on Alvarez's side, five feet away. After three or four minutes, with a clatter and a bang, the line started moving again, the jars coming down fast, side by side, maybe eighty percent full of sliced pickles. Alvarez started topping up the jars.

Sparkle watched for a while, took a couple of photographs with a point-and-shoot camera, and Alvarez said, "You seen it. It ain't gonna change for the next eight hours. Kills my legs." She kept topping the jars as she spoke; every once in a while a pickle slice got away from her and landed on the concrete floor.

"What happens if you miss a jar?" Sparkle asked.

"You don't miss any," Alvarez said. "If you make a bad drop—you know, you're working fast and you miss the jar—then you gotta catch that jar and work faster coming back to your station, getting them all full. If one gets away from you now and then . . . that's just what it is. If it's too many, they'll dock Leandro's pay. Say he came in late."

"Criminals," Sparkle said. She watched for another couple of minutes, then stepped back from the line as another woman came in with a broom and started pushing discarded pickles into piles and scooping them into a plastic bucket. Sparkle muttered to Alvarez, "I'll be back in a minute."

"What?"

Sparkle didn't answer, but stepped away, turned, and walked along the backside of the large stainless-steel tanks. She was the only one back there, and she slipped through the factory, taking pictures of women sorting cucumbers before they went into a huge vat; other women pulling cucumbers off a moving track into separate bins to be speared, sliced, or discarded; a woman monitoring a machine that dumped brine into the jars.

The place smelled like a huge wet cucumber, Sparkle thought, and so did she, after twenty minutes in the building.

She was looking at the brining operation when a heavyset man in a white shirt with a Castro label on the pocket walked out from behind a machine on the other side of the factory and saw her. He called, "Hey!"

Sparkle pretended not to hear and ambled away, and he shouted again, "Hey!" And then, to somebody out of sight, "Vic, grab that woman! Grab that woman!"

Sparkle still didn't see anybody, but she ran.

Thirty feet down the wall of the factory, she saw an intersecting hallway and took it, and down that, another thirty feet, two restrooms. She ducked into the women's restroom, realized it was a dead end, ran back out to a T intersection, took a right toward what looked like daylight.

Behind her, she heard a man shouting. She didn't look.

The daylight turned out to be an office with nobody in it. On the far wall was a line of old-style sash windows. She went to one not visible from the hallway, pulled it up, unlocked the outside window, pushed it open, clambered out, turned, and pulled the inner window back down, then pushed the outer window back in place.

She was on the side of the factory, with twenty feet of short scraggly grass between her and a line of trees. She dashed across the grassy strip into the trees, down into the sand of a dry, seasonal creek. Her car was parked off the side of the county road, four or five hundred yards from the factory. She jogged out to the road, looked both ways, then down the road to the car.

Elapsed time, from the moment the man shouted at her to the car, perhaps four minutes. She was breathing hard, her lungs aching when she got to the Mini. She drove out of the turnout, took a right, and rolled away from the factory.

Should she have been frightened? She didn't know. She didn't particularly care, either. With her photographs of fifty or sixty Mexican women working in the plant, on this single shift, she had her dissertation in the bag.

Virgil was sitting with his feet up on his temporary desk, talking with Sandy when he took a call from a Wisconsin deputy sheriff.

"This is Roger Briggs; I'm with the Pierce County sheriff's office over in Wisconsin. We've got a body here, in a ditch. It's missing its legs. Looks like they were cut off and we think it might be that guy you're looking for, Hayk Simonian. His face was down in the water, so it's messed up, but it resembles that mug shot you sent around and you had that other guy up north, who had his arms cut off. We think this one was shot."

"I'll be there in half an hour," Virgil said.

A half hour later, he stood on the side of a country road as two sheriff's department investigators prepared to pull the plastic-wrapped body out of the ditch and up onto the road. The ditch held six or eight inches of water down among the cattail roots, and the investigators wore gum boots as they worked.

Briggs, the deputy who'd called in the discovery, stood on the side of the road and told Virgil about it.

"Found by a farm guy who lives up the road. He saw three coyotes pulling on the plastic and got to wondering about it. He chased the coyotes off and walked over to the other side of the ditch and looked down, and he could see a hand, so he called us. I was the first guy here and called for help."

"Nothing around the body?"

Briggs shook his head. "He was pretty well wrapped up and obviously dumped here, killed somewhere else. The investigators will do the crime-scene thing here, probably send the rest of it down to Madison."

"I'll talk to the Madison guys," Virgil said. "We need whatever they can get, in a hurry."

"Talk to the sheriff. You could probably get somebody to drive the whole shootin' match straight down, have the lab working on it by the end of the day."

"That'd be good," Virgil said. "If that's Hayk Simonian in there, it'll be the second murder. There's a real bad guy out there."

The body was plugged into the mud at the bottom of the little roadside swamp, and once the investigators had freed it, and the plastic wrapper, they slipped the body easily over to the side of the road and hoisted it up to the dry surface. A funky sulfuric odor came with it. As they were doing that, a hearse came down the road to take the body.

The coyotes had chewed into the dead man's face, neck, and part of one upper arm. The body was naked from the waist down, although a pair of jeans was wadded up at one end of the plastic wrap, and Virgil could see the legs were missing from the hip down. Unlike the arms of Hamlet Simonian, the legs were not with the body.

The RV Simonians would not be happy. On the other hand, Hayk was apparently the same kind of asshole as his brother, Hamlet, not to be especially mourned, by Virgil, anyway. Further, he might be a hook into the information that the Simonians had, which had led them to the missing Barry King. If Virgil could get the news about Hayk to the Simonians, maybe he could blackmail them for whatever other information they might have. Something to think about.

As he was plotting, one of the Wisconsin investigators used a tongue depressor to move scraps of the plastic away from the face. There was enough left for Virgil to identify the body as Hayk Simonian.

"Yeah, that's him." He sighed and straightened up, said, "Tell your lab guys that they need to move some fingerprints to the feds, just to make one hundred percent sure, but that's him."

Briggs said, "He's a mess. At least we know the tigers are still alive."

Virgil: "Yeah? How do we know that?"

Briggs: "Where do you think the legs went?"

Virgil: "Oh . . . Oh, jeez." Briggs, he thought, could be right.

A car was coming down the road toward them, saw all the red lights clogging up the roadway, paused, then pulled into a farmer's field track, did a three-point turn, and disappeared back down the road.

Country people, Virgil thought, didn't like even the concept of a traffic jam, temporary as it might be.

Winston Peck VI saw the cop cars and the flashers and thought, *Uh-oh*. He pulled into a farmer's field track, did a three-point turn, and headed back the way he came. Barry King's body was in the back of the truck. The place where he'd dumped Hayk Simonian had seemed like a good one, so he'd come back to make another deposit. Not a good idea, as it turned out.

As he headed away from the cop cars, he looked in the rearview mirror. A guy standing on the side of the road in civilian dress, tall, lanky, blond . . .

Was that Flowers?

Whoa! Skin of his teeth!

Late in the afternoon, back at the office.

Virgil had talked to an investigator with the Wisconsin DCI. They were sending an agent to the area, because of the two bodies found on the Wisconsin side of the line, but they expected Virgil to carry most of the weight.

"Wisconsin's a dumping ground for something going on in Minnesota. If you get any indication that the tigers are on our side of the river, we'll give you all the help we can," the DCI guy said.

Catrin Mattsson called with the good news of the day: she thought she had identified the man who'd beaten up Frankie.

"It's a guy named Brad Blankenship. Got it from a not-so-good friend of his who said that Blankenship is walking around in long-sleeve shirts when he never wears anything but T-shirts in the summer. He said that Blankenship was drinking at Waters' Waterhole last night and his sleeve slipped up a couple of times and he could see a pretty good bandage under it. Blankenship has four previous arrests for fighting—worked as a bouncer at the Waterhole on Fridays and Saturdays when they have live music."

"What do you want to do?" Virgil asked.

"Well, first thing, the not-so-good friend says if Blankenship did it, the other person with him was almost certainly Frederick Reeves, who they call Slow Freddie. You know that song, 'If You're Gonna Be Dumb, You Gotta Be Tough'?"

"Sure. Roger Alan Wade."

"That's apparently Slow Freddie's life story. My source says he was in jail for theft a few years ago, and something really, really bad happened to him in there. I'm thinking rape, and it turned him mean. No smarter, but mean. It also gave him a permanent fear of being locked up, which means . . . we might be able to talk to him."

"Either that, or he'll shoot you," Virgil said.

"I said 'we.' I'd appreciate some company for this talk," Mattsson said.

"When?" Virgil asked.

"Now—as soon as you can get here."

"All right. Things are moving like glue up here, but we've got a second confirmed murder," Virgil said. "I'll help out, but you've got to front the thing—I don't want people saying I was down there working on a simple assault on my girlfriend and skipping out on a double murder."

"I'll front it," she said. "Besides, by the time it gets to court, you'll have the killers locked up, and nobody will remember the sequence of events."

"See you in an hour and a half," Virgil said. "Let's meet at the hospital. I can check on Frankie and hook up with you at the same time."

On the way to Mankato, Virgil decided that he really needed to get to the Simonians again. He needed to know where Hamlet Simonian's phone might be going and how the Simonians knew to pick up Barry King. They had a source of information that was better than any he had.

Although they were no longer answering his calls, he still had one good way to contact them. He got on the phone to Daisy Jones, the TV reporter. "You're going to owe me even more," he said.

"Is it like Texas barbeque or leftover porridge?"

"Hamlet Simonian's older brother, Hayk, that's H-A-Y-K, was found murdered in a ditch over in Wisconsin. I mean, murdered and dumped in a ditch. We think he was murdered somewhere else, and that probably means here in Minnesota."

"Give me the details," she said.

"Can't. I'm anonymous. You can call the Pierce County sheriff's office and they'll probably talk your ear off."

"The tigers are dead, right?"

He thought about it for a second, and then said, "No. Probably not."

"How do you know?"

"Masculine intuition," Virgil said. "Now go away and report the news, like you're supposed to. Your debt has now grown to huge proportions. Huge."

"Then why do I have a feeling I'm doing you a favor by putting this on the air?" she asked.

"Because you're a cynic, a terrible thing to see in a young person like yourself. I feel awful for you. Now go."

"Thanks for saying I'm young. . . ."

Virgil went to the Mayo Clinic to see Frankie, who'd been moved to a bed in a private room. Sparkle was sitting in a corner, reading the comics in a bent-up copy of the *Mankato Free Press*. "They're letting me out of here tomorrow," Frankie said. "It should be tonight, but the doc said he wanted somebody to watch me for a few more hours. That's the good news."

"What's the bad news?"

"No sex for six months," Frankie said.

Virgil sank into a chair and said, "I can understand that. A woman with a concussion wouldn't want to be intimately exposed to a jackhammer."

"How come," Frankie asked, "every time I want to get a little ribald, you take it farther into the ditch than I ever intended to go?"

"Speaking of ditches," Virgil said, "guess what we found in a ditch over in Wisconsin?"

He told them about Hayk Simonian, and the deputy's guess that the missing legs were feeding a tiger.

"That's gross," Sparkle said. "There's got to be some other reason."

"Think of one," Virgil said.

She thought for a moment, then, "I don't want to think about it. The whole idea is gross."

"But not entirely bad," Virgil said. "Hayk didn't need his legs anymore, because he was dead, and maybe the tigers are alive. You know, if they're feeding them."

"Gross," Sparkle said.

He told them about Catrin Mattsson possibly locating the guys who assaulted Frankie, and the plan to roust one of them that very night.

Sparkle was telling them about sneaking into the pickle factory when Mattsson showed up, sipping from a cup of coffee. She was dressed in dark cotton permanent-press canvas slacks and a beige canvas hunting shirt, with a pistol on her hip under her right hand. She was wearing hiking boots. A combat uniform, Virgil thought.

"That coffee's gonna make you all jittery," Frankie said. "You sure you want to be messing around with guns when you're jittery?"

"Jittery is always good," Mattsson said. "If you're holding a gun on somebody, and your hands are all shaking, that'll scare them every time. They'll lay right down for you."

That was the first sign of any sense of humor he'd gotten from Mattsson, Virgil thought, even if it was cop humor.

To Sparkle, Mattsson said, "I heard part of that pickle plant story. What happened next?"

Sparkle finished the story, the part about going out the window and running for her life. "I got it now—everything I need for my dissertation. I'd head back home to the Cities, except that I don't want to disappoint Father Bill."

Catrin looked at them all, and then said, "You know, you're an odd bunch of people."

Virgil slapped his thighs, stood up, kissed Frankie, and said to Mattsson, "Let's get this guy."

They were on the first floor, heading out the gate, when Sparkle shouted at them: "Wait! Virgil, Catrin! Wait!"

She was wearing flip-flops and ran flapping down the hall clutching her cell phone. She came up, grabbed Virgil's arm, and said, "My friend Ramona. My friend who got me into the factory. Some guys beat her up. Tonight, a little while ago. Her husband called. An ambulance is on the way here. Virgil, they beat her up! They beat her up bad."

20

▼ ▼ ▼

They waited in the emergency room for the ambulance to arrive. Alvarez had lived in an informal trailer park north of Mankato and well to the west, a long ride into town. A doc in the emergency room had spoken to the paramedics in the ambulance and relayed their account: "She was battered, knocked out; she's still only semiconscious. When she went down, they kicked her; probably has broken ribs, could have some internal injuries, depending on where they kicked her and how hard."

"Frankie all over again," Sparkle said. "Same goddamn criminals. Same men."

Virgil went back up to Frankie's room to tell her about it, but she already knew about the attack. Sparkle had still been sitting with her when the call came in, and she told Frankie about it before running off to stop Virgil and Mattsson.

"Sounds worse than I got it," Frankie said, after Virgil described Alvarez's injuries.

"Can't tell yet. I gotta get back downstairs. The ambulance is rolling fast. If she's conscious when she gets here, maybe I can have a few words with her."

"Go," Frankie said.

When he got back to the emergency room, he found that Father Bill had arrived, expecting to pick up Sparkle. Bill was in his bartending outfit of jeans, open-necked white shirt, and red vest with a small gold crucifix hanging around his neck from a gold chain.

When he saw Virgil, he walked over and said, "It's my fault. I was supposed to sit on Sparkle. She got away from me and Ramona helped her sneak into the pickle plant. It's my fault."

"I wouldn't get weird about it," Virgil said. "It's really the fault of the guys who beat up Alvarez and Frankie. That's the fact of the matter. You didn't do anything wrong or immoral, and neither did Sparkle. They did. They *will* be sorry."

"I certainly hope so," Bill said. "If there's anything I can do . . ."

"Catrin and I'll take care of it."

Bill turned toward the door, where Sparkle and Mattsson were looking out at the driveway that came up to the emergency room doors. He said, "Listen, Virgil—I can tell you that I wouldn't want to cross that young woman, Catrin. She has controlled the anger about what happened to her, but it's still down there in her gut. It burns particularly hard when it comes to men hurting women."

Virgil looked over at Mattsson. There had always been an aura of control about her. Even when she smiled, which she'd done a few times when they were sitting in Frankie's hospital room, the smile seemed constrained by a permanent internal tension.

"You're telling me to be careful," Virgil said.

"I'm telling you to be careful *for her*," Bill said. "There's a violence inside her that might be looking for a way to get out."

"That's true of a lot of cops," Virgil said. "It might even be necessary."

They heard the ambulance before they saw it, and a moment later it was in the driveway, lights flashing and siren wailing into the night, and the doctor and three nurses were going through the doors, led by an orderly pushing a gurney. The lights and siren quit and then an ancient Nissan huffed in behind the ambulance as the back doors on the ambulance popped open and they began moving Ramona Alvarez onto the gurney. An oxygen mask covered the bottom of her face and a gauze pad covered her forehead. A saline line was plugged into her arm.

Sparkle had run out into the driveway and when Alvarez was lifted onto the gurney she could see the other woman's face and she pressed her hands to the side of her own face and moaned, and Bill put her arm around her shoulders and pulled her tight.

One of the paramedics was talking fast to the doctor, saying, "She drifted off, partway back, she comes and goes . . ."

A burly Latino in a cotton plaid shirt and jeans had gotten out of the Nissan and was hurrying toward the gurney, and Virgil had time to think, *Husband*, when the man stepped past the gurney without looking at it, up to Sparkle, and with no warning, hit Sparkle in the face. She went down in a heap and Virgil went that way fast, with Mattsson a step behind, but Bill was behind the man and wrapped him up and lifted him off his feet and walked him away from Sparkle.

As he did that, Bill turned his head to Virgil and said, "I got him, help Sparkle."

The Latino was a big guy, and he struggled, but Bill had clamped two heavy arms around him and carried him away. When they'd been skinny-dipping, Virgil noticed that Bill had some serious muscles. Now that was working for him, and nothing that the big man did got him loose.

Sparkle tried to get to her hands and knees, but Mattsson knelt next to her and said, "Stay down, just turn over, let me look . . ."

A nurse had come over and Virgil squatted and they all looked, and Sparkle's eye was already starting to close and she sputtered, "It hurts . . ."

The nurse pressed a cold compress against her forehead and cheekbone and said, "If you can stand up, we can get you inside . . ."

The three of them helped Sparkle get to her feet and the nurse helped her get inside and Sparkle looked back at Virgil and Mattsson and said, "Don't do anything to Leandro. Don't do anything to him."

Bill had pushed the man into an inside corner of a wall, blocking his way out: he was talking to him quickly but quietly, and as Virgil and Mattsson walked up, the man reached out and touched Bill's crucifix and Bill patted him on the shoulder and said something in Spanish.

"We okay?" Virgil asked.

"We are," Bill said. "This is Leandro Cortez, Ramona's husband. He told her not to take Sparkle into the plant, but she did anyway. He doesn't know how the Castro people found out about Ramona, but they did, obviously. He thinks he'll probably be fired tomorrow."

"No, he won't," Mattsson said. To Cortez: "What time do you go to work?"

"Seven o'clock," the man said, in heavily accented English.

"I will see you there," she said. And, "We should charge you with assault, which would get you thrown out of the country and probably banned for good, but Sparkle doesn't want to do that. If she's hurt bad, we'll do it anyway. If she's only got a black eye, we'll probably let it go."

The man looked at Bill, who translated, and he nodded.

"That woman, she says to Ramona nothing would happen . . ." Cortez looked close to crying, and Bill patted him on the shoulder again.

"I'm sure this will work out," Bill said. He said something more in Spanish, and the man nodded, and Bill said in English, "Let's go see about Ramona."

Inside, a nurse told them that Ramona's vitals were being reviewed by the doctor, and then she'd be off to get a full-body scan. Bill explained that to Cortez in Spanish, and Mattsson asked Cortez exactly what had happened.

With Bill translating, Cortez told them that they lived in an informal trailer park hidden away on a farm that supplied the Castro plant. Cortez had been watching a Cubs baseball game with a couple of friends in one trailer, while Alvarez was visiting with two other women at the other end of the park at a picnic table. The women were sitting outside, because the night was hot and most of the trailers didn't have air-conditioning. The one where the men were watching the ball game did have air-conditioning, and the windows were closed.

Which was why they didn't immediately hear the women screaming, that and the ball game.

According to Alvarez's friends, a red pickup truck stopped a short distance away, maybe a hundred feet, and two men got out and walked into the park. That Alvarez should be sitting outside was an accident, but the men knew who they were looking for, recognized her, came directly to the table. Without a word, one of the men began hitting her, and then, when she was on the ground, kicking her. The other man faced off against Alvarez's two female friends, blocking them from the assault.

One of the women went running to get the men, and the two attackers jogged away, jumped into the truck, and tore off. By the time the men had run to the other end of the trailer park, the truck was gone. The attack had lasted maybe fifteen seconds.

The two attackers, one of Alvarez's friends told Cortez, wore Halloween masks, a man's face. Nobody knew whose face.

That was all he knew.

Mattsson said to Virgil, "Same guys. Wish I'd moved sooner."

"You needed the backup," Virgil said. "You think we ought to check the trailer park first, see if we can get more details?"

She shook her head: "We ought to move on this guy. Nail him down now."

"You're leading on this," Virgil said. "We'll do it your way."

Mattsson nodded and said, "Let's check on Sparkle. Make sure she's okay."

Sparkle had taken a good shot to the eye, but no bones were broken. She'd have a shiner for a while, a nurse told them, but there wasn't much to be done except to keep the cold compress on. "Me 'n' Frankie sort of match now," Sparkle said, looking into a mirror.

Virgil nodded and said to Mattsson, "You ready?"

"Yeah. Get your gun on," Mattsson said.

"Such a fascist impulse," Virgil said. "But okay."

Their first target for the night was Frederick Reeves, aka Slow Freddie.

"I'm pretty sure he's the blocker, not the hitter," Mattsson told Virgil, as they left the hospital parking lot in Virgil's truck. "Everybody says he's a really big guy. Fat. The other guy, Blankenship, is built more like you. Tall and wiry, strong and mean."

The idea, they agreed, would be to get Reeves to roll over on his partner. "We know he's scared of the lockup, like claustrophobia. We're gonna have to lock him up for a while, but if he thinks we might lock him up for *years*, maybe he'll talk about Blankenship. And maybe Castro."

"It's Blankenship that we could get on DNA from the bite on the arm," Virgil said.

"Right. But we need a reason to serve a warrant on him. If we can even get Reeves to mention his name, we got him. That's why we need to whisper in Reeves's ear."

Reeves lived in the town of St. Peter, a few miles north of Mankato, in a neighborhood of manufactured homes, which were exactly like single-wide trailers but with foundation skirts instead of wheels. The houses were all set end-on to the streets.

The neighborhood was neatly kept, with lawn sheds outside many of the homes and a boat parked here and there. At one of the homes, a half-dozen people were sitting at a picnic table with a woman playing a guitar. Virgil's window was open, and when they passed, they could hear the group singing what Virgil recognized as "Ablaze," a Lutheran religious song. *The darkness is deepest where there is no light. . . .*

"They sing that in my old man's church, the youth group," Virgil said.

"Neat to hear it passing by," Mattsson said. "You don't hear much outside music anymore, except in malls. Elevator music."

Reeves lived with his grandmother, Mattsson said. When they arrived at the address she had, they found a trailer that looked black in the night, but turned out to be navy blue when their headlights panned across it. There were lights on inside. A white pickup sat on the parking pad beside it, and Mattsson grunted, "Good. That's his truck."

Virgil pulled in behind the truck, blocking it. With the end of the house just in front of it, there'd be no way for the truck to get out.

"I'll knock, if you want to stay back a bit," Mattsson said. "Be more likely to open up for a woman."

"Okay."

The house had a two-step concrete stoop. Mattsson climbed the stoop and banged on the aluminum screen door; Virgil could hear TV voices inside. A moment later an elderly woman looked out through a hand-sized, diamond-shaped window, and the door rattled as she pulled it open, then cocked her head at Mattsson. "What?"

"State Bureau of Criminal Apprehension," Mattsson said. "We need to talk to Fred Reeves."

The old woman was dressed from head to toe in black—a loose black sweatshirt and sweatpants and fleece-lined slippers. She had a cigarette hanging from her lower lip. She looked off to her right and said, "Fred! Cops want to talk to you. Get over here."

They heard some movement, then another door banged and Mattsson shouted at Virgil, "He's gone out the back."

Virgil was already running, down the side of the house and around the back corner. There, probably forty feet away, a very large man was running toward the back corner of the neighboring house. Running slowly, like a tub of Jell-O with legs, though pumping his arms like a sprinter.

Virgil caught him in five seconds between the neighboring house and the next one over, and employing a technique shown to him by Jenkins: instead of trying to stop the man, he simply ran slightly behind him, a couple of feet away, and spoke to him. "Not getting away, Fred. I run three miles every night; I can keep up with you running backward. Want to see me run backward and keep up? Look at this, Freddie, I'm running backward."

Virgil didn't really run backward, but Reeves turned to look and stumbled, and finally stopped, bent to catch his breath, hands on his thighs, which was as far as he could bend; his pants rode down and his T-shirt up, exposing six inches of butt crack. Mattsson came up and said, "You should never have beat that woman up at night, Fred. Should have waited until it was light outside."

Reeves was breathing hard after his forty-yard sprint and gasped, "What?"

Mattsson said, "See, if it was during the day, you could see some daylight. Now it's gonna be a long time before you see daylight again, Freddie. Gonna lock your ass up and throw away the key. That Alvarez woman, looks like she could die."

"I never touched her," Reeves said. "Honest to God, I was just standing there."

"Yeah, but you were there, you had to be Brad's buddy," Mattsson said. To Virgil: "Put the cuffs on him, Virgil. Airmail his bubble butt to Stillwater prison."

She went back to Reeves: "How much did Blankenship pay you, Fred? A hundred bucks? We hear old Castro gave him a grand to slap Ramona around. Did he give you half? Did you get your whole five hundred?"

Reeves's breathing had slowed and he stood up straight and said, "He didn't get no grand. Who told you he got a grand? He said two hundred."

He was facing Mattsson and Virgil had stepped up close behind his shoulder with open cuffs in one hand. He caught Reeves's left arm just above the elbow, but Reeves yanked it away and then snapped it back, with a lot more speed than Virgil had seen when he was running, and the quick heavy slap caught Virgil on the chin and Virgil staggered backward, caught a heel, and fell on his butt. Reeves went right at Mattsson with two canned-ham-sized fists, and as Virgil pushed himself awkwardly back to his feet, Mattsson sidestepped and slapped at Reeves and Reeves fell down shouting, "Oww! Oww! Oww!"

He was facedown in the dirt and Virgil sat on his back and with Mattsson's help he bent his two arms together and cuffed them. Virgil caught one heavy arm and tried to help Reeves to his feet, but the huge man seemed disoriented and for a few seconds Virgil thought he might be having a heart attack or a stroke, but his eyes cleared and his mouth popped open and a thin stream of blood drizzled out.

Mattsson knelt next to Reeves's head and started the routine: "You have the right to remain silent . . ."

"What happened there?" Virgil asked, when she finished. "Why'd he go down like that?"

"Slapped him with mother's little helper," Mattsson said. She slipped a hand in her pocket and pulled out a flat leather-covered sap, nine inches long and an inch and a half wide. Virgil hadn't seen one like it since his days as an army MP captain. "Don't tell."

Virgil nodded. "Get him on his feet."

They got him up and Virgil asked him, "Where did you last see Blankenship?"

"He dropped me off," Reeves said. "Don't know where he went. Probably down to the Waterhole. Don't put me in jail."

"You think he only got two hundred?"

"That's what he said," Reeves said. "C'mon, I'll talk to you. Don't put me in jail. I didn't hit nobody."

"Gonna have to put you in jail for a while, but if you're good, and you tell the truth about what happened, it might not be too long," Mattsson said.

The old woman came walking around the corner of the house, carrying a can of beer. "You taking him?"

"Yeah," Virgil said.

"Come and bail me out, Grandma," Reeves said.

"Yeah, with what?" the woman asked. To Mattsson and Virgil she said, "He don't get along so well in jail. You gotta tell the jail people that. If you leave him a belt, he'll hang himself."

"We'll tell them," Mattsson said.

"Come get me, Grandma," Reeves said. He began to cry and shake, tipped his head up to the sky and wailed, "Don't put me in jail . . ."

"Shouldn't go beating up women," Mattsson said.

They locked Reeves to a steel ring that was welded to the floor of Virgil's truck, then got together outside, where Reeves couldn't hear, and Mattsson said, "I cruised that Waterhole place. Not a good spot to make a bust. Gonna be a few guns in there."

"So we take Reeves back to Mankato, let him look at the lockup, and interview him. I think we can squeeze him for whatever we need. Then we go over to Blankenship's and bust him there. You know where he lives?"

"Yeah, I got an address." She thought a moment, and then said, "That all sounds pretty good. Let's see what we get from Reeves."

"We need to ask him about Frankie, too."

"Yup."

They hauled Reeves into the Blue Earth County jail, stopping at Virgil's to get his BCA-approved recorder. After they booked Reeves in, they took him to an interview room, read him his rights with the recorder running and the jail video turned on, and suggested that he spill his guts, which he did.

"Don't put me in jail . . ."

He said that he'd worked with Blankenship doing security work at concerts and bars, and that Blankenship had told him that some dirty Mexicans had been sneaking left-wing union organizers into the Castro plant, and that somebody at the Castro plant—he didn't think it was old man Castro himself—wanted to teach them a lesson.

They'd only spanked a couple of people, he said, one of the

left-wingers at a Kwik Trip and then the Mexican earlier that night. Blankenship told him that they were protected, and there was no chance that the cops would even look into it.

"He said all the cops around here were on Castro's payroll," Reeves said.

"He was lying to you," Virgil said.

"Why would he lie to me?"

"Because he wanted a chump to go along and watch his back while he beat up people," Mattsson said.

"He didn't really beat them up; he slapped them," Reeves said.

"And kicked them a few times," Virgil added.

Reeves turned away and muttered, "Yeah, Brad does that when he gets excited."

When they'd wrung him out, a couple of jailers led him away to a cell. He was shaking uncontrollably as they led him away, and one of the jailers assured him he'd be alone in the lockup.

"Hope he doesn't hurt himself," Virgil said.

Mattsson: "At some point, even dumb people have to take responsibility for what they do. He wore a mask: he knew what they were doing was wrong."

"Yeah, I know, but . . ."

"Stop being an asshole," Mattsson said. "Let's find Blankenship."

They didn't, that night. Blankenship wasn't at home. Virgil walked into the Waterhole five minutes before closing time, asked around, but nobody had seen him. With the bars closed, they sat outside his house for a while, but he never showed.

"Maybe he's got a girlfriend," Virgil suggested.

"I'll get him tomorrow," Mattsson said. "I can get a sheriff's deputy to back me up, if you can't make it."

"I gotta stay with the tigers," Virgil said. "Jon would be pissed if he knew I was out here with you. There's not much I can do with the tigers except wait for a break, but still: they want me up there staring at the telephones."

"You go ahead and stare," Mattsson said. "I'll take care of Blankenship."

"Deal," Virgil said.

21

▼ ▼ ▼

Virgil went back to his house and bagged out, Honus at the foot of the bed; he spent a few minutes thinking about Mattsson and decided, before he went to sleep, that a prudent man would stay on her right side. Mattsson could wind up running the BCA someday, he thought, unless she decided to go into politics, in which case, she could wind up running the whole state. Frankie was already one of her fans, and Frankie wasn't that easy to impress.

The next morning he took Honus for a run, fed him, dropped him at the farm, and left for the Twin Cities with six hours of sleep, groggy but functioning. Frankie called and said Sparkle would take her home, whenever the docs let her out of the hospital.

On his way north, he started working the phones, called Barry King's girlfriend, who said she hadn't heard from him since he dropped her off the morning before, and that his phone was off-line.

There were no further tips on the BCA tip line, and Virgil was feeling stuck, when the Simonians called: "This is Levon. Is it true?"

"About Hayk? I'm afraid it is."

There was a collective moan on the other end of the phone line, and Virgil asked, "How did you know about Barry King?"

"Hamlet told the name to his mom," Simonian said. "She wrote it down."

"You don't have King now, do you?"

"No, he didn't want to go with us anymore, so we let him go. I mean, you know, we dropped him off."

"Well, we can't find him. I hope you didn't do anything else, like murder him."

"No, we didn't," Simonian said, although, from his tone of voice, Virgil understood that murder was among the range of acceptable possibilities. "We haven't seen him since we dropped him off. He didn't know anything about the tigers."

"You sure?"

"No. We talked to him for a pretty long time, though, and in the end . . . we believed him."

Virgil interrupted. "Did Hamlet's mom mention anyone else besides King?"

Simonian covered the microphone on his cell phone, although enough noise leaked through that Virgil understood that an argument was going on. Then Simonian came back and said, "Hamlet's mom, you know, she doesn't speak the English so good. She tells us that Hamlet says the name Larry King who works at the zoo. We look at the zoo, there is no Larry King, but there is a Barry King. We tell ourselves, this is the man. Hamlet's mom, she used to watch Larry King every night on TV, she makes this mistake. We think. But we're not sure. This is why we didn't talk to him longer."

"You were probably right, though," Virgil said. "You really didn't beat anything good out of Barry?"

"No. He was very stubborn. We think maybe he doesn't know anything . . ." There was some more mumbling in the background. "But of course, we never would beat up this man. That is not the Simonian way."

"Okay. Now, are you leading up to something with this Barry King story?"

"Yes. Hamlet's mom, she doesn't speak so good English. She writes down another name, but we can't find this man's name."

"What's the name?"

"She watches *The Simpsons* on TV, you know?" Simonian said.

"Okay, but what . . . ?"

"We think she makes a mistake again. She writes down Simpson Becker. Do you know this name?"

"Simpson Becker? Never heard of him," Virgil said. And he thought, *Holy shit, it's Winston Peck.* "You have any idea of what he does?"

"He is the big brain behind this operation," Simonian said. "That is what we know."

There was more mumbling in the background, then Simonian added, "My brother Dikran says we should tell you that there might be two big brains, one here, one from California. Hamlet and Hayk were hired in California, but we don't know who."

"Well, I'll keep an eye out for them, and thank dickweed for mentioning that," Virgil said. "It's time you guys went home. If you don't go home, you'll wind up in a Minnesota prison. All six of you."

"We think of this, but I tell you, Virgil: we are a valuable resource. A treasure in Armenian clothing. If you find this Simpson Becker, you give him to us. We speak to him, and he will tell the truth about the tigers. And Hamlet and Hayk."

Virgil got the Simonians off the phone and called Duncan: "Can I have Jenkins and Shrake? Only a couple of days?"

"We've got to have them back before the action starts at the fair," Duncan said. "You got something?"

"Maybe. It's possible that I've identified the guy who's got the tigers and probably killed Hamlet and Hayk Simonian, but I've got no proof. We need to spend some time watching him. The good thing is, he's got to be working with the tigers . . . you know, like processing them."

"Don't say that," Duncan said. "I'm still praying that they're alive."

"That's not realistic, Jon . . . the longer it goes, the smaller the chance," Virgil said. "At this point, we'd be lucky to get one of them back."

Virgil arranged to hook up with Jenkins and Shrake at a French bakery in St. Paul, where Jenkins liked to go to watch the madding crowd and Shrake liked to go for the scrambled eggs and croissants. They'd gotten a table and Virgil cut through the crowd and sat down next to Shrake, looked around, and asked, "You guys come here all the time?"

"All the time," Jenkins said. "The girls take me back to my college days."

"I didn't think they had girls at East Jesus Community College," Shrake said. And: "Virgie, what've you got?"

"I think a guy named Winston Peck has our tigers and probably killed the Simonian brothers. We need to watch him until he takes us to wherever the cats are."

"We have any proof that he killed the brothers?"

"No. All we've got is the fact that the brothers were helping with the tigers. If we get him with the tigers, though, we can tie Peck to the Simonians as a felony murder, even if he didn't personally kill them. Though I suspect he probably did. I don't think there were a whole bunch of people involved in stealing the tigers—no more than you could get in a van."

"Good enough," Jenkins said. "You know where Peck is right now?"

"At home, I hope," Virgil said. "He operates out of his house."

After talking it over, they decided that Virgil would go to Peck's house, with Shrake and Jenkins trailing in their cars. They'd find a spot to watch the house, while Virgil knocked on the door to make sure that Peck was home. They cooked up a thin excuse for Virgil's appearance at Peck's place—Virgil would show Peck the mug shots of the dead Simonians and ask if he'd seen them in any place linked to traditional medicine.

But Peck wasn't home. Virgil knocked on his door, and a neighbor, backing out of his garage, stopped long enough to say, "Dr. Peck isn't home. He pulled out an hour or so ago."

Virgil walked across the grassy strip separating Peck's driveway from the neighbor's, and said, "I'm an agent with the Bureau of

Criminal Apprehension. Dr. Peck is helping us with a case, but I haven't been able to contact him. Are you sure it was him pulling out?"

"Yeah, I saw him. The guy with the Ferrari was there, and Dr. Peck came out of the house with the Ferrari guy and they were talking in the driveway, and then he went in his garage and got in his truck and pulled out. It looked like he was following the Ferrari guy somewhere."

"Sure it was a Ferrari, and not, you know, a Corvette or something?"

"No, it was a Ferrari. Red. Driver was an Asian guy," the neighbor said.

"You didn't happen to see the plates on the Ferrari?"

"I did, but I don't remember any numbers. I do know that there were too many numbers and letters on it. I think . . . don't quote me on this . . . it might have been from California."

"Thanks," Virgil said. "That helps."

"Is Peck in trouble?"

"We're just trying to get some information, actually," Virgil said.

"That's what you always say when a guy's in trouble. I've got kids at home after school . . ."

"We're not going to shoot anybody," Virgil said. "We want to talk to Dr. Peck about his area of expertise."

"If you say so," the neighbor said.

That was all the neighbor had. Virgil called Jenkins and Shrake and told them that Peck was gone, and about the Ferrari.

"Probably get on to the communications center and find that

Ferrari in fifteen minutes," Jenkins said. "Can't be more than a dozen of them in the metro area, and probably only one with California plates."

"I'll do that, but what are you guys going to do?"

"We can sit here and watch and read our iPads," Jenkins said. "If he shows up, we'll call you. If not, at least we've educated ourselves."

With no better ideas, they settled in to watch Peck's house. Virgil spread the word about the Ferrari; forty minutes later, he took a call from a highway patrolman named Jason Rudd who was running a speed trap near the airport: "I think I got your Ferrari. Red, Asian driver, one passenger, also Asian, California plates. He's heading west on 494. I think he just came out of the airport."

"Can you run the plates?"

"Doing that now, but I thought you might want a little subtlety here, so I went on past him and I'm sitting on the overpass at 77. They're about to go by me."

"Wait a minute. The highway patrol has gone subtle?"

"We have that capacity, though we seldom need to call upon it," the patrolman said. "Okay, he's still on 494, out in front of me again. It's not like I'm going to lose a red Ferrari."

"Stay way back, see where he's going. I'm heading that way," Virgil said.

Virgil called Jenkins and Shrake, told them to stay put, and drove over to I-94 and went west. A minute later, the highway patrolman called again. "Okay, he's on I-35 going north into Minneapolis. He's doing about eighty, so I could pull him over anytime. Still want me to stay back?"

"Yes, but when we get to where he's going, I might want you to block him in, get some ID, give him a ticket. We'll talk about that when we get there."

"I already got an ID on the owner. It's a Zhang Min, sixty-five, of San Marino, California, if that means anything to you," Rudd said.

"It doesn't yet, but file that. I'm on 94, going across the river bridge. I'll be in downtown Minneapolis in a couple of minutes."

"Then you're ahead of us. You ought to get off at Eleventh Street and find a place to pull over and wait. He'll go right past you if he's going into town, and if not, you can jump back on the highway right behind us and catch up."

"I'll do that. Stay with me."

Five minutes later, Rudd called back. "He's getting off. He's coming into town. Where are you?"

"Right by the Hilton."

"He'll be coming by in fifteen seconds."

The Ferrari went by a few seconds later and Virgil pulled out behind it. The Ferrari driver apparently knew where he was going, as he threaded through town with Virgil a few cars back. They caught a couple of stoplights together, and the Ferrari eventually turned into the Loews Hotel.

Virgil called the patrolman, who was a few more cars behind him, and asked, "Let's not ticket him. Not yet. Can you hang around for a while?"

"Sure. I already talked to the boss and he's okay with it," Rudd said.

"Then stick your car where they can't see it from the hotel, I'm going to take a look at these guys."

A valet met Virgil at the front entrance, as another one spoke to the Ferrari's driver. "Checking in?" the valet asked.

Virgil held up his ID. "No, I'm checking out, so to speak. Leave the car here. I'm taking my keys. I'll move it if I'm going to be more than five minutes."

"Well, you *are* The Man," the valet said.

Virgil got his travel bag out of the back and hurried to the hotel door, slowed to an amble, and came up behind the two Asian men. The older of the two, who looked to be in his sixties and might therefore be Zhang Min, had produced an American Express black card. The younger man was looking around the lobby; he checked Virgil, then Virgil's bag, a tan canvas bag from Filson, dismissed him, and his eyes moved on to a better-dressed man with a diamond earring.

Another receptionist asked Virgil if she could help, and Virgil shook his head: "Waiting for a friend. He'll be here in a couple of minutes."

The two Asian men got the penthouse suite and disappeared behind a bellhop pushing a luggage rack.

Virgil called Jenkins, told him where he was. Jenkins said, "Old Asian man, California, Ferrari, penthouse suite. That sounds like a client for some tiger chops."

"I'm trying to think that without being a bigot," Virgil said. "He could be here for our Peking duck."

"I'm thinking not. What are you going to do?"

"Same as you," Virgil said. "Wait."

He waited for a long crappy hour, parked illegally in a handicapped spot across the street at the Target Center. Halfway through the hour, he called Rudd, the highway patrolman, and told him he could take off. Another half hour, and the valet brought the Ferrari around, and Virgil called Jenkins, who said they hadn't seen anything of Peck, and Virgil said, "We're moving here. If they come anywhere close to you, I'm going to want you to drop into the box. Shrake can stay where he's at."

"Got it," Jenkins said.

The two Asian men walked out of the hotel and got into the Ferrari. The driver wheeled out of the parking circle and again threaded his way through town, this time out to I-94, east toward St. Paul. Virgil called Jenkins, who said he'd be waiting at Snelling Avenue, if the Ferrari got that far.

It did. Jenkins pulled onto the highway behind it, let the Ferrari move away. Virgil fell farther back. They tracked the red car all the way through St. Paul and east out of town to Radio Drive, where the Ferrari got off, took a right, and pulled into a Cub supermarket parking lot.

Peck seriously stank. Stank to the point where he could barely stand it.

Part of it was tiger poop, part of it was meat that was beginning to go bad, and part of it was his own sweat: with five dryers going at once in the closed-off barn basement, he was probably working in 110-degree heat. The male tiger was almost done. He'd take the night off, kill the female in the morning, and start processing her. With the female, he was thinking that he'd take only the glands, the various important organs, the eyes, and the bones. Fuck this jerky thing: it was killing him.

He'd taken to hosing himself off with cold well water, but nothing really seemed to help. He needed some kind of strong soap, he thought. Then Zhang Xiaomin called, said his father was coming to town, and wanted to see the tigers for himself. Zhang said the old man was bringing along another hundred grand.

What was he supposed to say to that? No thanks? He popped a Xanax and said, "Sure. Meet you at the same place, that Cub grocery store. If we don't arrive at exactly the same time, I'll see you by the battery rack. Ask a clerk for the battery rack."

Peck was sitting toward the back of the lot staring at the "24-Hour Savings" sign on the front of the Cub store when he saw the Ferrari rolling through the lot to park in a slot near the front. Peck had wanted to be sure that Zhang Xiaomin got out of the car with an elderly Asian man, and not some marble-faced West Coast killer, as described by the late Barry King.

But an elderly Asian man got out of the Ferrari, his legs wobbling as he did so; Peck knew him from a half-dozen earlier meetings. Old man Zhang, all right. Zhang stopped to kick a tire and wave a hand at his son. He seemed to be saying a Rolls would be better than a low-slung sports job. The younger Zhang said nothing, but with his head down, led his father into the store.

Peck started the engine on the Tahoe and eased over toward the Ferrari, which had drawn a couple of Minnesotans in golf shirts, who were looking in the windows at the dashboard. "Fuckin' dumbass and his fuckin' Ferrari," Peck muttered.

He parked a few slots away . . . and saw Virgil Flowers hop out of a 4Runner on the far side of the lot, put on a cowboy hat and some aviators, and walk toward the entrance of the Cub grocery store.

Flowers. Again. Peck slid down in his seat.

Flowers was obviously either following the Ferrari or conspiring with them. If he was conspiring with them, why would they meet here? Not so they could put the finger on Peck—Flowers already knew what he looked like.

Flowers had gotten onto Zhang Xiaomin. Somehow, some way. And that little Chinese prick would sell Peck out in a minute, if he could keep himself out of jail by doing it.

He started his truck again, swung out of the parking lot, and called Zhang Xiaomin. Zhang answered on the second ring, and Peck said, "You miserable piece of shit. Are you working with Flowers?"

"What? Flowers? What flowers?"

He was confused, and to Peck's ear, not faking it. "Listen, a cop followed you into the store. He's the guy who's investigating the tiger theft. He's tall, long blond hair, wearing a white straw cowboy hat and dark sunglasses. He's onto you—I don't know how. You need to buy some groceries, go back out to your car, drive back to the hotel, and wait. I will call you. We need to figure this out."

"How could this happen?" Zhang sounded totally sincere.

"I don't know, but we need to stay away from this guy. Go back to your hotel. Wait. Maybe . . . I don't know. I will call when I think of something."

"Oh! I saw him. He's down the aisle, he's looking at beer. We're going. We'll go back to the hotel."

"Go."

The Ferrari led Virgil and Jenkins back to Minneapolis, all the way to the Loews. Halfway back, Virgil called Jenkins and said, "Notice how fast he's driving?"

"Pretty slow for a Ferrari," Jenkins said.

"Pretty slow for a Yugo. On the way over here, he was driving a casual eighty, in and out of the traffic. Now he's five miles an hour below the speed limit, in the slow lane."

"He made us," Jenkins said.

"I think so. I don't know how. I'd be interested in knowing, because I swear to God they didn't know when they went into the store." Virgil thought about it for a few seconds, then said, "You know what? They were meeting Peck. Peck was in the goddamn parking lot and saw me go into the store. That's the only thing that makes sense."

"Could have been," Jenkins said.

At the Loews Hotel, the two Asian men took a bag of groceries out of the car and disappeared into the lobby as a valet took the Ferrari.

"Goddamnit," Virgil said.

"What do you want to do?" Jenkins asked.

"I don't know. If they know we're watching them, then staking out Peck's house won't work. You and Shrake might as well go catch some lunch. Go to a movie. Hang out. I'll call you when I think of something."

22

▼ ▼ ▼

Zhang Xiaomin drove his father in near silence back to the Loews Hotel, the silence broken only by the elder Zhang's muttered expletives in Chinese. Zhang Xiaomin spoke only fair Chinese, having left China when he was seven years old. He didn't recognize all of the words his father was using, but he recognized the tone.

His father was the kind of man who'd grown up rough, out on the countryside, without phones, running water, or indoor toilets. When he arrived in Shanghai, at exactly the right time to make money, he'd made it, and that had conferred on him, in his own eyes, a kind of nobility.

That reaction to new money wasn't confined to Zhang Min, by any means, or even to nouveau riche Chinese; but Xiaomin's old man had it bad. He was a tyrant at work and at home; and when Xiaomin was a boy, he would beat him mercilessly and bloodily for even small faults, or even non-faults, if alcohol was involved.

Xiaomin never fought back.

When he was seven, his father, then with his first flush of real money, began secretly moving some of it to the United States, out of reach of China's authorities, should they come looking. He invested primarily in real estate—houses—another great move in the California of the eighties. He sent his wife and son to look after the houses. Xiaomin had grown up in San Marino, speaking Chinese to his mother, English everywhere else.

When they got back to the hotel, Zhang Min stalked without expression through the lobby, with his son padding along at his heels, carrying the groceries. In the elevator, Zhang Min pushed the buttons for both the penthouse level and the skyway level, and when the doors closed, he began slapping his son's face, hard as he could, saying over and over, "Fuckin', fuckin', fuckin'" along with a few Chinese phrases, and Zhang Xiaomin took it, head down, the impacts batting his face back and forth. He knew if he raised his hands, his father's hands would close and the open-handed slaps would become blows with fists.

When the elevator doors opened at the skyway level, both men were staring straight ahead, and only a close examination would show signs of blood around Xiaomin's eyes, nose, and lips. Zhang Min said, "You disgust me. You are an insect."

He led the way into the skyway and Zhang Xiaomin asked, "Where are we going?"

Zhang Min didn't answer, but took a cell phone from his pocket, punched up an app, and called for an Uber car. One would meet them, a block away, in five minutes. They dumped the groceries in a trash can and a moment later passed a fast-food place, where Zhang Min stopped long enough to pull a few napkins from a dispenser. He handed them to his son and said, "Clean yourself. You are a weak bleeder. Clean yourself."

Zhang Xiaomin pressed the napkins to his nose and face while his father made another call. "Peck: we are not followed. We will take an Uber to the same exit, but to the other side. I saw a sign for a Best Buy there. One half hour."

He listened for a moment, then said, "Yes, I am sure. We were moving too quickly for them to set up on us. One half hour."

The two men continued through the skyways to a Macy's store, where, after a moment of confusion, they found their way down to street level. They waited inside the door until the Uber car showed, and in the car, Zhang Min told the driver, "A Best Buy store at Radio Drive east of St. Paul. I will point you when we get there."

"There are Best Buys that are a lot closer . . ." the driver ventured.

"This is business, that's the store we want," Zhang Min said, in his softly accented English. "I will tip you twenty dollars above your Uber fee when we get there."

"Outa here," the driver said.

Zhang Xiaomin kept his face down, dabbing at it with the napkins. Although outwardly submissive, he was raging inside. Having Hayk Simonian slap him around was bad enough, but Simonian was a professional thug. His father was a small man, and yet . . .

The Uber driver dropped them at Best Buy. Two minutes later, Peck called them on Zhang Xiaomin's cell phone.

"Are you absolutely positive you are clean?"

"Yes, my father knows how to do this, from the old country," Zhang Xiaomin said. He gave a quick explanation—the fast turnaround in the hotel, the sneak through Macy's, the Uber.

"I'm coming in," Peck said. Another two minutes, and he rolled his Tahoe up to their feet. Zhang Xiaomin got in the backseat, the old man in the front passenger seat, and from there he began shouting at the two of them.

"Two people are dead? Am I hearing this now? You have killed to get these tigers? Are you this insane? I have nothing to do with this now. Nothing to do with this. I know nothing of this . . ."

Peck said, "Since you're the one who employed the Simonians, I don't think the cops'll buy it. Besides, they don't know who killed them."

"Shut up! Shut up! They will know! They will! Because you two are incompetent fools, to kill someone for the tigers."

"It was Hamlet's fault—he left his fingerprints where the cops could find him. Hamlet was the guy you picked, not me," Peck said. "Soon as they put pressure on him, he'd have rolled over on us. Had to be done . . ."

"Shut up! Shut up!" The old man stormed on, out of control, all the way to the barn. "No more money from me. No more money." To his son: "You can get a job or you can starve."

At the barn, he waved a hand at the house and asked, "Who is living here? Are they seeing me?"

"Nobody lives there, except me, for a while," Peck said. "The animals are in the barn. When we finish with them, I plan to soak it in gasoline, along with the house, and burn them both to the ground. They're wrecks, and I know for a fact that they're insured, and people will think that the owner burned them for the money. No reason even to look for a tiger hair."

Zhang Min walked once through the barn, stood a moment inspecting Katya, who inspected him back, then looked at the hanging corpse of Artur, and finally turned on his heel and said, "I have seen enough."

He marched back to the truck and got in the passenger seat. Zhang Xiaomin trailed behind with Peck, and on the way said, "I have had enough. We will kill this old piece of shit. You think of a plan and we will do it. When I have the money, I will give you one hundred thousand dollars."

"I don't think so," Peck said. "You'll inherit something more than a hundred million. The fiancée goes away. For helping get this flea off your neck, I want one. One million dollars cash. Then I will go away and you will never hear from me again."

They got to the truck and Peck got in the driver's seat and Xiaomin got in the seat behind him.

Zhang Min said, "I was the bigger fool—the bigger fool for getting involved with the two of you."

Zhang Xiaomin said to the back of Peck's head, "Yes."

Peck stopped the truck and said, "Wait one minute. I forgot my phone."

He went back inside the barn, where Hayk Simonian had strung up the body of Artur with quarter-inch brown nylon rope. He picked up Simonian's skinning knife, cut a four-foot length from the original roll, did a quick wrap around his fingers, stuck the wad of rope in his hip pocket. He took his iPhone out, turned the movie app on, picked up Simonian's jacket, and walked back out to the car.

At the car, he walked around to the passenger side and pulled open the back door, handed the jacket to Zhang Xiaomin, who was sitting on the other side, and said, "Throw this in the back, will you?"

The old man was staring straight ahead, muttering something. Perfect. Peck pulled the rope out of his back pocket, threw it around the old man's neck, yanked it back as hard as he could.

The old man fought and gurgled, tearing at the rope with his fingernails, breaking the manicured tips, and Peck handed the ends of the rope to Zhang Xiaomin, and shouted, "Pull, dummy. Pull the ropes."

Xiaomin began dragging on the ropes, which were looped around the metal bars of the front seat head restraints, and Peck eased off the backseat and Xiaomin leaned across to get a better angle and began shouting "Die! Die, you old fuck."

It took a while, three or four minutes before Zhang Min stopped thrashing, and a couple more minutes after that, before Xiaomin was satisfied that his old man was dead.

Peck filmed most of it; he tried to be subtle about it, holding the phone's camera up by his chest, half turned away, but it wouldn't have mattered. Xiaomin was so focused on his thrashing father that Peck could have used a full-scale movie camera and Xiaomin wouldn't have noticed.

When it was over, Xiaomin began weeping, dropped the rope, and fell out of the far side of the car, where he crawled around in the dirt for a few seconds, then ran around to the passenger side and pulled open the door and said, "My father, my father, you shit, you asshole . . ."

The spasm of grief—or whatever it was—took a couple more minutes, with Peck filming as much as he could. Then Xiaomin asked, wiping away tears, "Now what?"

"Now we wrap him up in some plastic sheets and take him back to Minneapolis with us."

"What?"

"Then you sneak back into the hotel, going through Macy's, like you did on the way out. Stop in Macy's, buy some workout shorts and gym shoes and a T-shirt. Pay cash. Go to the hotel, call down to the desk, find out where you can get a workout. They've probably got a gym of some kind. Get a trainer if you can. You're establishing your presence."

"What about Father?"

"I will leave him somewhere," Peck said. "You should call his phone a few times during the afternoon and evening. There won't be an answer. About nine o'clock, talk to the police about your missing father."

"You think that's safe?"

"I think it's perfect," Peck said. "When the police come to talk to you, think about the things your father's meant to you—the good things. Cry a little, but don't fake it. When they come to you about his body . . . then you can break down. Don't fake it, but work your way up to it. You really want to be distraught. But you can't fake it; you have to feel it."

"I already feel it."

"Well, feel it more."

They took Hayk Simonian's pickup to Minneapolis: a risk, but a necessary one. On the way, they talked alibis.

"What about this Flowers?" Zhang Xiaomin asked. "He followed us. The only reason I can think of is, he saw my car at your house."

Peck had to think about that complication for a while. Eventually, he said, "Your father came here to meet business associates. You were taking him to a meeting in Stillwater, about a property purchase, but you don't know who with. The associate had to cancel for some reason, you don't know what, and you pulled into the Cub supermarket to get a snack before you went back to the hotel . . . That explains that. Then, you came to my house because your father bought medications from me. I even have a bunch of e-mails from him, about medication and not about the tigers. You came over to pick up the medication to give to him when he arrived. Next time I talk to Flowers, I'll confirm that, and even let him see the e-mails."

"That is very . . . not so good," Zhang said.

"Not great, but it's simple and unbreakable," Peck said. "Keep it that way, and you'll inherit a hundred mil."

"What will you do with Father?"

"You told me once that he liked strip shows. Pole dancers, lap dancers. Hookers."

"Yes?"

"Keep thinking about that," Peck said. "When the cops say they've found him, you can be surprised, but not too surprised."

"What?"

"I'll take care of it—you be surprised. And freaked out and broken up. He's your father, for crissakes, and now he's dead. When they ask you, think about what you did to him. Almost cut his freakin' head off."

Zhang Xiaomin buried his face in his hands and began to weep again.

"That's very good," Peck said. "Do it just like that."

When he'd dropped Zhang, Peck wheeled around to the alley behind the Swedish Bikini Bar. There was a Dumpster in the alley that backed up to a wall; you couldn't see behind it, but there was a space back there. Peck had often stood next to that space, during his brief adventure with crack cocaine, smoking with the woman who dealt it to him.

Now he got out of the truck, checked around for witnesses, dragged the body out of the back—hit the ground with an *oof* sound—and around behind the Dumpster.

There, he unwrapped the plastic sheeting and threw it back in the truck, and after a last look around, he got the hell out of there.

23

▼ ▼ ▼

During the hunt for the tigers, every day had been hotter than the next. Temperatures climbed toward the hundred-degree mark as Virgil sat in his 4Runner, engine running to keep the air conditioner on, barely around the corner from Peck's house. He'd positioned himself so he could see the front of Peck's garage, his front door, and the whole stretch of street in front of Peck's house.

He was there, he thought, due to a failure of imagination. He was waiting for a call from the BCA's duty officer. Every police department in the metro area, plus the highway patrol, was looking for Peck's Tahoe.

That kind of a net could work with a Ferrari, Virgil thought, because everybody looks at Ferraris. But who looks at a Tahoe? And how often do you look in your rearview mirror and find a cop behind you, where he could read the license plate? Not very often, so the possibilities seemed thin, and even thinner if Peck was deliberately hiding.

The fact that he had to keep the truck's engine running was also annoying, because it was a waste of money and gasoline. He read a book as he waited, called *Too Big to Fail*, about the financial crisis the decade before, and which was rapidly making him even more irritable: not the book itself, which was fascinating, but the stories of the enormous collection of assholes who created and profited from the disaster.

He'd been waiting for three hours when he saw Peck's Tahoe turn the corner three blocks away and, a moment later, pull into the garage. Virgil pulled up directly behind Peck's Tahoe as the garage door was coming down. He got out and walked up the steps to the front door, started banging on the door and pushing the doorbell.

"Dr. Peck," Virgil called.

Peck came to the door, left the screen door closed, and scowled at him. He was red-faced and harried. "I am very busy right now."

Virgil moved up and squared off against the other man. "I need to talk to you about the Simonians."

"The who?"

Virgil thought that Peck had almost pulled it off: he sounded right, but there was a flash of alarm in his eyes. He knew the dead men all right.

"The Simonians. The guys who helped you steal the tigers. Their mother had two names written down, in case something bad happened to them: Barry King's and yours."

"That's absurd. I don't know anybody by that name," Peck said. "Never heard of them, or of Larry King."

"Barry King," Virgil said. "He worked at the zoo and provided the key that gave the thieves access to the tiger cages."

"Well, I don't know him, whoever he is," Peck said. He shook a finger at Virgil. "You know what? You can take a hike. I'm going to talk to my lawyer about you. If you want to talk to me again, you're going to have to do it with my lawyer sitting in, and at his convenience, not yours."

"That's not the way it works," Virgil said. "If I need to talk to you, I'll haul your butt downtown and you can call your lawyer from the BCA offices."

"Then fuck you. Haul me down. I want a lawyer and I'm not saying another word to you," Peck said. "I have nothing to do with any tigers and I never heard of these Somalia people or Barry King. So—are we going downtown? If we're not, I've got work to do."

"How about Zhang Min? Do you know Zhang Min, from Los Angeles? Owns a red Ferrari . . ."

Peck started to turn away, but stopped. "I shouldn't say another word to you, but what does Mr. Zhang have to do with this?"

"What is he to you?" Virgil asked.

"A patient. He also will occasionally refer one of his friends to me," Peck said. "I spoke to his son a couple of days ago and provided some herbal medications for Mr. Zhang's rheumatism. And I believe the Ferrari belongs to his son, not to Mr. Zhang."

"No, it actually belongs to Mr. Zhang. Have you spoken to Mr. Zhang in the past few days?"

"To his son, but Mr. Zhang lives in Los Angeles. I believe the last time I saw him was at the Traditional Medicine Expo in San Pedro, almost a year ago."

"You didn't know he was in Minneapolis?"

Peck shook his head and said, "No, and I'm surprised that you say he is—he would have called me, but he hasn't."

"Would you mind if I look at your phone?"

Peck put his hand in his pocket, started to pull his phone out, then frowned, put it back and said, "I really don't, but you've pissed me off—so you can look at my phone when you get a warrant.

I want to see the warrant and I want my lawyer to see it as well. When you do that, I'll hand it over."

Virgil peered at him for a long moment, then said, "I believe that you know where the tigers are. I think you know who killed the Simonians. I'm going to prove it, and you're going to prison. Don't leave the area, Dr. Peck. We will be talking again. Frequently."

"I'll tell my lawyer you said so," Peck said, and he turned and started into the house.

Virgil said to his back, "You know there's a whole pack of Simonians in town? Cut from the same cloth as Hamlet and Hayk, and they're looking for you. I'd walk very carefully, Dr. Peck. I warned them off, but they're looking for the man who dismembered their brothers, and they won't go away. They told me that when they find you, they expect to keep you alive . . . for several days."

Peck looked over his shoulder, and now the fear was alive in his face. He shook his finger at Virgil and said, "If you set me up . . . if you . . . I'm calling my lawyer."

Virgil went back to his truck, sweating in the late afternoon sun. He called Duncan and said, "I braced Peck. He's in on it, but he's got a mile of excuses. I may want a warrant to look at his phone, but I've got no cause."

"Nothing at all?"

"Not yet. But I will have. Could we get Jenkins and Shrake to do some surveillance overnight? Maybe hang a GPS tracker on Peck's Tahoe?"

"I'll have to talk to legal about that. I'll get back to you. What are you doing next?"

"I'll tell you, Jon, I'm running out of rope. I know goddamn well that Peck is involved, and also a couple of West Coast Chinese who are staying over at the Loews in Minneapolis, and a zoo worker named Barry King who nobody can find. But I've got nothing to hang it on."

"You think King . . . ?"

"He may have run for it—unless Peck or these Chinese guys killed him. Since we've got two murders already, that looks like cleanup. It's possible that King is dead, too. I've got his tag number out there, but haven't heard anything. And I've got his girlfriend working with me, but she hasn't seen him. I had Sandy check and he hasn't been using his credit cards, either."

"I can send Jenkins and Shrake over. What's *your* next move?"

"Don't have one. We could put both Jenkins and Shrake on Peck full-time, right in his face, to see if we can shake him up, or we could put Jenkins over here, at Peck's place, and send Shrake over to the Loews to keep an eye on the Chinese. What do you think?"

"Well, since you braced Peck, he knows you're looking at him, so he probably won't go driving out to wherever the tigers are," Duncan said. "Maybe split between Peck and the Chinese."

"That's good," Virgil said. "I need to get some sleep. I dunno. We'll get Peck sooner or later, but I think we might have lost the tigers."

"Ah, man. Really?"

"I'm afraid so. I've got an idea to break Peck out, but it's not something you want to hear about. I'll let it go at that."

"Okay. Keep pushing, pal," Duncan send. "I'll get Jenkins and Shrake wound up."

"How are things over at the state fair?"

"Clusterfuck. Gonna be a cop every two feet," Duncan said.

"Lucas tells me there was a cop every two feet down in Iowa, and the Purdys still touched off the bomb."

"Not here. Not here."

"Good luck with that," Virgil said.

On the way to Mankato, Virgil called Daisy Jones, the TV reporter. "I owe you so much now, I might have to resort to sex to pay you back," she said.

"Hold that thought. Right now I'm in a pretty intense relationship," Virgil said.

"I was in a pretty intense relationship the last time the possibility arose, and you weren't. I often wondered about how you worked that out," Jones said.

"Don't think about it. And don't give up hope," Virgil said. "Anyhoo . . . I want to be up-front with you and I've got something to say, but I *cannot* have this come back to me. I would maybe get fired."

"I'd get fired myself before I'd give you up," she said. "You know I'm telling the truth."

"All right. There's a guy in town named Winston Peck. Actually, Winston Peck the Sixth, MD. There's a lot of stuff about him on the 'net. I'm sure he's involved with the tiger theft and that automatically means that he's probably involved with two murders. I don't know if he did them himself, but he's involved. I can give you his address in St. Paul . . ."

He did, and she took it down and asked, "What do you want me to do?"

"I want you to show up with a TV truck and a microphone and ask him if he stole the tigers. I want him on TV, denying it. I want his neighbors to know . . . I want him to crack, I want him to make a run for it."

"Huh. So I would actually be functioning as a cop."

"No. You have no arrest powers. You got a tip from a friendly cop and you're just chasing it down like any reporter would. If you shared this with somebody from another station, that would be fine with me, as long as my name didn't come up. I know you guys sometimes cover each other's butts, no matter what anybody says about competition."

After a moment's silence, she said, "If I do this, I think I'll owe you less, not more."

"Let's be adults for a minute," Virgil said. "You don't really owe me a fuckin' thing, and you know it. We talk because we like each other and help each other out."

"That's true, but it's fun to pretend. Okay, Virgie . . . Video at ten. Oh, I might call you for a comment."

Frankie was in bed, propped up on a bunch of pillows, watching a movie on her old MacBook Pro.

"How are the ribs?" Virgil asked.

"Hurts when I torque them, cough, or laugh, so I try not to do that."

"I've got a sleeping bag and an air mattress," he said. "If you need me to sleep on the floor, I can."

"We should be okay; you don't usually flop around much," she said. "Besides, this new mattress . . . why did we wait this long? This thing is wonderful, it's like a cloud."

Virgil sat on it, careful not to rock her, and told her about the day. When he finished, she asked, "What happens if this Peck sits on his ass? If there's somebody else helping him besides the Simonians, they could be cleaning up while Peck has your attention. He does nothing. Then what?"

"That's the worst case," Virgil said. "I don't need him to have a backup guy; I need him out in the open, shit-faced panicked."

Virgil got his own laptop and checked on a couple of outdoors forums that he hadn't had time to read in a couple of days, wrote a couple of quick notes, then went into the living room to watch the ten o'clock news. Channel Three led with the Peck story—Jones tried to interview him through the screen door. Peck's face was barely visible, other than as a vaguely white oval, and he threatened to sue the TV station if they mentioned his name or used the video.

Jones mentioned Peck's name about twenty times and even asked why he couldn't practice medicine, and Peck slammed the door and Jones said, with one of her patented gotcha smiles, "Dr. Peck refused to answer any further questions about whether he was involved with the theft of the Amur tigers. . . ."

Frankie had eased into the living room to watch over Virgil's shoulders, and she said, "Man, she really screwed him, didn't she?"

"Well, he's a killer and a tiger snatcher," Virgil said.

"Wonder where she got his name?"

"She's got good sources," Virgil said. "Lot of cops kinda like her looks."

"And that BCA leaks like a sieve," Frankie said, giving him a cuff on the head. She'd heard Jones mentioned before, and not in a critical way. "If you ever get appointed director, you have to stop that."

"Yeah, I'll get right on it, the day the promotion comes through," Virgil said.

24

▼ ▼ ▼

After Flowers left, Peck popped a couple of Xanax and sat on his couch and tried to think it over, although the drug fogged him up for a while—enough that he later realized that he'd lost some time. He came back when the doorbell rang. Thinking it might be Flowers again and feeling simultaneously angry and chemically mellow, a confusing combination, he went to the front door and yanked it open.

An attractive thirtysomething woman was standing there, a smile on her face. He didn't immediately pick up the microphone in her hand or the cameraman standing off at an angle. What he felt first was the heat coming through the screen door; it was like opening an oven.

The woman said something and he frowned and asked, "What?"

She repeated herself: "Dr. Peck, we've heard from a number of law enforcement officials that you are suspected of being involved in the theft of the tigers from the Minnesota Zoo."

As she said that, a light came on to his left, blinding him, and he realized that he was talking to a reporter.

"That's ridiculous! Who are you? If you make this ridiculous charge public in any way, you'd better have a very good lawyer because I will sue you for every dime you have. . . ."

He went on for a while and then slammed the door.

Outside the house, Daisy Jones said to her cameraman, "That's about it; there ain't gonna be no more."

"Sounded pretty fucked up, man. That was drugs talking," said the cameraman, who'd know.

They got back in their van and started away from Peck's house, and a block and a half down the street, she noticed a familiar Crown Vic parked at the curb.

"Pull over next to that car," she told the cameraman, who was driving.

The cameraman pulled over next to the apparently empty Crown Vic, and Jones hopped out and walked around the back of the van and knocked on the driver's-side window. Jenkins had slumped over onto the passenger seat, trying to hide, but now he sat up and rolled down the window and Jones said, "You can't do surveillance from a Crown Vic, Jenkins. You need a Camry or something."

"Don't fit in a Camry," Jenkins said. "You get anything hot from Peck?"

"Yeah. A hot threat to sue us."

"You going with it?"

"Well, he didn't *exactly* deny taking the tigers; he said the charge is ridiculous and threatened to sue," Jones said. "So—yeah, we'll probably go with it. You and Virgie are using me to break him out, right?"

"We wouldn't do that, honeybun," Jenkins said.

"You call me 'honeybun' again, I'm going to jerk your tongue out of your mouth," Jones said.

"Honeybun, honeybun," Jenkins said. "You are a honeybun, Daisy. Anyway, why don't you go away so I can go back to being alert?"

"Right. America needs more lerts," Jones said. She looked down the street toward Peck's house and said, "If we put it on the air that he's under surveillance . . . could make him more nervous."

"Yeah, but it'd embarrass me with my boss," Jenkins said.

"Tough. I'll let my editor make the call on that one. Anyway, give me a ring the next time you're gonna beat up somebody. If it bleeds, it leads."

"I'll do that, if you don't say that thing about Peck being under surveillance," Jenkins said. "Now go away."

When the TV reporter left, Peck staggered into the bathroom and took down the tube of Xanax and looked into it. There were only seven little blue pills left and in one clear corner of his brain he thought, "My God, there were sixteen pills in here yesterday."

He put the tube in his pocket and tried to remember what he'd said to the TV reporter, but none of it was too clear. He went back to his reading chair and turned on the television, which was showing some horseshit cop show.

Another blank space went by, maybe an hour, and he came back when he saw his own face on the television, standing behind his own screen door. He sounded guilty in his own ears, and a little nuts, too: "I'll put some sue on your shirt. . . ."

"What?"

The woman said he was under surveillance. Really? He went to the front door and stepped out on the porch and looked both ways up and down the street. There were a few cars around, but he didn't see anybody lurking. The clear spot in his brain, which had grown a bit larger, said to him, "You won't see them, dummy. They're hiding."

He went back inside and sat in his reading chair. The weather report had come up on whatever TV channel he was on, and the weatherman, who looked like he'd been waxed, said it was hot outside. How hot was it? So hot that the hookers outside the Target Center were sucking on snow cones . . .

What? The weatherman hadn't really said that. . . .

Jenkins and Virgil were talking and Virgil, who'd seen the news broadcast after refusing to give a comment to Jones, said, "I don't know—he sounded like a chipmunk. I think he's been pounding his own medication or something. Then she went and said he was under surveillance. Thank you very much."

"Well, he was watching Jones, because right about the time the news came on, he came out on the porch and looked both ways. We got him on edge, that's for sure. I was thinking, maybe we ought to call Shrake and put him out behind the house, in case he tries to sneak out and make a run for it."

Virgil thought for a second, then said, "Let's keep Shrake in bed. I may need him tomorrow."

Peck slowly got sober. He was being watched. That fuckin' Flowers. Who did he think he was, anyway?

Good question: Who was he?

Peck got his laptop and typed in "Virgil Flowers BCA."

He still hit a few mental blank spots, when he found himself waking up without ever being aware that he had gone to sleep—or had gone somewhere, since he didn't think his eyes had closed—but over the next couple of hours, he gathered information about Flowers, who turned out to be a fairly dangerous man. Peck even remembered some of Flowers's cases, like the one with the Vietnamese spies and the one with the methamphetamine war out on the prairie with the maniac preacher.

Most interesting were two stories in the *Mankato Free Press*. One had come from the day before, reporting that a woman identified as a "close friend" of BCA Agent Virgil Flowers had been beaten up at a convenience store, according to Mankato police.

A BCA investigator named Catrin Mattsson had been sent to Mankato to determine whether there was any connection between the assault and Flowers's law enforcement activity. Flowers, Mattsson, and the victim, identified as Florence Nobles, a businesswoman who ran an architectural salvage operation, all refused to comment to the newspaper.

The other article, back a couple of years, reported that an unknown person had firebombed Flowers's garage. The fire was extinguished, with significant damage to the garage, but the piece mentioned that Flowers had managed to save his fishing boat, which had been parked inside. The really interesting thing about that article was that it listed Flowers's address.

Peck closed the laptop and closed his eyes at the same time, and sank back in his chair. Thought about it—mostly thought about it, there were still a few blank spaces in his internal time sequencing. He turned the computer back on, went to Google, typed in "How to make a Molotov cocktail."

The instructions he found were clear and simple, and he further reviewed the possibilities on YouTube. He shut the computer and thought some more. Ten minutes later, he was on his feet, a much larger clear place in his mind now; large enough that he considered taking another Xanax, but didn't.

Instead, he dug around in his kitchen drawers and found the two lamp-switch modules he used when he was out of town, which turned his lights off and on. He got a lamp from the living room, connected the lamp to the timer, and plugged it into an outlet in his main bathroom, next to his bedroom.

The other one he connected to a second lamp in the living room, and set it to turn the lamp off at two o'clock in the morning. The bathroom lamp would come on a minute later, and five minutes after that, turn off. From the outside, it would look like he quit working at two o'clock, had gone into the bathroom, spent a few minutes there, and then had gone to bed.

That done, he went into his bedroom and pulled on a dark blue shirt and black Levi's, black socks, and black Nikes. He found the ski mask he'd made Zhang Xiaomin pull down over his face the first time they went to the barn. He hesitated, then went to his bedroom closet, dug out the box at the bottom of it, lifted out a photobook, and below that, found the .38-caliber revolver that had belonged to his grandfather, and the half box of cartridges that went with the gun.

He loaded the gun carefully and put it in his sock. The gun pulled the sock down; that wasn't going to work. He remembered some knee-high compression socks that he'd bought for airline flights, and those worked fine and held the gun snugly to his calf.

There was still enough Xanax in his system to keep him calm about all of this, but he could feel a puddle of fear gathering in his stomach, ready to burst out. He pushed it down and went to the back door and sat and looked out the window. *Do it*, he thought, *or not*.

He did it.

When he saw neither movement nor light to his left or right, or in the house behind his, he slipped out the back door, into some bridal wreath bushes along the neighbors' property line, and sat and watched and listened again. Nothing. Moving carefully, he crossed behind his house, snuck across the alley, then between the two houses that backed up to his.

Emerging on the street on the other side, he set off for downtown St. Paul. Three miles, more or less, should take him forty-five minutes, if he moved right along.

And he moved right along, the gun seriously chafing at his calf; he was hot, but nearly invisible in the dark of night. Not invisible enough, though: he got mugged as he was walking down Selby Avenue, past Boyd Park, when a man stepped out of the trees and said, "Give me your fuckin' wallet."

The guy didn't look like a TV mugger: he was blond, well fed, was wearing a Town & Country Club golf shirt, tan pants with pleats, and tasseled loafers without socks. He crowded up on Peck, who tried to shrink away and cried out, "Don't hurt me," and the man said, "Give me your fuckin' wallet," and Peck fell on his butt and rolled on his side and said, "Don't hurt me," and the robber said, "Listen, man, give me your fuckin' wallet or I'll cut your nose off," and in the shifty illumination of a streetlight, flashed what to Peck looked like a screwdriver.

Peck had pulled up his jeans leg and he cried out, "All right, all right, don't hurt me."

The man looked around nervously and said, "Keep your voice down, shithead, gimme the fuckin' wallet. You got a watch. Is that a watch? Gimme the fuckin' watch and the wallet."

Peck pulled the gun out of his sock, but kept it behind his leg. "Can I ask you one question?"

"Give me the fuckin'—"

"Why'd you bring a fuckin' screwdriver to a gunfight?"

A few seconds of confused silence, then: "Whut?"

Peck pointed the pistol at the man's heart and said, "Back off."

The man said, "Listen, dude . . ."

Peck eased himself to his feet, kept the gun pointed at the man who was backing away, nervously watching the hole at the end of the gun's muzzle, which was shaking badly, and the man said, "Dude, I just wanted to get something to eat."

"I'll give you something," Peck said. "Gonna give you three steps. You know that song? I'm gonna give you three steps and then I'm gonna shoot you in the fuckin' kidneys. You better run . . ."

The man turned to run and Peck said, "No, no. Not that way—the other way."

The man turned and ran the direction Peck had just come from. When he was ten steps gone, Peck ran toward downtown. A block along, he stopped to look back, saw he wasn't being chased, and put the gun back in his sock. Now he really was hot, his shirt and socks soaked with sweat.

Ten minutes later, he was at the parking garage where he'd ditched Hamlet Simonian's car. He walked down a flight of stairs, which stank of years of damp and urine, and went to the car and pulled open the door. The keys were still jammed into the crack of the seat, and he got inside and closed his eyes.

Good so far.

25

▼ ▼ ▼

As Peck was running away from the mugger in St. Paul, Virgil and Frankie were falling asleep, holding hands. Virgil didn't intellectually blame himself for Frankie's injuries, but emotionally—well, he was supposed to take care of her, and she was supposed to take care of him. She hadn't gotten fully taken care of, so a bit of guilt was dog-paddling through his subconscious.

An hour and a half later, Frankie's phone went off. Virgil started, his eyes popped open, and he asked, "What the heck is that?"

"My phone . . . you'll have to get it . . . it's on the floor next to the bed. I forgot to turn it off."

Virgil walked around the bed and picked it up, as the ringing stopped. "It's Sparkle," he said. "She hung up."

"She knows better than to call now. There's trouble," Frankie said.

Virgil's phone started ringing on the windowsill. Virgil picked it up: Sparkle.

"Yeah?"

"Virgil! Are you in the Cities, or . . ."

"At my house, in Mankato."

"We're locked in the back bedroom—people are running through the yard here. I've got Bill and the kids with me . . ."

"What do you mean, running through the yard?"

"What I said! People are running through the yard. We can't see them, but we heard somebody yell. We don't know what to do."

"Stay locked up. If something bad happens, call me again," Virgil said. "I'm on my way, but it's gonna be fifteen minutes."

"Hurry, Virgil!"

Frankie asked, "What?"

"There's somebody running through the yard at your place, and no, you're not coming. I'm gonna have to hurry and the ride would kill you. I'll call you every five minutes."

Frankie tried to get out of bed, but groaned and sank back down. "Don't get hurt, Virgil. Don't get hurt."

Virgil pulled on his jeans and a Polo shirt and his running shoes, and he was out the door. In the garage, as the door rose up, he opened the back of the truck, unlocked the storage bin and took out his twelve-gauge and a box of FliteControl double-ought shells, and a high-powered LED lantern.

He stashed the gun and lantern in the passenger-side footwell and fifteen seconds later he was out of the garage and out of the driveway, hit the flashers, and rolled out of town at sixty miles an hour. Nice night, but hot, and late, not many cars on the road.

He drove north on 169 for a couple of miles, and then cut cross-country to Frankie's place. Since he drove it every day, he knew every pothole and bump in the road, but not every deer. He jumped a couple of does a few miles out, eye sparkle and a chamois-colored flash in a ditch. Hit his brakes as they ran through his headlights and bounded over a fence, still alive.

He was driving one-handed, talking to Sparkle on the cell phone in his other hand: there'd been more people running through the yard. Were they trying to frighten Sparkle and Bill, or was something else going on?

Virgil came up to the farm and saw, parked on the side of the road, a half-dozen vehicles, including one older pickup and five modest cars. His first thought was illegals: they looked like vehicles driven by illegal immigrants.

He drove down the driveway, and far ahead, saw a running man in a red shirt disappear into the field past the barn. At the house, he gathered up the shotgun, loaded it, and the LED lantern, then hopped out of the truck and crossed the porch and said into the phone: "Sparkle, I'm outside."

A minute later, Bill popped the door, with Sparkle and the youngest three of Frankie's kids crowded behind him.

"Who are they?" Bill asked.

"I don't know, but I saw one of them," Virgil said. "You guys stay here, I'm going to take a look."

"I'll come with you," Bill said.

"I really don't—"

"I'm coming," Bill said.

Virgil was happy to hear that and didn't protest any further. "C'mon then. They went out behind the barn."

Virgil told Sparkle to lock the doors and then he and Bill crossed the yard to the barn and Virgil walked past it, the shotgun pointed in the air, and then they heard people talking . . . female voices . . . and laughter.

"Ah, shit," Virgil said.

"What is it?"

"The cars were kind of messed up, so I thought it might be illegals," Virgil said. "You know, somehow pissed off about Sparkle. But it's not."

"What is it?"

"Best guess? High school kids skinny-dipping in the swimming hole. There are a few of them that know about it—they've been out here with Frankie's older boys."

Bill listened and sighed, and said, "I think you're right. I'm sorry we got you up. We didn't even think of that possibility, with people being beaten up."

"I don't blame you," Virgil said. "I want to go down and make sure."

"Maybe I should go tell Sparkle . . ."

Virgil held up the phone. "You can if you want. But I could call her."

"Maybe I'll come, then. Call Sparkle and tell her to call Frankie."

Virgil called Sparkle as they walked across the end of the hayfield in the moonlight, then walked past the "Occupied" sign and down the path to the swimming hole. It was dark in the hay field, and even darker back in the woods, but the people in the swimming hole had flashlights, so there was a bit of ambient light around, and Virgil and Bill emerged at the swimming hole where people were laughing and splashing in the cool water, and Virgil called, not too loud, "Hey, everybody! It's the cops."

Somebody groaned, "Oh, no," and Virgil turned on the LED lantern and found ten or twelve faces peering up at him from the water. A case of beer sat on the bank and the light scent of marijuana lay easily on the hot summer air. One of the girls, who wasn't totally covered by the water, said, "We're not causing any trouble. We wanted to get out of the heat."

"Yeah, well, you scared the heck out of the people in Ms. Nobles's house," Virgil said. "She was attacked a couple of days ago and beat up, and you know, running through the yard like that . . . they were afraid it was more trouble."

One of the boys said, "Jeez, I heard about that. You're Virgil, right?"

Virgil said, "Yeah."

The kid said, "I'm Cornelius Cooper's son. We used to come down here with Tall Bear. I thought it'd be all right. I'm sort of responsible."

"Okay. It's Chris, right? Listen guys, nobody drown, okay? And be quiet when you leave. Don't run and yell, just sneak out."

The Cooper kid said, "We can do that. Thanks."

"And call ahead the next time," Bill said.

There was a chorus of "Yeahs," and a few "Thanks, dude."

Virgil turned off the light and said, "Have a good time. Nice night for it. And . . . don't pee in the creek."

Virgil and Bill walked out of the woods, and Bill said, "You didn't say anything about the beer. I'm not sure they were all twenty-one."

Virgil laughed and said, "I don't think any of them were twenty-one. Chris Cooper was a senior last year, I think. I'm not really a good guy for arresting people for underage drinking. Or weed, either."

"You have some experience with that?"

"A lot of experience, actually," Virgil said. "You don't want to talk to my old man about it—he still gets pissed."

"Say, did you see the . . . ah, never mind."

"Yeah, I did," Virgil said. "Hormones gone wild."

"Beer, weed, and skinny-dipping," Bill said. He sounded happy about it. "It is just sort of Minnesota in the summertime, isn't it?"

26

▼ ▼ ▼

There was something terribly wrong with the air conditioner in Hamlet Simonian's car. The stench rolling out of the vents was so bad that Peck had to turn it off and roll the car windows down, as he motored east out of St. Paul to the farmhouse. Sweat began running in rivulets out of his hair and down his face, back, and chest.

By the time he pulled into the barnyard and got out, he was gasping for fresh air.

The farmhouse itself was barely functional and parts of it had actually been stripped out by vandals, but in the basement, there were at least a hundred Ball jars, once used for canning. He went down the basement stairs, batting face-sticking spiderwebs out of his way, and got the biggest jar he could see that also had a lid. The jar looked to be quart-sized, and old and delicate.

Out in the barn, Katya hissed at him like an alley cat—a really huge alley cat. Peck ignored her. When the tiger processing was complete, Peck and the Simonians had planned to fill the house and barn with corrugated cardboard moving boxes, douse them with gasoline, and burn the buildings to the ground.

The cardboard would guarantee a fast hot fire that would obliterate any sign of the stolen tigers, and Peck guessed that the fire—which would clearly be arson and which he didn't care about—would be blamed on the absentee owner.

Nice and tidy.

In preparing for that, they had collected four five-gallon cans of gasoline. He popped the top on one of the cans and filled the Ball jar to the top, put the lid on, and screwed the top down. Hayk Simonian's cotton-canvas butcher's apron still hung from a nail in the wall, and Peck cut off a thick strip of it, and wrapped it around the jar, creating an efficient Molotov cocktail.

With that done, he killed the barn lights and went back to the car, took it around the Cities exactly at the speed limit, and from the southwest corner of the metro area, turned it south down Highway 169 toward Mankato.

Toward Virgil's house.

His thinking was simple: he needed a day, or perhaps two, to finish as much as he was now planning to do with Katya. Most of Artur had come out of the dryer and needed to be run through the meat grinder, but that would only take a few hours at the most. He could do the work much more efficiently if he could get Flowers off his back. If Flowers's house burned, he suspected Flowers would be off his back, at least for long enough, looking for the people who'd first beat up his girlfriend and now had tried to burn down his house. Once Peck had burned the farmhouse and barn, and the processed tigers were on their way to California, Flowers could suck on it.

Peck had a vision of himself sitting in a rocking chair, smiling at Flowers, saying, "No, no, no, no, no . . ." He'd have to get a rocking chair.

The heat in the car became insufferable. He turned the air conditioner back on and suffered the stink. It actually smelled, Peck thought, like Simonian had taken a dump on the engine. But why would anybody . . . ?

Ten minutes after making the turn down Highway 169, the chemical remnants of the Xanax came back to bite him in the ass and he found the driver's-side tires running off the left edge of the highway. The bumping shook him awake and he jerked the car back into its own lane. The sudden change of direction knocked the jar of gasoline over. The seal wasn't quite tight, and gas started leaking into the car's backseat carpet.

As soon as Peck smelled it, he reached behind the seat and managed to get it upright, but the fumes were added to the residual stink of whatever was contaminating the air conditioner. He began to gag and finally turned the air conditioner off and rolled the windows down again. He drove stupidly into the night, and farther on, he wasn't sure how much, he crossed the Minnesota River, and about fifty large yellow-gutted insects splatted across the windshield, and a few whizzed past his ear into the backseat, where they spattered on the inside of the back windows.

Hunched over the steering wheel, barely able to see, Peck muttered, "A nightmare. A fuckin' nightmare."

The drive seemed to go on forever, but didn't. He pulled into an all-night gas station in St. Peter, wiped off the windshield, and sped away without going inside; being able to see made things better. An hour and a half after he left the barn, he drove slowly and quietly into Mankato.

The Xanax-free space in the back of his head began hinting

that his whole plan was insane, but the Xanax-saturated part ignored it.

Peck had drawn a quick sketch of the location of Flowers's house on a legal pad before he left his own home, but in the dark, he missed a few turns and had to go back a couple of times—and once saw a Mankato patrol car cross a street ahead of him.

"Not good for morale, Winston," he muttered. "Not good."

When he finally got onto Flowers's street, he found it to be narrow and moon-shadowed by trees arcing over the blacktop. Pretty in the daytime, dark as tar in the night. A lot of the houses either had no numbers, or no numbers that could be seen in the dark. One white house had a bright yellow porch light on outside, and he could see that the idiot owners had painted the house numbers white. How could anybody see them?

The first set of numbers he *could* see suggested he was two blocks from Flowers's place. He idled on down that way, through two stop signs, saw a number that suggested he'd passed Flowers's, went on another block, did a careful U-turn, and came back. He had a choice of three houses: one of them had to be Flowers's, but they were all dark.

The first house looked to be too high on the numbers list. The middle one had an attached garage and he remembered from the firebomb newspaper story that Flowers's garage had been the target of the bomber. The next house down the street had a detached garage, and why would anyone bomb a detached garage if they were targeting the owner?

Logic had spoken: had to be the middle one.

Peck was sweating even more heavily now, fear adding pressure to the heat, all of it still ameliorated by the residual Xanax in his brain. Do it, or not?

The residual Xanax won.

He fumbled the jar out of the backseat, unscrewed the top enough to leak some gasoline onto the apron rag, made sure he had his Bic lighter, left the car running, got out, ran across the yard to the side of the house—ran so he wouldn't have a chance to change his mind—fired the Bic lighter into the rag, which ignited with a low-running yellow flame, and heaved the jar through a side window.

There was an instantaneous mushroom of fire inside the house and he ran back to the car and took off, turning the first corner he came to.

Now he was exultant. "Did it, did it," he said aloud. "People sometimes meet guys like Winston Peck the Sixth, and they say, 'I didn't think he could do it, I guess I just didn't know.' Yeah, you just didn't know, you asshole. . . ."

An hour and a half later, still talking to himself about the bombing, and after another encounter with the yellow-gutted bugs crossing back over the Minnesota River, he found a parking spot six blocks from his house in St. Paul, and did a reentry that was exactly the opposite of his exit.

Once in the house, he peeled off the ski mask and went into the bathroom to wash his face. There, he caught sight of himself in the mirror: he'd never seen anything like it. Winston Peck the doctor had been replaced by Winston Peck the terrorist-attack survivor.

His thinning hair, soaked with sweat and dirt, stood away from his head like the Cowardly Lion's in *The Wizard of Oz*. His face was a fiery red, and a rash had broken out across his nose and cheeks. His mouth hung open, and he really couldn't seem to keep it closed.

He stood in a cool shower for five minutes, dried off, collapsed naked on his bed, but his mind was still screaming. He lay rigid for three minutes, maybe five minutes, his brain rerunning the gasoline explosion, then crawled out of bed and found the tube of Xanax.

"Just one more," he said to himself. He popped two, on second thought, and went back to the bed and was out before he had time to pull a sheet over himself.

27

▼ ▼ ▼

Virgil was on his way home when Frankie called: "I was going to wait for you to get here, but I'm exhausted. I've got to get to sleep. Everything is okay at the farm, right?"

"Yeah, Sparkle said she talked to you . . ."

"Some kids out skinny-dipping."

"Yup. I had to talk your boys out of going down there," Virgil said. "If they'd gotten a good look at those girls, they'd have been locked in the bathroom for the rest of the summer."

"But that wouldn't apply to you?"

"Nah. I'm well taken care of."

"Thank you. I'm taking a couple of painkillers and going to sleep. Try to be quiet when you come in."

Virgil stopped at a convenience store and bought a bottle of orange juice, rolled his truck windows down—it was finally beginning to cool off—and put his elbow out and drank the juice.

With the windows down, he could hear the sudden blast of sirens from Mankato.

If it was cops, Virgil thought, there's a riot going on. More likely the fire department. He rolled across the Highway 14 bridge into town and realized that the sirens seemed to be heading toward the general area of his house, which didn't worry him much, until he got off at the North Riverfront exit and realized that the sirens, and now the flashing lights, were really close to his house, and when he turned onto his street and saw the lights straight ahead, and a cop blew past him with sirens screaming through his open windows, he thought, *Holy shit, that IS my house.*

He instantly thought of Frankie, who'd taken those painkillers to knock herself out, and he floored his truck and blew through a couple of stops signs until . . .

Wait. That's not my house.

It was, in fact, the house next to his house. He couldn't get all the way down to it, because of the fire trucks, and he had to park on the block behind his house. All the neighbors were out in the yards watching, and Virgil saw the couple who owned the house behind his, and he called, "Jack, hey, you guys—what happened?"

Jack's wife, Emmy, said, "We thought it was a gas explosion or something, but when we ran out here, we could smell gasoline. Not natural gas, car gas."

"Did the Wilsons get out?"

"Yeah, we talked to them. They said something blew up in their kitchen. I think they're around in the front."

Virgil trotted over to his house and let himself in through the back, and Frankie called, "Virgie?"

"Yeah. I was afraid it was here, and you'd be asleep."

She was standing in the front room, wrapped in a terry-cloth robe, looking out through the side windows. "The firemen came pounding on the doors, said I might have to leave, but they put the fire out and they came back and said I was okay. For ten minutes, it was like the end of the world around here."

"You okay?"

"Not entirely. I gotta go back and lie down. I'm not sleepy anymore, but those pills got me feeling like the undead."

Virgil took her back to the bedroom, tucked her in, and said, "I gotta get out there and find out what happened. Jack and Emmy made it sound a little strange."

"Like how?"

"Like there was gasoline involved. I'm gonna talk to the fire guys."

"Careful."

A fire lieutenant named Carl Beard saw Virgil walking through the crowd of neighbors and came over and said, "You gotta quit this shit, Virgil."

"What happened?"

"The Wilsons were sleeping and something blew up in their kitchen, and Kyle went running in there and found the whole place on fire. Janet called us and Kyle sprayed it with his fire extinguisher and knocked it down a little, and then the extinguisher ran out and they went outside and waited for us. We shut it down, but you could smell gasoline all over the place—and Kyle said there was no gasoline in the house."

"It's like when . . ."

"Yeah. Like when that preacher firebombed your garage. Same deal. After we put the fire out, I looked in the kitchen, which is pretty scorched, and the kitchen sink is full of broken glass and there's a piece of burnt rag in there. . . . It was a bomb."

"Goddamnit. You think it was aimed at me?"

"Kyle sorta hinted at that. He said nobody's mad at him, but a lot of people might be mad at you. You've been in the newspaper, a little bit, with your girlfriend."

Wilson worked as the service manager at a car dealership and was generally known as a friendly guy. He had, on occasion, mown Virgil's grass when Virgil had been out of town a few days too many, and they'd always been invited to each other's barbeques.

"I better talk to him," Virgil said.

"Maybe you better—but I'll tell you, Virg, this wasn't any prank or anything like that," Beard said. "The dipshit who threw the bomb wanted to burn the place down and he didn't care who got hurt."

The Wilsons were standing on the other side of the fire trucks. Virgil went over and found them talking to their insurance agent, who was also Virgil's agent and who lived in the neighborhood. When Kyle Wilson saw Virgil coming, he prodded his wife with his elbow and said, affably enough, "We were thinking about remodeling anyway."

Virgil said, "Hey, Kyle, Janet. Uh . . . I kinda know what you might think. I hope it's not true."

Janet said, "Who knows? We can't think of why anybody would do this to *us*. If it really was a firebomb."

Kyle said, "We're pretty sure it was a bomb. We actually heard it hit, we heard the window break and glass shatter, then *whoosh*."

"Nobody upset about a car repair or anything?"

Kyle shook his head. "Wouldn't be aimed at me, even if it was. I don't do the customer contact and I don't fix the cars—I supervise the mechanics and everything I do is in-house. You'd have to fish around to even find my name."

Virgil nodded. "All right. I helped arrest a guy last night. He's in jail, but he had an accomplice and he's still out there. We'll nail him down pretty quick, and I'll find out whether he did this."

The insurance agent said to Virgil, "Their policy covers all the damage, and we'll get an adjuster on it tomorrow. It'd be helpful if you or the Mankato police could find out who did it, and let me know. There would be the possibility of some civil recovery from the perpetrator, if he has any assets at all."

"I'll call you," Virgil said. He looked up at the house. "What a mess."

Virgil got back to the house, took a quick shower, and got back in bed. Frankie, talking in the dark, asked, "You think it was you? Or us?"

Virgil rolled toward her, had to think about it for a moment, then said, "Probably. It's hard to see the house numbers in the night and the guy that Catrin is looking for is no genius. I don't know why he'd come after me, though."

"Because he's pissed off and he's a mean redneck?"

"He's gotta know by now that we're looking for him and that we're not going away," Virgil said. "He'd know it'd be an aggravating circumstance if he was identified, and he's no virgin. A couple of years in prison for assault is way different than an ag assault charge, or attempted murder, or even murder, if there'd been somebody standing in the kitchen, or even arson, for that matter. He could be doing a six-pack for throwing the bomb."

Frankie said, "Hmm." And a moment later, "What if it's the people who stole the tigers? Trying to make you go away?"

"That occurred to me," Virgil said.

"What do you think?"

"I don't know what to think," Virgil said. "It could even have been aimed at the Wilsons. But there have been two murders tied to the tigers. Winston Peck? It's possible, but I really don't know. I will know, though. Sooner or later, I'll know."

28

▼ ▼ ▼

Jenkins could barely remember what it was like doing surveillance before he got his phone-linked iPad, but he could remember the feeling: it was brutal. An overnight watch could still be deeply boring, but now he could prop the iPad on the steering wheel and browse the 'net while still keeping an eye on the target, and, in the end, get the BCA to pay for his Verizon text charges.

Until four o'clock in the morning, the target had been pretty quiet. After he'd stepped out on his porch to look for surveillance, Peck had gone back inside and hadn't stuck his head out since. The television had gone off before two o'clock, though there was still a light in the living room. Then that went off, and a light in the back of the house had come on—bathroom or bedroom, Jenkins thought—and then that one went off, too.

Jenkins read a couple of investment forums, a news forum, a forum that specialized in Chuck Norris jokes ("What do you get when you play Led Zeppelin's 'Stairway to Heaven' backward? The sound of Chuck Norris banging your mom."), and a gun forum and was browsing men's Purple Label suits on the Ralph Lauren website when things began to pick up.

A few minutes after four, as Jenkins was checking out a white silk gabardine suit for $4,995, an RV pulled up outside Peck's house and six heavyset men spilled out into the street.

Jenkins said, "Oh, shit," and picked up the phone and called Virgil.

Virgil groaned when the phone went off, groped for it on the windowsill next to the bed, and asked, "What?"

Jenkins said, "The Simonians just arrived in their RV. They're going up to Peck's house. What do I do if they kidnap him?"

Virgil took a second to pull his head together, and said, "Ah, man—Jenkins, you gotta get over there and break it up."

"You know, if they beat on him a little bit, it might encourage . . ."

"No! Daisy knows you're sitting there. She'd know that you let them take Peck," Virgil said.

"Ah, shit, you're right. I'm going," Jenkins said.

"Try not to shoot anyone."

"Gotta go, they're beating his door down."

"Call me back!"

Frankie said, "Now what?"

Virgil said, "Tell you later" and fell facedown on his pillow and was almost instantly asleep. Peck, at that same moment, was knocked out of bed by what sounded like an earthquake. With the two Xanax holding him down, he didn't notice that he was naked, and not only naked but sporting a substantial erection. He lurched out of the bedroom to the front door, which he yanked open. A crowd of men stood on his porch, and all seemed to step back when they spotted his hard-on pointing at them, then one of them tried to yank open the locked aluminum door and, when that didn't happen, punched a fist directly through the screen.

Peck almost lost his balance and tried to turn to run, but then a siren bleeped in the street and an unmarked car pulled to the curb showing police flashers, and a large man jumped out of the car and shouted, "Get out of there. Simonians—get out of there."

Peck slammed the door and stood in the hallway for a moment, wondering what he was doing standing naked in the hallway with an erection. Maybe he'd been masturbating? He didn't think so. He stumbled back to bed and fell asleep.

On the porch, the Simonians confronted Jenkins, who said, "I oughta arrest every fuckin' one of you guys. You can't go driving around town kidnapping people, for Christ's sakes. . . ."

"He cut the arms off Hamlet and the legs off Hayk," said Levon Simonian, their spokesman. "We gonna cut off his pecker and make him eat it."

"That's a worthwhile thought, but not here," Jenkins said. "It'd cause all kinds of trouble. You guys get back in your RV and get the fuck out of here. I don't want to see you back here again. If I do, I'll kick your ass."

"You think you can take all of us?" the youngest of the Simonians asked.

Jenkins did a quick survey—except for the youngest one, they were all middle-aged and fat, though they showed signs of having done a few million bench presses—and said, "Yes."

They spent a few seconds in a stare-down and then Levon Simonian said, "We should complain to the police force in St. Paul that this man walks around free, while Hamlet has no arms and Hayk has no legs."

"You do that," Jenkins said. "First thing tomorrow morning. Right now, let me tell you about Mickey's Diner. . . ."

Five minutes later, he had the RV on its way to Mickey's, and Jenkins called Virgil.

"What?"

"I ran them off. You want me to sit here some more? Peck saw me," Jenkins said.

"No. Go home. Sleep. Don't call me again," Virgil said.

"You sound a little snappish."

Click.

"And very un-Virgil-like," Jenkins said to the dead phone.

He went home.

At seven-thirty in the morning, Virgil was getting into his second round of REM sleep when the phone rang again and he vaulted out of bed, grabbed it, and shouted, "What?"

After a couple of seconds of silence on the other end, a man's voice said, "This is Rudd. I'm the highway patrol guy who helped you follow that Zhang Ferrari into Minneapolis?"

"What?" Confused now, and quieter.

"I thought I should call and tell you, in case you hadn't heard, the Minneapolis cops just pulled old man Zhang's body out from behind a Dumpster at a strip club."

"What?"

Rudd had gotten the news by monitoring his radio, and finally by a call to the Minneapolis cops because of his involvement with tracking the Ferrari. When he was told that Zhang was dead, he thought to call Virgil.

"Thank you," Virgil said. "This is a big deal—this is the third murder in the tiger hunt."

Frankie was awake now and she groaned and said, "Bad night."

"I gotta go," Virgil said.

"You okay?"

"I feel like somebody hit me on the head with a phone book."

He stood in the shower for five minutes, switching between hot and cold, shaved, got back in the shower, and dressed. Frankie had eased out of bed while he was cleaning up and gave him a thirty-ounce Yeti Rambler container of coffee to take with him. Forty-five minutes after Rudd's call, he was headed back north to the Cities; he'd had maybe four hours of sleep after a whole series of sleep-deprived nights and was feeling it. The coffee helped.

On the way north, he called the Minneapolis cops and talked to a homicide detective named Anderson Huber. "A garbage guy found him about five o'clock this morning when they were moving a Dumpster. Missing his wallet, a five-carat diamond pinky ring, and a watch that his kid says is worth a hundred grand, though that's a little hard to believe. He said it was a Filipino something-or-other. My partner wrote it down, if you're interested. Anyway, he'd been dead for several hours, but a good time of death might be hard to come up with because his body was superheated. . . ."

"How's that?" Virgil asked.

"He was behind the strip club, that's the Swedish Bikini Bar, and they got a stove vent that comes out of a wall right above the Dumpster. Warm enough that you get bums sleeping back there in the winter. Last night, might have been a hundred and fifty degrees back there, so . . . he was superheated. On the upside, he smells like a whole lot of expensive cheeseburgers."

"Shot?"

"No. Strangled. Rope was still around his neck, nylon rope, pretty small diameter, that parachute-cord stuff, you can get it anywhere," Huber said. "I wouldn't be surprised if the killer has rope creases or bruises on his hands, because this thing really got dragged on."

"What does his son say?" Virgil asked.

"We're talking to him now. He's pretty screwed up. He tried to file a missing persons report last night; he called 911 a couple of times, but you know . . . the old man was an adult, nothing wrong with him, not mentally ill or incapacitated, and the son told the 911 operator that his old man sometimes liked to go out and look at girls. We thought maybe he'd found a hooker and was getting his ashes hauled."

"You look at the kid's hands?"

"Yeah. Nothing there. I'll tell you what, Virgil, it's possible, I guess, that the kid killed him, because as I understand it, the Zhang guy's got a lot of money, and the kid stands to inherit. But when he freaked, it's hard to believe that he was faking it. Me and my partner went to tell him—we knew about him because of the 911 calls—and if he was faking, he ought to get an Academy Award. We had to sit him down to keep him from falling down, and he was bawling like a little girl. Not fake bawling, real bawling. Then when we took him to identify the body, he started all over again."

"All right, I'm going to tell you who did it, or at least who knows who did it."

"I'd appreciate that."

Virgil gave Huber everything he had on the tiger case and told him that he believed Peck was involved in at least two murders, and now, quite possibly, a third. "I believe if he didn't do it, he knows who did. He does know the kid."

"I'll go ring his doorbell," Huber said.

"Before you do that, ask the kid if he thinks Peck was involved in the murder. Sneak up on him, and then whack him with it. See what his face says."

"Where are you at right now?"

"Highway 169 south of the Cities. I'll be up there about nine-thirty," Virgil said.

"How about we keep him here until then, and *you* whack him—since you've got the background, you might be able to riff on something we don't even know about."

"Happy to. I'll see you then," Virgil said.

Traffic was bad going into town, but Virgil found a police-reserved parking spot next to City Hall and put out his BCA dashboard sign, then hustled into what he believed might be one of the ugliest city halls in the country. He found Huber, who took him down to the office of a homicide lieutenant named Kevin Howser, where Zhang Xiaomin was sitting in a visitor's chair, typing on a laptop, while the lieutenant was talking on his phone.

Zhang's face looked raw, Virgil saw, as though he'd been weeping all night, and his eyes were bloodshot. He looked up when he saw Virgil and his eyes shifted. Virgil thought, *Okay, he knows who I am.*

Howser got off the phone and crooked a finger at them and said, "Virgil, how you doing?"

"Could be worse," Virgil said. Then: "Wait—let me think about that."

"You haven't found the tigers."

"Not yet," Virgil said. Zhang was sneaking peeks at him. "I'm hoping Mr. Zhang can help us with that. He's good friends with our leading suspect who we think might also have murdered his father and a couple of other people. What about that, Mr. Zhang?"

Zhang pretended to be startled, but he wasn't, and the three cops exchanged a quick flicker of glances. Zhang said, "What are you talking about? Who are you?"

"You know who I am," Virgil said. "We met in the Cub supermarket, but I didn't know it at the time. Who tipped you off? Was Peck out in the parking lot?"

Zhang's head seemed to sink an inch or two into his chest, and he said, "I don't know what this officer is talking about. I know this Peck man, but I only get medicine for my father."

"Tiger medicine?" Virgil asked. "Was your old man the West Coast distributor?"

Zhang's head seemed to sink an inch farther into his chest: "I don't know their business. My father didn't tell me. I only bought small medicine from Dr. Peck, for my father."

Virgil said, "You're full of shit, Zhang. I know you're involved and I'm gonna put you in prison for it. The big question now is, did you help kill your father?"

Zhang's head came up and he shouted, "I did not kill my father. I did not. You go away. Go away."

Virgil jerked his head at Howser and Huber to get them out in the hall, and Huber said in a low voice, "Okay, I see him now. He's involved."

Virgil said, "Do me a favor. Get your crime-scene guys to take a look at his dirty clothes and the driver's seat in his car. If they pick up a single tiger hair . . ."

"We can do that," Howser said. "I agree with Huber—he knows something that he's not telling us. I didn't see that in him until now. Since we talked to you on the phone, we took a look at old man Zhang online, and there's an article in *Forbes* that said that he got out of China with more than a hundred million dollars, and another small item from a Chinese American society rag from LA that says he's about to get married again. His kid might think that money is going away."

Howser asked Virgil to make a formal statement about his observations of Zhang; they could already go through the father's belongings at the hotel because there wasn't any question of a crime in his case, and because he'd ridden in a car under suspicious circumstances, they could also look at the car. What they needed from Virgil was anything that would allow them to look at the son's possessions. Virgil didn't have much, but with the right judge, they might get a warrant.

Virgil was making the statement when Catrin Mattsson called: "I think I found Blankenship. You still in bed?"

"No, I'm up at the Minneapolis PD," Virgil said.

"Great. He's at a biker friend's house in Falcon Heights. I'm on my way up there. What are you doing up so early?"

Virgil told her about the murder of Zhang, and she whistled. "That's three. The tigers don't look so important anymore. You've got to get this guy off the street."

"Yeah, I do. Did you hear about the fire?" Virgil asked.

"What fire?"

He told her about the fire, and the question of who might be behind it. "We'll get Blankenship and squeeze his turnip-like head," Mattsson said. "I got his location from his brother, who hates him. His brother got it from their mom, who also apparently hates him."

"How far out are you?"

"I went through Jordan a few minutes ago," Mattsson said. "What's that, forty-five minutes?"

"I'll meet you at the office in forty-five minutes. If this guy is with a biker friend, maybe I ought to get Shrake to back us up."

"I'll buy that."

Virgil called up Jon Duncan, told him about the murder of Zhang and about the pending arrest of Blankenship. "I need Shrake, if I can get him."

"I saw him here a few minutes ago," Duncan said. "If you had to guess . . . how long before you wrap the tiger thing?"

"Tomorrow? The Minneapolis cops are going to squeeze Zhang the younger, and I doubt that he'll hold out. Not completely hold out, anyway. I wouldn't be surprised if he gives up Peck. I think Zhang will know about the tigers."

"Good. That's good," Duncan said. "Man, three dead. This really turned into something. Virgil? Remember what I said about you and Blankenship. You can go, but let the other guys carry the load. We don't need him walking around loose, but we don't need him shoving a lawyer down our throat, claiming that you violated his civil rights or some shit like that. Don't touch him."

"I won't even take my gun with me."

"I wasn't worried about you shooting him, Virgil. You couldn't hit the side of a barn from the inside—"

"Hey!"

"I was worried about you breaking his face. Oh, yeah, I was supposed to remind you: you're up to qualify again. Get your pistol and stop by the range as soon as you're done with this tiger thing. So: day after tomorrow? At the range?"

29

▼ ▼ ▼

Shrake had called Jenkins, who had been getting up anyway, so both the BCA thugs met Virgil and Mattsson in Jon Duncan's office at BCA headquarters. Duncan himself was at a meeting to discuss security at the state fairgrounds, trying to figure out what might blow up, if anything might. The Secret Service wanted the state to hire septic system inspectors to put cameras down all the water lines, but the state was pleading poverty.

"If I was involved in that particular disaster, I might go looking for a security-guard job at the Mall of America," Shrake said.

Jenkins asked Mattsson, "Blankenship's brother hates him? What'd he do to his brother?"

"Both Brad Blankenship and his brother, George, were interested in the same woman, one Ellen Frye of Henderson, Minnesota. I talked to her yesterday. She's a hot little number, but not entirely what you'd call a one-man woman," Mattsson said.

Shrake said, "Ah. The brothers became competitive."

"If it was only that, there might not have been any trouble," Mattsson said. "Ellen Frye sees that Brad is not such a good risk, and so she slides on over to George. One thing leads to another, she gets pregnant, and George does the right thing and marries her. They're married for two days when a DVD arrives in the mail, from Brad. Seems that she and Brad had done a little experimentation on camera. Even worse, it wasn't a selfie porno. There was a cameraman in the room. George is an unhappy man right now."

"It's exactly this kind of thing that can create stress in a family tree," Jenkins said.

Virgil raised a finger. "I'm as interested in porno gossip as the next guy, but uh . . . any hint that Blankenship might carry a gun? You know anything about his biker friend? I'd hate to run into some cop-hating Nazi without seeing it coming."

They all looked at Mattsson, who said, "I ran the biker—name is Dougie Howe—and he's been picked up a few times on dope charges, small amounts of weed and small amounts of heroin, and twice for DUI, plus a boatload of speeding tickets. That's about it. No violence on the record. He runs a home-based motorcycle customizing business called Harley Heaven. Blankenship is the guy we have to worry about. He's flashed guns a few times, but never pulled a trigger, as far as we know."

Shrake asked, "Armor up?"

Virgil said, "It's really hot."

"I don't think we'll need it," Mattsson said. "A Sibley County deputy told me Blankenship's a puncher, not a shooter."

Jenkins said, "Yeah, fuck it. Who's driving?"

They went in two cars: Virgil's 4Runner and Shrake's truck. Mattsson rode with Virgil and said, "Alvarez is out of the hospital. She looked worse going in, but wasn't actually as bad as Frankie."

"Frankie's gonna be hurting for a while," Virgil said. "She can't find a comfortable way to sleep."

"I know—but don't take it out on Blankenship. You really do have to be a little careful here."

"I already got the lecture from Jon," Virgil said. "I've also got the TV people hanging on me about the tiger thing. They haven't figured out that Zhang is connected, but they will. I gotta get back on that, but I want to do this one, too. I want to be there when you get him."

After a moment, Mattsson said, "You know, the only reason Blankenship is getting any attention at all is because you're a BCA agent and the whole question of why Frankie was beaten up. We know the answer to that, and it doesn't have anything to do with you. Or Frankie. They got the wrong woman. Ordinarily, an assault, even a bad one, isn't going to pull in four BCA agents."

"I know, I know. But when it's all said and done, Frankie's still hurt—and then, there's the firebomb last night."

"Yeah. The firebomb. You agree that it's possible that the firebomb could have come from the tiger job, if it was aimed at you at all."

"Possible. I want to see what Blankenship has to say about that. I want to see his face."

Dougie Howe lived in a neighborhood of ranch-style houses a few blocks from the University of Minnesota's golf course, where Virgil had whiled away some time as a bad golfer: he'd always preferred team sports to solo games like golf or archery. Howe's house was visible from two blocks away. It didn't exactly have a bluetick coonhound lolling in the shade of a short-block

Chevy engine that hung from a sassafras tree in the front yard, but it was over in that direction, with bits and pieces of motorcycles lining the driveway and scattered around the front yard. A bumper sticker on the side of the mailbox said, "Forget the Dog, Beware of Owner."

A red Ford pickup was parked at the curb in front of the house next to Howe's, and Mattsson said to Virgil, "That's Blankenship's truck. He's here."

"Good," Virgil said. "We can tie it up here."

Shrake called on Virgil's cell, which Virgil switched over to the speaker: "Who's gonna knock?"

Mattsson said, "You and me, Shrake. I want Jenkins on the side of the house to the left, because he's the sprinter among us, and Virgil down the side of the house to the right. Everybody good with that?"

Everybody was good with it.

Shrake and Mattsson walked up to the house. The front door was open, although there was a screen door in front of it. Mattsson pushed the doorbell, which didn't work, so she knocked on the aluminum screen door, and a man yelled, "C'mon in, whoever it is. I'm in the kitchen."

Virgil got a phone call: a BCA number. He rejected it for the time being.

Out front, Mattsson and Shrake looked at each other and Mattsson said, "Sure." Shrake pulled his pistol and held it by his leg, and they both walked back to the kitchen where Howe was sitting at a counter with a little girl, both of them eating bowls of cereal. Howe was a fat man, bald, with a blond beard that had been twisted into a number of pigtails; he wore rimless glasses, a T-shirt, and cargo shorts. He asked, "Who are you?"

"We're with the Bureau of Criminal Apprehension," Mattsson said. "Where's Brad?"

Howe cocked his head back and asked, "Cops? He didn't say anything about the cops looking for him."

"Well, we are," Shrake said.

Howe shrugged and shouted, "Hey, Brad, there are some cops here looking for you."

Two seconds later, a door banged open in the back of the place and Howe said, "Shit, he ran out the back patio. . . ."

Shrake ran toward the sound of the door and Mattsson ran back out the front door and yelled, "He's running, he's running. . . ."

Virgil had some problems on his side of the house. He'd been standing near the back corner of Howe's house when a woman screamed from the house next door, "Dan, Dan, there's a man, there's a man, there's a man looking in the bedroom window."

Virgil turned that way and a man shouted out the window, "What the fuck?"

Virgil said, as quietly as he could, and still be audible, "I'm a cop and I'm not looking in your window. . . ."

The man looked at Virgil's long blond hair, the band T-shirt, and the cowboy boots and said, "Bullshit you're a cop."

The woman, somewhere inside but not visible, shouted, "Get your gun, Dan. . . ."

At that moment, from the front of the house, Mattsson screamed, "He's running, he's running. . . ."

Virgil turned to Howe's backyard and saw Blankenship bolt across the yard, stepping through ankle-deep water in a child's plastic swimming pool as he went. There was a chain-link fence across the back of Howe's lot, and he vaulted the waist-high fence with Jenkins, and then Shrake, behind him. Virgil followed as far as the fence, then thought to turn back to the house, in case Howe might be a threat, but a barefoot Howe had come out on the patio with the little girl. He said to Virgil, "He didn't say nothing about cops looking for him."

"How long has he been here?" Virgil asked.

"Since yesterday."

A man ran around the corner of the house. He was carrying a huge shiny revolver, saw Virgil, pointed the pistol generally in Virgil's direction, and hollered: "Hold it."

Howe shouted, "What the fuck are you doing, Dan? These are cops."

The man hesitated, then said, "Oh," and pointed the gun at the ground.

Virgil said, "There are three other cops here. If they see that gun, they could kill you."

A woman jogged around the corner of the house in a bathrobe. She stopped behind Dan, pointed at Virgil, and said, "That's him, Dan."

Howe said, "They're cops, Jane. They're gonna kill you guys if they see that fuckin' gun."

Dan said to the woman, "We better get back inside."

The little girl said to Virgil, "My dad said 'fuckin'.'"

"That happens, sometimes, honey," Virgil said. He heard Jenkins shouting something from what seemed to be down the block, but more toward the front yard. Virgil said, "I better get out there."

He ran back down the side of the house and, in the front yard, saw Blankenship sprinting toward his truck, with Jenkins twenty yards behind. Shrake was out of sight somewhere, but Mattsson was standing near the back end of Blankenship's truck, raking leaves. The rake had the fan-type thin, wide blades made for lawn care, rather than the heavy tangs of a garden rake.

It worked well enough, though, especially when Blankenship tried to run past her, and she lifted the rake and swatted him in the face. He went down on his back, and Jenkins was on top of him before he got reorganized, flipped him over, and snapped on the cuffs. Shrake came puffing up a minute later as Jenkins and Mattsson were putting Blankenship in the back of Virgil's truck. Blankenship was bleeding from three fan-shaped cuts on his face.

"What happened to him?" Shrake asked.

"Catrin hit him in the face with the rake," Virgil said, nodding to the rake that was now lying on the neighboring lawn.

"I'm liking this chick better all the time," Shrake said. He looked down at his tan pants, which had two-foot-long grass stains on the legs. "I fell or I would have been here for it. Goddamnit, I miss all the fun stuff."

Blankenship was cuffed to the ring welded to the floor in the back of Virgil's truck. He said, "I'm gonna sue you motherfuckers. . . ."

"Shut up," Virgil said, as he got in the truck, "or I'll tell all your friends in Mankato that you got your ass kicked by a woman."

"She ambushed me," Blankenship said.

"I'd lie about it," Virgil said. "Now shut up."

"I want a lawyer."

"Yeah, yeah, yeah. Shut up."

"My face is all cut up. I'm bleeding," Blankenship said.

"Throw a little dirt on it," Virgil said.

Mattsson added, "And shut up."

They went by the BCA, and Mattsson picked up her car and followed Virgil over to the Ramsey County jail, where she took Blankenship inside and told Virgil, "Go find the tigers."

"Yeah. Catrin: thanks. I appreciate what you've done."

He couldn't decide whether to shake Mattsson's hand or hug her, but didn't do either when she simply nodded, stepped back, and said, "Nice working with you, Virgil. Let's do it again."

30

▼ ▼ ▼

Virgil left the jail and, as he headed out of the parking lot, checked his phone. Two missed calls from the same personal number, and he thought it might belong to Sandy, the BCA researcher.

He was right. "Virgil," she said. She sounded breathless. "Where have you been?"

"Arresting a guy, nothing to do with the tigers. What happened?"

"You know I was tracking that phone that belonged to Hamlet Simonian? Well, I figured it out."

"Where is it?"

"It *was* in Oakland, California—at a FedEx place. Whoever sent it, shipped it ground so we'd think somebody was driving it across country," Sandy said.

"Ah, hell. Is it still there?"

"No, it's in a truck heading south, toward Los Angeles. It should be there in a couple of hours. But here's the thing—it's an iPhone, and iPhones have their location services on by default. That means if we get the phone and if it's not password protected, and he hasn't turned off the location services, we can open up the privacy section and see everywhere the phone's been. Like, if he went to where the tigers were, we would probably get an exact address."

"We need that. Right now. You think the phone is headed toward LA?"

"Yes. Probably in a semitruck, which would be a huge load of packages, but I talked to FedEx and everything on the truck will be sorted for local delivery, which means we can probably narrow it down to one delivery truck. From there, we ought to be able to find it."

"Do you have a date this evening?" Virgil asked.

"What?"

"If I get Jon to put you on a plane, are you up for a quick trip to LA?"

"Well . . . sure. But I gotta tell you, it could be password protected, and Apple doesn't help you crack those. Even if you're a cop."

"I know all about Apple and I also know that when we searched Hamlet Simonian's room, we found a little book that seems to be full of passwords. Pack your party panties and get out to the airport—you're going," Virgil said. "I'll call Jon right now and get him to authorize a ticket. And a hotel with a pool."

"Oh my God. All right. I'll be on my phone."

Virgil called Duncan, who said he'd fix it and put Sandy on the first flight into LAX.

If Sandy could find out where Hamlet Simonian had been, Virgil thought . . . and then he thought, *Wait a minute. We've got phones closer than LA.*

He called Minneapolis homicide, got Howser on the phone. "Does Zhang have an iPhone?"

"Yeah. He's also got a lawyer, who's standing right behind him," Howser said. "And we really don't have enough to hold him."

"Damnit. Ask him anyway; ask him if he'll let you look in his iPhone. Don't specify what you're looking for, but you might hint you want to look at his messages. Then you go to the privacy settings, see if the location services are turned on, and if they are, look at the phone's history and tell me where it's been the last few days."

"I can ask, but I'll tell you, he's got Horace Turner here. You know him, the attorney? No? Well, Horace is an asshole of Jovian dimensions. The chances of him letting me look are slim and none."

"And slim is out of town."

"Not just out of town, he's in fuckin' Transnistria," Howser said. "But I'll try."

Virgil headed over to the BCA building and was nearly there when Howser called back. "Turner told me where I could stick my request, and it's not a place you'd want to visit. I have one fact that you'll find interesting, and a thought."

"I'll take both," Virgil said. "What's the fact?"

"Found a couple of hairs on the old man's shoes. Crime Scene isn't promising anything, but they could well be from a tiger. Definitely animal hair, or fur, or whatever it is, and the right color for a tiger."

"Excellent. That's great. What's the thought?"

"If his old man was in on this, if he was killed by this Peck guy . . . well, we have the old man's phone. We don't need anybody's permission to look at that, since he's, like, dead."

"Despite what people say, you are a man of average intelligence," Virgil said. "I'm on my way."

Zhang senior's phone was sitting on Howser's desk when Virgil arrived back at Minneapolis homicide. It had been processed by the crime-scene people and sent to the evidence room, where Howser had collected it. He dumped it out of a plastic bag, and they stood around and looked at it.

"Not an iPhone," Howser said. "What the hell is a Jazzpod?"

"There's some Chinese writing on it," Virgil observed.

"Must be a Chinese brand," Howser said. "Turn it on."

Virgil did, and they found that the phone's top language was English, and that it was fingerprint protected. Howser said, "Goddamnit. So close."

Virgil, thinking of the prints they'd taken from Hamlet Simonian, said, "Well, we've *got* his fingers."

Before going to the medical examiner's office, where Zhang's body was being held, Virgil and Howser went back to the homicide office, where a cop was being harangued by Horace Turner, the younger Zhang's attorney.

"We're already deep into the lawsuit. You've got no reason to hold my client . . ." Turner spotted Howser and said, "It's about time. This has gone beyond any reasonable hold and into physical abuse."

Howser looked at the other homicide cop and demanded, "Have you been beating up Mr. Zhang?"

The other cop yawned and said through the yawn, "Only with my dry wit."

Howser said to Turner, "Does dry wit fall under the Civil Rights Act?"

"Let my person go," Turner said. And, "For you cops, that's what we call a play on words. Anyway . . . let him go. Now. I am instructing him not to say another word to you. Not under these conditions."

Virgil said to Turner, "I think he choked his father to death for the inheritance. I think he was involved in the theft of the tigers. I think he's involved with at least a triple murder, and maybe four murders."

"No!" Zhang said.

Virgil said, "I'm not talking to you."

"Show me a single thing and there's a slim possibility that I won't sue you for abusing my client," Turner said.

"His father's shoes had tiger hair on them. That's a single thing. This guy"—Virgil pointed at Zhang—"drove his father everywhere. His father didn't even have a car here. They took junior's Ferrari when they wanted to go somewhere."

"He took Ubers," Zhang blurted.

"Shut up," Turner said to Zhang.

Virgil said, "Really. Ubers? I bet there's a record of that. Thanks, that helps. You mind if we look at your shoes?"

"If you've got a warrant," Turner said.

Howser said, "Why don't we keep Mr. Zhang sitting here for a while longer, while we go get a warrant, then?"

"I had nothing to do with . . ."

"Shut up," Turner said. "Not another word." And to Howser: "Get your warrant, if you think you can."

They left Turner, still complaining, and Zhang, now sourly silent, sitting in the homicide office. Virgil and Howser went off to the medical examiner's office, and another cop went to apply for a warrant, and a fourth one sat with Zhang to make sure he didn't rub the soles of his shoes too hard on the carpet.

The Hennepin County medical examiner's office had the same shoe-box ambience as the Ramsey County medical examiner's office, but instead of being simply plain, it was aggressively beige. An investigator pulled Zhang senior's nude body, and Virgil looked away as the experts figured out how best to get a fingerprint.

One of the examiner's employees, apparently an expert on cell phones, said, "There's no way to know which finger he used until we try them."

"Try his right hand first," said the investigator, a tall thin man with a hipster's goatee.

"Based on . . . ?"

"The fact that ninety percent of the people in the world are right-handed," the investigator said. "Try his right index finger first."

They hit it on the first try and the phone opened up. Virgil said, "I'll take it out in the waiting area . . . but let Mr. Zhang hang on here, in case we need the finger again."

"You could take the finger with you," the investigator said.

"Ah . . ."

"Just kiddin'. A little medical examiner humor there. Zhang parts ain't going anywhere."

Virgil and Howser went out to the waiting area, where it smelled less funny, and Virgil, who'd rehearsed on his own phone, poked his way through the menus of the Jazzpod to the location history, and the history opened up.

Most of the locations shown on the phone were in downtown Minneapolis or St. Paul, but one was in Washington County, east of St. Paul and adjoining the St. Croix River and Wisconsin.

The problem was, all the locations were much more general than they were on iPhones. Instead of addresses, they got areas: for Washington County, they got a location circle that Virgil figured was ten miles across. From previous such calculations during fugitive searches, Virgil knew that a circle ten miles across would cover almost eighty square miles, and in this case, a nice chunk of suburbs and probably a few thousand homes.

"That help?" Howser asked.

"It does, some," Virgil said. "We tracked the kid and his old man out that way, but they got onto us and turned around. We never did find out where they were going."

The medical examiner's investigator had an iPad and a Wi-Fi connection, and they called up a mapping program's satellite photos and compared it to the phone location. That part of Washington County had dozens of small lakes and ponds, most of them isolated from the road system, and many with houses around them.

"That's a rat's nest of streets out there, twisted around all those lakes. You need a better location," Howser said. "You can't just go out there and drive around."

"Yeah. I maybe got a better location coming. In the meantime, talk to Zhang about his old man's travels through the countryside out there . . . maybe crank up the pressure a little."

As Virgil left the medical examiner's office, Sandy called from a plane that was on the runway at Minneapolis-St. Paul International: "Got here by the skin of my teeth—Jon had to shout at Delta Air Lines to get them to hold the plane for five minutes. Everybody's looking at me. They think I'm a movie star or something."

"I can see that," Virgil said.

"You should. Anyway, they're telling me to turn off my phone. I'll be in LA in four hours."

"Call me," Virgil said. "Hey, where's the FedEx truck?"

"Going into San Bernardino, last time I could look. Gotta go, or they'll throw me off the plane."

The pressure to find the killer, and the tigers, had grown intense, especially with Channel Three now running a clock on the number of hours and minutes the animals had been missing.

Virgil considered the possibilities, and went to lunch.

While he was working his way through an egg-salad sandwich at the Parrot Café, he called around to see if he could find a human being at Uber. He eventually found one, who passed him up through several levels of management to a guy who said he couldn't call every Uber driver in the Twin Cities—he said there were thousands of them, though Virgil thought he might be exaggerating. "I can get a mass e-mailing to them, but I can't guarantee that they'll read it," the Uber guy said. "Tell me again exactly what you're looking for?"

Virgil described the two Zhangs and suggested that they may have been taken to Washington County the previous day, from downtown Minneapolis. He gave the Uber guy his phone number and authorized him to give it to anyone who called back with information.

"I'll do all that, but I wouldn't hold your breath," the Uber guy said.

Before he rang off, Virgil asked, "Has anyone ever asked you if you're like an Uber manager, you know like . . ."

"Like an Obersturmbannführer in Nazi Germany? Yeah, people ask me that all the time, because they think it's funny. I tell them that for one thing, in Germany it was spelled with an *O*, not a *U*, and for another thing, shut the fuck up."

"Thanks," Virgil said. "You've been really helpful. Really."

A television in the corner of the café began running a midday news program, and the first thing shown were the faces of two tigers, and an all-caps caption that said, "DEAD?" Virgil didn't need to have the sound turned up to know what was being said.

He finished the egg-salad sandwich and tried to figure out what to do next.

31

▼ ▼ ▼

Peck was at a Walgreens off I-94, pushing a Xanax prescription across the counter, hoping it wouldn't bounce. The clerk looked at it, typed into a computer for a while, then asked, "Do you want to pick these up later or wait?"

"How long if I wait?"

"Fifteen or twenty minutes," the clerk said. The clerk seemed to be looking at him oddly, but Peck couldn't think why.

"I'll wait," he said.

Drug secure again, he wandered off to the magazine rack, popped the last Xanax in his pill tube, and started paging through *People*. The magazine confused him: Who were all these celebrities? A few of the names were vaguely familiar, but most were not. One prominently displayed woman seemed to have an enormous ass and was famous for it. This was an ass that should have been on a balloon in the Macy's Thanksgiving Day parade. Yet, as awkward and obscure as they were, all these people seemed to have media skills, either smiling directly into the camera lens or hiding bruised eye sockets behind dark glasses. Or showing off their asses.

These people, both the smiling ones and the bruised ones, needed to take more Xanax, he thought.

He noticed that his left foot was tapping frenetically on the floor and stopped it. He got down another, cheaper celebrity magazine and was sucked into an apparently imaginary story about Jen. Jen's last name was never mentioned, and he had no idea who she was, although he thought he might have remembered her from some TV show a long time ago. That was confirmed when he got to the last paragraph of the story: the show was *Friends*, and it had ended eleven years earlier.

Eleven years: Peck would give everything to have had those eleven years back. For one thing, he wouldn't have messed around with those women in Indianapolis. If he'd gotten a regular doctor job, he'd be driving the big bucks now, fixing everything from Aarskog syndrome to Zika virus.

Mostly with Xanax.

Done with the magazines, he started pacing the aisles, trying not to look impatient or worried. Trying to look cool. He went by a cosmetic counter and caught an image of himself in a mirror. Even with the calming drug flowing around his brain, he knew why he'd gotten the odd look from the clerk: he was wearing a green golf shirt, but it was on backward, the collar up so it looked like a turtleneck.

He wandered some more, purposefully now, until he saw a sign for the restrooms. There was only one, a unisex, but it was open. He went inside, locked the door, turned the shirt around, splashed some water on his face, checked his fly, smiled at himself, and went back out.

Five minutes later, he got his new tube of Xanax with no further comment or looks from the pharmacy clerk, and he went out to the parking lot and spent fifteen minutes searching for his car. He eventually remembered that it had a remote panic alarm on the key fob, and he set it off, found the car, and crawled into the driver's seat, where he went to sleep, still clutching the paper sack that contained the new tube of pills.

He woke sometime later, with a woman rapping on the partially rolled-down driver's-side window. He looked at her and she stepped back and asked, "Are you okay?"

"A little sleepy," he said. His mouth tasted like chickenshit smelled. "I'm fine."

She went away and he muttered after her, "Mind your own business, you old bitch." He smacked his lips, realized the temperature inside the car was near the boiling point—would have killed a dog, he thought—and he started the car, put the AC on high, and wheeled out of the parking lot. The sun was much lower in the sky than it had been when he went into the Walgreens. How long had he been asleep? He looked at his watch and was surprised to see a mole on his wrist, but no watch. Must have forgotten to put it on. And where was he going? He had some other mission besides the pills. . . .

He sat at the stop sign and had to think a moment. He knew it was close by, and so it must . . .

Ah! Walmart. He needed a meat grinder. Hayk Simonian had not yet picked one up, at the time of his unfortunate accident.

He drove over to Walmart, a trip of five minutes or so, and when he got there, sat in the parking lot, trying to remember why he was there. Remembering was tough. He tried running through the alphabet, thinking of things he might need starting with an *A*, then a *B*. . . .

He'd gone all the way through to Z and was still sitting stupefied in his car, when he remembered: meat grinder. Before getting out of the truck, he automatically touched his pocket, checking to make sure he had his medication. He could feel it on his leg: he pulled the amber-colored tube out and almost panicked when he found it was empty.

But he distinctly remembered Walgreens and looked at the passenger seat, where he saw the white paper bag with the new prescription. A surge of relief. Drug secure again. But the old tube, the date . . . the date on the tube was two days earlier. Could that be right? He took out his cell phone and checked the date, and it *was* right. He'd taken thirty Xanax tabs in two and a half days? Jesus: he might have a problem here.

Had to slow down with that shit. Maybe . . . three a day. Okay, maybe four. No more than four, and only on bad days.

He went into Walmart, functioning better now, found a hand-operated meat grinder. As he was walking down the aisle toward the checkout counters, a woman, talking on a cell phone, accompanied by a clutch of children who appeared to be about seven, six, five, four, and three years of age, was approaching with an overloaded shopping cart. He tried to dodge but she crashed the cart into his legs, looked up, and said, "Hey, watch where you're going, asshole." As she walked away, he heard her say, "Some weirdo walked right into my cart."

The Xanax worked to keep his temper under control—he put it

all down to a Walmart moment—and Peck continued to the checkout. He paid cash for the meat grinder, went back to the car, drove out to I-94, and turned east. He was ten miles from the farm, with a stack of tiger jerky to grind up and another cat to kill. He really didn't want to do it anymore, the whole thing had spun out of control.

But he needed the money. It had to be done and he had to do it by himself; nobody to help old Peck now. A tear gathered in his left eye, and he wiped it away. Nobody to help old Peck.

Five miles down I-94, Peck passed a Minnesota highway patrol car sitting in the median, running a speed trap. He reflexively tapped the brake and looked at his speedometer, found that he was only going fifty miles an hour. He hadn't noticed that all the other cars were passing him, but they were. He sped up a bit, the patrolman looking at him as he went past. He kept an eye on his rear-view mirror, but the patrolman never moved.

The sight of the cop made him nervous, and when he got to the farm, he drove his car around behind the barn, where it couldn't be seen from the road.

In the barn, the cat stood up and hissed at him. She really hated him, he knew, and he found that amusing. He picked up the rifle, carried it close to the cage, and the cat pressed against the wire mesh. He aimed the rifle at her eyes.

"Who's the big dog now?" he asked her.

He pulled the trigger. Nothing happened. He worked the bolt and looked down into the chamber. Nothing there, and nothing in the magazine. Fuck it.

The temperature inside the barn must have been a hundred

and thirty, he thought; one of the dryers was still running, and he walked over and turned it off, and then opened the door, which he propped open with a rock. The incoming air felt cool on his skin, compared to that inside the barn, but he knew the outside temperatures must still be in the nineties, after touching a hundred earlier in the day.

He went back to the dryer, opened the door, and looked inside. The last of the tiger meat was more than crispy: it looked like bacon that had been hard-fried for ten minutes too many. He left the door open to cool the meat and went to the worktable, where he'd piled up three stacks of dried meat, each a foot high.

He took the grinder out of its box, used the screw clamps on the bottom to clamp it to the worktable, and started grinding. After a while, the silence got to him, and he turned on Hayk Simonian's radio, which Simonian had tuned to the public radio station, and listened to *All Things Considered*.

Last thing up was a commentary on the missing tigers, with an interview with a state cop named Jon something.

"I can tell you that we're picking up more and more material, more and more evidence, to work with, and we're going to solve this. I was talking to our lead investigator this morning, and he thinks we'll have a break of some kind today or tomorrow. We're keeping our fingers crossed: we hope the tigers haven't been hurt, but we have to live with the possibility that they have been. I don't want to upset anyone, but that's the reality of the matter."

The interviewer said, "We've seen an intimidating list of crimes that the thieves could be charged with. Do you really think that the perpetrators could be charged with anything like what we've seen? Fifteen or twenty separate crimes, possibly even including murder?"

"From what we know now," the cop said, "we believe there

have been at least two murders committed in the course of this crime—we've got the bodies of two brothers who we *know* were involved. Persons involved in this crime now fall under the felony murder statute, which means that they didn't have to pull a trigger, or even know about the murders, if they were involved in the initial crime. When we catch them, they're going to prison. Thirty years in Minnesota, no parole. There is, of course, the matter of prosecutorial discretion: if somebody involved were to come forward, to help us clear this matter up, a prosecutor could well decide to recommend leniency. That would have to happen soon, because I believe we're going to solve this crime on our own, in the next day or so, and start rounding up the perpetrators."

Peck changed to a classic rock station and continued grinding.

When he was done, he had fifty or sixty pounds of rough-ground dry meat, which he packed into five plastic buckets from Home Depot. The meat would eventually be poured into plastic tubes the size of his pill containers, and sold for anything up to twenty-five dollars.

He had, he thought, at least fifty thousand dollars' worth of meat right there, and he hadn't even gotten to the good stuff yet.

The bones would have to be broken up with a hammer before they could be ground. Hayk Simonian had bought an anvil at an antique shop for that purpose, along with a heavy ball-peen hammer.

Peck was too tired for that. Maybe dehydrated from the heat. He needed a quart of cold water and an icy margarita and a nap. Xanax for sure. He picked up the rifle and the box of cartridges and started for the door. Katya hissed again, and he turned and said, "When I come back, I'm gonna blow your brains out, kitty cat. Right after I take my nap. Look forward to it."

32

▼ ▼ ▼

Virgil spent part of the afternoon making phone calls, staying in touch with Minneapolis homicide about the younger Zhang, checking the tip line, talking to people at the zoo, avoiding calls from the media. Most of it was unpleasant, from his point of view.

Brad Blankenship had been picked up by a Blue Earth County deputy and taken to the jail in Mankato, but Mattsson had called to tell him about a chat with the Blue Earth County attorney. "He's going to try to push Blankenship into a corner, try to get him to deal up for Castro, but he doesn't think it's going to work. Blankenship made a call to an attorney from the jail here, and the county attorney tells me that that guy is also Castro's attorney. If what happens is what I think is going to happen, Blankenship will be out on bail by tonight, on Castro's money."

"Then he's probably not going to deal up," Virgil said.

"Probably not."

"What if we said he was a danger to witnesses?"

"The bail will probably get larger, but that's all," she said. "We're still going to get the guy, but . . ."

"It's not exactly what we were hoping for. It'd be nice if we could deal up and get whoever paid him, but I want to see Blankenship doing time, too."

"I was hoping you'd say that, because that might be what we're gonna get. If you're happy, I'm happy, and I already talked to Frankie about it, and she's okay with it. Alvarez . . . I think Alvarez and her husband are probably headed back to Mexico. Sparkle isn't too happy about that, but Sparkle doesn't have to go back to the pickle factory," she said.

"I don't much care what Sparkle is happy about," Virgil said.

Mattsson said, "Okay, then. Listen, I'm up for the rest of the day—do you need help with the tigers?"

"I don't even have enough for myself to do," Virgil said. "If I need help, I'll call."

"Do that."

Howser called from the Minneapolis homicide office and said they hadn't gotten a warrant for Zhang's shoes. "Got the wrong judge, in the wrong mood, and we were a little thin to begin with. Goddamn Zhang went out of here dragging his shoes on every carpet he saw."

"How about the Ferrari? It was titled to his old man."

"We're all over that. Crime Scene's down there with vacuums, looking for tiger hair."

That was about it. No tips, no ideas from the zoo. Late in the afternoon, he went over to Peck's house and pounded on the doors, but there was no answer, and the house felt empty. Should have left a round-the-clock stakeout on Peck, he thought. He was probably with the tigers.

With no place left to go, he looked at his watch: Sandy should be in Los Angeles, but she'd call if she actually got anything. Last gasp: he drove out to Washington County to the middle of the large circle on the older Zhang's Chinese telephone and started driving around.

The countryside was lush with the end of summer coming up, the tall grasses showing gold on the edges, a few yellow leaves popping out in the aspens, birches, and soybean fields. His favorite time of year, but south Washington County was not becoming his favorite place.

The roads ran all over the place, and many of the houses were set so far back from the road, or so deep behind sheltering trees, that he could see almost nothing—and he suspected that wherever the tigers were being kept, that place would be hard to see. With nothing else to do, he kept driving, up one road and down the next, gravel to blacktop and back to gravel, redwing blackbirds perched on cattails, rabbits warming their feet on the gravel shoulders, what might have been a mink making a dash for a culvert: and the sun slowly sank down to the horizon.

The fair-weather clouds were showing orange crinkles from the setting sun when Sandy called. "This place is a nightmare," she said. "It took an hour and five minutes to drive from LAX to Pasadena. Thirty miles."

"I don't have a real tight grip on where Pasadena is," Virgil said. "You have a reason for going there?"

"Yes. The FedEx packages have been dropped at a place here, and the phone is in this building. I'm going to start calling it, and we'll have a bunch of people listening for it. There are about a million packages and I'm hoping he hasn't turned the ringer off. Anyway, I just got here, I'm dealing with the manager, I'll call back when we get something. *If* we get something."

Virgil called Mattsson: "You still free?"

"Sure, for a while, anyway. I'm starting to get a little off-center. I've been up since five o'clock."

He told her where he was, and she said she'd drive out.

Fifteen minutes later, Sandy called back: "We got it. The ringer was turned off, but he had the vibration thing turned on, and we can feel the box vibrating when I call it. It's addressed to a Jack in the Box. I don't know what that's all about, but the manager says as long as I give him a written statement that the owner is dead and this is for a police investigation, we can open it here."

"Then do it. Now," Virgil said.

"I'm doing it," she said. "The box is right here and I'm typing out this statement. I hope it doesn't get us in trouble."

"Hamlet's dead, Sandy. Who's going to complain?"

"Hang on . . ." As he hung on, he dug in his briefcase and found Hamlet Simonian's password book. Sandy came back and said, "Got it. It wants a password, four numbers. You got a four-number password?"

He looked. "I do. I've got three of them, unidentified."

"Give them to me."

They hit it on the second one and Sandy said, "It's opening up—that's it, Virgil. Okay, I'm paging through here. Location services are on . . . Oh my God."

"Oh my God, what?"

"He was at the zoo three times," Sandy said. "He was at the zoo the night the tigers were stolen, it's all right here, it actually says the Minnesota Zoo and has the time."

"Aww . . . kiss yourself for me. On the lips. What else? I mean, where else?"

"A few places in St. Paul . . ."

She read off the addresses and Virgil said, "That's Peck's place . . . that's his apartment . . . that's the place over in Frogtown, where they sent the dryers. Don't know what the other ones are. . . . What about Washington County?"

"Doesn't say Washington County but there's a place out east of St. Paul, must be it. He's been seven times."

"That's it. Where is it?"

She read off the address. Virgil wrote it down and said, "We need to keep that phone secure. We need a list of witnesses who saw you open the FedEx box, and who saw you put the password numbers in and who saw you open up the phone. We need names and addresses for all of them. Be sure to save the box and any documentation that comes with it, and make friends with the witnesses."

"I can do that. The manager here asked me what I was doing later tonight . . ."

"Jesus, Sandy . . ."

"Messing with you, Virgil. I will do that, I'll document everything. I haven't touched the phone except to put in the password numbers, and I did that with a stylus so I wouldn't put my own fingerprints on it. Simonian's should be all over it. Maybe Peck's, if he's the one who shipped it."

"You are so good," Virgil said.

"Are you going to his place in Washington County?"

"Soon as the backup gets here," Virgil said.

"Jenkins and Shrake?" Sandy asked.

"Catrin Mattsson."

"She's as good as Jenkins and Shrake—she's sort of my new heroine. Virgil—be careful, huh? Both of you. Please?"

"Got it covered," Virgil said, as he hung up.

33

▼ ▼ ▼

Virgil cruised the address Sandy had given him and it looked perfect as a tiger hideaway. The place was surrounded by tall trees, but he could see a light in a main house and a barn or an oversized garage in back, all down a long gravel driveway. Details were hard to pick out as the daylight diminished, but it was clear that if someone had wanted to unload tranquilized tigers, he could have done it privately.

A mailbox said "Hall" with the house number under that, so he had the right place.

When he'd seen as much as he could from the road, he drove out to the closest intersection of I-94 and parked off the road. Mattsson arrived five minutes later and pulled up behind him.

"How does it look?" she asked, as they rendezvoused at Virgil's front bumper.

"I could see at least two buildings from the road. We'll have to scout it before we go in. I'd suggest we park a couple hundred feet away from the driveway. . . . Let me get a legal pad."

He got a legal pad from his briefcase, and a pencil, and drew a quick schematic of the target address, showing what he'd been able to see of the house and the outbuilding, and shaded some areas that were heavily wooded.

"The ditches are dry, so we'll be able to walk through them. If we come in from this side, we'll have to climb at least two fences, but from this point"—he tapped his sketch—"we should be able to walk all the way around the place without anyone seeing us."

"Any vehicles?"

"Not that I could see," Virgil said.

"After we scout it, one of us should run back to the trucks and use one to plug the driveway before we go in," Mattsson said. "If we're on foot and they make a break for it, they could be gone before we could get to our own vehicles."

"Yes. You run, I've got these goddamn cowboy boots on and you've got sneakers, so you'll be quicker."

"Getting dark: we better move."

Virgil led the way to the parking area he'd spotted while scouting. They got out, quietly as they could, and Mattsson whispered, "Virgil: get your gun."

"Oh, yeah."

He got his Glock out of the back, with the clip-on holster, and pressed his back against the truck door, so it closed with a *click* instead of a *slam*. He led the way down the road toward the target address and, fifty feet short of the driveway, through the roadside ditch and over a fence with a single barbed-wire strand on top, and into the trees. Another fence, old, in poor condition and barely visible, stopped them a few feet in, and they took a minute getting over it. Darkness was coming on fast now, but they had enough light to navigate.

They moved slowly through the trees, stumbling over the occasional downed branch or hole in the ground, to where they could see the house and the building behind it. There were no open doors, nothing visible through the windows.

"Driveway's the only way in or out," Mattsson said, next to Virgil's ear. She slapped at her own face: they were in a swarm of mosquitoes.

"Yeah." Virgil led the way around the open lot, staying back in the trees, both of them swatting at mosquitoes as they walked. When they'd gone all the way around, they'd learned nothing more, other than only a single light was shining in the house, and it was possible that nobody was inside.

When they got out to the ditch at the other side of the house, Virgil whispered, "I'll go down to the driveway; you run to get your truck."

"Car coming," she said, and pointed.

The car had turned onto the road a half mile away and was coming toward them. They stepped back into the trees so they wouldn't be caught in the headlights. The car slowed, turned into the driveway—they could see it was a Toyota Corolla or something like that—and pulled all the way past the house. Somebody, they couldn't see who, got out of the car, and a moment later, a house door slammed.

"*Now* there's somebody home, if there wasn't before," Virgil said quietly.

"Probably a woman," Mattsson said.

"Why?"

"Because this far out, with a large lot and a barn or a toolshed, a guy would probably be driving a truck, not a small sedan," she said.

Virgil said, "Huh. Okay. That's not necessarily good. I was thinking it'd be a place where they could kill the tigers and cut them up, not somebody's home."

"We'll see," Mattsson said. "I'll get the truck."

She jogged off through the dark, and Virgil saw the lights go when she opened the truck door. At that same moment, another truck turned the corner, slowed as it passed Virgil's and Mattsson's vehicles, then came on, slowed again, turned down the driveway. Virgil heard the truck door slam and somebody go into the house.

Mattsson followed a minute later, turned down the driveway, stopped her truck at the narrowest spot in the driveway, effectively blocking it.

When she got out of the truck, Virgil asked, "What do you think?"

"Well, you think the tiger thieves have murdered three people. We gotta be ready."

"Let's knock," Virgil said. "Get your gun out; keep it out of sight behind me. Don't shoot me in the back."

They walked up to the door in that odd formation, Mattsson behind him but very close, Virgil's Glock loose in its holster, his hand resting on the stock—inconspicuously, he hoped.

The interior door was open and Virgil heard a woman call, "Tom, I think somebody's in the driveway."

Virgil reached out and pushed the doorbell and heard the *ding-dong* inside. Mattsson whispered, "You step eight inches left and I'll have a clear shot inside."

A few seconds later, a man in a brown UPS uniform trotted down some interior steps and looked at them through the screen door. "Can I help you?"

Virgil held up his BCA identification and said, "We're agents with the state Bureau of Criminal Apprehension. Are you Mr. Hall?"

"Yes." He pushed open the screen door to come out and Virgil and Mattsson took a step backward, still locked in the too-close formation to hide Mattsson's weapon. "What can I do for you?"

He was too . . . Virgil looked for the right word and came up with "querulous." Hall was too questioning, too void of worry.

Virgil half-turned his head to Mattsson and said, "I think we're okay."

She said, "I do, too," and Virgil felt her step back farther away.

"What's going on?" Hall asked.

Virgil gave him a brief explanation, and Hall's wife, Alice, came to the door, carrying a towel, and said, "The man was here? His telephone was here?"

She was disbelieving.

"That's what came up on the phone," Virgil said. "This specific address."

"We're gone during the day," she said. "There hasn't been any sign of anybody around. We don't know anyone named Simonian."

Virgil went to his phone, called up the BCA website, and showed the Halls the mug shots of Hamlet and Hayk Simonian, and they both shook their heads. "I've never seen them," Tom Hall said. "We would have noticed strangers hanging around."

Alice said, "Tom, take them out to the garage. Make them look in there, so they know there's nothing out there. . . ." And to

Virgil, she said, "We wouldn't be skinning tigers in the house, would we?"

Virgil had to smile. "Probably not."

"So go out and look in the garage."

Virgil knew it was pointless, but he and Mattsson went and looked, and found a bunch of lawn equipment and a workshop. They thanked the Halls and left.

Wonder what happened?" Mattsson asked, at her truck.

"Don't know, but I can't believe those guys knew anything," Virgil said. "I'll talk to Sandy, see what she has to say."

Mattsson left, headed for home and a nap. Virgil watched her taillights as they disappeared around the corner and scuffed down to his truck.

He called Sandy, who said, "I can't believe the address could be that wrong. I'll look at the numbers again, maybe I got something backward." She looked at the house numbers again, but they were correct.

"I can't explain it," she said. "Maybe . . . I don't know . . . Maybe Hamlet was coming or going from somewhere else and he wouldn't turn his phone on until he got to that address. You know, like he didn't want to give away where he really was."

"I haven't gotten the impression that Hamlet was a big thinker," Virgil said.

"Then I guess I can't help," Sandy said. "Actually, I don't know exactly how the locator gizmo works. I'll try looking it up on the 'net and get back to you if I find anything."

Virgil told her to hang on to Hamlet Simonian's cell phone and everything else. "When do you get back?"

"Tomorrow night, if nothing else comes up."

"Probably see you then," Virgil said.

Virgil thought about driving around some more, but it was so dark that he wouldn't be able to see much at all. Discouraged, he headed out to I-94, saw a convenience store on the other side of the highway, and across from that, Red's County Bar & Grill. He pulled into the gas station and filled up, went inside to pay and to get some cheese crackers and a Diet Coke.

Back in his truck, he opened the crackers and sat crunching on them, looked at the "Red's" sign with its flashing neon red rooster. After a moment he said, "Huh," and turned the truck that way.

There were maybe twenty trucks and cars, mostly trucks, in the bar's parking lot. There were no other bars in the neighborhood, as far as Virgil knew. He clumped inside in his cowboy boots: Not much going on, a lot of people in booths eating hamburgers and drinking beer, two or three more on bar stools, and a couple of guys in the back shooting pool at a coin-op table. Nobody paid any attention to him, and he walked over to the bar and the bartender put a napkin in front of him and asked, "What can I get you?"

"Is the manager around?"

The bartender was a square white-haired man with a tightly cut beard and rimless glasses sitting on a round nose; he might have been Santa Claus except for the boxing scars under his eyes. "We don't rightly have a manager," he said. "What we have is an owner, who is me."

Virgil pulled out his ID and explained his problem and how the bartender/owner might help him. "If you don't mind . . ."

"Well, it's weird, but I guess I don't mind," the bartender said. "Give us something to talk about when you're gone."

"Thanks," Virgil said. He stepped to the middle of the bar and called out, loud enough to break through the chatter, "Hey, everybody! I'm a cop. I need your attention for a minute."

The chatter stopped, and the pool players backed away from the table, and everybody looked at him, and Virgil said, "I'm with the Bureau of Criminal Apprehension, and I'm looking for the stolen tigers. We think they might be in this neighborhood—well, on the other side of the highway, anyway. Someplace south of here. What I want to know is, have any of you seen anything even a little unusual in the area?"

He described the Halls' place as the most likely general location and waited. There was a buzz, but people were shaking their heads, then a woman said, "I don't know, but I know who would."

"Who's that?"

"Buddy Gates."

Somebody said, "Oh, hell yes."

"Who's that?" Virgil asked.

The woman said, "The rural route carrier out here. He knows every single house."

"Of course," Virgil said.

Nobody knew how to get in touch with Buddy Gates, but somebody knew he worked out of the post office in Lakeland, which, of course, was closed. There was a general head-scratching until somebody said, "I think he does live in Lakeland. You could ask down there."

Somebody else said, "Buddy does drink a little. You could ask down at York's."

York's, it turned out, was the only bar in Lakeland. Virgil drove down to Lakeland, parked at the bar, went inside, and asked the bartender about Gates. The bartender introduced him to a woman named Judy, who told him that Gates lived in kind of a hard place to identify, but she'd be glad to show him the way.

Virgil followed her down the highway a few hundred yards, then back into a neighborhood of 1960s ranch houses and pointed out her window at a house with lots of lights in the windows.

Virgil waved at her, and she headed back to York's. Gates was home, smelling strongly of marijuana, and when Virgil told him what he wanted, he said, "I wondered what those dudes were up to."

Gates led the way to the back of his house, where a woman with glossy blond hair was sitting in a La-Z-Boy with her feet up, watching *The Vampire Diaries*. Gates said, "Gotta help a cop find the tigers," and she said, "Shhh . . ."

Gates turned on his computer, brought up a Google map, switched to a satellite view, found the spot.

"Here's where you was," he said. He touched the screen with a pencil. "That's the Halls' house, right there. And here's where these guys was."

He touched the screen again, where Virgil could see the roofs of a house and barn. The structures were on the other side of the Halls' back woods, probably no more than a hundred and fifty yards away.

"The reason the Halls didn't know about them was, they're on a completely different road and the two roads don't hook up with a crossroad for almost a half mile either way," Gates said. "No reason for anybody on either road to go onto the other one. The reason it didn't come up on the telephone was, it's not an official address anymore. This guy from out of state bought about five places over there, as investments, and merged them into one new subdivision. The closest official address is the Halls'."

Virgil showed him the pictures of Hamlet and Hayk Simonian, and Gates said, "I'm not completely sure, but this one"—he touched the Hayk photo—"I think I talked to him just a day or two ago."

The woman in the chair said, "Would you guys shut up?"

Virgil went back to the front door, where Gates filled him in on the countryside around the house and barn where he'd seen Hayk. Virgil thanked him, and as he was leaving, said, "I wouldn't necessarily recommend you invite a cop inside, when you've been smoking dope."

"It's medicinal," Gates said. "Besides, does anybody really care anymore?"

Virgil thanked him again, went out to his truck, and called Mattsson. The phone rang, but she didn't answer. He left a message on her voice mail and tried Jenkins. Jenkins answered, but he and Shrake were in St. Cloud, which had to be the best part of a hundred miles away.

Virgil decided to wait for Mattsson, but until she called, he'd go scout the house that Gates had identified. He drove back through the rat's nest of roads to the Halls' house, then past it, a half mile down, over another quarter of a mile, then back toward the target address.

He found the driveway and eased on past, but could see nothing down the driveway except one dim light in the house; he couldn't see the barn at all, which Gates had described as "dirt-colored."

Virgil left his car a hundred yards down the road, on the side away from I-94. If Peck was in the house and decided to drive out, he'd probably be going out toward the interstate.

On foot now, Virgil snuck back to the driveway, crouched at the entrance, listening, then walked down toward the house, staying as much as he could in the brush along the side of the drive. Took his time: no rush now.

As he got closer, he could see the thinnest rime of light in a rectangular shape, out past the house. A door, he thought. He kept moving, slowly, slowly, listening all the time, his pistol in his hand now.

Went past the house, stepped on something, dropped his hand to it: an electric cord, snaking off toward the barn. Another few steps, something else. A hose.

Took his time, listening. No sound at all from the house, no sign of a vehicle. He thought about that, wondered if Peck had gone somewhere else. The light in the house was nothing you'd read by. . . .

Another minute and he was next to the barn door. The door opened inward. He thought about it for a moment, listened some more, then pushed on it. The light inside was bright and cut a pencil-thin shaft across his jeans. He pushed a bit more and now could see inside.

And he could smell what was in there, and it was awful: a combination of spoiled meat and rotten blood and maybe tiger shit, he thought. Nobody there—then something moved at the back and two lamp-like eyes turned toward him from behind a chain-link fence.

A goddamn tiger, he thought. He'd found them. Or one of them.

He caught the door with his fingernails, pulled it closed again, and turned to the house. As he did it, the phone in his pocket began to vibrate. He didn't answer, but slipped around the corner of the barn and walked down the side of it until he was nearly to the back.

Shielding the phone screen from the house, he looked at it: Mattsson.

Called her back and she picked up on the first ring. "I was in the shower. . . . Missed your call."

"I found them," Virgil said. "They're in a barn at a house right behind the Halls', but on a different road, a road that's parallel to the one the Halls are on. You can see them both on the Google satellite. One tiger's alive. There's nobody in the barn, except the tiger, but may be somebody in the house."

"You got your gun with you?"

"Yes."

"I'm on the way," Mattsson said.

34

▼ ▼ ▼

Peck had been asleep in the farmhouse. There was no furniture in the place, but Hayk Simonian had brought in a foam pad, and Peck passed out on it, partly from exhaustion and partly from the drugs. He awoke in the dark and was disoriented: the first thing he recognized was the smell of the place, mostly dry rot, rodent shit, and dust, with a lingering stink from the tiny bathroom.

None of the plumbing worked, but Simonian had used the toilet anyway. He'd later tried to flush it with a bucket of water, but the pipes were screwed up and he was only partially successful. The electricity still worked, but since they didn't use the house for much, Hamlet Simonian had installed only one lightbulb, in the kitchen, leaving his fingerprints all over it, Peck assumed.

Peck had dragged the foam pad into the mudroom, which still had functioning screens, because the house was too hot and the cross-ventilation from the open windows kept the Hayk Simonian stink at bay. In the dim light of the sixty-watt bulb, he pushed himself up, popped a Xanax, opened the door, took a step down, unzipped, and peed off the side of the back stoop.

As he was doing that, he saw a crack of light to his left, at the barn. And a figure in the light: that fuckin' Flowers, no question about it.

Caught in midstream, he tried to get back inside the house without peeing on himself, and succeeded, mostly, except for one hand, but did pee all over the foam pad and in the doorway to the main part of the house. At that point, figuring he was near the end anyway, he finished peeing on the kitchen floor, wiped his hands on his pants, and got the rifle.

Getting as close to the kitchen lightbulb as he could, without throwing shadows that might give him away, he carefully extracted the magazine from the bottom of the rifle, cursing himself for not loading it earlier, and began to fumble cartridges into the magazine. He didn't know exactly how many rounds the magazine would hold, but he managed to press in eight or nine before he knocked the cartridge box off the kitchen counter, and the metallic cartridges hit the floor like a rain of steel bolts.

That panicked him. He tried to shove the magazine into the rifle, but got it backward, couldn't make it fit, realized what he was doing when he saw the pointed end of the top bullet aimed at his eye. He turned the magazine around and managed to seat it, and he worked the bolt to chamber a round.

Two Xanax-calmed thoughts about Flowers: he had to go because he stood between Peck and his truck; he had to go because the barn was full of live tiger and dead tiger parts and, more troubling, fingerprints left by Winston Peck. The whole quarter-million-dollar dream was going down, but if he could kill Flowers, he could dump the gas cans in the barn and the house and burn them to the ground. That would take care of the prints and any DNA that might be around, as well as the man who had somehow tracked him here.

If he could kill Flowers, he had a chance.

Virgil snuck back to the front of the barn to peek at the house, and when he did it, he saw a flicker in the light from the kitchen, and seconds later, the sound of metallic cartridges falling on the floor. He knew the sound because . . . he and his hunting buddy Johnson Johnson had dropped any number of metallic cartridges on the floor of any number of hunting cabins.

The sound meant that somebody—probably Peck—was loading a gun, which meant that the gun wasn't quite loaded. Virgil ran as softly as he could to the front of the house, because the kitchen, where the light was, was in the back. He took his gun out and climbed the sagging front porch steps. At the top, he tried to see through the glass rectangle in the front door, but it was dark inside, and he could see nothing. The porch boards creaked underfoot as he moved to the door, and Virgil hesitated, listened, then took another step forward.

When he put his foot down, the porch board collapsed with a noisy clatter, and Virgil went through up to his right thigh. As he struggled to get out of the hole, the boards under his other foot began to crack, and he could go neither up nor down easily. He set his gun aside and tried to pull himself out of the hole with his hands, as if he'd fallen through lake ice.

Peck had stepped out on the urine-soaked back stoop, thinking that he might see Flowers either coming or going from the barn. He wasn't confident of his combat skills, but he had little choice. Flowers had to go and the range would be short. He put the rifle up to his shoulder as he'd seen soldiers do on news broadcasts, wrapped his finger around the trigger, and waited.

And heard Virgil fall through the porch floor.

He knew exactly what had happened, because he'd almost gone through himself. If Flowers had fallen through, he'd be at least temporarily discombobulated, and Peck might shoot him from the range of six feet.

He turned and ran down the side of the house, looked under the porch railing, saw Virgil on his hands and knees. Virgil saw him at exactly the same moment and Peck pushed the gun through the railing directly at Virgil's chest and pulled the trigger.

The trigger didn't move and Peck's brain froze. Virgil saw that, knew what had happened—Peck's gun's safety was on, but it could be off again in a quarter second—and launched himself at the front door, smashed it open and rolled inside. Straight ahead was a stairway leading to a second floor and a hallway that led to the kitchen. If he took the hallway, he'd be silhouetted in the thin kitchen light.

He took the stairs.

Peck wasn't as quick on the uptake as Flowers, but realized in the next second that the gun's safety was on. He thumbed it off and ran around to the porch stairs in time to see Flowers topping the stairs inside, and fired a single shot, wildly off-target; a plume of plaster dust exploded from the ceiling of the second-floor landing, two feet above and three feet to the right of Flowers's head.

He saw Flowers launch himself into a bedroom. That bedroom was a dead end: he worked the bolt on the rifle, chambering another round, climbed the porch steps, careful now . . . and kicked

Flowers's pistol. He had an idea of what it was, because Flowers had been clambering out of the hole in the porch with both hands open and hadn't had time to scoop it up before crashing through the door.

Peck picked up the pistol, thinking it would be handier in an up-close fight, though he knew almost nothing about handguns. He tried to find a safety, failed, and pulled the trigger instead. He'd been holding the gun nearly upright when he did that, not expecting it to go off, and when it did, the recoil not only wrenched his hand backward, but he nearly shot himself in the nose. Additionally, something hit his left eye, like a piece of sand, but a hot, burning piece of sand, and his eye shut of its own accord. When he tried to open it, it flooded with tears.

Worse, when the pistol went off, he'd been so startled he'd dropped it, and it had fallen through the hole in the deck of the porch. He was back to the rifle and half-blinded. He shouted up the stairs, "Hey, Flowers . . . lose your gun?"

Flowers yelled back, "Can't talk now, I'm on my cell phone, telling my partner exactly where you're at and everything that's happened tonight. You're fuckin' toast, asshole. Better give it up or you're gonna die here."

Peck pointed the gun at the bedroom door—he could see only an edge of it from the bottom of the stairs—and pulled the trigger, worked the bolt, pointed it again, and pulled the trigger again. His eye hurt like hell, but when he wiped it with his shirtsleeve, the tearing seemed to have stopped, and he got some vision back in that eye.

He worked the bolt again, climbed halfway up the stairs, and fired another shot through the wall of the bedroom.

Virgil was lying on the floor under the bedroom window. As long as Peck stayed down the stairs, it'd be hard to get a slug to him. If he came up the stairs, Virgil had a major problem: the bedroom wasn't much bigger than a modern closet and Peck could stand back and blow holes in it all night long, depending on how much ammo he had. Sooner or later, Virgil would get hit.

And the third shot, because of its angle through the wall, seemed to Virgil to come from the stairway, not from the bottom floor.

He had to move.

He waited, waited, and Peck shouted, "Gotcha, Flowers," and Virgil yelled back, "I don't believe you do," and when the fourth shot came through the wall, knowing that Peck would have to work the bolt, he stood up and kicked the rotten double-hung window right out of its frame. He struggled through the window, exposed now, afraid Peck would run down the stairs and catch him, but another shot came through the wall, missing him by three feet. Virgil hung for a moment from the window ledge, looking down in the dark.

Couldn't see anything at the bottom, but figured his feet were no more than six or seven feet off the ground.

He let go, hit the stone edging of an ancient flower bed with both feet, the pain lancing through both ankles and up past his knees as he fell down. He'd sprained both ankles, he thought: goddamn cowboy boots. He got to his feet and tried to run away, but he heard the bedroom door smash open—Peck must've heard him kicking the window out—and he started juking back and forth as he ran toward the nearest cover, which was the barn. He was ten feet away, waiting for the impact of the bullet tearing through his back, when Peck fired and the bullet . . . missed.

But it was close enough to hear it go by, an actual *zing* sound that was unmistakable if you'd heard it before.

Virgil hit the barn door like a linebacker and sprawled inside, in the bright light, rolled out of the line of fire as another bullet smashed through the rebounding door. Virgil rolled over next to it and kicked it shut.

And here he was, no gun, his ankles screaming at him.

Beside a door that was as good as a target, in the basement of a building with no other door and no windows. One good thing: the walls were made of stone, so Peck wouldn't be knocking holes in it.

He looked for something he could use to block the door, which opened inward, but nothing seemed likely to be heavy enough: there was a table, but it was made from a sheet of four-by-eight plywood laid over sawhorses. He limped over to one of the dryers, but it probably didn't weigh more than twenty pounds.

And he had no time. Peck was coming.

His best chance, he decided, would be to try to take the guy in the dark. There were three bright lights overhead, and Virgil grabbed a knife off the plywood table and stabbed the first bulb, smashing it, smashed the second one, and as he was about to smash the third one, noticed an unremarked-upon feature of the whole tiger-cleaning lash-up.

There, he said to himself, *is an interesting possibility.*

He smashed the third light and in the sudden impenetrable darkness, fished his cell phone out of his pocket, punched the recall button for Mattsson, and clutching the knife in one hand, crawled into the vacant tiger cage left behind when the Simonians dragged out the dead Artur.

Mattsson answered the phone and said, "I'm on the way . . ."

"Listen!" Virgil said. "I'm in deep trouble. I'm trapped in the barn in back and Peck is coming for me with a rifle. I lost my gun . . ."

Peck was crossing the barnyard with his best Airborne Ranger combat-killer simulation, his rifle at his shoulder, one round visually confirmed in the chamber, the safety off, ready to go.

As he got closer, he could hear somebody talking inside the barn, and not, he thought, from right behind the door. Sounded farther away than that. He tiptoed up to the barn door and listened.

Flowers was saying, "Don't let him quit. If he gets me, kill him. He's got that rifle, you'll have every chance in the world, and nobody will question it. Kill the motherfucker."

Peck was quite calm about it, hearing his own death sentence. It was apparent that Flowers had given up on some level, but on another level, was making sure that Peck would pay.

Peck started to tear up again: that wasn't fair. He'd *won*. He'd beaten Flowers fair and square, and now Flowers was ratting him out to the world?

He didn't burst into the barn to stop it, though. Instead, he pushed the door open a quarter inch and put his good right eye to it. Everything inside was dark, except the cell phone, and as he watched, he could see the reflection off Flowers's face.

There was no kind of tricky thing going on, like with the cell phone being in the back of the barn, while Flowers hid behind the door. He kept his eye to the door, fished out his own cell phone, brought it up, and turned on the flashlight app. He pushed the door open with his foot, aimed the rifle at Flowers, and stepped inside in the dark.

He said, in his best Airborne Ranger combat-killer voice, "You're all done."

Flowers's cell phone light went out as Flowers apparently dropped it facedown in the dirt. That didn't help him, though, as Peck aimed his own cell phone light at the back of the barn and stepped out across the barn floor. Flowers, he realized, had hidden himself in Artur's cage.

Flowers said, from across the barn floor, "I still don't think so."

"Know what I'm going to do?" Peck asked. "I'm gonna dump twenty gallons of gasoline on—"

Flowers interrupted: "You know what I already did?"

Peck couldn't help himself. "What?"

"I let the other tiger out."

Peck momentarily froze, or most of him did. His hair didn't: it stood up all over his body. Mouth open, Xanax totally failing, Peck turned the cell phone light to his right and saw two amber coals glowing in the dark.

Close. Getting closer.

What Virgil had seen before he smashed out the last light was the two simple snap-shackles that locked the chain-link farm gates of the tiger cages. They were secure enough—a tiger wasn't going to figure them out—but they were also easy enough to undo. If he knelt inside of the empty cage, he could reach over the half-closed door of that cage and unshackle Katya's door.

He did that, in the light of his cell phone, and pulled his own door shut, and shackled it just to be sure the cat couldn't somehow get in.

Katya didn't move right away, but when she did, it was all at once, the big golden orange-and-black cat rolling to her feet, nosing out through the open door.

The barn door opened inward, so Virgil thought the cat probably couldn't get out of the barn on her own; but if he could get Peck inside, without getting shot himself . . .

Peck did like to talk. Would probably want to claim victory.

Now Peck's cell phone flipped up in the air as he tried to bring his rifle around but he was way, way too late.

Katya hit him like a furry cannonball and Virgil put his hands to his ears and closed his eyes, not willing to witness the rest of it, even in the dim light of a cell phone. Thankfully, the screaming ended with a loud crunching of skull bones.

Then Katya roared.

A full-bore, full-throated, Siberian forest, after-the-kill roar, and some atavistic gene in Virgil's personal gene pool sat up and screamed, "Run, dummy."

He couldn't. He sat and listened to Katya make a *dug-dug-dug* sound. A moment later, she started dragging Peck's body back to her lair. She had trouble getting the body across the gate stop-bar on the floor, but managed after tossing her head for a moment or two, settled in the far corner, and after giving Virgil an appraising look, went back to work on Peck.

Virgil eased his cage door open, one inch, two inches, ready to slam it back in place. At six inches, he reached one arm out, and managed to hook Katya's cage door and pull it shut. Katya stopped chewing, gave him another look, and went back to Peck.

Still kneeling behind his own door, Virgil got a snap shackle back in place on Katya's cage, then pushed his own cage door farther open and got the second shackle on.

He turned back into his cage and picked up the phone; Mattsson was shouting at him.

"I'm okay," he said.

"Where's Peck?"

"He's uh . . . uh, Peck's at dinner."

35

▾ ▾ ▾

When Mattsson turned her truck into the barnyard, her headlights played across Virgil, who was sitting in the barnyard in the dirt, his legs out in front of him, talking on his cell phone to Jon Duncan.

She hopped out of her truck and heard him say, "We need everybody out here—Crime Scene, medical examiner, the zoo people, and tell the zoo people to bring a tranquilizer gun. We've got to get that tiger out of its cage before she eats the rest of Peck."

Virgil clicked off the phone as she trotted over to him and asked, "What happened?"

"That's a little hard to explain," Virgil said. "It got really complicated."

"Why are you sitting in the dirt like that?" she asked.

"I sprained both my ankles when I jumped out of a second-story window."

"What?" She turned to look at the farmhouse, where in the reflected headlights of her truck, she could see a window frame dangling from a few nails on the second floor.

"I told you, it was confusing," Virgil said. "Help me up. I need to find my gun."

"What happened to your gun?"

"Well, see . . . I fell through the floor of the front porch . . ."

Mattsson supported him with an arm around his waist, and he put one of his arms around her shoulders, as they limped over to the front porch. On the way, he gave her the whole sequence from the time he arrived at the farm, until he managed to lock Katya back in her cage with Peck's body.

"If it was anyone else, I wouldn't believe it. With you, I think, 'Yeah, probably,'" she said. At the porch, they didn't see a gun and Virgil said, "Peck must have picked it up. He never fired it, though."

They worked carefully around the hole in the porch deck and stepped inside the house. There was no pistol in the entry and Mattsson climbed the stairs to the second floor and returned empty-handed.

"There's some .308 brass on the bedroom floor up there, so I was in the right room, but I didn't see any 9mm," she said. "I'll get a flashlight."

She got a Maglite from her truck and left Virgil sitting on a porch step, contemplating the quiet of the night, as she traced Peck's route from the bedroom down to the barn. She came back and said, "Nothing in the barn. The tiger's sitting there staring at Peck, what's left of him, anyway. I don't see a gun on his body. Really stinks in there."

Virgil thought for a moment, then said, "Look down the hole in the porch."

She did, shining the flashlight down it, and a second later said, "I see it. Can't reach it, though."

"Embarrassing as hell," Virgil said. "But if you'd been here . . ."

Mattsson said, "Yeah," and "Just a minute." The porch had a skirt of weather-worn wooden slats, in no better condition than the rest of the porch. She kicked out a half-dozen slats, then crawled under the porch, got his gun, backed out, and handed it to him. She said, "Maybe we won't have to mention the whole gun thing."

"Yeah, we will—because if we don't, the whole rest of it doesn't make any sense." There was some tall uncut grass growing up next to the porch steps, and Virgil pulled out a blade and chewed on the stem, savoring the sweetness of it, and tried to forget the pain in his ankles.

"You got a tiger back," Mattsson said. "That's a wonderful thing, Virgil."

"I suppose," Virgil said. "But basically, it was just more crazy shit."

Mattsson cocked her head and asked, "Hear that?"

Sirens. Several of them, still a long way out. "About time," Virgil said.

Mattsson sat on the porch next to him, looked out at the road. A greenish yellow light blinked in the weeds out along the road and she said, "Last firefly of the year."

Fireflies weren't supposed to last this deep into the summer, Virgil knew. Maybe he was getting a signal from God, from one of God's bugs. But what would a yellow light mean? Caution? A little late, huh?

Virgil's ankles were on fire, but he couldn't leave the scene until all the relevant crime-scene processing was under way. Mattsson met the first responders, a couple of Washington County sheriff's deputies, and asked them to park in the road because most of the barnyard was a crime scene.

Two BCA agents were next and they began taping off the scene. An ME's investigator arrived, followed the BCA crime-scene crew, followed by Jon Duncan.

"The zoo people are getting their stuff together; they'll be here in a half hour or so. I talked to the TV stations; they all got something on the end of their newscasts. They'll be sending out some trucks to get video for tomorrow."

"I'm kinda hurting here," Virgil said. "Could you and Catrin talk to them?"

Duncan and Mattsson could. The TV trucks got there before the zoo people; Virgil was making a recorded video statement on the porch of the farmhouse when the zoo people arrived with a truck and a man with a tranquilizer gun.

There was some back-and-forth between the zookeepers and the crime-scene crew, but eventually one zoo guy was allowed inside the barn. He shot Katya, and he and two crime-scene crew members lifted the unconscious cat onto one of Peck's dollies, and they rolled her out to a truck.

The TV crews were allowed to stand on the shoulder of the road and film the transfer of the tiger to the zoo truck. A minute later, the hatch was closed and the sleeping Katya was on her way back to the zoo.

"Hope she makes it," Mattsson said, looking after the truck. "The zoo guy told me that tranquilizing them can be dangerous."

The ME's investigator and the crime-scene people began consulting about the removal of Peck's body. The investigator told Virgil, "She didn't eat him much, but she did crush his head like an English walnut."

Jenkins and Shrake arrived way too late to do anything—in fact, they weren't even supposed to be at the farm, but when they heard what happened, they'd driven out hoping to get in on the action. Instead, Duncan asked for a volunteer to drive Virgil first to a hospital for X-rays, and then home. Jenkins volunteered to drive him and Shrake would follow with Virgil's truck.

Jenkins and Shrake helped Virgil out to Jenkins's Crown Vic; the process was filmed by the TV crews, and Jenkins said, "We're all gonna be famous."

"For tomorrow," Virgil said. "The day after, not so much."

At Regions Hospital, the ER was enjoying a low-key night, and Virgil got the X-rays done and examined in an hour: getting his cowboy boots pulled off hurt almost as much as the original fall. The doc said, "Nothing broken. You need some RICE." Rest, ice, compression, and elevation; Virgil had been there before. The doc wrapped his ankles and gave him a supply of cold packs, then Virgil was driven home by Jenkins, with his tightly wrapped, freezing feet up on the Crown Vic's dashboard.

Virgil talked to Frankie as he and Jenkins drove south through the Cities, and she met them on Virgil's porch. She'd already asked him how bad the ankles were, and now she asked, after kissing him, "You can't walk?"

"I can, but it hurts," Virgil told her. He was carrying his cowboy boots.

"He's being a sissy," Jenkins said. "I've been hurt a lot worse than this and still played basketball."

"Bullshit, Jenkins," Frankie said. "I've seen you stung by a wasp and you cried like a baby. Anyway, get him inside. I won't be able to help much. . . ."

Shrake arrived, and they all got Virgil on the living room couch, with his feet up on a couple of cushions, and put the used cold packs in the freezer. Jenkins and Shrake left to go back to the Cities, and Frankie, who was a bit of a cop groupie, settled into a chair opposite him and said, "I've heard enough about your ankles. What I want to hear is, what happened when you figured out where he was? I want it minute by minute, with all the blood and spattered-out brains and stuff."

He told her, minute by minute; she flinched when he told her about being shot at in the upstairs bedroom, but was nothing but delighted when he told her about the walnut-crunch sound of the tiger crushing Peck's head.

"Deserved every bit of it," she said. "Go, Katya."

If anything, Virgil's ankles hurt worse in the morning, a shooting pain when he moved that told him to stay off his feet. At ten o'clock, he got a call from Bea Sawyer, head of the crime-scene crew.

"Can you talk?"

"Yeah, it's my ankles that hurt, not my tongue," Virgil said.

"Okay. Anyway, we found Peck's cell phone on the barn floor, and guess what? It was another one of those fingerprint-password things. The tiger hadn't eaten his fingers, and we still had the body, so we opened it up and changed the settings to eliminate the password. . . ."

"Yeah, yeah, and what?"

"Roger went through his photos, to see if he'd documented all of this, and he found the most amazing documentary film. It shows a younger Asian man strangling an older Asian man in the front seat of Peck's truck."

"Aw, man," Virgil said. "You gotta call Howser at Minneapolis homicide."

"It's done," she said. "That Zhang guy was leaving for the airport when they snagged him."

"Bea: thank you."

"One more thing," she said.

"Yeah?"

"That firebomb that was thrown through the window of your neighbor's house? We're thinking it came from Peck's barn. A Ball jar was used to hold the gasoline in the firebomb, and the basement in the farmhouse is full of old Ball jars. There's a piece missing from an apron in the barn, and it looks like the same fabric used on the bomb."

"Oh, boy. I'm going to have to do some patching up with the neighbors."

He watched the noon news and Shrake had been right: they were heroes for the moment. There was some question about whether Katya would have to be put down, since she'd killed a human being. On the other hand, Jon Duncan—did he have a tear in his eye?—told the story of Virgil using the tiger to defend himself against a mass murderer, so there was a solid argument that the killing had been justified.

As they'd sat waiting on the farmhouse porch for everybody to arrive, Mattsson told Virgil that Blankenship had bailed out of the Blue Earth County jail. "Freddie has already made a deal with the county attorney. He's given them a statement saying that

Blankenship was the person who did the beating in both assaults. They've already gotten a gum scrub from Blankenship for the DNA match, so that should nail it down. He's going to jail, or maybe even prison, but he probably won't get as much time as you want."

"Can't know that yet," Virgil said. "Frankie's friends with every judge in Blue Earth and Nicollet counties. So . . ."

That all became relevant as Virgil sat on the couch at home that afternoon, with his feet up in the air. Frankie was at her salvage shop at the farm. Sparkle called in a panic. "That Blankenship guy who beat up Frankie and Ramona—me and Bill were out on the road, getting mail, and he cruised us. I'm almost sure it was him. It was a red Ford truck and I got the license number. He was looking at us."

"Ah, man. All right, let's get the sheriff on it," Virgil said. "If the tag number checks out, he can have somebody go over and talk to him. Warn him off."

"Virgil, the guy's not only mean, he's insane."

"I'll talk to the sheriff now."

That evening, every news channel that Virgil saw reported that the population of Minnesota was in an uproar about the possibility that Katya might be put down. The possibility was evaporating.

By the second day, after a continuous regime of rest, ice, compression, and elevation, and a couple of long chats about life with Father Bill, Virgil started moving around the house with the help of crutches that Frankie got from a drugstore.

He was alone in the house, headed back to the couch, when an RV pulled up to the curb. Virgil said to himself, "The fuckin' Simonians. Exactly what I needed."

Sure enough, six of them got out and seemed to arrange themselves by age and size. Levon led the way up Virgil's porch and pushed the doorbell. Virgil pulled the door open and said, "You might as well come in. I can't move around so well."

The Simonians followed him into the living room. The youngest one asked, "You need anything? Painkillers, a little weed, some liquor, anything to make it easier?"

"I'm fine," Virgil said. "What's up with you guys?"

Levon said, "We will go back to Glendale, thank the Good Lord, as soon as we wind up our business here, the arrangements for Hayk and Hamlet."

"I'm sorry they were killed," Virgil said. "We think Peck might have murdered another man as well, but there's no body, and Peck, of course, can't tell us one way or the other where he might be."

Levon said, "We see this on the television news. We have also researched this 'Virgil Flowers' on the Internet, because we have a large Simonian problem."

Virgil: "Which would be?"

"This man Peck murders two of our Simonians. We wanted to deal with this ourselves, but that did not happen. Then we find out that our friend Virgil Flowers feeds Peck to a tiger, and this is better than anything we could think of."

"I didn't exactly feed him . . . but anyway, uh, I don't see a Simonian problem there."

Levon said, "We have a large debt to you. Our Simonian honor requires that the debt be paid, so we come here and ask, what does Virgil Flowers want?"

"A little peace and quiet, that's about all," Virgil said.

Levon pulled on his chin, glanced out to the street, as if checking for cops, and said, "I tell you, Virgil, coming from LA, you have here more peace and quiet than I could stand."

"Yeah, okay," Virgil said. "But, guys, what happened was my job. I got paid for it. You don't owe me anything."

"This is where you are wrong," Levon said, and the other five Simonians all nodded. "Anyway, we tell you, we will pay this debt. We will be here, the medical examiner says, for another week, maybe ten days, but since the murderer is dead, and there will be no trial, they will not have to hold the bodies of our Simonians longer than that. We will find a way to pay."

Virgil said, "*You don't owe me*. Get that through your heads. Anything you give me, I'd have to turn in to the state. I can't take any kind of payment outside my job—that would be considered a bribe."

Levon nodded and said, "Stupid law. We will go around it."

They all filed out, each of them giving Virgil a slap on the back or an elbow nudge, and when the RV pulled away from the curb, Virgil collapsed on the couch, grateful for the thickness of his peace and quiet.

The sheriff talked to Blankenship and told Virgil, "He denied being out there, but he was lying. I told him that if he messed with Ms. Nobles or her sister or you or anybody else, or even looked at any of you, I'll jerk his bail so fast his head will be spinning for a week."

Mattsson came down to give a statement in the Blankenship case and stopped at Frankie's farm on the way back home. They all had a nice chat and Virgil again didn't know whether to hug her or shake hands when she left, as she stepped away and said, "See you around."

When she was gone, Sam, the youngest, said, "That chick is *really* hot."

They all looked at him, but he didn't back off. When you're right, you're right.

On the third day, Maxine Knowles was charged with another count of attempted murder for her assault on Toby Strait, and her bail was pulled on the first count. A newspaper story said that the trial on the first count was scheduled to start in a month and a half. That was actually at the bottom of the news story: at the top was a long feature about a rich animal lover named Crewdson from Minnetonka who had donated a quarter-million dollars to Knowles's animal refuge and its elderly caretakers.

Virgil would never suggest that newspeople were cynical, but the story concluded with, "Questioned by a reporter, Crewdson agreed that the contribution, made to Knowles's charitable organization, would be fully tax deductible."

That same day, Jon Duncan called and said that since Virgil had a job-related injury, he wouldn't be required to qualify with his pistol until the following year. "We thought that would be best for everybody," Duncan said.

By the eighth day after Peck's death, Virgil was walking without crutches, though his ankles still hurt and felt wobbly. A doc told him that without the RICE, it might have taken him a month or more before he could jog. He thought Virgil might start jogging in another week. Virgil, he said, probably had a grade-one sprain, on the border of a grade two, whatever that meant.

By that time, Katya the tiger's future was not only assured, but the zoo had announced that they'd stored semen from her former mate, Artur, and she would be impregnated the next time she came in season, and she would be expected to produce three or four cubs. Robert McCall, the wealthy chairman of the zoo's board of directors, announced that he had agreed to fund an animal psychologist, to be flown in from San Diego, to treat Katya for any psychological trauma she may have incurred during her imprisonment.

On the tenth day, Brad Blankenship rolled his red Ford pickup into the parking lot of Waters' Waterhole, his favorite bar, and sat for a moment, waiting for the gravel dust to settle. Another hot day. The next day was supposed to be even worse, with a flood of humid air coming up from the Gulf of Mexico. He picked up the seed corn hat from the passenger seat, put it on, and got out of the truck as a six-door white Mercedes-Benz stretch limo pulled up a few feet away.

A wedding limo, Blankenship thought, exactly the kind rented by eight or ten horny young bridesmaids before they went out to a bar and got wasted and laid. He'd never seen one at the Waterhole, which was basically a rural dive, but nevertheless, it might be an opportunity; there was hardly anyone else around in the midafternoon, so he'd have the ladies to himself.

He lingered near the front of the Benz, checking out the fat driver. Then the three doors on the far side of the limo popped open and several heavyset men climbed out into the parking lot. He'd never seen them before, but they were looking at him. He noticed that one of them was carrying a baseball bat; maybe they were a bar team.

"What are you guys supposed to be?" he asked, curling a lip. "The New York fuckin' Yankees?"

Well, no.

Virgil's ankles still hurt, but he could swing a baseball bat. He had three fielders spread out across the barnyard: young Sam, Father Bill, and Honus the dog. He smacked a grounder out toward Sam, who flinched as it popped up in his face, but he smothered the ball, picked it up, and threw it back.

Virgil hit a sharper drive at Honus, who went to his right, snagged the ball on the second bounce, and ran it back to Virgil.

He was about to send one out to Bill when his phone chirped. A text message from an unknown phone. The message said, "We're all square." It wasn't signed. He contemplated the phone for a moment, then put it back in his pocket.

He was still out there, hitting balls, when his phone went off again. The sheriff asked, "You got some witnesses where you're at?"

"I'm hitting baseballs at a young boy, a Catholic priest, and a dog named Honus, up at Frankie's farm. I got witnesses all over the place."

"Well, good. Because about fifteen minutes ago, somebody caught Brad Blankenship out at the Waterhole and broke his arms and legs. *All* his arms and legs. And his fingers."

"Wasn't me," Virgil said.

"Didn't think it was," the sheriff said. "You take it easy there, Virgil."

"I'll do that."

Frankie came out on the porch, chewing on an apple. She was wearing a white T-shirt and ripped blue jeans and sandals, blond braid falling down her back; she was an American dream. "It's awful hot," she said. "You guys come on inside, I've made some lemonade."

Sam and Bill started toward the porch, but Honus hung back deep in the imaginary infield.

When Sam and Bill were inside, Frankie called, "You coming? Maybe you and me and Sparkle and Bill could go on down to the swimming hole after the lemonade?"

Virgil took off his baseball cap and wiped away the sweat on his forehead. Really was hot.

He said, "That sounds terrific. Minnesota in the summertime, huh? But let me hit a couple more grounders out to Honus."